The Magician's Death

ALSO BY P. C. DOHERTY

The Magician's Death

A HUGH CORBETT MEDIEVAL MYSTERY

P. C. DOHERTY

Minotaur Books ✠ New York

THE MAGICIAN'S DEATH. Copyright © 2004 by Paul Doherty. All rights reserved. Printed in the United States of America. For information, address St. Martin's Press, 175 Fifth Avenue, New York, N.Y. 10010.

www.minotaurbooks.com

Library of Congress Cataloging-in-Publication Data

Doherty, P. C.
  The magician's death : a Hugh Corbett medieval mystery / P. C. Doherty. — 1st U.S. ed.
    p. cm.
  ISBN-13: 978-0-312-56562-6
  ISBN-10: 0-312-56562-3
  1. Corbett, Hugh (Fictitious character)—Fiction. 2. Great Britain—History—Edward I, 1272–1307—Fiction. 3. Code and cipher stories. I. Title.
  PR6054.O37M29 2009
  823'.914—dc22

2009007935

First published in Great Britain by Headline Book Publishing, a division of Hodder Headline

First U.S. Edition: July 2009

10 9 8 7 6 5 4 3 2 1

In memory of my brother,
Francis Patrick Doherty [1950–2004]

Foreword

Philip IV of France and Edward I of England were arch-rivals. Philip saw himself as a new Charlemagne. He wanted to give France natural boundaries and, through his family the Capets, dominate the other monarchies of Europe. He therefore spent a great deal of his reign plotting against Edward of England for two reasons: to acquire the wine-rich province of Gascony in south-west France, still held by the English; and to see his own grandson crowned as King of England at Westminster. He viewed the latter as the best way of securing the former. Edward I manoeuvred to avoid such entanglement but events conspired against him. In May 1303, under extreme international pressure, particularly from the Papacy, he agreed to the Treaty of Paris, whereby he solemnly promised that his eldest son, the Prince of Wales, would marry Isabella, Philip's only daughter.

At the beginning of the fourteenth century international intrigue was rife and ripe, as it is today. It was also a time of considerable change as the great writers of the day began to push back the boundaries of knowledge. One of these writers was the Franciscan scholar Roger Bacon, who had died some thirty years earlier, the custodian of many great secrets . . .

Consequently, we have before us the notable regions of northern Europe.

Roger Bacon, *Opus Maius*

Prologue

The Royal Palace at Poissy: Feast of St Barnabas the Apostle, June 1303

Philip IV of France, nicknamed 'Le Bel', knelt on the prie-dieu in the small royal chapel overlooking the fountain in the court-yard of the Palace of Poissy. Philip loved this little church, with its exquisitely tiled floor of black, white and red lozenges, the cushioned oak prie-dieu, the splendid tapestries depicting the exploits of his great predecessor, the Capetian Louis IX, now St Louis, proclaimed so by the Universal Church. Philip knelt before a statue to his glorious ancestor and stared up at the saintly carved face, studying it carefully. He would have words with the sculptor. He wanted Louis' face to look like his own; that was not blasphemy, for wasn't Philip a direct descendant? Didn't the same sacred Capetian blood flow in his veins?

Philip knelt immobile. Despite the warmth, he had a fur-lined blue cloak embroidered with gold fleurs-de-lis about his shoulders. His light blond hair, parted down the middle, fell below his ears; his moustache and beard of the same colour were precisely clipped; the light blue eyes which so many of his subjects found terrifying in their gaze moved now and again, distracted by the flames of the countless tapers and candles which surrounded this statue. The memorial to St Louis stood on the left side of the chapel altar in a chantry specially built according to Philip's precise instructions. This was the place

Philip would retreat to to give thanks to God, whom he regarded as an equal, as well as to talk to his sainted ancestor, whom he viewed as his envoy at the heavenly court.

Philip joined his hands, fingers raised heavenwards. He had so much to thank St Louis for, and putting aside his usual icy demeanour, he leaned across and kissed the base of the statue. Philip had nourished dreams, and these dreams, thanks to the intervention of St Louis, were to become a reality. He had married his sons to the daughters of the three great dukes in his kingdom, ensuring that provinces such as Burgundy would be brought firmly under Capetian rule. The only obstacle had been the wine-rich duchy of Gascony in the south-west, controlled and owned by Edward of England. Philip allowed himself a smile, for that too was changing. Philip had threatened Edward with outright war, exploiting the English king's troubles in his campaign against the Scots. Oh, success tasted so sweet! Last month, by the Treaty of Paris, Edward of England had been forced to concede that in the matter of Gascony, Philip of France was his overlord. Edward had also solemnly sworn that the Prince of Wales would marry Philip's only daughter, the infant Isabella, she of the light blue eyes and golden hair, a true daughter of her father.

Philip looked up in rapture at the carved face of his ancestor. 'One day,' he whispered, 'my grandson will wear the crown of the Confessor, my daughter will be Queen of England and her second son will be Duke of Gascony.' Philip could have hugged himself. He had finished what this great saint had begun; he would give France natural boundaries, the great mountain range to the south and the wild seas to the north and west. The Low Countries would become his clients and the power of France would be felt as far east as the Rhine. Philip's smile faded at the cough behind him. He crossed himself slowly and rose elegantly from the prie-dieu. Taking the silk gloves from his belt, he put them on as he stared at Monsieur Amaury de Craon, Keeper of the King's Secrets.

'Your Grace asked to see me?' De Craon did not like the harsh look on his master's face.

'Amaury, Amaury.' Philip's face broke into a smile, and striding across, he grasped de Craon's face between his hands and squeezed tightly. 'We have matters to discuss, Amaury.'

He led this red-haired, most secretive of councillors over to a small bench halfway down the chapel in a narrow enclave, where he usually met his confessor to whisper his sins and seek absolution. Philip didn't really believe he needed absolution; after all, God was a king and he would understand. Nevertheless, this was an ideal place to meet and plot where no eavesdropper could lurk or spy take note.

'Well, Amaury.' Philip sat down, pulling his robes about him, gesturing for de Craon to sit next to him. 'I read your memorandum.' He played with the red tassels on the silken glove. 'You have insisted,' he whispered, 'that I face two problems.'

'The first, your Grace, is Sir Hugh Corbett.'

'Is he a problem, Amaury, or the result of your hatred for him?'

'Your Grace.' De Craon bowed imperceptibly. 'You are as astute as always. I hate Corbett for what he represents, for what he leads, that Secret Chancery with its legion of spies.'

'True, true.' Philip nodded.

'And the University of the Sorbonne.'

De Craon kept his head down, but he knew from the long sigh from his master that he had hit a mark.

'The lawyers,' Philip hissed. 'Those men from the gutter who believe my will does not have force of law.'

'Your Grace, there are measures we can take.'

Philip leaned closer, like a priest listening to a penitent, as there, in that House of God, the French King and his Master of Spies spun their bloody tangled web to draw Edward of England deeper into the mire.

The King, being in Oxfordshire, at a nobleman's house, was very keen to learn about this famous friar.

The Famous Historie of Fryer Bacon

Chapter 1

Paris: August 1303

Walter Ufford was good at peering through keyholes. He claimed to have a natural talent for it, and on that Friday, the eve of the Feast of St Monica, the Mother of St Augustine, he was using his talents on behalf of his master, Sir Hugh Corbett, Keeper of the Secret Seal of Edward I of England. Ufford was enjoying himself. In fact, when he visited the shriving pew to confess his sins at the beginning of Advent, he would confess to this. Walter Ufford was busy spying on Magister Thibault, Reader in Divinity and Master of the Schools at the University of the Sorbonne in Paris. He glanced quickly up and down the gallery. It was deserted. Only the creak of floorboards and the scampering of vermin echoed along that gloomy passageway. Magister Thibault would not want any distraction; after all, it was his house, a soaring three-storey mansion in the Rue St Veuve, only a walk away from the stinking, turbulent Seine. Ufford strained his ears. From below he could hear the sounds of revelry, the music of the rebec, flute and tambour. The dancing had begun. Those dark-eyed moon girls would be cavorting like Salome, drawing lustful glances and rousing the hot passions of the spectators.

'There'll be little schooling done tonight,' Ufford whispered to himself. He pressed his eye against the keyhole. He was so pleased that Magister Thibault had removed the key. The gap was large and provided Walter with a clear view of the old lecher's bedchamber, a grand place with its polished floor and woollen rugs, the walls covered in costly drapes. A fire crackled merrily in the mantled hearth, whilst the candles placed around the chamber lit up the tableau taking place on the blue-draped four-poster bed. Magister Thibault, naked as the day he was born, was busy cavorting with Lucienne, *fille de joie*, one of the best the House of Joy could provide. Ufford groaned quietly to himself. Lucienne was a thing of beauty, with her lustrous red hair and snow-white skin. She had the figure of a Venus and the face of an Aphrodite. He watched in quiet surprise at the agility of this old master of the schools. He could hear his groans of pleasure and Lucienne's cries of joy.

'He is occupied?'

Walter whirled round, hand going for the hilt of his dagger, then relaxed. Despite the scarlet robe and the gilt mask covering his face, he recognised his companion, William Bolingbroke, like Ufford an eternal student of the University of Paris, a man who immersed himself in the *scientia naturalis*.

'He's truly enjoying himself,' Ufford whispered.

'Put your mask on!'

Ufford hurried to obey, though he didn't like the thing. It was supposed to be a fox. He had caught a reflection of himself in a shiny brass jug and considered the mask too life-like. The same went for Bolingbroke's, an evil animal mask with slanted eyes, fierce snout and horns curling out on either side.

'It's so hot,' Ufford muttered. 'I am sweating like a bitch on heat.'

Bolingbroke grasped him by the elbow and took him further down the gallery to the small seat under the window casement. He climbed up, opened the latch door and took off his mask, inviting Ufford to do the same. For a moment they both stood revelling in the cool night air.

'Will he come?'

'He had better do.' Bolingbroke turned his face away from the window. He looked pale and drawn, the deep-set eyes ringed in shadow, a sheen of sweat on the broad forehead beneath his close-cropped sandy hair.

Ufford felt a spasm of fear and clutched his stomach. He shouldn't have drunk so much wine but, as Bolingbroke had said, they had to enter into the spirit of the evening. The masters of the school had organized a party to celebrate the beginning of term, to eat, drink and enjoy themselves before they returned to the rigorous discipline of their studies.

'Are you sure all is well?' Ufford whispered.

'They are as drunk as sots downstairs. Magister Thibault is lost in his pleasures and the rest couldn't distinguish Alpha from Omega.'

Ufford smiled quietly to himself. Bolingbroke the scholar, always ready to show his learning at the most inappropriate occasions.

'We had best go.'

Ufford heard the sign, the clanging of the bells from a nearby church marking the hour of Compline. He put on his mask and followed Bolingbroke down the gallery. They paused at the top of the stairs.

'Take care!' Bolingbroke urged.

They went down the wooden staircase, on to the second gallery, past various chambers, from where the noises of love echoed loud and clear, down a second side staircase, along a stone-paved passageway, dark but sweet-smelling of spilt wine, and into Master Thibault's so-called Great Hall. This long wooden-panelled chamber had been transformed for the night's rejoicing. The trestle tables on either side were littered with fragments of food, splashes of wine, ale and beer. Cups, goblets, beakers and platters lay strewn about, catching the glow of the many candles and torches which lit the room yet also provided shadows deep enough for those who wished to continue their pleasures in private. The benches had been pushed aside. Magister Thibault's guests stood in a ring, watching three young olive-skinned women, hair black as a raven's wing, garbed in a motley collection of garish rags, dance and whirl to the click of castanets and the tinkling of little silver bells. The moon women moved to the blood-stirring tune of the musicians, who took their beat from the small boy holding a tambour, almost as big as him, which cut through the rhythm and quickened the pace. Most of the spectators were drunk; even as Bolingbroke and Ufford entered, one broke away to stagger off into the shadows to be sick, kicking aside the great hounds which roamed the halls and jumped on to the tables looking for scraps.

Bolingbroke and Ufford pushed their way through the throng. Ufford felt as if he was in one of the circles of Hell, surrounded by men and women in gaudy robes, the air reeking of their cheap perfume, their faces hidden behind the masks of dogs, badgers, hawks, griffins and dragons. Eyes glittered, fingers snatched at his clothing; he was pushed and knocked by those eager to watch the dance and join the rest as they edged closer and closer to the twirling Salomes. When the dance stopped, who ever had won the women's favour enjoyed their bodies.

Ufford felt slightly sick, and tried to curb the panic seething within him. These were doctors of the law, masters of logic, professors of divinity, now giving themselves up on a fool's night to every whim of taste and passion. He was sure he recognized Destaples and Vervins, who were easy to distinguish by their height. Across the hall, as if to distance himself from the orgy, sat Louis Crotoy, whilst fat Pierre Sanson plucked at Bolingbroke's sleeve only to be pushed away. At last they were through, going under the minstrels' gallery and into the kitchens. Revellers had slunk here to satisfy their thirst and see what extra wine they could filch from the servants and scullions. Elsewhere the servants were busy either washing down the blood-soaked fleshing tables or helping themselves to the remainders of the feast. No one paid Ufford and Bolingbroke much heed as they went out into the cobbled yard, a dark, dank place, rich with the stench from the stable. Bolingbroke slipped across the yard with Ufford following closely in the shadows, opened a postern gate in the high curtain wall and whistled softly into the darkness. The whistle was returned. Ufford, peering through the gloom, saw a shape move, and the Le Roi des Clefs, the King of Keys, stepped in close. Bolingbroke rebolted the gate and all three men crouched in the shadows.

Le Roi des Clefs was as thin as a wizard's wand. His hair, prematurely white, parted down the middle, fell just below his ears. His peculiar face fascinated Ufford, so thin, the chin so pointed, it looked like the letter 'V'; close-set eyes, a beaky nose above a small mouth. Ufford smelt the fragrance and recalled Bolingbroke's observation that this master housebreaker hated hair on his own face as well as on the face of anyone he did business with. Naturally, early that evening, both he and Bolingbroke had shaved themselves well.

'You are ready?' Bolingbroke asked.

Le Roi des Clefs peered around. 'You are by yourself?' His English was good, the soft voice emphasizing every word.

'Of course we are!'

'One gold coin.' The King of Keys stretched out a hand, the tips of his fingers visible in the dark leather mittens. Bolingbroke handed over the gold coin. The King of Keys held it between forefinger and thumb, bit it, pronounced himself satisfied, and went back to the gate. He returned with two leather sacks. The larger one he handed to Bolingbroke, whilst the other he tied to the belt strapped around his leather jerkin. Bolingbroke undid his own sack and took out two war belts, each carrying a sword and dagger. He and Ufford strapped them on, and digging into the sack again, Bolingbroke brought out two small arbalests and a stout leather quiver of bolts.

'We are ready.'

They slipped across the yard and into the kitchen, their cloaks hiding both the war belts and the arbalests. The servants were now fighting over a juicy piece of lamb, whilst in the far corner a greyhound stood staring at the place where he usually lay, which was now occupied by a reveller busy lifting the skirts of a kitchen slattern. No one noticed the three newcomers as they opened the cellar door and went down the ill-lit stone steps. At the bottom they stopped and grouped together. Bolingbroke took one of the torches from the sconces on the wall and led them further into the darkness. On either side stood barrels, vats and casks, most of them broached for the evening's feasting so the ground was slippery underfoot. At the far end of the cellar they reached a stout wooden door reinforced with metal studs. The King of Keys crouched down, whispering to Bolingbroke to hold the torch closer as he emptied his sack of small rods and key-like instruments. For a while he just knelt, crouching, whispering to himself, cursing in the patois so common in the slums of St Antoine.

'Can you do it?' Bolingbroke whispered.

The King of Keys paused in his fiddling and gave a cracked-toothed grin.

'Be it the Tabernacle of St Denis, or the treasure house of King Philip, there is not a lock in Paris I cannot break.' He held up one of the devices. 'No lock can withstand these; it's only the poor light which hinders me.' As if to prove his point, he inserted the small rod and Ufford sighed in relief at the satisfying click.

The door opened. The chamber inside was no more than a whitewashed box, the ceiling, with its heavy black beams, only inches above their heads. Around the room were ranged chests, coffers and caskets: Magister Thibault's treasures. Bolingbroke ignored these, leading them across to a heavy iron-bound coffer, dark blue in colour and decorated with golden fleurs-de-lis. The coffer had three locks at the front and one on either side. The King of Keys pulled it closer and stared at it curiously.

'What does it contain? A king's ransom?'

'The *Secretus Secretorum*,' Ufford replied.

'The what?'

'The Voice of God,' Ufford retorted.

The King of Keys stepped away. 'This is not black magic, is it? It does not contain some malignant root or book of spells? Messieurs, I am frightened of magic.'

'It is not magic,' Ufford soothed, 'but knowledge. It contains a manuscript of the secret writings of Friar Roger Bacon, once a scholar at the Sorbonne.'

'What?' the King of Keys laughed. 'You have hired me, the Master of the Locks, the King of Keys, to steal the manuscript of a Franciscan?'

Ufford's hand fell to his dagger. 'You have been well paid, Monsieur, whoever you are. One gold piece to be hired, two for opening that coffer and two more when we part. Now upstairs Magister Thibault rides his young filly while his guests acquaint themselves with all the sins of the flesh. You must hurry.'

The King of Keys returned to the coffer. Bolingbroke went back to close the doors and make sure all was well. Ufford crouched against the wall, willing his stomach to quieten itself and his sweat to cool, all the time watching the King of Keys, his hands now free of those leather mittens, fondling the locks as he would a lover's hair, chuckling quietly to himself.

'Monsieur, this is the work of craftsmen,' he declared, walking over to Ufford.

'*Domine miserere!*' Ufford whispered. 'They always come back for more.' He glowered at the King of Keys, noticing how thin and spindly his legs were in their dark woollen hose, how his feet seemed to swim in those flat-heeled boots.

'Two more gold pieces.' The Master of the Locks held out his hands.

Ufford glanced at Bolingbroke, who opened his purse and handed the coins across. Ufford lifted up his arbalest, pulled back the cap to the quiver, took out one of the barbs and placed it in the polished slot. The King of Keys, however, just pocketed the gold, winked and returned to his task.

'I hope you open it,' Ufford called out. 'Either you do and we leave with that manuscript, or . . .'

'Don't threaten me,' the King of Keys hissed back, now busy with another lock.

Ufford fell silent. Cradling the arbalest, he leaned back, staring at the ceiling. He would be glad when this evening was over. It would be good to return to England and receive the praise and rewards of Sir Hugh Corbett, the Keeper of the King's Secrets! He smiled to himself. He liked Corbett, a man of few words, a good master with no illusions about the great Edward of England. He recalled the last time he and Bolingbroke had met Corbett. When was it? Eight weeks ago, around the Feast of Corpus Christi? Corbett had come to Paris on the pretext of some diplomatic incident and had met his two secret clerks, as he called them, at a small auberge beyond the city walls, on the road to Fontainebleau. He had not told them much; he didn't need to, for both Ufford and Bolingbroke were scholars of the natural sciences as well as the Quadrivium and Trivium, the logic, metaphysics, philosophy and ethics of the Masters. They had been in Paris for three years now, collecting information on behalf of the English Crown. Now their task had changed . . .

Corbett had hired a chamber at the auberge, and had seated them close around a table whilst his henchman, Ranulf of Newgate, dressed in black leather, guarded the door. Ufford was constantly surprised at the contrast between Corbett and Ranulf. Sir Hugh was dark-faced with deep-set eyes, his clean-shaven face and regular features always composed. 'A man of clean heart and clean hands,' as Ufford secretly called him.

Ranulf was different, red-haired, those slanted green eyes and pale face always watchful, a fighting man, expert with the sword, dagger and garrotte. Ufford had listened to the rumours, how Ranulf had once been a riffler, a roaring boy, from London's stinking alleyways, rescued by Corbett from the gallows. Ranulf had educated himself, unlike Corbett, who had studied at the Halls of Oxford. A man of bounding ambition with the talent to match, Ranulf was now Principal Clerk in the Chancery of the Green Wax.

'There, I have it!' the King of Keys exclaimed.

Ufford broke from his reverie at the sound of a click. The King of Keys had opened the two side locks and was working busily on the three at the front.

'Hurry up,' urged Bolingbroke, leaning against the door.

Ufford stared at his companion. Bolingbroke was usually a serene man, composed and rather elegant in his ways, fastidious in his habits, but tonight he was clearly agitated. Ufford knew the reason. One of the *magistri* upstairs was a traitor. Neither Bolingbroke nor he knew which one, but after all their searches they'd been informed how the University of the Sorbonne did possess a copy of the *Secretus Secretorum* of Friar Roger Bacon, and how its scholars were busy studying its cipher. The mysterious traitor had offered to sell the *Secretus* to the English Crown. At first Bolingbroke and Ufford had been cautious; they were being watched, suspected of being Secret Clerks. But, there again, it was a question of much suspected and nothing proved. Now it had all changed. Somebody had learnt about their secret meeting with Corbett. How the Keeper of the King's Seal had urged them to find that manuscript, or a copy, steal it and bring it immediately to England . . .

Ufford lifted his hand in the sign of peace, Bolingbroke smiled thinly back and stared down at the King of Keys busy on the coffer. Neither Bolingbroke nor Ufford knew the source of their information; letters were simply left at their lodgings in the Street of the Carmelites, above the Martel de Fer tavern, describing how the *Secretus Secretorum* had been handed to Magister Thibault, who kept it in a coffer in the strong room in his house.

'D'accord!' Another click. The King of Keys turned and ceremoniously lifted the clasp.

'For God's sake,' Ufford whispered hoarsely, and gestured at the other two locks. The hour was passing, the revellers upstairs might want some more wine and they must not be disturbed. If they were arrested . . . Ufford closed his eyes; he could not bear the thought.

During the last few days, whilst they had planned the robbery, both he and Bolingbroke had been aware of dark figures standing at the mouths of alleyways watching their lodgings. Corbett had warned them to be careful of Seigneur Amaury de Craon, Keeper of the Secrets of his Most Royal Highness Philip IV of France. He was Corbett's mortal enemy, dedicated to frustrating the designs of the English Crown, and he had a legion of spies and informers at his disposal, nicknamed the 'Hounds of the King'. Ufford and Bolingbroke had discussed the danger but they had no choice. Yet if they were caught? Ufford grasped the arbalest tighter. They would be taken to the Chambre Ardente, the Burning Chamber beneath the Louvre of Paris, questioned by the Inquisitor, strapped to the wheel of Montfaucon and spun while the hangman smashed their limbs with mallets, before they choked on one of the soaring gibbets near the gates of St Denis. Ufford closed his eyes and prayed. He had visited Notre Dame this morning, lit three tapers in the Lady's Chapel and knelt on the hard stone floor, reciting one Ave Maria after another.

To break the tension, Ufford got to his feet and walked across to his companion.

'Why?' he asked. 'Why is the manuscript so valuable?'

Bolingbroke shifted his gaze and put a finger to his lips.

'Bacon was a magician,' Bolingbroke whispered. 'He discovered secrets, the hidden knowledge of the Ancients. He said . . .' He paused as the King of Keys freed another lock and moved to the last one. 'You know the rivalry between Philip of France and Edward of England; either will do anything to frustrate the other.'

'But Roger Bacon was a friar,' Ufford pointed out. 'They are always hinting at secrets.'

'Did you know—' Bolingbroke broke off, moving away from the door. Ufford had heard it too, the sound of footsteps. At the far end of the strongroom the King of Keys also recognized the danger. Ufford winched back the cord of his arbalest. Bolingbroke, grasping the torch, quickly went round the chamber dousing the candles, hissing at his companions to join him in the corner. Ufford, heart racing, skin clammy with sweat, stood beside his companions, the pool of light from the torch dancing around them. He prayed it was only a reveller coming down for more wine or ale. Then the footsteps drew nearer, a woman laughed, and to Ufford's horror the door at the far end opened in a pool of light and a man and woman entered the chamber. Both had drunk deeply. Ufford heard a strident voice, speaking quickly in French, wondering why the strong-room door was open. Heart thumping, Ufford realised what had happened. Magister Thibault, together with the fair Lucienne, had come down to inspect the treasure room. The old goat was showing off, eager to impress this beautiful court-esan, but he was too drunk to fully realize what had happened, and instead of retreating, he closed the door behind him and staggered across the room, lifting the tallow candle he carried.

'Qu'est-ce que c'est?' What is this? He swayed in the pool of light, cursing sharply as a piece of hot wax dropped on to his hand.

'Kill him,' Bolingbroke whispered. 'Kill him now!'

Magister Thibault walked towards them.

'Who's there?' he screeched.

Ufford stepped into the pool of light, the arbalest still hidden beneath his cloak.

'Magister Thibault, good evening. My friends and I became lost and found ourselves down here.'

Thibault, full of wine and hot from the pleasures of the bed, blinked his watery eyes.

'Why, it's Ufford the Englishman, who is always asking me questions about Albert the Great.'

Ufford took a step closer. The Magister studied him quickly from head to toe. Thibault's mood was changing.

'What are you doing here?' Thibault stepped back in alarm. The woman, leaning against the wall, was falling asleep. She seemed unaware of any danger, thumb in her mouth, laughing softly as if savouring a secret joke.

'You shouldn't be here.' Thibault stepped back further. Ufford brought up the arbalest and released the bolt, which thudded deep into Thibault's chest, sending him staggering back. The candle dropped from his hands as he went to clutch the feathered barb embedded deep in his chest. At first, unaware of the pain or the blood pumping out, he opened his mouth to scream, but Ufford leapt forward and struck him on the side of the head with the arbalest. The Magister slumped to his knees, groaning in pain, coughing on the blood frothing between his lips. Ufford simply pushed him to one side and raced towards Lucienne, who stood, hands still to her mouth, staring as if it were all a dream. Ufford felt a pang of pity at that beautiful face, the lovely lips, the pale ivory skin. He clutched the young woman by the neck and drove his dagger deep beneath the heart, drawing her closer on to the blade, watching the life-light die in those exquisite eyes.

'I'm sorry,' Ufford whispered.

'I . . .' Lucienne's eyes rolled in her head, she gave a cough and a sigh. Ufford lowered her corpse to the floor.

'We'll hang!' The King of Keys gazed in horror at the two corpses. Blood was snaking out, pools forming and running down the lines between the paving stones.

Ufford couldn't stop trembling.

'I had no choice,' he gasped. 'If I didn't we would have hanged. Finish what you're doing,' he snarled at the King of Keys, and running over, he pulled across the bolts securing the door.

The lock-breaker returned to his task. Ufford paced up and down, while Bolingbroke simply slumped by the wall, staring at the stiffening corpses. Ufford started as Thibault's corpse twitched and a gasp of air escaped from his stomach. The King of Keys, sweat-soaked, concentrated on the last lock. He gave a cry of triumph at the click, threw back the lid and plunged his hand inside, only to give the most hideous scream. Ufford spun round. Bolingbroke moaned quietly, like a man caught in the toils. The King of Keys turned, and Ufford stared in horror. Little caltrops, balls, their spikes as sharp as razors and as long as daggers, had pierced the hand and wrist of the King of Keys. He staggered towards Ufford, arm out, staring beseechingly, blood pumping from his wrist like water from a drain.

'My hand,' the King of Keys moaned, 'my hand. I shall never . . .' His face was a liverish white at the shock of what had happened. 'God damn you!' he whispered.

The sudden horror of this hidden device had made him unaware of the seriousness of his wound, but Ufford knew enough about medicine to realise that a large vein had been cut.

'Help me!' the injured man pleaded. 'For God's sake!'

He slumped to his knees and tugged at the spike in his wrist, but the pain sent him writhing to the floor. Ufford ran across and, helped by Bolingbroke, tried to extract the caltrop, but it was embedded too deep. The King of Keys was shaking, the blood gushing from the wound so fast Ufford knew he couldn't staunch it.

'Help me, please!' the King of Keys repeated.

'Of course, of course. We need to cut some cloth.'

Ufford drew his dagger, one hand going to cover the King of Keys' eyes, the other slicing the blade deeply across the man's throat.

'We can do no more.' He stared at Bolingbroke grasping the King of Keys' sack, who now asserted himself as if waking from a dream.

'True, he was dead already.'

They went across to the casket and, grabbing it by the lid, tipped the contents on to the floor. They fell with a crash, more of those deadly caltrops bouncing across the paving like some dangerous vermin escaping from a hole. Bolingbroke, however, sighed in relief at the leather bag tied at the neck which also fell out. He picked this up, undid the knot and slid out a bound book. He took it beneath the sconce torch, undid the leather clasp and quickly leafed through the pages.

'Do we have it?' Ufford demanded.

'We have it!' Bolingbroke replied. 'The *Secretus Secretorum* of Friar Roger Bacon!'

They fled the strongroom taking their weapons and the leather sack with them. Ufford stopped at the wine cellar, fingers to his lips, staring at the small casks and vats above the wine barrels. Climbing up, he took one down, prised the bung hole loose with his dagger and shook the oil on to the floor as he and Bolingbroke made their way back to the steps. When it was emptied, he threw it down and raced up the cellar steps. At the top, grasping the torch, he stared down at the glistening oil, then tossed the torch in and slammed the door shut.

They raced through the kitchen, past sleepy-eyed scullions. In the yard two revellers were being sick over the horse trough. Bolingbroke and Ufford pushed them aside and hastened to the gate and out into the shadowy side streets of Paris. As they reached the end of the alleyway, the faint sounds of clamour rose behind them. Looking back, Ufford saw a glow against the sky. The fire he had started was now raging.

'Why?' Bolingbroke asked.

'Why not?' Ufford gasped for breath. 'It will create what the French would call a *divertissement*. Come, let's go.'

They walked quickly, but did not hurry. The watch were out, groups of halberdiers dressed in the city livery, but the clerks carried passes and were allowed to go unmolested. They avoided the main thoroughfares where the chains had been drawn across, or the open squares lit by torches and candles placed around the statues of the local patron saints. In the shadows stood crossbowmen, city bailiffs, ready to apprehend any law-breaker. Ufford took a deep breath. He regretted the deaths, but what could he do? The King of Keys would have died anyway. And as for Magister Thibault? Ufford's lip curled. The Magister was a stupid old man who should have fallen to his prayers. It was Lucienne's face he could not forget: those lovely eyes, her pretty mouth gaping, the smell of her perfume, the touch of her soft warm body. In a way she had reminded him of Edelina Magorian, the merchant's daughter in London who sent him such sweet letters and was so eager for his return.

They were now approaching the Porte St Denis and the great gallows of Montfaucon. The long-pillared, soaring gallows standing on its fifteen-foot mound, the execution ground, the slaughteryard of Paris, with its hanging noose and ladders stark against the starlit sky and, in the centre, a deep pit to receive the corpses. Ufford shivered and looked away. He would make sure he would not be taken alive, thrown into the execution cart, battered and bruised and forced to dance in the air for the delight of the mob. He gripped the leather sack more tightly. They would never come back to Paris and he was glad. There would be other assignments, though Corbett would not be pleased that such deaths lay at his door.

'Walter?'

Ufford started and realized they had reached the mouth of the narrow alleyway leading to the Street of the Carmelites. Bolingbroke pulled him deep into the shadows of an over-hanging house. 'For God's sake, man, keep your eyes sharp!'

Ufford swallowed hard. He could feel the night cold as he peered down that alleyway, the crumbling houses jutting out above their neighbours, almost blocking out the sky. Here and there a lonely candle burned in a casement window. A river mist hung thin in the air, blurring the light of the lantern horns slung on hooks outside some of the tenements. He narrowed his eyes. The street was the same; that stinking sewer down the centre. He could see the corner of a runnel, the place where footpads lurked, but this appeared deserted.

'I can see nothing wrong.'

Keeping to the line of the houses, they edged down towards the small tavern known as the Martel de Fer, the Sign of the Blacksmith, above which they had their room. The tavern was closed and shuttered for the night, as was the small apothecary opposite. Ufford stared across at this, looking for any chink of light, but all was cloaked in darkness. They went up the outside stairs into their narrow, shabby chamber with the paint peeling off the walls and the air rancid with the smell of cheap tallow candles. Even as Bolingbroke struck a tinder to light these, Ufford could hear the scampering mice. Yes, he would be glad to leave this place. The candles glowed, and Ufford stared around at the hard cot beds, the battered chests, the rickety table and stools. On the wall, just near the arrow slit window boarded up against the night, hung a crucifix on which the gaunt white figure of Christ writhed in mortal agony. Ufford looked away. He could not forget Lucienne.

He placed the leather sack under the bed, built up the brazier and began to destroy sheaves of paper from the secret compart-ment hidden beneath one of the chests: letters and memoranda they had received from England. Bolingbroke was doing the same. Then they took down leather panniers from hooks on the wall and filled these with their pathetic possessions, sharing out the gold and silver the English Ambassador had given them when he'd met them amongst the tombstones at St Jean. They washed their hands and faces, and divided their remaining food – a loaf of bread, some cheese and a small roll of cooked ham –

whilst they finished the jug of claret purchased from the tavern below. At last all was ready.

'We should go now.' Ufford picked up the leather sack. 'Who shall carry this?'

Bolingbroke drew the dice from his wallet.

'Three throws?'

'No, just one.'

Bolingbroke grinned, leaned down and shook the dice on to the floor. 'Two sixes.'

Ufford picked up the dice.

'Do you wish to throw?' Bolingbroke asked.

Ufford shook his head and handed the leather sack over. Bolingbroke drew out the manuscript and began to leaf through the pages.

'It's in cipher!' he exclaimed. 'What does it contain, Walter? It has cost the lives of three people and could send us to our deaths. Oh, I know.' He raised his hand. 'I'm a scholar like you. I've read Friar Roger's *On the Marvellous Power of Art and Nature*.' He smiled. 'Or, as Magister Thibault would have said, *De Mirabile Potestate Artis et Naturae*.'

'You know what it says, William?'

'I can suspect,' Bolingbroke replied. He closed his eyes to remember the quotation. ' "It is possible that great ships and sea-going vessels shall be made which can be guided by one man and will move with greater swiftness than if they were full of oarsmen." ' He opened his eyes.

'What did he mean by that?' Ufford asked

Bolingbroke pulled a face, closed the book, fastened the clasp and placed it carefully back in the leather sack.

'We should go,' Ufford repeated.

'We are not to be at the Madelene Quayside until the bells of Prime are being rung.' Bolingbroke cocked his head at the faint sounds of clanging bells. 'The alarm has been raised, the fire at Magister Thibault's must have spread. But no, Walter, we will stay, at least for a while.'

Ufford lay down on the bed, eyes watching the door, aware of the shifting shadows as the candle flame fluttered at the draughts which seeped through the room. He thought about being back in London, of sitting in the tiled solar at Edelina's house, a warm fire glowing, the air fragrant with the smell of herbs and spices; of cleaning his mouth with a snow-white napkin as he bit into tender beef or drank the rich claret her father imported.

Ufford's eyes grew heavy but he started awake, alarmed by a sound from the street below. He leapt from the bed and, hurrying across to the arrow slit, carefully removed the plank which boarded it and stared out. The cold night air hit him even as a stab of fear sent his heart racing. Dark shapes shifted in the street below and a light glowed from the apothecary's shop. He was sure he heard a clink of steel from the alleyway, the muffled neigh of a horse. He felt his legs tense as if encased in steel. There were people below; he saw a movement and caught the glint of armour. He whirled round.

'They're here!' he gasped, aware of the sweat breaking out on his face, his hands clammy.

'Nonsense!'

'They're here,' Ufford repeated. 'The Hounds of the King, de Craon and company.' He picked up his war belt and strapped it round his waist. Then, snatching his cloak and saddlebags, he opened the door and stood at the top of the stairs. He was aware of Bolingbroke breathing behind him. The alleyway below was empty.

'Down the steps quickly,' Bolingbroke urged. 'Separate. If I am caught I'll destroy that manuscript. Remember, the Madelene Quayside, the boatman in the scarlet hood – he'll take you downriver to *The Glory of Westminster*, an English cog. Its captain's name is Chandler.'

Ufford nodded and raced down the steps. When he reached the bottom, he turned left and ran up a runnel, blind walls on either side. He didn't know which way Bolingbroke had gone but his companion was forever wandering off by himself and knew the city like the back of his hand, even better than Ufford did. Ufford ran like the wind. He was aware of beggars, with their white, pinched faces, crouching in doorways, of dogs snarling and slinking away as he lashed out with his boot. He passed a small church, its steps crumbling; he glimpsed the face of a gargoyle and thought it was Magister Thibault laughing at him. He kept to the poor quarter, ill-lit and reeking with offensive smells, slums rarely patrolled by the watch or city guards. One thing he kept in mind: the map he had memorized. He reached the Street of the Capuchins and stopped to catch his breath, to ease the stabbing pain in his side. He resheathed his dagger, squatted down and, fumbling in his pocket, found a piece of cheese. He tried to chew on this but his mouth was dry so he spat it out.

Ufford tried to make sense of what was happening. They had stolen that damnable manuscript, Bolingbroke had it, and now they were only hours away from safety. Once aboard that cog, de Craon and his Hounds could bay like the dogs of Hell, but they would be safe. Yet how had it happened? Ufford breathed in deeply, his ears straining for any sound of pursuit. Had he made a mistake or were the Hounds chasing poor Bolingbroke? He tried to soothe his humours by recalling Edelina's face, but it was Lucienne's that came to mind, that pretty mouth opening, the blood spurting out. Ufford half dozed. He recalled his question to Bolingbroke. What was so precious about that manuscript? London and Paris were full of magicians! Friar Roger had made remarkable prophesies, but surely they were just vague imaginings? The pain in his side eased and Ufford tried to concentrate on his own predicament. It was Bolingbroke who had discovered where the manuscript was, liaising with this mysterious traitor, but what then? Was it that traitor who'd betrayed them? Was it a trap? Was the manuscript Bolingbroke carried genuine or a forgery?

Ufford peered down the Street of the Capuchins. From where he squatted he could see glimpses of the river and caught the glow of the quayside torches fixed on their poles. Perhaps the boatman would come early. He got to his feet and walked slowly down the street. From a casement window a child cried, a strident sound piercing the night. A dog howled and Ufford started at the swift swirl of bats in the air above him. From a garden further down an owl hooted, and he recalled old wives' tales about an owl being the harbinger of death. He was halfway along the Street of the Capuchins when he heard the clink of metal behind him. His hand went to the hilt of his sword, and he turned. A line of mailed men, heads cowled, had emerged from an alleyway. They stood silently, like a legion of ghouls spat out from Hell.

'Oh no!' Ufford gasped.

'Monsieur,' a voice called. 'Put down your arms, and return that manuscript.'

Ufford peered through the gloom. He could make out the livery, the silver fleur-de-lis on a blue background: the Hounds of the King! He drew his sword and dagger and turned to run. He was finished. A second line of men had appeared, blocking any escape to the quayside. Again the voice, loud and clear: 'Monsieur, put down your arms, we wish to talk to you about what you have stolen.'

Ufford recalled the gibbet of Montfaucon, black and stark, the rumbling of the execution cart, the whirl of the wheel as the torturers broke legs and arms with their mallets.

'I cannot lay down my arms, I have no manuscript.' He spread his hands. 'I demand safe passage.'

The line of men facing him, dressed like the others, began to walk towards him, ominous figures of death. Ufford murmured an act of contrition and crouched, sword and dagger out, and the silence of the street was shattered by the clash of arms and the hideous screams of the Englishman as he died.

In a narrow, reeking runnel scarcely a mile away, William Bolingbroke crouched in a filth-strewn corner, his leather bag between his feet. At the mouth of the alleyway squatted a beggar who'd told him that the Hounds of the King were swarming along the riverside. So what should he do now? The waiting cog was out of the question. He tried not to think of Ufford, but reflected instead on their master, Sir Hugh Corbett. What would he expect Bolingbroke to do? What was the logic of the situation? This was his best protection, his sure defence against any danger, now or in the future. Bolingbroke chewed on his lip and carefully plotted his way through the maze confronting him.

Corfe: October 1303

The ancient ones believed that Corfe Castle in the shire of Dorset was the work of giants, a grim mass of masonry which stretched up to the sky. Towers, battlements, crenellated walls and soaring gateways dominated the fields, meadows and thick dark forests which stretched down to the coast. On that freezing night, the Feast of Saints Simon and Jude, the castle was shrouded in darkness broken occasionally by the glint of light from the flaring torches and crackling braziers ranged along the battlements to provide light and warmth for the sentries.

The outlaw known as Horehound, however, was glad of the freezing cold. No parties would leave the castle, so its constable would not be hunting him and his companions. The outlaw hid deep in the shadows of a great oak tree. A more pressing problem was hunger. The roe deer had been too fleet, whilst such a hunt would always provoke suspicion. Consequently Horehound had laid his rabbit traps and, with his leather sack over his shoulder, intended to see what the early-evening harvest had brought in. He grasped his crossbow and sought reassurance by touching the knife thrust through the leather belt around his waist. He felt comfortable in the clothes he had stolen from a merchant taking wine to the castle, a foolish knave who thought he could sit on his cart and rattle along the trackways of the forest without surrendering the usual toll, a skinflint who hadn't bothered to pay out for an escort. Horehound had taken his clothes and his wallet but let him keep his wine, cart and horse. The outlaw appreciatively rubbed his woollen jerkin and pulled the heavy black cloak closer. He listened to the darkness for any sound. Sometimes the constable sent out his verderers and huntsmen, but Horehound could hear nothing in the dark of the night.

Horehound picked himself up and decided to move on. He knew the paths and could use the castle like a sailor would a star on an unknown sea. He moved easily; he knew there would be no one in the forest tonight. No danger lurked there. He loped like some hunting dog taking its time, certain of its quarry. The real danger was out in the open, in the meadows or pasturelands, or the great expanse before the castle. The track snaked before him. Now and again Horehound paused to crouch and sniff the air before continuing. He reached where he had set his traps, only to be bitterly disappointed: the rabbits caught had already been devoured by the vermin of the forest, some fox, weasel or stoat pack. Nothing was left but the remains caught in the wire or the tarred wooden rope. Horehound cursed under his breath. He had what? Eighteen or twenty souls to feed, three of them old, five women, two children.

He continued on, reaching the broad track which would lead down to the main castle gate. He looked to his left and right. The forest path, bathed in faint moonlight, was empty; no danger there. Horehound kept to the verge, ready to slip back into the trees should danger threaten. The further he went, the more he picked up new smells, not of wet wood or leaf meal, but wood smoke and the delicious odour of burning meat. He was now approaching the Tavern in the Forest, a favourite meeting place for the surrounding villagers and all those doing business with the castle, but that was usually in fairer weather, not when winter swept in cold and hard. Horehound slipped back into the forest, approaching the tavern from the rear. He was wary of its owner, mine host Master Reginald, with his fierce dogs. The outlaw gave the tavern a wide berth and passed by its rear wall. The smells from its kitchen drifted rich and tantalising, and Horehound looked longingly at the distant gleam from its windows and the smoke billowing up from its fires. Sometimes Master Reginald would tolerate him and a few of his companions, to sit in the inglenook and warm themselves, gobble a bowl of rabbit stew in return for whatever they had caught in the forest.

Horehound moved on. Now and again the trees gave way to some dripping glade or treacherous morass. As usual, he circled these and continued his journey. The trees thinned. Horehound was now out in the open, climbing the slight escarpment from which the castle reared up into the sky. This was a favourite place for rabbits. Corfe had its own warren and some of the rabbits bred there often escaped to begin colonies of their own. The previous night Horehound had set traps very near the moat. He hoped the bitter cold and darkness would blunt the sentries' vigilance. As he approached, he could smell the rank stale water, and grateful for the mist now beginning to boil, he searched out where he had laid his traps and was delighted at the soft plump corpses waiting for him.

He'd almost filled his sack when he came across the corpse. The young woman lay sprawled on the edge of the moat, hidden beneath some gorse, opposite a narrow postern gate to the castle. Horehound almost screamed with fright. Edging closer, he felt the girl's face and her long hair, and touching her neck, he felt the coldness of death as well as the feathered quarrel embedded deep in her chest. He glanced up at the pinpricks of light along the battlements. There was nothing he could do, and retreating into the night, he returned to the forest by a different route, skirting the nearby village.

He reached the cemetery of the church of St Peter's in the Wood and stopped before the lych gate. Should he go in and seek Father Matthew, a kindly, honest-faced priest? Surely he too must be concerned about the stories. How many now? Two or three young women, and tonight's victim made possibly four, all brutally murdered. Two of the corpses had been found in the castle itself, and the third, like tonight's, on the approaches to it. Horehound was deeply troubled. He did not want to think of the other nightmare, which he called 'the horror of the forest', that lonely glade, the sombre oak tree and that corpse hanging like the victim of some barbaric sacrifice. The outlaw stared across the cemetery. He could glimpse no light from the priest's house, whilst the church was a sombre mass of stone, black against the night. Such matters would have to wait. Horehound loped on.

Inside the church, Father Matthew knelt, enveloped by the darkness. He was crouching just within the sanctuary, his back against the communion rail, staring at the small lantern which hung next to the pyx above the high altar. He crossed himself once again and quietly murmured the Confiteor, the 'I Confess', reciting his sins and begging pardon and penance for them. It was the same every night. Whenever he could, Father Matthew doused the lights of his house and came to pray in the cold darkness, an act of reparation, allying himself with Christ's agony in Gethsemane. He recalled the words of Psalm 50: 'A pure heart create for me, oh God, put a steadfast spirit within me.' His dry lips and tongue stumbled over the word 'steadfast'.

Father Matthew laughed bitterly to himself; he could pray no more. The cold darkness also reminded him of that cell, and above all of that voice whispering its secrets through the darkness. Such memories provoked tears, reminding Father Matthew of his mysterious past. Putting his face in his hands, he wept bitterly for what he had done, as well as what he should have done but had failed to do.

Others hide their secrets . . . by their method of writing.

Roger Bacon, *Opus Maius*

Chapter 2

Horehound, with his companion Milkwort, hid amongst brambles and undergrowth, quiet as dappled roe deer. They crouched as if carved out of stone, watching the trackway which wound out of the forest to climb the chalky downs to Corfe Castle. Six weeks had passed since Horehound had found the murdered girl out near the castle. Since then there had been another one, Gunhilda, her battered corpse discovered amongst the rubbish heaps on a piece of wasteland within the castle itself. Father Matthew had preached vehemently against these gruesome murders both in his pulpit and again at the market cross. Yet what good would that do? Killing was part of life. A reward had been posted on Horehound's head because he and Milkwort had to hunt to live, poaching Lord Edmund's deer and filching whatever they could. They had spent November hunting, trapping deer and rabbit, drying the flesh and salting it in vats of brine deep in the forest. The Ancient One, a member of their group, had advised them to fill their larder against the winter; he had prophesied how the snows would come and how life, once again, for Horehound and his band would balance on a knife edge.

Advent had arrived, and the church was preparing for the birth of the infant Christ. Father Matthew had already decked the nave of St Peter's with evergreen, whilst his parishioners were collecting wood in the cemetery and common land to build a crib. All this had been swept aside by fresh news and busy rumour; everyone was agog with excitement. Strangers were moving into the area! Corfe Castle was to be the meeting place for a council between the clerks of France and England. Horehound did not know who the King of France was. The Ancient One had told him that the Kingdom of France lay across the Narrow Seas and had once been ruled by the kings of England. Horehound had listened to the gossip. He'd acted suitably impressed as he squatted amongst the trees at the rear of the Tavern in the Forest, sharing gossip with the pot boys from the tap room who could so easily be bribed for local news and information in return for a basket of succulent fresh rabbit meat. He depended on such news, ever vigilant lest the Sheriff of Dorset move into the area with his comitatus, ready to hunt the likes of Horehound down. He'd questioned the pot boys closely. At first they teased him as he sat between Milkwort and Angelica, Milkwort's woman. The pot boys claimed royal justices were coming, their execution cart trundling behind them surmounted by stocks, gibbets and whips, to punish Horehound and his coven. One boy, more insolent than the rest, even hinted that Horehound was responsible for the death of the local maids. The outlaw had yelped his innocence until the others laughed and reassured him. 'One-ear', so called because a dog had bitten off the other one, claimed it was because of 'Ham', which provoked more laughter, until he correctly recalled the details he had learnt from a sottish man-at-arms: how the Council was to discuss a Franciscan called Roger Bacon, a local man, born at Ilchester, just over the Somerset border. Horehound listened round-eyed. Even he had heard stories about the magical friar who'd travelled far to the east to study in some great city.

'Why would they want to talk about him?' he had asked. The boys had simply shaken their heads and returned to discussing the gruesome murders.

The finger of suspicion for the deaths pointed directly at someone in the castle rather than anyone from the forest or one of the local villagers. After all, as One-ear pointed out, and he was regarded as wiser than the rest because he could count to ten and knew his letters, the corpses of the poor maidens had been found either in the grounds of the castle itself or near its gateway. Horehound wasn't concerned about such murders, as long as he and his ilk weren't blamed. Yet the presence of

King's men in the area alerted him to danger, whilst the 'horror of the forest' still cast a deep shadow over both himself and his group. Horehound wished he could be free of all that, as well as gossip about what might be glimpsed in the forest.

Last night rumour, like a mist, had swirled up the secret forest paths. The King's men were on their way. So Horehound and Milkwort were ready. They had to make sure about these strangers, and what better opportunity than a mist-strewn morning at the beginning of December when the light was poor and the forest dripped with damp, whilst their bellies were warmed with viper broth and chunks of steaming rabbit meat?

Horehound tensed. The strangers were coming, the clip-clop of their horses echoing like a drumbeat. He peered down the track. The riders emerged out of the thinning mist, four in all, three riding abreast, the last bringing up the rear, trying to manage a vicious-looking sumpter pony. The rider in the centre was talking, gesturing before them at the castle. As the line of trees thinned, just opposite where Horehound and Milkwort crouched, the riders reined in to take a full view of Corfe Castle. They did not speak in Norman French but English, so that the fourth man, the moon-faced, blond-haired groom, with a clear cast in one eye, could understand what was being said. The leading man, whom Horehound immediately christened 'the King's henchman', was describing the history of the castle. He had a strong, carrying voice as he informed his companions about how, in the ancient times, a king had been stabbed in its gateway whilst princes of the blood had been starved in its ancient dungeons.

Horehound watched most closely. The speaker was the first King's man he had seen for years and he wondered about his title. Turning his head, he caught the name 'Sir Hugh'. He was tall and slender, with dark skin and large oval eyes, a sharp nose above full lips and a clean-shaven chin. A peregrine falcon, Horehound reflected, and he felt his stomach curdle. Horehound lived on his wits, and he knew this man was dangerous, just by his calm manner, the authority with which he spoke. He was dressed simply enough, in a dark blood-red cotehardie above pale green leggings pushed into high boots on which glittering spurs jingled. A ring sparkled on his finger, and beneath the cloak he wore some collar of office around his neck. As the King's Man turned, pushing back the cowl of his cloak, Horehound could see that his black hair was tinged with grey, swept back and tied at the nape of the neck.

Horehound shifted his attention to the others. The nearest to him sat astride a big-girthed horse with gleaming saddle and harness. This second King's man was dressed like a raven in his black leather, a broad war belt slung diagonally across his chest, whilst the cross hilt of his sword was looped over the saddle horn so it could be drawn swiftly and easily. The black leather garb accentuated the narrow pale face under the fiery red hair. 'The fighting man' was how Horehound would describe him later, a clerk but also a killer, just from the way he sat, hands never far from his weapons. The rider on the far side was sandy-haired and looked like a clerk in his sober cloak, his hair shaven close to his ears.

Horehound turned to Milkwort and winked. His companion grinned; his leader was satisfied. The King's men hadn't brought soldiers, so they wouldn't be hunting them.

'Shall we go?' Milkwort whispered. As he moved his foot, the bramble bush shook. Horehound, horror-struck, gazed back at the trackway. The King's men had stopped talking and were staring directly at where they were hiding. Both outlaws stiffened. The red-haired one, the fighting man, following his master's gaze, swung easily out of the saddle, drawing his sword as he did so. He edged across the path, his left hand going behind his back to find the dagger strapped there, drawing closer to the line of brambles and tangled weed which stretched like a net between the trees. Horehound nudged Milkwort.

'Now,' he whispered.

Both men turned and, at a half-crouch, raced back into the darkness of the mist-hung trees.

'Let it be, Ranulf.' Sir Hugh Corbett, Keeper of the Secret Seal, gathered up the reins of his horse. Ranulf resheathed his sword and returned to his own mount.

'Are you sure, Master?'

'As God is in Heaven. I thought someone was there.' Corbett pulled a face. 'Perhaps children from the village; their curiosity must be stirred.'

Ranulf of Newgate, Principal Clerk in the Chancery of the

Green Wax, wondered how long Sir Hugh had known about the secret lurkers. He was convinced they weren't children; he had glimpsed broad shoulders and a tangle of hair, and one of them had definitely been carrying a crossbow. But there had been no real danger.

'Master Longface', as Ranulf called Sir Hugh whenever he was discussing him with Chanson the groom, was only intent on letting their horses rest before the steep climb to the castle gates, hence the brief pause. Ranulf glared at Chanson, who was now grinning wickedly at him.

'They may not have been children, Ranulf,' whispered the groom, 'but very big rabbits. They grow very large around here.' Chanson was pleased to have the opportunity to tease Ranulf, whose one fear, as he had openly confessed himself, was the countryside, with its menacing woods, lonely open meadows and stretches of land with no sign of human habitation, the only sound being the screech of birds and the ominous crackling amongst the trees either side of the track. Ranulf was a child of the narrow lanes and runnels of London, and was quick to pine for what he termed 'the comforting stink and close warmth of a town or city'. Ranulf slipped his boot into the stirrup and remounted.

'If they had rabbits as big as a house,' he retorted quickly, 'you still wouldn't be able to hit one.'

William Bolingbroke, Clerk of the Secret Seal and recently returned from Paris, heard the remark and joined in the teasing. Amongst the clerks of the Secret Chancery, Chanson's lack of skill as an archer was notorious. Given any weapon, this Clerk of the Stable, with such a notable cast in his eye, was judged to be more of a danger to himself than any mailed opponent.

'We must go on. Sir Edmund will be expecting us.' Corbett leaned over and gripped Bolingbroke's wrist. 'William, I am content you are with us.' He winked. 'Though I am certain that the Seigneur de Craon will not be so easily pleased.' Corbett pulled back his hood. 'You are well, William?'

'Curious, Sir Hugh.'

'Of course, but remember, those things done in the dark will soon be brought into the light of day.' Corbett urged his horse on. 'Or so Scripture would have us believe.'

They left the shadow of the trees, spurring their horses over the grassy chalkland up towards the castle built on its successive mounds, one above the other, which provided it with its impregnable position. Corbett had visited Corfe years before. His parents had farmed land in Devon and they had taken their favourite son to see the glories of the King's builders and stonemasons. He had worked in London and Paris, yet even the sights of those cities, not to mention the passing of years, had done little to diminish his awe at this formidable fortress, with its lofty crenellated walls, soaring towers, battlemented turrets and thick-set drum towers. From the keep, on the top of the hill, fluttered the royal banner of England, the golden leopards clear against their scarlet background, and next to it the personal standard of Sir Edmund Launge, the Royal Constable, silver lions couchant against a dark blue field.

At last they reached the castle, clattering across the drawbridge and in under the sharp teeth of the raised portcullis. They crossed the outer ward or bailey, as busy as any market square with its stalls, smithies, stables, cookhouses and ovens being hastily prepared for another day's business. Somewhere a bell clanged, and a hunting horn brayed, almost drowned by the baying of a pack of hounds, hungry for their first meal of the day. On tables just inside the gateway, where the blood ran like water, the warrener was laying out the skinned corpses of game for the flesher to gut after he had finished hacking at a whole pig, the severed head of which lay forlornly in a tub of brine, frightening the curious hunting dogs with its still, glassy stare. Fires and braziers crackled. Children shrieked and danced around them, pushing aside the mastiffs which drooled at the smell of salted bacon being laid across makeshift grills to sizzle until brown. Washerwomen struggled to carry baskets of stinking clothes to the waiting vats. Verderers hung more game from poles while the whippers-in fought to keep back the dogs as they placed bowls underneath the cut throats of beast and fowl to collect the blood. Further up, a horse suspected of being lame was being led out of the stables for a horse-leech to inspect. Men-at-arms and archers lounged about, their weapons piled before them as they grouped round a fire and broke their fast on coarse rye bread, spiced sausage and a jug of ale. No one challenged Corbett or his retinue; they were allowed to pass through the bailey, across a second drawbridge spanning a dry fosse, and into the inner ward, a more serene place, dominated by its soaring keep and towers. Guards lurked in the shadows beneath the portcullis, more in the bailey beyond, whilst archers on the battlements turned to watch the newcomers arrive. Corbett reined in and dismounted, glancing across at the Great Hall, a manor house in itself. Built of good stone and fronted with ashlar on a red-brick base, it boasted a black-tiled roof and two low, squat chimney stacks. This was the Constable's personal dwelling, comprising hall, kitchen, solar and buttery, with his private chambers above. Sir Edmund Launge, accompanied by his wife and daughter, was already hastening down the steps to greet them. Ostlers and grooms hurried up to lead away their horses. Sir Edmund strode across, sending chickens and ducks squawking away in protest.

'Sir Hugh!'

'Sir Edmund!'

They clasped hands and exchanged the kiss of peace. Corbett went to show his commission from the King, but Launge waved it away with his fingers, demanding to be introduced to the rest of his party. Corbett did so. Pleasantries were exchanged. Questions were asked about Corbett's wife, the Lady Maeve, and his two children, Edward and Eleanor, named after the King and his late lamented Queen. Corbett enjoyed the introductions, eager to view Ranulf's reaction.

Sir Edmund was small and thick-set, grey hair straggling down either side of a square face burnt dark by the sun. A sombre-eyed man, his beard and moustache neatly clipped, Sir Edmund was dressed in a green and gold cotehardie with a black leather belt around his waist. Corbett knew the Constable of old as a born soldier, a skilled jouster and one of the old King's comrades, entrusted with the care of this important fortress. Lady Catherine Launge was buxom and plump, her red-cheeked face and grey hair almost hidden by a voluminous old-fashioned wimple. Dressed in her dark blue gown with a silver girdle, she stood on tiptoe to greet Corbett before introducing what Corbett knew would be the source of Ranulf's astonishment, her truly beautiful daughter. Constance was tall and willowy, her glorious auburn hair plaited under a bejewelled net. She wore a pelisse across her shoulders, and her dark tawny dress ringed a swan-like neck. But it was her face which Corbett found so beautiful; oval, with pale ivory skin, perfect features made all the more exquisite by calm sea-grey eyes. Corbett winked at Ranulf, who now realised why his master had told him he would be surprised, and so to be careful to observe all the courtly etiquette at Corfe.

Once protocol had been observed, Sir Edward insisted on taking Corbett and his party on a swift tour of the keep and inner ward, introducing them to officers of the garrison. Ranulf, reluctantly bidding the Lady Constance farewell, had no choice but to follow. Corbett became aware of how truly powerful the castle really was, with its mailed force of knights, men-at-arms and archers, as well as a company of Welsh longbowmen trained to deliver massed volleys of their goose-quilled yard-long shafts. He became breathless as they climbed the keep and the towers of the inner bailey. He and his party were to be lodged in the Salt Tower, which lay to the east of the keep, a collection of rather shabby chambers furnished with the bare necessities. Launge apologized, saying he had done what he could. Corbett's chamber was on the second floor of the tower, while his three companions would share a chamber above. He brushed aside Sir Edward's apologies and pronounced himself satisfied; his room was circular, its walls lime-washed, the wooden floor covered in rugs. A four-poster bed stood in the centre of the chamber, warmed and protected by dyed woollen drapes. There was a table, chairs, stools and a chest for his belongings, as well as a sufficiency of candles and lanterns as the window was a simple square, closed by a wooden board. He realized Launge had tried to make it as comfortable as possible; at least the chamber had a hearth built against the outside wall, with small-wheeled braziers either side.

'I have reserved the best chamber above the long hall for the Seigneur de Craon.' Sir Edmund raised his eyes heavenwards. 'Though personally I would like to throw him into the moat.'

Corbett laughed and stood aside as Chanson, helped by castle servants, brought in his belongings, along with his precious chancery coffer, which Corbett insisted on immediately placing in the iron-bound chest at the foot of the bed.

'It's the stoutest in the castle,' Launge explained. 'Your chancery coffer arrived yesterday escorted by a troop of lancers, and spent the night in my strongroom. That chest is just as safe.'

'It's just what I want.' Corbett patted the Constable affectionately on the shoulder and went up the spiral staircase to inspect his companions' quarters.

Afterwards, Corbett, Ranulf and Bolingbroke met with the constable in the council chamber, a long, low-ceilinged room on the ground floor of the keep. It was so ill lit by the narrow loopholes and arrow slits that the air was thick with the smoke from candles and torches. Sir Edmund ordered the doors to be closed, waving Corbett to one end of the heavy oaken table. He served them some ale, bread and cheese, then sat on Corbett's right, facing Ranulf and Bolingbroke. He asked about the King, and Corbett replied tactfully. He didn't think it was appropriate to inform Sir Edmund about the King's sudden rages at being trapped in a peace treaty with Philip of France.

'What problems do you have here, Sir Edmund? The fortress is well manned; you have many soldiers.'

'Drawn in from outlying garrisons,' the Constable replied.

'And the reason?'

'Flemish pirates, a swarm of them, have been seen off the foreland; they are packed in herring ships guarded by cogs of war. According to rumour they have been raiding coastal villages in Cornwall, Devon and Dorset.'

Corbett drank his ale and tried to ignore the queasy feeling in his stomach. Pirates, sheltering in the ports of the Low Countries, were a constant threat, but why had these appeared now? Did it have anything to do with his meeting de Craon at Corfe Castle? Corbett had many spies in Hainault, Flanders and Brabant, port officials and sailors who provided him with information about these pirates. They were financed by merchants, powerful men in cities like Dordrecht who secured letters patent from their rulers to harass other countries' shipping in the Narrow Seas. They could also be hired by foreign princes, as Edward of England had often done in his wars against France, Scotland and Wales. Had they been employed now by Philip of France, or was this just the normal pirate activity which plagued the southern coast of England?

'You are worried, Sir Hugh?'

'Of course I am. Have they been seen off Corfe?'

Sir Edmund shook his head. 'This castle is too powerful. Why throw yourself against the rocks when you can gather a richer harvest in the fishing villages to the west?'

'And what else?' Corbett insisted. 'I heard rumours about young maids being brutally murdered.'

Sir Edmund put his face in his hands. 'If God be known, I wish they were rumours. Five corpses in all, killed at close range by a crossbow bolt.' He removed his hands and took a deep breath. 'Three of the corpses were found in midden heaps in the castle wards; two were found outside, one near the moat, the other in the approaches leading to the eastern postern gate.'

'When did these murders begin?'

'About two months ago ... yes, it must be.' Sir Edmund chewed the corner of his lip. 'The first was found after Michaelmas, a castle girl who served at the nearby inn, the Tavern in the Forest.'

'Three corpses found in the castle?' Ranulf asked. 'Two outside? The murderer must be someone who lives here.'

Sir Edmund glared at this red-haired clerk. 'I have reached the same conclusion myself, sir.'

'No offence.' Ranulf smiled, eager to placate the father of the beautiful woman he had just met and couldn't forget.

'My officers and I have investigated.' Sir Edmund took a deep breath. 'All five girls were from the castle. You know how it is. Corfe is a small village in itself; we have a leech, who also acts as an apothecary, we have a small market, a chapel served by old Father Andrew. People come and go: traders, tinkers, pedlars, the moon people and the road folk, the wanderers, the tinkers.'

Corbett held his hands up, fingers splayed. 'But five corpses?' The Constable was unable to hold his gaze. 'Five corpses in what, the space of two months? This bloody work can't be laid at the door of some itinerant. The assassin must live somewhere close, perhaps only a short walk from this room.'

Corbett pressed against the table, pushed back his chair and went across to one of the loopholes, standing on a ledge to peer out. He felt tired and sweaty; the fug in the room was thick. He had slept badly the night before, whilst the journey had been cold and hard. He did not relish his meeting with de Craon and was alarmed at the reports Bolingbroke had brought from Paris.

And now this! Corbett thought of similar murders he had encountered in Suffolk and elsewhere, evil men hunting down young girls, slaughtering them like a weasel would birds in a farmyard, falling on them like a hawk would a dove. There had been murders like this in London; even the Royal Council . . .

'Sir Hugh?'

'I was thinking.' Corbett returned to the table, patting Ranulf on the shoulder and glancing at Bolingbroke, who was half asleep in his chair. 'I was thinking,' Corbett repeated, sitting down, 'of similar murders. They have been discussed even at Westminster. Young women being slaughtered, often abused, their bodies thrown into a river, sometimes even buried beneath a screed of soil in one of the city cemeteries.'

'There have been murders since the days of Cain,' Launge pointed out, 'and maids have been ravished since time immemorial.'

'No, this is different.' Corbett raised his tankard against his cheek, relishing its coolness. 'Sir Edmund, you have heard how the Commons and the Lords have approved measures, statute law, to clear the highways and make the roads safer. Do you know the reason for that? They say that the countryside is changing. There's no longer any need to plough the land or sow a crop.'

'Just grass it over,' Sir Edmund declared, 'and let the sheep graze. It's happening all through Dorset and Devon. God forgive me, in my own manor I have done the same.'

'The foreign merchants can't get enough of our wool,' Corbett continued, 'and King Edward sells it to the Frescobaldi bankers in return for treasure to finance his wars. They say it takes twelve people to plough, sow and harvest a field, but one man to guard a hundred sheep. Villages are dying, the poor are becoming poorer and they flock to the cities, London, Bristol, York, Carlisle, or to the great castles like Corfe, young maids looking for employment, sometimes without kith or kin or a place to lay their head. In Southwark alone there are five thousand whores, easy prey for the foxes, the hawks and the weasels, those with killer souls.' Corbett paused, half listening to the sounds of the castle carrying faintly through the thick walls of the keep. For a few moments he felt a deep pang of homesickness and wondered what the

Lady Maeve would be doing. 'What hour is it?' He turned to Sir Edmund.

'It must be about nine.' The Constable apologized for the hour candle not being lit.

'If we can,' Corbett sighed, 'we shall help trap this murderer. Do you suspect anyone?'

Launge shook his head.

'The hour hurries on.' Corbett drew himself up. 'We must come to the business in hand. When do the French arrive?'

'They should be here late this afternoon. They landed at Dover three days ago. Seigneur de Craon, four professors from the Sorbonne, de Craon's bodyguard and a few royal archers. Why this meeting?' Sir Edmund leaned forward. 'And why here?'

'Seven months ago,' Corbett replied, 'Edward of England sealed the peace treaty of Paris with his beloved cousin Philip of France. They promised to settle all differences over shipping in the Narrow Seas, as well as Philip of France's claim over certain territories in dispute in the English Duchy of Gascony. Our King was forced to agree to a marriage between the Prince of Wales and Isabella, Philip's only daughter. The French King is beside himself with glee; he sees himself as a new Charlemagne – the king before whom all other kings and princes will bow. He looks forward to the day when one of his grandsons sits on the throne at Westminster whilst another is made Duke of Gascony. He hopes this will weaken English control over south-western France and make it easier to absorb Gascony into the Capetian patrimony. Philip sees himself as the glorious descendant of St Louis. He claims that his family, the Capets, are of sacred blood. He is helped in all this by the Papacy, who, as you know, because of family feuds in Rome, have moved to Avignon in southern France.' Corbett placed his thumb against the table top. 'The French have the Pope there.' He pressed his thumb even harder. 'The Treaty of Paris is protected by the most solemn penalties imposed by the Pope.'

'And our King wishes to escape it.'

'Of course,' Corbett agreed. 'He would love to tell Philip to tear the treaty up, leave Gascony alone, stop meddling in Scotland and allow the Prince of Wales to marry whom he wishes. In truth, Edward is trapped. If he breaks the treaty he will be excommunicated, cursed by bell, book and candle, an outcast in Europe. He would love to go to war, but the barons of the Exchequer say the treasury is empty.'

Corbett paused for effect. Everything he said the Constable knew. Both he and Corbett had fought in Scotland, where the Scottish princes refused to bow to Edward. More and more armies were being sent north, more treasure drained away.

'And so we come to Friar Roger Bacon. He was born in the last years of King John, our present King's grandfather, at Ilchester in Somerset. He proved to be an outstanding scholar, studying at Oxford and Paris. While in Paris he came under the influence of Pierre de Marincourt. People claim that Marincourt was a magician who had discovered secret knowledge.'

Corbett glanced at his two companions; Ranulf was listening intently, as he did to anything on education or knowledge. Bolingbroke had roused himself, eager to discover the true reasons for his flight from Paris, and Ufford's hideous death.

'Bacon became a Franciscan,' Corbett continued. 'He wrote a number of books, *Opus Maius, Opus Minus* and *Opus Tertium*. He also disseminated a number of treatises, such as *The Art of the Marvellous* and *How to Prevent the Onset of Old Age*. At first Friar Roger was supported by the Papacy, but eventually he fell under the suspicion of heresy, and until shortly before his death in 1292, some eleven years ago, he was kept in prison. His writings were frowned upon, and they say that when he died, his brothers at the Franciscan priory in Oxford nailed his manuscripts to the wall and left them to rot. Friar Roger's disciples dispersed. We know of one, a scholar called John whom Bacon often sent to the Holy See. After Friar Roger died, these followers disappeared like puffs of smoke on a summer's day.'

'This secret knowledge?' Ranulf asked.

'I have studied Friar Roger's works,' Corbett replied, 'as has Master William here. His theories are truly startling. He talks of being able to construct a series of mirrors or glasses which will make places miles away appear so close you could touch them. He claims that Caesar built such a device before his invasion of Britain.' Corbett warmed to his theme. 'He talks of carts which can travel without being pulled by oxen, of machines which can go to the bottom of the sea, of ships which don't need rowers, even of machines that can fly through the air. He also talks of a black powder which can create a thunder-like explosion, a mixture of saltpetre and other substances.'

'But these have been talked of before.' Bolingbroke spoke up. 'Even the great Aristotle claims it is possible to build a machine to go along the bottom of the sea.'

'I know, I know,' Corbett conceded, 'but Friar Roger is different. His Grace the King and I have been through his papers. Bacon actually insists that he has seen some of these experiments work.' Corbett sat back in his chair, gazing around this stark whitewashed chamber, so simple and bare, nothing but a crucifix and a few coffers and a side table for jugs and goblets, such a contrast to what he was describing.

'Impossible!' Sir Edmund breathed. 'This is witchcraft, magic, the ravings of a warlock.'

'Is it?' Ranulf retorted. 'In the Tower, the King's engineers are working on bombards which can throw a stone harder and faster against a castle wall than a catapult. The Flemings are building a ship with sails different from ours which make their cogs faster yet sturdier.'

'I know, I know.' Sir Edmund sipped from his tankard. 'But why should his Grace the King be interested in all of this? The schools are full of new wonders; new manuscripts are being discovered; even I, an old soldier, know this. As you do, Sir Hugh. You have debated in the Halls of Oxford and listened to the schoolmen.'

'I would agree.' Corbett smiled. 'I've heard the whispers about a magical bronze head which can speak all manner of wisdom, whilst they claim the Templar order have discovered the secrets of Solomon, but it is,' Corbett grinned, 'as if someone claims to be able to call Satan up from Hell. He may be able to, but will Satan come?' His words created laughter, which lessened the tension. 'Friar Roger, however, is different. During his captivity he wrote another book, the *Secretus Secretorum*, or *Secret of Secrets*, in which he revealed, in great detail, all his secret knowledge. He wrote the book then copied it out again. The original went to Paris, whilst the copy stayed in England.'

'That's why Ufford died?' Bolingbroke interrupted.

'Yes,' Corbett replied more sharply than he intended.

'We stole the original?'

'No,' Corbett shook his head, 'you only stole a second copy; that's what you brought back to Westminster. The original is still kept by King Philip himself in his treasure house.'

'What!' Bolingbroke would have sprung to his feet, but Ranulf gripped him by the wrist, forcing him to stay seated. Bolingbroke knocked the tankard off the table. 'A copy? Is that why Walter died? We failed!'

'You didn't fail.' Corbett's voice remained calm. 'Edward of England wanted to know if his copy and the copy kept in Paris were the same. I am pleased to say they are.'

'What does it say?' Sir Edmund ignored Bolingbroke's outburst.

'That's the problem.' Corbett got to his feet and went to retrieve the tankard. He refilled it and placed it in front of his clerk, patting him gently on the shoulder before resuming his seat. 'The *Secretus Secretorum* is written in a cipher no one understands. Whoever breaks that cipher will enter a treasure house of knowledge. For months, the clerks of the Secret Chancery have tried this cipher or that in a search to find a key. We know de Craon's clerks have been doing the same, to no result. Edward knows Philip has the *Secret of Secrets*; the French know Edward has a fair and accurate copy.'

'Ah,' Sir Edmund sighed. 'Now I see. Philip has invoked the peace treaty, the clauses stipulating how he and Edward are to work together.'

'Precisely.' Corbett steepled his fingers. 'Philip has demanded, especially since the theft of the copy from Paris, that both kingdoms share their knowledge. He knows I am responsible for the secret ciphers of the Chancery, so he called for this meeting.'

'Why here?' Ranulf asked.

'Philip is being diplomatic. He wants to reassure Edward. He simply asked that the meeting place be in some castle on the south coast, not Dover or one of the Cinque Ports, well away from the hustle and bustle of the cities. Edward proposed Corfe, and Philip agreed. De Craon will bring with him four professors from the university, experts in the study of Bacon's manuscripts, men skilled in breaking ciphers. They will meet myself, Bolingbroke and Master Ranulf here.'

'Who are they?' Bolingbroke asked. 'What are their names?'

'Etienne Destaples, Jean Vervins, Pierre Sanson and Louis Crotoy.'

Bolingbroke whistled under his breath. 'They are all pro-fessors of law as well as theology, leading scholars at the Sorbonne.'

'Of course,' Corbett agreed. 'I know one of them, Louis Crotoy; he lectured in the schools of Oxford, a formidable scholar, with a brain as sharp as a knife.'

'I don't believe this.'

'You don't believe what?' Ranulf smiled.

Bolingbroke just shook his head. He took off his cloak and threw it over the table, fingers going for his dagger in its leather sheath. 'Philip means mischief; there is treachery here.'

'Which is why we are meeting here,' Corbett retorted. 'Tell me again, William, why Ufford killed Magister Thibault.'

'He had to.' Bolingbroke sat down and rubbed his face. 'We were in the cellar trying to open that damnable coffer.'

'But why?' Corbett insisted. 'Why should Thibault, whom Ufford last saw cavorting with a buxom wench, leave his bed sport, his warm, comfortable chamber, and, on a night of revelry, take that woman down to a cold cellar? What was he going to show her? A precious manuscript she couldn't under-stand?'

'Perhaps he was boasting,' Ranulf said. 'He wanted to impress her?'

'But why then?' Corbett insisted. 'At that specific moment on that particular night?'

'I don't know.' Bolingbroke shook his head. 'But yes, I've thought the same. You've asked me often enough, Sir Hugh; now Thibault's colleagues are coming, you ask again. I truly don't know.' He sighed in exasperation. 'I have also wondered how Ufford was trapped and caught.' He took a deep breath. 'Are you sure the manuscript we stole was genuine? Or has Philip simply put fools' caps on all of us?'

The wise have always been divided from the multitude.

Roger Bacon, *Opus Maius*

Everyone ought to know languages and needs to study them and understand their silence.

Roger Bacon, *Opus Tertium*

Chapter 3

Alusia, the butterymaid, daughter of Gilbert, understeward of the pantry at Corfe Castle, moved amongst the gravestones and crosses in the large cemetery of St Peter's in the Wood. Alusia, small and plump, with curly black hair and dancing eyes, was very pleased with herself. The arrival of the King's men at the castle had caused a great deal of excitement. People pretended to go about their normal business but, as her father remarked, 'a stranger is a stranger', and everyone stared at these powerful men from the distant city of London. Alusia had been frightened by the sombre-faced clerk with the black hair and silver-hilted sword, but already the girls were talking about the red-haired one, just the way he swaggered, those green eyes darting about ready for mischief.

Alusia would have loved to have stayed and listened to the gossip, but Mistress Feyner had declared she would leave promptly at noon, and Mistress Feyner was to be obeyed. The castle girls called Mistress Feyner 'the Old Owl', because she never missed anything. Hard of face and hard of eye, strong of arm and sharp of wit, Mistress Feyner was chief washerwoman. She knew her status and her powers as much as any great lady in a hall. Indeed, matters had grown worse since Phillipa, Mistress Feyner's daughter, had disappeared on Harvest Sunday last. Gone like a leaf on the breeze, and no one knew where. Of course, none of the other girls really missed her. Phillipa, too, had been full of her own airs and graces, especially when Father Matthew gathered them in the

51

nave on a Saturday afternoon to teach all the girls of the area the alphabet and the importance of numbers. A strange one, Father Matthew, so learned.

Alusia looked up at the leaden-grey sky. Was it going to snow? She hoped not, but if it did, at least she'd come here on Marion's name day to honour her friend's grave. Alusia blew on her frozen fingers and watched her hot breath disappear. Rebecca should have come with her, but Mistress Feyner had been most insistent that if she wanted a ride in the laundry cart down to the church, she'd have to leave immediately. Mistress Feyner had linen to deliver to Master Reginald at the Tavern in the Forest, and Rebecca would simply have to run to catch up. Alusia could not quarrel with that, but now, in this deserted graveyard, she thought that perhaps she should have waited. Oh where, she wondered, had Rebecca got to? When would she come?

Alusia paused next to her grandmother's gravestone and stared up at the church, an old place of ancient stone. The nave was like a long barn, though Sir Edmund had recently retiled the roof and done what he could to dress the stone of the soaring square tower. From one of the narrow tower windows candlelight glowed. Father Matthew always lit that as a beacon when the sea mist swirled in and cloaked the countryside in its thick grey blanket. Only the glow of the candles, as well as torches from the castle, could guide people, for Corfe was a dangerous place. To the north, east and west lay a thick ancient forest, full of swamps, marshes and other treacherous places. The girls talked about the sprites and goblins who lived beneath the leaves or sheltered in the cracks of ancient oak trees, of strange sounds and sights, of will-o-the-wisps, really ghosts of the dead, which hovered over the marshes.

Alusia stared round the sombre churchyard; a mist was creeping in now, even so early in the day, its cold fingers stretching out from the sea. She hitched the cloak she had borrowed from her father close about her, a soldier's cloak of pure wool and lined with flock, with a deep cowl to go over her head. She wondered whether Father Matthew was in the church, and if he would come out. She would pretend she was searching for herbs, but of course, the real herbs didn't bloom until May, and spring seemed an eternity away.

Alusia was looking for a grave, Marion's tumulus, that small mound of black earth which marked her close friend's last resting place. Marion, bright of eye, always laughing, whose corpse had been found beneath the slime of the rubbish in the outer ward of the castle. She had been the first to be killed, a crossbow bolt, shot so close Alusia's father said it almost pierced poor Marion's entire body. The castle leech, together with Father Matthew and old Father Andrew, assisted by Mistress Feyner, had dressed the body for burial. Alusia and the rest of the girls were excluded, but she had stolen up that afternoon and slipped through the door. Now she wished she hadn't. Marion's face had been a gruesome white, dark rings around those staring eyes, from which the coins had slipped. Flecks of blood still marked her mouth, whilst so many cloths had been wrapped around the wound her chest appeared to have swollen.

Alusia found the grave, marked by a simple cross, with *Marion, Requiescat in Pace* burnt in by the castle smith. She knelt down and, from beneath her cloak, took a piece of holly she had cut, the leaves sparkling green, the berries bright. She placed this near the cross. She would have liked to have brought flowers, but it was the dead of winter. Didn't Father Matthew say the holly represented Christ, the evergreen, ever-present Lord, whilst the berries represented his sacred blood? Alusia scratched her nose and tried to recall a prayer. Father Matthew had taught them the Our Father in Latin. She tried to say this. Latin was more powerful, it was God's language. She stumbled over the words *Qui est in caelo*, 'Who art in heaven', and gave up, simply satisfying herself with the sign of the cross. Then she sat back on her heels. Why would someone kill poor Marion, and the others? One by one, in the same manner, a crossbow bolt through the heart, or in Sybil's case through her throat, ripping the flesh on either side. Who was responsible? What had the victims been guilty of? The castle girls, in their innocence, were full of gossip about young men, eagerly looking forward to this feast or that holy day, be it Christmas when the huge Yule log crackled in the castle hearth, or May Day when the maypole was erected under the sheer blue skies of an early summer. Yet what crime in that?

Alusia lifted her head, staring back towards the lych gate. For a moment she thought she had seen someone. The church bell began to toll, the sign for midday prayer; not that many people listened. Alusia made the sign of the cross again and got to her feet. The other girls were buried nearby. Why had they died? The gossip said they hadn't been ravished, so what was the purpose? Poor girls with nothing in their wallets, not even a cheap ring on their finger.

Alusia walked slowly to the lych gate and on to the narrow trackway leading up to the castle. The trees thronged in on either side, and the mist had grown thicker. Alusia walked briskly, then paused at a noise behind her. She turned swiftly, but there was no one. She walked on until she noticed a flash of colour on the verge beside the track. Intrigued, she hurried over. It was a bundle of cloth, dark greens and browns, and a glimpse of reddish hair. Alusia stood, gripped by a numbing fear. Wasn't that Rebecca's hair? Weren't those her colours? Breath caught in her throat, she stooped and pulled at the bundle. The corpse rolled back: sightless eyes, a blood-caked mouth, and just beneath the chin, that awful bloody wound with the crossbow quarrel peeping out. It was Rebecca, and she was dead yet alive, for Alusia could hear a terrible screaming.

The discussion in the council chamber had grown more heated, Bolingbroke striding up and down, obviously angry that he and Ufford had risked their lives, with Ufford paying the ultimate price, merely to steal a copy.

'It was necessary,' Corbett shouted. 'His Grace the King has taken a deep interest in Friar Roger's writings. We had to make sure that the book we held, our copy of the *Secretus Secretorum*, was accurate. I have compared the two, and as far as I can see, with all their strange symbols and ciphers, they are in accordance.'

Sir Edmund sat watching this confrontation; Ranulf was quietly enjoying himself. He liked nothing better than watching old Master Longface in debate. Moreover, he knew Bolingbroke of old as a passionate man, and Ranulf, who had done his share of fleeing from those who wished to kill him, sympathised with his anger.

'What we must look at, William,' Corbett kept his voice calm, 'is the logic of the situation.'

'Logic?' Bolingbroke retook his seat. 'Sir Hugh, I know as much about logic as you do, we are not in the schools now.'

'Yes we are.'

Corbett smiled, then paused as the servant whom Sir Edmund had summoned brought in a fresh jug of ale and soft bread from the castle ovens. He was glad of the respite as the drink was poured and the bread shared out.

'We must apply logic.' He spoke quickly as Bolingbroke filled his mouth with bread and cheese. 'What concerns me is not the copy, or what happened when you stole it, but why Magister Thibault came down to that cellar on that night of revelry. Why did he bring that young woman with him?'

'Ufford had no choice but to kill them!'

'I'm not saying he did. Walter was a dagger man through and through. What I suspect is treachery. Let me describe my hypothesis. Here we have two clerks of the English Secret Chancery, scholars from the Halls of Oxford, pretending to be scholars at the Sorbonne. The order goes out, our noble King wants the French copy of Friar Bacon's *Secret of Secrets*. You and Ufford cast about, searching for it. A traitor emerges from amongst the French, this mysterious stranger who offers you the manuscript.'

'He didn't offer,' Bolingbroke answered, his mouth full of cheese. 'He simply told us where it was and promised that we would receive an invitation to Magister Thibault's revelry.'

'Do you know who this person was?' Ranulf asked.

Bolingbroke shook his head.

'No, we never met him; he communicated through memoranda left at our lodgings. I have shown you those I kept; the others I destroyed.'

Corbett nodded. He had scrutinized the scrawled memoranda. The Norman French was written in a hand he didn't recognize, providing information for his two secret clerks.

'What I do know,' Bolingbroke continued, sipping his ale, 'is that a month before Magister Thibault's revelry, this Frenchman discovered what we were looking for and, in return for gold, told us where it was and how we could take it. I think that somehow or other he alerted Magister Thibault and brought him down to that cellar. We were to be trapped there but Magister Thibault was an old sot, full of wine and lust, and perhaps he refused to believe what he was told or didn't realize the significance. More importantly, this traitor also told Seigneur Amaury de Craon and the Hounds of the King what was happening. We were fortunate. We were supposed to be trapped either at Magister Thibault's or at our lodgings in the Street of the Carmelites, but we escaped. We separated; they probably thought Ufford was more important and pursued him—'

'Did you see him die?' Ranulf interrupted.

'I was near the Madelene Quayside when I heard the clamour. A beggar told me how royal troops had been in that quarter since the early hours. I decided to leave Paris by another route. I joined a group of pilgrims journeying to Notre Dame in Boulogne.' Bolingbroke pulled a face. 'It was easy enough. I pretended to be a French clerk. It was simply a matter of reaching the port and securing passage on an English cog.'

'Who do you think this traitor was?' Corbett asked.

'It could have been de Craon himself, or one of the men he is bringing with him.'

'And why do you think is he bringing them to England?' Ranulf asked.

'Two reasons,' Bolingbroke replied, 'and I have thought deeply about this. First, I am sure Philip of France would love to discover the secrets of Roger Bacon. He is genuinely interested and wants to see what progress, if any, we English have made.'

'And secondly?'

'Secondly, Sir Hugh, what if . . .' Bolingbroke paused, running his finger round the rim of his tankard. 'What if we turn the game on its head? What if Philip of France has broken Friar Roger's secret cipher and has discovered the hidden knowledge? How to make a glass which can see something miles away, or turn base metal into gold.'

'And?' Corbett asked.

'What if de Craon is bringing the *periti*, the savants of Paris, to discover if we have done the same? And if we haven't, to confuse us further, hinder and block our progress?'

'There's another reason, isn't there?'

'Yes, Sir Hugh. Philip of France does not like the University of the Sorbonne. Oh, if it agrees with what he says he is all charm and welcoming, but if it doesn't, Philip's rage blazes out like a fire. I wonder if he has already broken the secret cipher, and is sending these men to England so that they can be killed, murdered, and the blame laid at our door.'

'Nonsense!' Launge shook his empty tankard as if it was a sword.

'No, no.' Corbett raised a hand. 'I follow your logic, William.' He smiled. 'What if Philip has broken the secret cipher, and what if he wants to rid himself of the *periti*, men who have also discovered that knowledge? The last thing Philip would want is one of these professors claiming the knowledge for himself and writing his own book, eager for fame amongst the universities and schools of Europe. We all know our doctors of divinity and theology, how they love fame as much as gold; indeed, the two often go together.' He paused. 'More seriously, Philip is looking for a crisis. He has bound our King by treaty, he wishes to depict Edward of England as the oath-breaker, the wily serpent. He knows that Edward's motto is "Keep Troth", yet he realizes Edward would storm the gates of Hell if it meant escaping from the Treaty of Paris. Let's say, for sake of argument, something happens during this French embassy to England. Philip will turn and scream for the protection of the Pope, who will bind our King even closer with heavier penalties and dire warnings.'

'But you must have considered this before you accepted the French embassy?' Bolingbroke asked.

'Of course I did,' Corbett replied. 'I have shared similar thoughts with the King, though not as detailed and sharp. As God is my witness, both Philip and Edward richly deserve each other, two cunning swordsmen circling each other in the dark, each looking for the advantage.' He laughed drily. 'Do you know, gentlemen, isn't it ridiculous – or as they would say in the schools of Oxford, *mirabile dictu*, marvellous to say – that the one thing which unites Edward of England, Philip of France, Amaury de Craon and myself is the belief that something will happen during de Craon's stay here at Corfe. Only the good Lord knows what.'

'So what do you propose?' Sir Edmund asked.

'The French are to be given good secure chambers.'

'They won't want guards, they never do,' the Constable retorted. 'They will only accuse us of eavesdropping or treating them like prisoners.'

'Make sure they are given the keys to their chambers,' Corbett tapped the table top, 'and that they eat together in the hall. As for the castle, let them go wherever they wish.' He pushed back his chair, a sign the meeting was over. 'But if they leave the castle they must have an escort.'

Sir Edmund rose to his feet, bowed and left. Bolingbroke asked if there was anything further. Corbett shook his head. The clerk departed saying he needed to change, wash and sleep.

'What now?' Ranulf asked.

He lounged in his chair, playing with the dagger sheath on his war belt. He placed this on the table before him and peered up at Corbett.

'You really do expect mischief, don't you?'

Corbett walked to the door which Bolingbroke had left half open. The gust of cold air was welcoming, but as he pulled the door shut, he noticed the first snowflakes fall.

'I don't know what to expect, Ranulf. You know Edward of England; he rejoices in the title of the Great English Justinian, he has a passion for knowledge. Once he becomes absorbed in something he becomes obsessed. He has been through Bacon's writings time and time again, like some theologian poring over the scriptures. He has insisted that I do the same. I have his copies of Friar Roger's works in that coffer.'

'Was the friar a magician?' Ranulf asked.

Corbett drew the trancher of bread towards him, cut a piece, dabbed it in the butter jar and put it in his mouth. 'Ranulf. Again it's logic. Have you ever lain in the grass,' he grinned, 'by yourself, stared up at the sky and watched a bird hover? Have you ever wondered what it must be like to fly, to be a bird? Or leaned over the side of a ship and wondered what really happens beneath the waves?'

'Of course,' Ranulf agreed. 'Your mind wanders.'

'People like Roger Bacon go one step further. Is it possible? Can it be done? They speculate,' Corbett continued, 'they become intrigued, and so the experiments begin.'

'Do you believe in this secret knowledge?'

'No, I don't.' Corbett swirled the ale round his jug. 'I believe in logic and deduction. If something is possible, does it become probable? What is the relationship between an idea and a fact? If we build a machine such as a catapult, to hurl rocks at a castle wall, is it possible to construct another machine to throw them even further and harder? Go down to the castle yard, Ranulf, study those Welsh bowmen. They don't use an arbalest but a bow made of yew which can loose a yard-long shaft. In Wales I watched a master bowman fire six such arrows in the space of a few heartbeats whilst a crossbowman was still winching back the cord of his own weapon.'

'When the French come . . .' Ranulf decided to change the subject. He knew from past experience how Corbett's military service in Wales always brought about a change in mood. Sir Hugh still suffered nightmares about those narrow twisting valleys and the cruelties both sides perpetrated on each other. 'When the French come,' he repeated, 'will de Craon accuse Bolingbroke of theft and murder?'

'Great suspicion but little proof.' Corbett laughed drily. 'Oh, he'll know and he'll know that I know, which will make us both very knowledgeable, but de Craon is too cunning to accuse anybody. He may make references to it, but no outright allegation. He might talk about a housebreaker called Ufford, a scholar and an Englishman, being killed, but that is as far as he will go. The dead do not concern de Craon. Like a fox which has killed a pullet, it has only whetted its appetite for—'

Corbett started at the shouting from outside.

'Woe unto you who has done this! Limb of Satan, fiend of Hell, innocent blood cries for vengeance and justice! Cursed be ye in your thinking and in your drinking . . .'

The rest of the proclamation was drowned by a soul-chilling scream, followed by shouts and yells. Corbett and Ranulf hurried to the door. The snow was swirling under a biting wind, but the flurry of winter was ignored as members of the castle, men, women and children, ran towards a tall balding man, his lower face covered by a luxuriant beard and moustache, who stood, dressed all in black, beside a small hand barrow. Corbett ran down the steps, forcing his way through the throng. On the hand barrow sprawled the corpse of a young woman, the sheet which had covered her pulled back to reveal a bloodless face, staring eyes and a quarrel high in the chest which had rent flesh and bone. A line of blood coursed down from the girl's gaping mouth. A woman knelt beside the hand barrow, fingers combing her grey hair as she threw her head back and shrieked at the low grey sky. A man beside her, dressed in a leather jerkin, tried to comfort her. Others were gathering around, shouting words of comfort and condolence. Another young woman, hysterical with grief and fear, crouched holding on to the barrow until others prised her fingers loose and led her away. The crowd was turning ugly with shouts and curses, and Corbett became aware that the main accusations were levelled against an outlaw band and its leader, Horehound.

Sir Edmund, along with his wife and daughter, had arrived. Constance, her beautiful face shrouded by the hood of her cloak, took the distraught mother, lifting her up and pressing her body next to hers as she led her away. Lady Catherine hastened to help. Sir Edmund ordered his men-at-arms to keep the crowd away, shouting at them to go back to their business. After a while order was imposed. The grieving parents were taken into the long hall. The young woman's corpse was inspected by the dry-faced castle leech, who introduced himself simply as Master Simon. He carefully examined the body and shook his head.

'No bruises, no violation; death must have been instant. Sir Edmund, there is nothing I can do.' He pointed to the quarrel dug deep into the flesh. 'Except take that out and prepare her for burial.' He walked away shaking his head, muttering about the girl's death being similar to the rest.

Corbett crouched down beside the barrow, whilst Sir Edmund led the black-clad priest away, having introduced him to Corbett as Father Matthew, parish priest of St Peter's in the Wood. Father Matthew had a strong face, lined and ashen, and hollow eyes red-rimmed from lack of sleep. He was shaking slightly and muttered an apology about his outburst, putting it down to the horror of what he had seen. Sir Edmund called for a servant to bring a cup of posset. The snow was falling heavily now, covering the sheet-white face of the murdered girl. A flake settled on her half-open eye; others mingled with the dry blood. Corbett's finger brushed the feathered quarrel, a stout, ugly dart, embedded so deeply the feathers mingled with the ruptured flesh. When he glanced up, the priest had returned and was staring down at him.

'So you are the King's man?' Corbett noticed the fear in the priest's eyes. 'I apologise once again, but . . .' Father Matthew stumbled as he gestured at the corpse. 'It was in the lane outside the church, crumpled like a bundle of rags. I was in my sacristy when I heard Alusia's chilling scream. She's the girl who found the corpse. Apparently she'd arranged to go down to the cemetery to visit the grave of another victim, her friend Marion. This lass,' he gestured at the corpse, 'was meant to go with her. Poor Rebecca! Anyway, Alusia left on Mistress Feyner's cart, thinking Rebecca would join her later. Of course, she didn't. When Alusia left the cemetery she stumbled across her corpse.' The priest shook his head. 'Such horror! I'd forgotten the warning of the ancients, *Praeparetur animus contra omnia.*'

'Prepare your soul for the unexpected,' Corbett translated. 'You are a student of Seneca, Father?'

'Many years ago.' The priest seemed pleased at the arrival of the old chaplain Father Andrew, who came hobbling across almost hidden by his cloak, a walking stick in one hand, a small reed basket in the other.

'Have you performed the rites?' the old priest asked.

'No, Father, I haven't. I forgot.'

Father Matthew knelt, the snow swirling around him, and whispered the words of absolution, '*Absolvo te a peccatis tuis,*' 'I absolve you from your sins.'

'And now the anointing,' Father Andrew cackled. 'For God's sake, man, don't forget the anointing. Extreme unction is one of the Sacraments of the Church. I can't do it myself.' Father Andrew's light blue eyes peered at Corbett. 'It's the rheums in my legs, you know.'

Father Matthew snatched the phial of holy oil from the basket and began to anoint the palms of the dead girl's hands, then her feet, slipping off the coarse leather sandals, before anointing her eyes, ears and mouth. Corbett looked over his shoulder. Ranulf stood watching avidly. Corbett recalled his henchman's ambition, one he voiced now and again, that if the path of preferment meant ordination as a priest, he would seriously consider it.

Once the anointing was finished, Sir Edmund ordered some men-at-arms to take the corpse down to the small shed which lay behind the castle chapel, St John's Within-the-Gate, near the entrance to the first bailey. Then he stared up at the sky, a sea of iron grey, the snowflakes shifting in the sharp breeze.

'Sir Hugh, my apologies, you haven't eaten, well, not properly.'

He invited the priests to join them, but the old castle chaplain declared he would watch by the corpse and pray. They watched him go, then hurried across to the Constable's quarters. The hall was a welcome relief from the bitter cold and the grim, sombre council room. It was a long vaulted chamber, its beams painted a deep black, its walls covered in white plaster as background for a series of beautiful paintings of angel musicians, all playing different instruments: lutes, harps, viols, pipes, clarions and shawms. Sir Edmund, to ease the tension, explained how Lady Catherine had a fascination with angels, adding that the hall's tapestries and gaily coloured cloths celebrated similar themes.

'We call it the Hall of Angels.' He gestured around. The hall was certainly comfortable and tastefully decorated, its hard-wood floor polished and free of the reeds and rushes which collected filth and could reek like a midden heap. At the far end was a minstrel's gallery, and down either side long trestle tables of good stout walnut, polished until they shone in the light of cresset torches and candles. In the centre of the hall, almost facing the principal doorway, was a large mantled hearth, a yawning cavernous fireplace protected by a wire mesh grille, behind which a stack of logs burned merrily. At the other end of the hall, under heraldic banners, stood the high table on its dais, and in the centre of the table rested a beautiful silver castle which served as the great salt holder. Sir Edmund, pointing out various features of the hall, took them up to the table and grouped them round it. Servants hurried from the kitchens behind the dais with steaming bowls of barley soup, followed by platters of towres, a delicious veal omelette, with buttered bread and a dish of diced vegetables. Sir Edmund poured the wine, a sparkling white, especially imported from vineyards of the Rhine. To keep their fingers warm, small ornamented chafing dishes, filled with charcoal and sprinkled with thyme, were placed along the top of the table. Father Matthew, declaring himself famished, ate quickly, and when he had finished accepted a dish of rather fatty lamb cutlets served in a mint sauce.

'You are fasting, Father?' Ranulf teased.

'I haven't eaten since yesterday. Sir Edmund,' Father Matthew nodded towards the Constable, 'insists that I dine with him here.' He grinned. 'So I thank him by prayer, good works and fasting for the next meal.'

'Father,' Corbett waited until the chuckling had subsided, 'you have brought in the sixth victim.'

'Aye, it is; six in all. Five buried in my cemetery, five requiem masses, five sprinklings of holy water, five crosses, five mothers and fathers to console.'

'And you have no suspicion why this has been done?'

The priest shook his head. 'That is the first corpse I have found. The rest? Well, Sir Edmund will tell you about them. Just lying there she was. Crumpled, like a bundle of cloth tossed aside. But why?' The priest talked as if to himself. 'She was only a poor maid, she had nothing but her comeliness.'

'I heard people blame the outlaws.'

'Outlaws,' Sir Edmund interrupted. 'You would think they were William Wallace. A paltry group of men and women,' he explained to Corbett, leaning across the table. 'Poachers and petty thieves. Oh, they've done enough to hang, but why should they kill young women? Three of the seven victims have been found in the grounds of the castle.'

'I thought it was six?'

'One is missing,' Sir Edmund explained. 'Phillipa, Mistress Feyner's daughter, she is the principal laundrywoman here. About ten weeks ago, just after the harvest was brought in, Phillipa disappeared after Sunday Mass. According to common report she claimed she was going for a walk but never returned. I sent out men-at-arms and riders who scoured the countryside; they went as deep into the forest as they could. I asked the fishermen along the coasts to watch the tides, but no corpse has ever been found.'

'I organized my parishioners,' Father Matthew added. 'Every dell, wood, copse, ditch and cave on Purbeck Island was searched but nothing was found. Mistress Feyner now believes her daughter is dead, the first victim of these horrid murders. A time of tribulation, the worst since I joined the parish.'

'How long ago was that?' Corbett asked, scooping up a piece of omelette with his horn spoon.

'About eleven years. I originally come from Durham, but was unable to obtain a benefice there.' The priest swiftly reverted back to the murders. 'Truly this is a time of fear; as Ovid says: *Omnibus ignotae mortis timor*, "In all creatures lurks a fear of unknown death." No one understands why these young women have been killed in such a brutal fashion.'

Corbett leaned over and whispered to Sir Edmund, the Constable turning his head to listen intently.

'Is there anything,' Ranulf asked, 'that all these victims have in common?'

The priest pushed away his platter, cradling his wine cup. Corbett noticed how, despite his burly appearance, Father Matthew's fingers were long and slender as a woman's.

'What do they all have in common? I understand your logic.' He raised his eyebrows. 'But I do not know your name.'

'Ranulf, Ranulf atte Newgate, Chief Clerk in the Chancery of the Green Wax.'

'Those things,' the priest replied, 'which are equal to the same thing are equal to one another. The same rule of logic applies to all these victims. They are poor, they are young, they live in the castle, they all look for work, either in the castle, or the great prize, being a slattern or maid at Master Reginald's inn, the Tavern in the Forest.'

'And there's your school,' Sir Edmund added.

'Oh yes, my school.' The priest smiled. 'Every Saturday afternoon I gather all the young women into the nave of the church to teach them the basic rudiments of reading and writing. There must be about thirty girls in all. Some are very quick, young Phillipa certainly was. I give them some butter-milk and freshly baked bread and, in summer, the best honey from my hives. On Sunday it's the turn of the young men. I'm very proud of my school,' he added.

'So would I be,' Corbett replied. 'That's where I began, the transept of St Dunstan's church, followed by cathedral school and after that, the Halls of Oxford. Small sparks can be fanned into flames.' He paused as a servant carrying a leather bag entered, then bent over and whispered into Sir Edmund's ear.

'They'll be here in a short while, but in the mean time . . .' The Constable pushed across the leather bag. Corbett took out the wicked-looking quarrel which the leech had removed from Rebecca's chest; at one end were sharp barbs like those on a fish-hook, at the other a flight of stiffened feathers. It had been cleaned but Corbett noticed how the impact had bent one of the barbs, and even the ugly tip was slightly blunted.

'Do you recognize it, Sir Edmund?'

'There are thousands like it in the castle.'

Corbett weighed the quarrel in his hand. 'Rebecca was found on a trackway; at a guess her killer stood only a yard away. Now here was a young woman fleet of foot and sharp of ear. If she felt threatened, she would run, but she didn't. She was facing her killer, she must have allowed the assassin to draw very close. Now tell me, sirs, on a lonely, misty trackway, on a cold December morning, in a place and at a time when hideous murders have taken place, why should this young woman not show any fear?'

'Before you say it,' Father Matthew's voice was hard, 'she would allow her priest to walk close, but I was in my church.'

'Pax, pax,' Corbett whispered. 'No one accuses you, Father, let alone suspects you. Who else?'

'A friend,' Ranulf declared, 'another young woman, or someone old and frail? Rebecca was not frightened.' He paused at the clamour around the hall door. Sir Edmund shouted at his guards to let them pass and a group of men and women shuffled into the hall, staring round in wonderment before turning to bow towards Sir Edmund.

'They are the parents,' Sir Edmund whispered, 'of the dead girls. I've gathered them as you asked.'

Corbett waited until they all stood just inside the doorway before going down to greet them. The rest of the company on the high table followed. Sir Hugh asked the parents to sit, then introduced himself.

'Have you been sent down here?' A small, slender woman with wiry grey hair and fierce eyes in a sweat-soaked red face stared eagerly at Corbett. 'Has the King himself sent you down here to seek justice for our daughters?'

'Yes, yes,' Corbett replied quickly, 'that is one of my tasks. Sir Edmund, perhaps we could serve our guests a cup of warm posset; their hands are chapped and their lips blue with the cold.' His words were welcomed, and for a while there was some confusion as the cooks and scullions from the kitchen brought out a bowl of heated wine, muttering under their breath about interfering clerks whilst they doled out the hot spiced drink. Corbett himself took a cup and toasted his guests sitting either side of the trestle table. He turned to the woman who had addressed him.

'You are?'

'Mistress Feyner, chief washerwoman of the castle.' She hitched her tattered shawl about her shoulders. Corbett noticed how the smock underneath, although threadbare, was spot-lessly clean, whilst the woman's chapped red hands glistened with oil.

'I am a widow, sir, and my only daughter Phillipa was the first victim, although she has never been found.'

'I've heard this,' Corbett replied, 'but is there anything you can tell me about why your daughters should die in such a hideous fashion?'

At first there was silence, but then the clamour of replies began. Corbett listened carefully before holding his hands up for silence.

'But there are no strangers in the area.'

'There's the outlaws,' Mistress Feyner shouted. 'Horehound and his coven.'

She was immediately contradicted by the others, and Corbett sensed she was not popular amongst the others.

'That's ridiculous,' a man who introduced himself as Oswald retorted. 'Horehound is a poacher, a petty thief, one of us but fallen on hard times. Why should he slay our daughters?'

'It must be someone we know,' a voice shouted. 'Here in the castle.'

Corbett glanced down the table at the old woman, dressed in dusty black, her long white hair falling to her shoulders, Corbett detected a slight accent and commented on it.

'You've got sharp ears, clerk. I'm not from these parts, I'm from Gascony.'

'And your name?'

'To you and everyone here, Juliana, Mistress Juliana they call me, clerk. My granddaughter was killed near the castle moat but the others were placed near midden heaps. How can it be Horehound? He never comes into this castle.'

Corbett allowed others to speak, and as he did so stared at their lined, grimed faces, the anger and desperation in their sad eyes, the way they raised their chapped hands, sometimes joined as if in prayer, looking expectantly down at him, the King's Man, ready to dispense justice. He felt as if he had gone back in time, gazing at the faces of his own mother, father, aunts and uncles. Men and women tied to the soil, 'earthworms' as his mother described them.

Despite Ranulf's muttering and a tap on his ankle, Corbett publicly promised what he quietly prayed he could carry out: to hunt down the assassin of their daughters and see him hang. The group slowly began to take their leave. Father Matthew assured Corbett he was always welcome in his church, and left. Sir Edmund shook his head and quietly whispered how he hoped Corbett would keep his promise but that he too could not stay any longer as he expected the French to arrive before nightfall.

'Can you do that?' Ranulf asked as he followed Corbett across the castle bailey, head slightly turned against the sharp breeze, the snow now falling heavily, coating everything in a sheet of white. Corbett cursed as he slipped on the cobbles but then steadied himself.

'I have to, Ranulf. Could you not feel the sea of misery in there?'

They entered the Salt Tower and went up to Corbett's chamber.

'You'll rest now?' Ranulf asked, alarmed to see his master slip on his war belt and lift up his thick grey cloak.

'The French will be here soon and the snow is falling.' Corbett patted Ranulf on the shoulder. 'We might become prisoners of Corfe and I want to look where we are. There's no need for you to come.' And before Ranulf could reply, Sir Hugh, spurs jingling, was halfway down the stairs.

Ranulf closed his eyes. For a few short heartbeats he cursed Corbett. Old Master Longface expected Ranulf to follow; that was why he hadn't locked the room. Ranulf stared at the ironbound coffer at the foot of the bed. It looked secure enough to hold what Corbett called his treasures of the Chancery, his bible of secrets and manuscripts of symbols. These contained the ciphers and hidden writing the Keeper of the Secret Seal used to communicate with his spies, from Berwick on Tweed in Scotland to the far-flung outposts of the Teutonic knights far to the east of the River Rhine. Corbett had brought these, and other books of secrets, with him as he always did, to continue the day-to-day business of the Chancery as well as a possible means to translate Friar Roger's enigmatic puzzle.

'As I can bear witness!' Ranulf whispered. He had been with Corbett, burning the candles low in the Chancery rooms at Westminster, the Tower and even Leighton Manor. Corbett had neglected the Lady Maeve and his children, totally immersed in his task, only to grow increasingly frustrated.

Ranulf went across to the coffer and, crouching down, examined the three stout locks, the work of a craftsman. Then he blew out the candle glowing under its cap and, removing the key, locked the door from the outside and raced up the steps to his own chamber. He would have preferred to go wandering around the castle until, by accident of course, he met the Lady Constance. Perhaps he could persuade her to sit with him in a window seat? His mind was busy with all sort of chivalric notions, snatches of poetry, fitting similes and those subtle compliments a gentleman should pay to a lady. But now, there was more pressing business. Ranulf could not forget that last meeting of the Secret Council at Westminster. Edward of England, roaring like a bully boy, kicking over chairs and stools, pounding the table like a spoilt child as Corbett explained how Friar Roger's cipher could not be broken and that they might learn more after meeting with de Craon. Once the meeting had ended, the King had taken Ranulf aside, as he was growing more accustomed to do, and pressed him against the wall, his elbow digging into the clerk's chest as he whispered in his ear. The warning had been simple: the King loved Corbett as a brother but de Craon was a most venomous viper in the grass. Edward had made Ranulf swear an oath on life and limb that if de Craon threatened Corbett, or worse, did him injury, Ranulf was to take the Frenchman's head.

'But he is an envoy!' Ranulf gasped, fearful yet flattered by the King's attention.

'Then he is a dead envoy.' The King smiled drily. 'I am not asking you to take his head literally. I will be content that de Craon dies of some mishap. You do understand, Master Ranulf, what a mishap is?'

'Yes, your Grace.'

'Good.' The King had smiled and dug his elbow deeper. 'Because if you fail, some mishap might occur to you.'

In all matters the freedom of the will is preserved.

Roger Bacon, *Opus Maius*

Chapter 4

The bell of the castle chapel was tolling mournfully as Corbett, accompanied by Ranulf and Chanson, clattered under the yawning gate, across the drawbridge, disappearing into the whirling storm of snow which was now beginning to cover the grassland and shrubs around the castle. Ranulf had kicked Chanson awake, screaming at him to put his boots on and get down to the stables as quickly as possible. Of course Chanson took an age to wake. Ranulf had to put the groom's boots on for him, even if it meant the left on the right foot, then, dragging him by the scruff of the neck down the stairs, bundled him across the yard, ignoring Chanson's wails of protest and the strange looks they drew from passers-by. Corbett had been waiting in the stables, cloak fastened, his head and face hidden by the deep cowl of his cloak.

'I thought I'd better wait,' he murmured.

Ranulf muttered something obscene under his breath and helped Chanson saddle the horses. Now they were out in the open countryside, Ranulf felt the panic seething within him. He pushed his horse alongside Corbett's.

'Sir Hugh, why are we out here?'

'I told you.' Corbett's voice sounded hollow from the cowl. 'We will soon be prisoners enough. I want to know where we are.'

Ranulf's panic was replaced by a chill of unease.

'What do you fear, Sir Hugh?'

'I'm concerned.' Corbett reined in his horse, clicking his tongue as it shook its head. 'Why are Flemish pirates patrolling in the dead of winter? True, there are easy pickings, but . . .'

They rode on silently for a while, then Corbett turned his horse and stared back at the black mass of the castle. 'We have,' he stretched out his left hand, 'about six miles to the north-east the fairly large town of Wareham. The French envoys probably lodged there last night. All around us, shaped like a crescent, spreads thick forest; to the south of Corfe, about another seven or eight miles, lies the sea. To the east there's an estuary, and to the west an even smaller one, which makes this part of the shire almost an island. They call it Purbeck Island.' Corbett wiped the snowflakes from his face. 'For the rest, let's see for ourselves.'

They entered the trees, turning right, following the trackway, and passed a village slumbering under the snow. The cottages looked deserted; only the lonely cry of a child or the bark of a dog and the curling black wood smoke showed any sign of life. They rode on. Corbett, glimpsing the tower of St Peter's church, realized they must be following the same path Rebecca used that morning. They dismounted at the lych gate, tethered their horses and walked up the cemetery path to the Galilee porch built on to the side of the church. The door was open and they entered the cold mustiness of the nave, a gloomy place, its paved floor lit by the occasional shaft of light piercing the high narrow windows. Nevertheless, it was a hallowed spot, an ancient chapel with squat pillars, narrow transepts and white-washed walls. Baskets of herbs stood at the base of each pillar and successive priests had hired itinerant painters to cover the walls with deep glowing paintings, not very skilful, but their reds, browns and greens displayed a robust vigour in their depictions of harvest scenes or images of Christ and His Mother.

The sanctuary was small, cordoned off by a simple Eucharist rail rather than a rood screen. Beyond that, to the left, was an ancient Lady Chapel with a carved wooden statue of the Virgin Mother holding her child, and on the right a Chantry Chapel to St Peter, a statue of whom stood on a plinth, in one hand the keys of the Kingdom, in the other a net. The sanctuary itself was simple, niches and small alcoves to the right and left for the Offertory cruets and other sacred vessels. The high altar was built against the end wall with steep steps before it. On the right of the altar hung the silver pyx in its Corpus pouch, and beneath that a candle glowed under its red glass cap. Corbett genuflected towards this and crossed himself. He was fascinated. Most churches smelt of incense and wax, but this one was different. A sharp, acrid tang which he couldn't place.

Corbett went through into the small sacristy, a bare lime-washed chamber with a large aumbry, coffers and chests, and, beneath a black crucifix, the vesting table where the robes for Mass were laid out. He turned the key in the side door, drew back the bolts and looked out. This part of the church land was reserved for the priest. At the far end stood a simple grey-brick two-storey house, steps leading up to the main door, the windows on either side boarded up. The house looked old, but the slated roof was gleaming black in the patches not yet covered by snow. From the trellis fences and raised mounds of earth, Corbett deduced that Father Matthew was a keen gardener. He glimpsed a statue of a saint and wondered if it was one of the many holy men or women the church claimed as patron saints of gardens and herb plots.

'What are you looking for, Sir Hugh?' Ranulf asked.

Corbett walked back to the sacristy and stood before the small gate in the Eucharist rail.

'I'm thinking of those young women who have been murdered. The one thing which binds them together, apart from their age and sex, is that they all meet here. I wonder if their deaths . . .'

Corbett let his words hang in the air. He returned to the Galilee porch, made sure the door was secure, and walked down towards the main entrance, stopping to admire the font and the image of St Christopher holding the Christ Child painted on a nearby pillar. He opened the door and walked out into a flurry of snow. There was a sound like the rush of bird-wings and a crossbow bolt smacked into the stonework above him. Corbett stepped back hastily, slamming the door behind him. Ranulf, alarmed, drew his sword, Chanson his dagger. The groom was now fully alert but blinking and muttering to himself.

'They know we have no bows. Whoever it is, they don't mean to attack us! That crossbow bolt was meant as a warning.'

'King's man.' The voice carried through the closed door. 'King's man, we intend no harm.'

Corbett lifted the latch, only to be pushed aside by Ranulf, who opened the door and stepped through before Corbett could stop him. He and Chanson went out on to the top step. A figure moved from behind a battered gravestone. He was hooded, snow covered his cowled head and shoulders. Corbett glimpsed ragged hose, though the boots were good, whilst there was no mistaking the arbalest he held. Other men appeared, at least half a dozen in number.

'King's man.' The hooded one walked closer, lowering his crossbow. Ranulf, sword drawn, clattered down the steps. 'No further,' the man shouted harshly. He lifted his head; a ragged mask covered his face. 'King's man, whatever you hear in the castle, we are not responsible for the deaths of those maids, nor for what you might see in the forest.'

'What might I see?' Corbett shouted, joining Ranulf at the bottom of the steps.

'The horror hanging in the woods,' answered the man. 'But we are poor people, truly dust of the earth; we only kill to eat, remember that.' The cowled figure lifted his hand, and the outlaws turned and ran, scaling the cemetery wall and disappearing into the trees beyond.

The three companions stared into the falling snow for an instant, before gathering their horses and turning back towards the castle. The sombre greyness of the day deepened as the light faded. The snowstorm was subsiding, but it had turned the countryside into a silent white wasteland, emphasizing the blackness of the trees and bushes above which solitary birds soared, whilst the gorse and undergrowth crackled as the snow dripped and slipped to the ground. They reached the path stretching across the open downs up to the main gate of the castle, where pitch torches and braziers glowed fiercely along the battlements.

'It looks like a donjon from Hell,' Ranulf muttered, yet he was eager enough to reach the gateway and escape from the chilling stillness of the countryside.

They clattered across the drawbridge where Corbett reined in. Leaning over to Ranulf and Chanson, he gave strict instructions not to tell anybody about the confrontation in the cemetery. Chanson took their horses, while Ranulf went to the buttery claiming he was still famished and Corbett returned to his chamber. A servant was waiting outside. Corbett unlocked the door and the man busied himself lighting the capped candles. He used a pair of bellows to fire the brazier and quickly strengthened the weak fire in the hearth, placing fresh logs over a bank of charcoal strewn with herbs which gave the chamber the smell of summer.

'My Lord.' The man sweated as he used the bellows, urging the flames to spurt up and fire the wood. 'You'll be as comfortable soon as a pig in its sty.'

Corbett grinned at the analogy. He helped the servant until he was satisfied, then gave him a coin and, when he had gone, locked the door behind him. He kicked off his boots and was about to settle before the fire when he heard a faint singing. Going to the window, he opened the shutter and listened intently. He recognized plainsong drifting up from the chapel of St John's Within the Gates and all exhaustion forgotten, quickly thrust his boots back on, left the chamber and ran down the stairs. He met Ranulf just outside the tower, and grabbing his henchman by the arm, they hurried into the icy gloom, slipping and slithering as they made their way to the castle chapel. Ranulf made to protest but knew it was futile. As he had remarked to Chanson, 'The one thing Master Longface loves is the opportunity to sing.'

The chapel of St John was a long, whitewashed barn-like structure, though the walls had been covered by paintings and the raised floor of the sanctuary was tiled with beautiful stone. The altar, of Purbeck marble, seemed to glow from the light of the candles placed either side. Father Matthew, assisted by Father Andrew, was busy organising members of the garrison into a choir to rehearse the hymns of Advent.

'Why, Sir Hugh.' Father Matthew beckoned them forward. 'You heard the chanting?'

'Angels' teeth,' Ranulf whispered. 'Of course he did.'

Corbett immediately became involved in the singing, and for a while stood and listened as the choir, under Father Matthew's direction, sang the *'Puer Natus Nobis'*, 'A Child is Born For Us'. The choir was composed of young boys and old men, but the real chanting was provided by the Welsh archers, whose voices Corbett particularly admired. He stood tapping his foot, gently moving his fingers as if he could catch the very essence of the hymn. Ranulf quietly conceded that the choir, the archers in particular, had beautiful carrying voices. In his manor at Leighton Sir Hugh had organised his own choir, composed of servants and manor tenants, and once the hymn was over Corbett was drawn into a passionate argument with the two priests over what they termed the 'arrangement of voices'. Sir Edmund and his officers drifted in and stood fascinated as the sombre Keeper of the Secret Seal argued vehemently about who should stand where, and whether the choirs should alternate or sing together. Ranulf's heart skipped a beat as the Lady Constance, with her damsels-in-waiting, also entered the little chapel now thronged with people and ablaze with light as Father Matthew lit more candles and tapers.

At last the priests were persuaded and the choir regathered, under Corbett's direction, to sing the *Introit*, the entry antiphon to the dawn Mass for Christmas Day: *'Dominus dixit ad me, hodie genu tei'* – 'The Lord said to me this day I have begotten you'. First the choir had to be taught to memorize the words. Corbett translated the Latin – a lengthy exercise, but, as at Leighton Manor, the rhythmic chant of the music helped them remember it. After a great deal of shuffling, they stood in three rows to reflect the varying tones, with Ranulf in the middle line feeling rather embarrassed as the Lady Constance watched him intently. Once finished, everyone judged it a great success and they turned to something more popular, one of the great 'O' antiphons of Advent. Glancing quickly over his shoulder, Ranulf glimpsed Corbett, eyes closed, passionately singing the words. At the end Sir Edmund, and the congregation which had gathered, applauded loudly. Corbett became involved in yet another heated discussion whilst Ranulf edged towards the Lady Constance. She, however, as if sensing precisely his intentions, strode directly towards him, standing in front of him like the Lady Maeve would, head slightly forward, face stern, her beautiful eyes bright with mocking laughter.

'Master Ranulf,' she whispered, 'what are you trying to do? Do you want to play cat's cradle with me? If you want to talk, then talk! Or do you wish something else? To take me aside and whisper the sweet words of a troubadour?' Her eyes widened. 'Or will you appear beneath my window tonight with rebec and flute and chant how my skin glows like soft satin and my eyes, well . . .' She waved her hand. Ranulf blushed and quietly thanked God that Chanson wasn't nearby.

'My Lady,' he stammered, glimpsing Corbett moving towards the door. 'My Lady, certain tasks await me.' Face burning, he hastened after his master.

'Ranulf!' He turned.

'I wish you had,' Lady Constance whispered. 'I wish you would.'

Ranulf could take no more, but fled into the icy night, quietly whispering the *Deo gratias*.

Corbett was still full of the singing. 'You see, Ranulf, when you have more in the middle group, where the voice is not so deep as the line behind or the row in front . . .' He continued his lecture as they crossed the snow-filled bailey, torches spluttering against the falling snow sent sparks flying like miniature beams of light to sizzle on the icy cobbles. The bailey was full of noise as carts and barrows were pushed away, horses stabled and the castle folk sheltered and hastened their preparations against the encroaching icy darkness. Ranulf made his hasty farewells and Corbett, still full of the choir music, returned to his own chamber, where he closed the door, refilled his wine goblet and stretched out before the fire. De Craon, he realized, would soon be here. He thought of the choir at Leighton; perhaps it should be divided in two and arranged in stalls? His mind drifted to that snow-bound church, those hooded, masked figures in the cemetery. What did their leader mean by *the horror hanging in the woods* . . .

Ranulf shook his master awake. 'The French have arrived, we must prepare.'

Corbett struggled up. Ranulf had already changed into a cotehardie of Lincoln green edged with silver, over a white linen shirt and dark brown leggings; his face was shaven, his hair oiled, his fingers beringed, and round his waist was a narrow leather belt with a sheath for a stabbing dirk.

'The Lady Constance will think you are quite parfait,' Corbett teased, but Ranulf was already striding to the door; he did not wish to discuss that matter any further!

Servants came into the room struggling with buckets of boiling water for the lavarium bowls. Once they had gone, Corbett stripped, washed and shaved, donning a clean linen vest, drawers and cambric shirt. Humming the Offertory canticle from the second Sunday of Advent, he took from his travelling chest a cotehardie displaying the red, blue and gold of the royal household. He donned black hose, pushing his feet into soft leather boots and placing the silver filigree chain of office around his neck and the signet ring of the Secret Chancery on the middle finger of his left hand. As he was brushing his hair, Ranulf and Chanson came into the room.

'I've done the best I can.' Ranulf pointed at Chanson, resplendent in a new woollen jerkin, his hair looking even more spiked than ever. The teasing continued as Bolingbroke entered and described de Craon's arrival.

'I've been round this castle.' Bolingbroke sat down on the coffer at the end of the bed. 'It's a veritable rabbit warren, with more gaps and alleyways than any ward in London.' He looked at Corbett. 'There's talk about the promise you made . . .'

'I know, I know,' Corbett conceded. 'It's a promise I shouldn't have made.' He paused as the castle bell chimed, the signal that the feasting would soon begin.

Corbett led his retinue down through the bitter cold and across to the Hall of Angels. The long chamber now blazed with light and colour. Fresh greenery had been arranged, logs piled high in the hearth and the flames roared up into the stack. Braziers glowed and incense-holders from the church gave off their own spiced fragrance. Musicians in the gallery practised the flute and plucked the strings of a harp. The great table on the dais was covered in white damask and bright with gleaming jugs, goblets and flagons.

De Craon and his entourage were standing in front of the hearth, sipping cups of spiced wine. Corbett, a false smile on his face, but eager to observe etiquette and protocol, strode across. He embraced the russet-haired, dark-faced Frenchman who, he knew, wanted to kill him, and exchanged the *oscuum pacis*, the kiss of peace, with lips which had cursed him and clasped hands, eager to be stained with his blood. De Craon, too, observed the niceties. He stepped back, hands spread out, greeting Corbett in Norman French, conveying to him the good wishes of his most gracious master. Corbett's rival was also dressed in the livery of another royal household, a cotehardie of blue and white, emblazoned with silver fleur-de-lis. They stood exchanging pleasantries, toasting their respective masters, de Craon obviously smirking, making no attempt to hide the rancour in his eyes. Further introductions were made. Ranulf gave the sketchiest of nods to de Craon's black-haired henchman, Bogo de Baiocis. Corbett icily introduced Bolingbroke; de Craon clasped the clerk's hand, gripping it tight.

'You studied in Paris sir?'

'Why, yes, my Lord.' Bolingbroke deliberately answered in English. 'But I had to discontinue my studies because of certain matters.'

'If you ever come again,' de Craon's smile faded and he withdrew his hand, 'I must entertain you. There's a very fine cookshop near the Quai de Madelene.' Swift as a snake in the grass, he turned immediately back to Corbett. 'Sir Edmund has been telling me about your singing. I, too, have sung in the Chapel Royal at St Denis.' De Craon's hand went to his chest and he bowed. 'My master has congratulated me on my fine voice, and there is nothing better my daughter Jehanne likes than to join me in that beautiful song *'Companhon, farai un vers desconvenent'*. You know it, Sir Hugh? It was composed by William, Duke of Aquitaine, when Gascony was part of the domain of France.'

Corbett couldn't help laughing at the sheer insolence of de Craon's remark. De Craon decided to act surprised.

'You mock me, sir?' Corbett teased.

'Would I mock you, Sir Hugh? Don't you believe that I have a fine voice, or an equally fine daughter? When you are next in Paris, I must entertain you at my house.' De Craon's smile widened. 'It is far, far away from the Quai de Madelene, I assure you.'

Corbett hid his own surprise. He had always considered de Craon a villain steeped in subtlety and cunning, without family or interests. He could tell from Ranulf's grin that perhaps he and his French opponent had more in common than he might concede.

'And your companions?' Corbett asked.

De Craon hastened to introduce the four professors: Etienne

Destaples, a tall, gaunt professor of divinity; Jean Vervins, lanky and thin, with the lugubrious face of a man who reflected a great deal but spoke very little. He was, like Destaples, dry of skin and dry of tone, a man with tired eyes who kept fidgeting, whispering to Destaples and glancing around in disdain. Pierre Sanson, professor of metaphysics, was more convivial, his small, plump face wreathed in a perpetual smile. He, like the rest, was dressed in dark garb with a thick fur-rimmed robe around his shoulders. Louis Crotoy was introduced last, a small, aristocratic-looking man with rather elongated sharp blue eyes, his hair pure white. Unlike the others, he grasped Corbett's hand and drew him close, exchanging the kiss of peace. Corbett smelt that perfume with which Crotoy always anointed himself, a fragrance which took him back down the years to those sombre, dusty school rooms in the Halls of Oxford.

'It's good to see you, Sir Hugh, a little older but only just a little.'

He stepped away as de Craon came between the two. 'I understand you know each other of old?'

'A great honour on my part,' Corbett replied. 'Master Louis is once heard never forgotten. He lectured on logic in the schools of Oxford.'

'Sir Hugh was my favourite pupil,' Crotoy answered. 'Not because of his logic; I have just never met a man who takes things so seriously.' His remark provoked laughter. 'And now,' Crotoy continued, 'such seriousness is needed.' He spoke quickly in Norman French, and by the look in his eyes, Corbett realized that this old friend, this master of the sharp thought and the shrewd word, wished to talk with him in secret.

Sir Edmund clapped his hands, summoning the servants to replenish cups and serve soft, spiced slices of bread. The conversation turned to the weather, the horrors of the sea voyage and the history of the castle itself. Corbett tried to draw Crotoy into conversation, but whenever the Frenchman drew closer, de Craon or one of the others appeared at their side. Corbett plucked at Sir Edmund's sleeve and whispered about the seating arrangement; the Constable nodded, promising he would do what he could.

When a trumpet sounded from the minstrels' gallery announcing that the first course was to be served, Corbett found himself on Sir Edmund's left, with de Craon on the Constable's right, but more importantly, Louis Crotoy was seated between himself and Ranulf. The wine goblets were filled, toasts made and the first course was served: roasted salmon in an onion wine sauce, followed by spiced capon and chicken mixed with cumin and cream. The wine circulated, faces becoming flushed, voices raised. De Craon's retinue relaxed as the leader of the French envoys quietly conceded that he could do little to interfere between Sir Hugh and his old teacher.

'Do they trust you?' Corbett asked.

'Of course,' Louis replied. 'They are just curious.' He patted Corbett gently on the hand. 'De Craon attended the Halls of Cambridge, Destaples has lectured in this kingdom as well as at universities in Lombardy. Knowledge has no frontiers, Sir Hugh. You are well?'

For a while the conversation turned to personal matters; eventually Corbett pushed away his silver platter.

'Friar Roger Bacon?'

'I'm not too sure, Sir Hugh, whether he was a buffoon or a genius.'

'Have you translated the *Secret of Secrets*?' Corbett asked.

'Of course not,' Crotoy whispered, 'but there are rumours that Magister Thibault had begun to.' He kept his face impassive. 'You heard the news, Sir Hugh? Magister Thibault organized a great feast, an evening of revelry, but a dreadful accident occurred. They claim housebreakers tried to rob his cellar and, either by accident or design, began a fire which swept through the house. All the guests escaped safely, including myself, but the King's men who were sent down to investigate maintained that in the cellar they found three corpses, or what was left of them: the mortal remains of Magister Thibault, a young woman he was dallying with, and someone else, a stranger. A tumultuous evening! They say one of the housebreakers was English, a clerk called Walter Ufford. I saw him at the revelry that night, along with a man who looked very much like your companion Bolingbroke.'

Corbett glanced down the table at William Bolingbroke, deep in conversation with Destaples. He could hear the loud debate over the logic of the famous theologian Abelard, who had used his book *Sic et Non* to poke fun at other theologians and their misuse of scripture.

'I doubt if William was there,' Corbett turned his head, 'but if he was, and proof was offered, I would investigate more thoroughly.'

Crotoy laughed. 'And perhaps you should ask him if Magister Thibault's prize possession, his copy of the *Secret of Secrets*, came into his possession. Our royal master was furious.'

'What at?' Corbett asked. 'Magister Thibault's death or the theft of the manuscript?'

'His Grace,' Crotoy's voice was barely above a whisper, 'is angry at many things, Sir Hugh. He is angry at me and others of the university. He has surrounded himself with flatterers, men like Pierre Dubois, sycophants who recall the old adage of the Roman jurists, "How the will of the Prince has force of law". As he grows older Philip does not take kindly to opposition.'

'And his interest in Friar Roger's theories?'

'If your King is interested, so is mine. There is no doubt that our learned friar was a treasure house of secret knowledge, but whether it is worth a sou is for us to decide.'

'Had Thibault broken the cipher?' Corbett asked. 'When we meet we have to share such knowledge.'

'I think he had, or at least had begun to. Now I and my companions must earn the good grace of our master by finishing the task. I have spent many years on ciphers, Sir Hugh, the writings of Polybius and other ancients, but the device Bacon used to hide his knowledge is the most difficult I have ever encountered.'

'And Magister Thibault,' Corbett continued, 'the night he died, why should he be found in the cellar?'

'His strongroom was there,' Crotoy replied. 'I was in the hall of his house that evening. I had withdrawn from the revelry. People had drunk too much and the *filles de joie* were becoming more abandoned by the hour. I was near the door when Magister Thibault appeared. I asked him to join us, but he refused. The young woman he was with, an exquisite courtesan, remarkably beautiful, she too was objecting.'

'Objecting!' Corbett exclaimed.

Crotoy made a gesture with his hand for Corbett to keep his

voice down. 'Yes, objecting. She said it was cold and she didn't want to go down to a freezing cellar. "You asked me to," Magister Thibault replied. They left, and a short while later servants reported smoke and flames pouring up from the basement.' Crotoy shrugged. 'Now, Ranulf . . .'

Crotoy hastily turned away from Corbett, leaving the Keeper of the Secret Seal alone with his thoughts. Sir Edmund was now deep in conversation with de Craon, describing the fortifications of Corfe Castle and the building work which was to begin once spring arrived. Corbett sat staring into his wine cup. He had advised his own royal master that this meeting at Corfe was highly dangerous. Philip and de Craon were plotting something, but what? And although he had questioned Edward closely, the King would not reveal the reason for his own deep interest in the writings of Roger Bacon.

Corbett stared down the table at the various faces. According to Bolingbroke, who, flushed-faced, was still lecturing Destaples, there had been a spy at the University of the Sorbonne who had been prepared to sell Magister Thibault's copy of the *Secret of Secrets*. Ostensibly he had done it for gold and silver. Had that same person simply been a catspaw, the means to trap Bolingbroke and Ufford? But there again, de Craon could have brought his men to that cellar and apprehended them there and then. And why had Magister Thibault gone down to the cellar? According to Crotoy, it seemed as if Thibault had meant to meet someone there. Had Thibault been the spy? And why had de Craon allowed the copy of the *Secret of Secrets* to be stolen in the first place? Did that manuscript hold something very dangerous? Was that the reason for the meeting at Corfe?

Corbett raised his goblet to his lips but thought again. He needed to keep his mind clear. Sitting back, cradling the goblet, he smiled to himself. Logic could only be based on what happened, not what might happen, as Crotoy had taught him, so he would have to wait . . .

Alusia, daughter of Gilbert, was recalling the shock of discovering Rebecca's corpse. She had knelt beside it on that cold cobbled trackway, aware of someone screaming, and it was only when she heard Father Matthew approaching that she realized that she herself was making that terrible noise. The priest had raised her to her feet, his strong arms about her, one hand stroking her hair as he tried to comfort her. He had told her to stay beside the corpse whilst he hurried over to the church and brought back the hand cart. She'd helped place poor Rebecca's corpse on it, covering it with the stained canvas cloth the priest had brought with him. Once they had returned to the castle, Alusia had been comforted by her parents. They'd brought her a cup of warm posset from the kitchen and her father had hurried to Mistress Feyner for a few grains of valerian to help her sleep.

Alusia had slept long and deep, and only as she woke became truly aware of the horrors she had witnessed that day. Both Sir Edmund and Father Matthew had come down to question her but Alusia was confused, still suffering from the effects of the powdered wine. She explained how she and Rebecca, close friends, had decided to slip away from the castle and meet under the lych gate so that they could lay greenery on Marion's grave. After all, it had been her name day, and they wished to do something to mark their friend's passing. Alusia described the church and the snow-covered forest, how quiet it had been; she even recalled the cawing of the rooks and crows.

'But did you see anything?' Sir Edmund and Father Matthew had been kindly but persistent. Alusia had shook her head and babbled about the silence and the snow, about poor Rebecca lying like a bundle of cloth on the trackway.

'Did you see anything strange?'

Again Alusia had shaken her head. She couldn't recall anything, and yet now she was more awake and fresh, certain memories did come back. It was like waking up after last Midsummer's Day, when she had drunk deep of the cider and danced with the rest on the castle green. At first she couldn't recall anything, but then the memories had returned, how she had kissed that boy or this; more importantly, how Martin, that handsome man-at-arms, had caught her eye, studying her from afar. He had held her tight whilst the dancers whirled and the air was piped full with the wild music of the tambour, rebec and flute. Now it was the same. Her parents had told her what had happened to Rebecca's remains, lying cold and stiffening in the death house next to the castle church. How

Father Matthew had brought Rebecca's corpse and herself back to Corfe. How he had anointed the body . . .

Alusia, sitting up in her parents' bed in the loft of their small house built against the castle wall, tried hard to remember. Sir Edmund had said that sharp-eyed King's man might come to question her. So what could she say to him? Yet the memories were there. She was sure she had glimpsed someone, just for a moment, near the lych gate, and what was Father Matthew doing on the trackway? Alusia recalled how Father Andrew, about this time last year, had been called to give the last rites to a sentry who'd slipped from the castle parapet walk and fallen to his death. He had knelt down and whispered the words of absolution into the dead man's ear. Why hadn't Father Matthew done that to Rebecca? Hadn't that same Father Matthew taught them that the soul never left the body immediately, so absolution could still be given and the skin marked with the holy oils hours after death?

Alusia stayed in bed, warm and secure, until called down for the evening meal. Later she went out to join the other girls as they grouped round a large bonfire lit in the castle yard. A time to share the warmth and chatter and sip from a jug of ale made hot and spicy with burnt embers and powdered nutmeg. Martin had been watching her and she had stared boldly back. The fright she'd experienced the previous morning had made her braver, as if aware of how fleeting life had become. She had agreed to meet him at the usual place, in the far distant corner of the inner castle bailey, and Alusia always kept her promise.

She'd brought a tinder from her father's pouch and, though it was bitterly cold, stood now in the empty crumbling passageway leading down to the old storerooms, disused because of fallen masonry. Since the weather had turned cold, Martin and she would often meet here. It was dark, safe and quiet, and her parents would think she was with the other girls. She only hoped Martin would bring that bronze chafing dish, a gift from his elder brother, who had won it at a game of hazard from a passing tinker. The dish was capped and had a handle, and once full of charcoal or burning embers was so good to keep the fingers warm on a dark, cold night such as this.

Alusia heard a sound and, blowing out the candle, went deeper into the cellar. Someone was coming down the steps, a soft footfall, 'Alusia, Alusia!' The voice was soft. The young woman, eager to meet her lover, was already stepping out of the shadows before she realized her mistake. It was too late. She was aware of a dark shape blocking out the light. She heard a 'crick' and a 'click', and the crossbow bolt hit her high in the chest, sending her crashing back deep into the shadows.

One finds it in every town, every village, every camp...
Corruption and debasement of character whicih renders all
efforts futile.

Roger Bacon, *Opus Minus*

Chapter 5

Foxglove the outlaw was dying. Horehound, crouching beside him in the fire-lit cave, recognized the symptoms. Foxglove had been ill for days; now the old man's unshaven face was gaunt, his cheeks hollowed, his forehead sweat-soaked, his eyeballs rolling back in his head. A strange rattling echoed in his throat. Angelica had done her best, feeding him juice of the moss, but the fever remained unabated and Foxglove was seeing visions. He was calling on brothers, comrades who had died at the great battle of Evesham almost forty years before, when the old King's father had trapped Earl Simon de Montfort, killed him, hacked up his body and fed it to the dogs. Foxglove, as Milkwort reported, was now preparing for judgement, going back into the past, and yet he had one last wish.

'I need to be shriven,' the old man begged. 'I must have a priest to listen to my sins.' He gripped Horehound's hand. 'I'm going, but I want a priest to anoint me. I don't want my soul to go stinking into death.'

The rest of the outlaw band had agreed with him. Foxglove might be old, but in his time he had been precious, a skilled hunter, a loyal companion. Horehound moved to the mouth of the cave and crouched by the second fire, staring across the snow-covered glade. The storm had passed but the skies threatened more. Horehound chewed the corner of his chapped lip as he considered Foxglove's request. This had happened before, when old Parsley had died. Father Matthew had come, but that had been in the full flush of summer when the trackways were clear and firm and the priest welcomed a walk through the green dappled coolness of the forest. Now it was the heart of winter; even the outlaws had to be careful not to become lost, and they would have to stay off the beaten trackway. Horehound was fearful of that ancient oak and the corpse hanging there, the horror of the forest! Early in the evening there had been fierce debate about that very thing. Angelica and Milkwort, supported by Peasecod and Henbane, had argued that the corpse should be cut down and secretly buried. Horehound had been insistent in his refusal. He would go and fetch Father Matthew but bring him into the camp by more secret routes. The priest must not see that corpse; that was the kernel of Horehound's argument. If they touched the corpse they would be held responsible, and wasn't it ill luck to take such a body down? He smiled grimly. He had won the argument when he had posed the question, who would cut the rope? Nobody wanted to do that; indeed, no one had even approached it. They couldn't tell if it was male or female.

Horehound stretched out his hands towards the fire. He was deeply worried: their larder of salted meat was depleted; game was becoming increasingly rare and difficult to hunt, the prospect of plunder even rarer. Horehound's band was growing older, weaker; sometimes the temptation to leave them and go deeper into the forest was almost irresistible.

'What shall we do?'

Milkwort and Angelica joined him at the fire.

'We'll fetch the priest.'

'No, I don't mean that!'

Horehound could feel his companion's anger, whilst Angelica's broad, smooth face was deeply troubled.

'You know what I mean.' Milkwort gathered up his hair, tying it more securely behind his head with a piece of string. 'Here we are, in the heart of the forest, in the depths of winter, three of our companions ill, and we have very little food.' He threw a stick on the fire. 'We've even forgotten our names, hiding behind those of wild herbs. We are outlaws, wolfsheads!' He hawked and spat. 'But the law doesn't afear me, the sheriff doesn't give a damn about us; what frightens me is winter. It's not yet Yuletide but we're so short of food we're going to starve. I don't think,' Milkwort added bitterly, 'we should have threatened the King's man.'

'We didn't threaten,' Horehound snapped. 'If we are going to hang, let's hang for venison, for stealing some clothes from a merchant, but not the slaughter of young maids.'

'There was another killed,' Angelica intoned mournfully, shifting the hair from her face. She gazed back into the cave where Foxglove was gasping, fighting for his life. 'I understand that.' She jabbed her thumb back at the dying man. 'But not the brutal slaying of young maids?'

'You saw her?' Horehound was eager to change the subject and distract Milkwort.

'Yes, I told you, I was out near the pathway gathering nuts and whatever else I could find for the pot. I saw the girl in the cemetery. She was standing by the grave, she'd taken some holly, red with berries.'

'Yes, but did you see the one who was killed?'

'I saw no one else.'

'Have you seen any strangers?' Horehound asked.

'I think I have, mere glimpses.'

'There's none of them about,' Milkwort scoffed. 'No peddlers or chapmen, only the foreigners at the tavern. Cas . . . tel . . .'

'Castilians,' Horehound corrected him, proud of remembering what Master Reginald had told him. 'They are from Castile; it's in Spain.'

'Where is that?'

'It's part of France,' Horehound blustered. 'I think it's part of France, somewhere near the Middle Sea. They've come here to buy wool. They travelled from Dover.'

'Did you see them?' Milkwort asked. 'We could have stopped them.'

Horehound wagged a finger. 'Don't be stupid. There are five of them, all armed. Above all, they are foreigners. You know what happens if foreigners are robbed? They complain to the sheriff, or to their own prince, and as fast as Jack jumps on Jill, the sheriff's men will be in the forest, hunting us like deer. You heard what happened to Pigskin and his group? Moved further east they did, attacked some foreigners coming out of Dover.'

The group fell silent. They all knew what had happened to

Pigskin and his companions: hanged at the crossroads as a warning to others.

'If we don't get the priest soon,' Milkwort broke the silence, 'old Foxglove will be joining Pigskin.'

'Nah,' Horehound disagreed. 'Pigskin's in Hell, a killer he was, not like Foxglove; the worst thing *he* did was knock a man on the back of the head. But you're right,' he sighed, 'let's go.'

They left the camp, stumbling through the snow, cursing and muttering as they were cut by gorse whilst the snow resting on branches above sprinkled down to soak their clothes. Horehound drew his cowl closer about his head. They went in single file, Angelica bringing up the rear so that she could follow in their footsteps.

Horehound was truly frightened. The forest was silent, a bad sign at night, as if the freezing cold and snow had smothered all life and sound. Everything had changed: no longer the familiar trees and bushes; no longer the telltale stones placed where the trackway turned; no different colours; nothing but blackness broken only by the blind brightness of the snow. Horehound felt as if he was in a dream. He paused to see where he was. Concerned at becoming lost, he ignored Milkwort's protest and led them out of the forest on to the trackway which snaked through the trees. Eventually they left this, going back into the protection of the trees, following a secure route which would lead them to the Tavern in the Forest.

Horehound, summoning up his courage, knew they would have to cross that glade. When they reached it they all paused; even in the poor light they could see that macabre shape hanging from an outstretched branch, moving slightly as if it had a life of its own. Horehound crossed himself and moved on. He felt hungry, slightly weak, and even as he approached the pathway leading to the tavern, his sharp sense of smell caught the drifting odours of cooked meats and freshly baked bread. His mouth watered and his belly grumbled, and he decided that he could not let such an opportunity slip. He gestured to his companions to keep silent, and they slipped behind the trees at the rear of the tavern. Summoning up their strength they scaled the curtain wall, dropping quietly into the yard below and scrambling down the manure heap piled high between the two stretches of stables. The dogs on their leashes across the cobbled yard were immediately roused and, despite the cold, strained on their ropes, lips curled, barking raucously. This was as far as Horehound would go. He watched the rear door of the tavern open, the welcome sliver of light, smelled the odours of cooking, nigh irresistible, drifting across.

'Who's there?' Master Reginald, a crossbow in one hand, stood in the light. Behind him two tap boys grasped stout cudgels.

'Only Horehound, Master Reginald,' the outlaw called across. 'Foxglove is dying, we need food and drink.'

'And what do you have to trade?' Master Reginald came forward, shouting at the dogs to stay silent.

Horehound gripped the club he carried. 'We've nothing,' he grated. 'Even our salted meat is putrid. Master Reginald,' he whined, 'we need meat and bread. I can pay you back in the spring.' He edged forward, so hungry he was becoming angry. Master Reginald's buttery and kitchen were full of good meats, golden-crusted pies, soft pork, goose, chicken and other delicacies. His hunger made him bold. He walked across the cobbled yard swinging his cudgel; the taverner lifted his crossbow. 'Give us some food,' the outlaw repeated, 'and we will leave you in peace.'

From the tavern came a shout, a foreign voice. 'You have visitors?' Horehound asked. The taverner understood the threat in his voice. 'They will have to travel, so we will agree to give them safe passage.'

Master Reginald didn't realise how weak and impoverished the outlaw band had become. Again the voice shouted, and this time he reluctantly beckoned them forward into the sweet warmth and light of his kitchen. Horehound groaned in pleasure. Milkwort and Angelica just stood gaping at the meats spread out on the fleshing tables, the basket of rye bread and the small white loaves freshly taken from the ovens either side of the great hearth. Horehound stared around. Lamplight glinted in the polished bowls and skillets, and it was then that Horehound made his decision. He was tired of the forest; this was his last winter skulking amongst the trees. Emboldened by the prospects of a change, he walked across and stared through the half-open door of the tap room. The five foreigners were seated round a table. Master Reginald, his bitter face even more angry, ushered him away. A leather bag was brought, quickly filled with scraps of meat and hard rye bread and pushed into Horehound's hand. The taverner allowed them to take one of the fresh loaves and a morsel of cheese before opening the rear door and gesturing at them to leave. As Horehound passed, the taverner gripped the outlaw's shoulder.

'You remember this,' he warned. 'I want no trouble for my guests on the forest paths, and when spring comes I want to be repaid.'

Horehound and his two companions were only too delighted to agree. They crossed the yard, scaled the wall and crouched for a while in the icy darkness, congratulating themselves on their good fortune.

'I wonder why?' Milkwort's face, red and chapped, was twisted in disbelief. He crouched so close to Horehound the outlaw leader could smell his foul breath, the rancid sweat from his dirty rags.

'Master Reginald wanted us out,' Angelica whispered. 'He didn't want us there! He didn't want us troubling those merchants who must be paying him well.'

Now that he was out in the freezing night Horehound was even more suspicious. The taverner was not noted for his kindness; the tap boys had told them about how he liked to beat the slatterns. The foreigners must be paying well and Master Reginald didn't want any trouble. Horehound stared up at the black sky, and even as he did, fresh flakes wetted his face.

'What hour must it be?'

'Not long before midnight,' Milkwort guessed. 'We should hurry. They say a dying man always goes before dawn.'

They continued their journey through the trees, Horehound clutching his precious bag. Now and then they lost their way, cursing and grumbling as they were pricked by icy brambles. Horehound hissed at them to be careful. Near the church lay hidden marshes and he didn't want to become trapped. At last they reached the cemetery wall, and climbed this wearily, moving quickly around the tombstones and crosses towards the priest's house. Horehound now felt more comfortable. The priest kept no dogs and, being a kindly man, might have some food to spare. The outlaw carefully circled the grey-brick building, leaping up to catch a glimpse of light from the shutters, but the house lay in silence. The priest had his chamber at the back, on the second floor, yet the shutters here were closed too and betrayed no gleam of light.

Horehound searched amongst the snow and, gripping some dirt, flung it up, but no reply. He sent up a second hail of dirt and pebbles, shouting hoarsely, 'Father Matthew? Master Priest?' He started as an owl hooted in the far trees of the cemetery.

'Perhaps he is not here,' Milkwort suggested. 'Perhaps he stayed at the castle.'

Horehound was about to turn away when he glimpsed a gleam of light coming from a window in the church, a small oriel overlooking the entrance to the nave. 'He's in the church,' he whispered. He hurried across, thrust his cudgel at Milkwort and climbed the crumbling wall. The hard stone dug into his chapped, sore flesh but Horehound persisted.

The small oriel was full of thick stained glass, the gift of some wealthy parishioner. The image of a saint, hands extended, blocked any clear view, but the thickened strip of glass beneath allowed Horehound to peer through. He gasped and blinked. The porch of the church was bright with light from a ring of candles. Father Matthew, wrapped in a thick, heavy cloak, was squatting in the centre. On his left was a pot of fire, the flames leaping up from the charcoal, and before him a large deep bowl of gleaming brass. Horehound couldn't understand what was happening. Now and again the priest would stare down at a small book, the size of a psalter, kept open by weights on each corner. Horehound couldn't decide if he was chanting or talking to himself; his lips were moving, as if reciting some incantation. Just near the book was a small open coffer, the sort a leech would use to contain his powders. Father Matthew was taking grains of powder from this and sprinkling them into the bowl, cleaning his hands very carefully above it.

Horehound, fascinated, forgot the reason why he was there. He watched the priest sprinkle more powder before lighting a taper from the fire pot and throwing it into the bowl.

Horehound stifled a scream at the flash of fire which leapt up, so surprised he lost his grip and almost fell on to his waiting companions below.

'What is it?' Milkwort gasped.

Horehound, terrified, didn't even bother to reply but, grasping his cudgel, raced across to the cemetery wall, flinging himself up it and dropping down on the other side. Ignoring the shouts of his companions, he ran until he had reached the shelter of the trees. Milkwort and Angelica came panting up, the woman holding the precious sack of food.

'What did you see?' Milkwort asked.

'The devil,' Horehound hissed back, 'appearing in a tongue of flame!'

'Nonsense!' Milkwort protested.

'I know what I saw,' Horehound rasped, 'and when we go back to the cave, keep your mouths shut. Old Foxglove will be all a-tremble. I'll pretend to be the priest.' He gestured back towards the church. 'I'll do him more good than that one.'

Sir Hugh rose early the next morning. He loosened the shutter and gasped at the blast of freezing air. It was snowing again, though not as heavily as the day before. He placed the shutter back, went across to the lavarium, cracked the ice and splashed water over his face. Dressing quickly, he built up the fire, blowing at the embers and using the powerful bellows on the weak flames in the braziers. For a while he crouched, basking in the warmth. The chamber was bitterly cold and he hitched his cloak tighter against the icy draughts seeping under the door and through the shutters. He was glad he was clear-headed, pleased he had not drunk or eaten too much the night before, and he smiled as he remembered how he and Ranulf had helped Chanson to bed. The groom had sat with the other henchmen below the dais and drunk everything placed before him.

Corbett had lain awake in bed before summoning up enough courage to face the cold. He'd heard the tolling of the chapel bell and decided to go to Mass before doing what he planned. He finished dressing, pushing his feet into fur-lined boots, wrapping his military cloak securely about him and putting on a pair of thick mittens which Lady Maeve had bought from a chapman who traded between Leighton and Colchester.

Leaving his chamber unlocked he went down the steps, standing aside for servants bringing up buckets of scalding water as well as sacks of logs and charcoal for his chamber. He assured them they were not too late, saying he would return after he had attended Mass.

The small castle chapel seemed gloomier than the night before. Father Andrew was already vested in the purple and gold of Advent. Corbett knelt with the other early risers, mostly men-at-arms and servants, as they huddled together in the small sanctuary. Father Andrew intoned the Mass, all its readings and antiphons foretelling the birth of Christ and God's great promise of salvation. Corbett took the Sacrament and, once Mass was finished, lit a taper before the Lady Altar and waited, stamping his feet, until the priest left the sacristy.

'Father, I am sorry to trouble you, but the girl who was brought in yesterday . . .'

'I am saying her requiem at noon today,' Father Andrew answered.

'Has the corpse been coffined?'

The old priest paused. Sniffing and coughing, he gazed watery-eyed at Corbett. 'No, it's still in the death house. The leech has prepared her.'

'Can I see her, Father? I would like to scrutinize the corpse once more.'

The old priest shrugged, led him out of the church and around the side into a small barn-like building built against the castle wall. It housed two corpses. Father Andrew explained that one was a beggar man, found on the edge of the road, who had died suddenly the day before Corbett had arrived. The beggar was already shrouded in a thick canvas cloth, only the face-piece pulled away to reveal a thin, cadaverous face, sharp nose and hollow eyes. Next to him, also on trestles, was an arrow chest, so long and thin it looked as if Rebecca's corpse had been squeezed in. Corbett pulled back the shroud. She was now dressed in a white shift, her black hair falling down either side of her face. With the priest muttering under his breath about the stench, Sir Hugh carefully scrutinized the corpse. He tried to hide the deep sadness at such a waste, as well as a grumbling anger at the soulless violence. The quarrel had been removed, the wound filled with spices and covered with a herbal poultice.

'In life she must have been comely,' he whispered, lifting the shift to examine the girl's rounded thighs and flat stomach. As he pressed his hand down against the cold, hard flesh, he caught the faint smell of herbs.

'Sir Hugh, what are you looking for? This is unseemly.'

'Death is unseemly, murder is unseemly. I made a vow. I will see the person who killed this young woman hang.'

Corbett noticed the purple patches on the arm; they looked like bruises. He noticed also how the skin was scraped, and when he turned the corpse over, similar marks could be seen on the shoulders and the back of the neck. He heard voices outside, so he repositioned the corpse, pulling down the shift and covering it with the shroud cloth.

'What I am searching for, Father, is a solution to this mystery. How a young woman comes to be found on a lonely trackway with a crossbow bolt in her chest.' He tapped the makeshift coffin. 'When the corpse was brought in yesterday, you were there. How was she garbed?'

'A dark green gown, boots on her feet. I accompanied the leech back here. Beneath the gown she wore a kirtle, thin and patched; she was dressed like any other girl in the castle.'

'That's what I thought,' Corbett mused, walking to the door. He went out into the castle yard. Although it was still snowing, people were busy about their tasks. Small bonfires had been lit, water was being drawn from the well, stables opened, children and dogs chasing around. The blacksmith was firing his forge, shouting at his apprentices to bring more charcoal. A horse, more skittish than the rest, and glad to be free of its stables, whinnied, its hooves pawing the air. Bakehouses and ovens were lit, barrel-loads of food, slabs of salted meat and baskets of not-so-fresh bread being wheeled down to the tables, boards laid across trestles, where the garrison would muster to break its fast.

Corbett walked around, watching the people at their work, now and then returning a greeting. A young woman came tripping along the cobbles, a heavy basket in her hand. Corbett stopped her, took the basket from her and, looking down, realized they were greasy pots and pans from the kitchen being taken to be scrubbed in vats of boiling salted water. The girl was pretty, her thin white face shrouded by reddish hair.

'Why, sir, thank you.' Her accent was thick, rather musical, the words clipped, running breathlessly into each other.

'What's your name?'

'Why, Master, Marissa.'

'Tell me, Marissa . . .' Corbett carried the basket across the yard, and the other women stood back, gaping at this powerful King's man helping one of their own. He placed it down on the cobblestones, as far away from the fire as possible so that it would not be scorched. 'Tell me, Marissa,' he took a coin out and, grasping the girl's chapped hand, made her take it, 'do you have a cloak?'

'Oh no, Master.' She must have glimpsed the disappointment in Corbett's face. 'But I can always borrow one.'

'And if you were to leave the castle?'

'Then I wouldn't ask for one,' she grinned, 'otherwise people would know that I was leaving.'

Corbett turned away in disappointment, as he realised why Rebecca wasn't wearing a cloak.

'Sir Hugh.'

He looked round. Bolingbroke, nursing his sore head, came trudging through the snow.

'I drank too much,' he confessed. 'I had to go straight to bed. Now the cold is sobering me up.' He squinted at Corbett, who saw the cut marks on his cheek where the clerk had tried to shave himself. 'What are you doing here?'

'I'm prying.' Corbett smiled. 'I should say trying to discover something about that murder yesterday morning.' He gestured round at the inner ward, now busy as any marketplace. 'There's nothing, and de Craon has insisted on an early start.'

Corbett led Bolingbroke across to the hall to break their fast. Ranulf was already there, keen and sharp as a knife, trying to persuade Chanson, who looked much the worse for wear, to eat some bread and take a sip of watered ale. De Craon and his entourage entered, and pleasantries were exchanged before they adjourned to the solar, which was reached by going down the passageway which ran under the minstrels' gallery. A warm, comfortable chamber, sure protection against the freezing cold, its walls were cloaked in heavy woollen drapes of dark muted colours. The polished wooden floor was covered by turkey carpets and the fire in the great hearth was already merry and full, its flames roaring up. A long walnut table dominated the centre of the chamber, a high-backed quilted chair at each end, with similar chairs arranged along both sides. On the table lay writing trays containing ink horns, sharpened quills, pumice stones and a small jar of fine sand. At either end stood a hardened leather drum, its cap thrown back to reveal cream-coloured rolls of vellum and parchment. The Catherine wheel of candles had been lowered from the black-beamed ceiling. Each container held a costly beeswax taper, so as to provide good light for those at the table, and three sets of brass candelabra had also been lit for good measure.

The seating arrangement was agreed upon: Corbett and de Craon at the ends, their clerks and advisers along either side. Father Andrew came to intone the *Veni Creator Spiritus*. Corbett pronounced himself satisfied and, leaving Chanson to sit with the other henchmen on either side of the mantled hearth, took Ranulf and Bolingbroke back to his own chamber. He felt in the toe of one of his riding boots, took out a ring of three keys and crossed to the iron-bound coffer at the foot of the bed.

'This used to be the castle treasury,' he explained, slipping two of the keys off the ring. 'It's the work of a craftsman, constructed specially in the Tower of London. You'll not find its like anywhere. All three locks are distinctly separate; we shall each hold a key.'

He distributed the other two keys, the locks were turned, and Corbett pushed back the lid and, helped by Ranulf, lifted out the red quilted Chancery box. This, too, possessed two distinct locks, to which Ranulf always carried the other key. Corbett broke the red and green seals, and the locks were turned. Inside was a further lid which only Corbett could unlock in order to draw out the leather pouches containing the leather-bound copies of the *Secretus Secretorum*, and other manuscripts of Roger Bacon. Each pouch had been sealed by the King himself using his signet ring, pressing it into the blood-red wax.

'The King was most insistent.' Corbett smiled at his two companions. 'He regarded these as he would any treasure in the Tower.' He took out the *Secretus Secretorum*, with its dark red Spanish leather cover, its clasp containing a brilliant amethyst. 'This is not,' he winked at Bolingbroke, 'the manuscript you stole from Paris, but the King's very own.'

He put the pouches and what they contained on the floor.

'I've also brought my own ciphers, as well as the various ones used in the Secret Chancery, not to mention those used by myself.' He got to his feet, brushing the dust from his knees. 'Not that they have done any good,' he sighed. 'Friar Roger's cipher resists everything I know.'

Sir Hugh gave the manuscripts to Ranulf, telling him to put them back in their pouches and relock the coffers. They were about to leave when there was a pounding on the door, and one of Sir Edmund's stewards burst into the chamber.

'Sir Hugh, you best come, one of the Frenchmen,' he fought for breath, 'one of the Frenchmen has died from a seizure.'

Corbett shouted at Ranulf to guard the manuscripts with his life and, accompanied by Bolingbroke, hurried across the bailey to the Lantern Tower. The steward explained how three of the clerks were lodged there, with de Craon above the Hall of Angels, and Crotoy in the nearby Jerusalem Tower, so called because it once contained a small chapel. The door to the Lantern Tower thronged with men-at-arms. They stood aside as Corbett strode through, up the stone spiral staircase and into a stairwell which led into a chamber. The door, its leather hinges snapped, rested against the cracked lintel. The castle leech, with Father Andrew nearby, was bending over the corpse sprawled on the bed. De Craon and his three companions were standing near the ash-filled hearth, looking on anxiously.

Corbett stared at the corpse. Destaples had definitely died of a seizure. His narrow face was all mottled, eyes popping and staring, mouth open as if ready to scream. He felt the Frenchman's hand; the flesh was cold, hard and stiff.

'He's been dead hours,' the leech declared mournfully, wiping his hands on a napkin. 'The fire's gone out, the chamber is freezing; he must have died shortly after going to sleep.'

Corbett glanced quickly at the bedside table and the little coffer, lid open, full of miniature green leather pouches. He picked one of these up, undid the cord and sniffed, but detected nothing but crushed mint, and the same from the empty goblet nearby. He sprinkled the water dregs on his hand, then closed his eyes and thought of other chambers where men and women had died violent deaths, suicides who locked and bolted the door, victims who thought they were safe, not knowing that they were being as zealously hunted as any beast in the forest. How many corpses had he stood over? How many times had the questions been put?

'Are you certain it was a seizure?' Corbett asked.

'If you are looking for poison,' the leech replied, 'this is not the case. A true seizure, Sir Hugh, a stopping of the heart, a closing of the throat, swift convulsions. Death would have been instantaneous.' He gestured with his head towards the group of Frenchmen. 'They say he had a weak heart.'

'Oh, Sir Hugh.' De Craon came forward. 'I must admit my suspicions were roused.' He beat his chest like a mock penitent. 'I confess my evil thoughts, but Destaples was old, his heart was weak, the sea voyage wasn't pleasant.' De Craon gestured at the side table. 'This excellent physician has already examined all these pouches and the goblet. They contain nothing but mint. Etienne enjoyed an infusion mixed with water just before he went to sleep.'

Corbett didn't glance at Bolingbroke, even though he recalled the clerk's earlier warnings about why the Frenchmen had been brought to England. He gazed down at the corpse. 'Sir Edmund?'

The Constable, who had been standing near the window, arms crossed, deep in thought, walked out of the shadows.

'Did anyone approach the bedside table?' Corbett asked. 'I mean, when the door was forced?'

'Sir Hugh, Sir Hugh,' de Craon's voice was like a purr, 'I know your mind.'

'Do you?' Corbett snapped.

'You suspect foul deeds, but I assure you—'

'Monseigneur is correct,' Sir Edmund intervened. 'We were gathered in the solar. I noticed,' he gestured at the corpse, 'Monsieur Destaples was absent. I sent a steward to investigate. He reported back that he could not rouse him. I did not alarm anyone but came across myself. I eventually had the door forced and found what you see. I left a guard near the bed with strict instructions whilst I checked both the wine and water jugs. Sir Hugh,' the Constable shrugged, 'this man died of a seizure.'

Corbett gazed round the chamber, which was very similar to his own. Now the shock had passed, he noticed how cold it was, and yet everything was in its place, neat and tidy, more like a soldier's room than a professor's. He glimpsed the robes hanging from the wall. Destaples had changed into a linen nightshirt and must have been in bed when he had the seizure. A mass of white wax coated the candle pricket.

'He didn't even have time to douse the candle,' Corbett murmured.

'Gentlemen, gentlemen.' De Craon, clapping his hands for warmth rather than attention, walked over to the bed. 'Sir Edmund, I suggest we have a small respite and perhaps begin our meeting, shall we say,' he narrowed his eyes, 'at ten o'clock.'

The Constable agreed. Corbett left the tower, sending Bolingbroke back to keep Ranulf company.

'Do you think, Sir Hugh,' Bolingbroke came back across the yard, fully distracted by his own thoughts, 'do you think Destaples' death was natural?'

'I don't know,' Corbett rasped, watching his own breath hang heavy on the icy air. He was aware of the scenes in the bailey around him, how the noise of the people, the creaking of the carts, the neighing of the horses, seemed muffled on this sombre morning. According to all the evidence, Destaples had died in his sleep and there was nothing to be done. De Craon acted blunt and honest with not even a hint of accusation. And yet? He slapped Bolingbroke on the shoulder. 'Tell Ranulf to stay in my chamber.'

Corbett walked across to the stables and stopped halfway at the well, using the cover of the people milling there to watch the entrance of the Lantern Tower. De Craon and the others came out, each going their separate ways. Corbett went striding back.

'Louis, Louis, can I have words with you?'

Crotoy, muffled in his black coat, turned and smiled. 'Good morrow, Sir Hugh.' He clasped Corbett's hand.

'That's right, Louis.' Corbett kept his smile fixed. 'Just exchange pleasantries,' he whispered. 'Now, about these manuscripts?' He raised his voice and chatted about ciphers and vellum until de Craon and the rest were out of earshot. 'Well,

Louis.' He took the Frenchman by the elbow, gently steering him across the bailey towards the Hall of Angels. 'One of your comrades is dead.'

'He wasn't a comrade,' Crotoy declared. 'I disliked Destaples intensely; he was of narrow mind and sour soul. He once wrote a commentary on the first chapter of John's Gospel. By the time I had finished reading it I couldn't decide if Destaples thought of himself as St John come again, or even Christ. He seemed to have a natural knowledge about the divine, much deeper than us common mortals.'

Corbett laughed out loud. He had forgotten the intense rivalries which set these professors at each other's throats.

'I'll tell you two other things,' Crotoy continued. 'De Craon and his royal master disliked Destaples. He knew enough scripture to challenge Philip's authority. Do you remember the line, "Do not be like the pagans whose rulers like to make their authority felt"? Destaples constantly reminded Philip of it.'

'And the second thing?' Corbett asked.

'Why, Sir Hugh, weak heart or not, I don't believe Destaples died of a seizure. Somehow or other he was murdered.'

'What?' Corbett stepped back. 'You, a friend of de Craon?'

'I'm no friend,' Crotoy intervened, 'neither to him or his royal master.'

They paused as a cart trundled by, standing back so they weren't splashed by the icy mud.

'Let's go into the Hall of Angels,' Crotoy continued. 'Let's talk as if we are still exchanging pleasantries. How many years have I known you, Hugh, twenty, twenty-two?' He nudged Corbett. 'Do you think, because I'm French, I'm not your friend? Do you think because we are from different kingdoms we are not of one mind, of one soul?'

They entered the Hall of Angels, where servants were clearing away all the signs of revelry from the previous evening. They walked over to the fireplace, taking two stools, and sat basking in the warmth. Crotoy positioned himself so that he could watch the main door, whilst he quietly instructed Corbett to guard the entrance leading from the solar.

'If anyone comes,' he murmured, stretching out his hands, 'we are discussing the relative merits of Albert the Great and

Thomas Aquinas. Now, to your real question. Hugh, I don't know why I'm here. Yes, I'm an expert on ciphers. I have studied the writings of Roger Bacon but I judge him to be a boaster and meddler. Oh, a true scholar, but one full of mischief. His writings abound with his own pride and pre-eminence. I understand the attraction of finding the true worth of the *Secretus Secretorum*, but now I'm confused.' He leaned forward, using his fingers to emphasize the points he was about to make. 'Why are we here, Hugh? The real reason. To share knowledge?' He shook his head. 'Our royal masters despise each other. Secondly, why here at Corfe?'

'Because Philip asked for a castle near the coast and agreed you should come to us as a gesture of friendship.'

Crotoy made a rude sound with his lips. 'Thirdly,' he continued, 'why were I and the others selected?'

'Because of your scholarship?'

Crotoy shook his head. 'We have one thing in common, Sir Hugh. We are members of the Sorbonne, well known for our opposition to the more strident demands and claims of Philip of France.'

'And fourthly?' Corbett asked.

'Etienne Destaples.' Crotoy sighed deeply. 'Did you notice last night, Sir Hugh, how Destaples ate very little at the banquet?'

'He didn't trust his host?'

'No, Hugh, he doesn't trust his own kind. Destaples was very suspicious, as I am, about why he was brought here. You do realize, Hugh, none of us are friends of de Craon, and we do not enjoy the friendship of Philip of France. The same applied to Magister Thibault.'

Corbett stared into the flames. He recalled the banquet last night. In fact Destaples had had more to say to Bolingbroke than anyone else, whilst afterwards he had approached Ranulf to introduce himself.

'So why did you come here in the depth of winter?'

'We had no choice,' Crotoy murmured. 'We are servants of the King. If we displease him it is remarkable how swiftly, like Lucifer falling from Heaven, we can be dismissed from our posts. Look,' Crotoy edged closer, staring around the Hall of Angels to make sure they were not being watched, 'why are you here, Sir Hugh Corbett? Wouldn't you like to be closeted with the Lady Maeve, or playing with your children? You serve your King loyally, but do you trust him? Do you approve of everything he does?'

Corbett recalled Edward at the most recent council meeting, his iron-grey hair swept back, face flushed with anger, spittle-edged lips curled in a snarl; or meeting Scottish envoys in a church, garbed in black armour, seated on his great war horse Bayard, drawing his sword and shouting that its blade was the only justice the Scots would receive from him.

'There's a difference,' he mused. 'My Lord the King is a difficult man but he likes me, he trusts me; sometimes I can temper his rages.'

'Philip is different. His power grows from year to year. He does not listen to our "Parlements" but to his brothers, Louis and Charles, and a small coterie of lawyers. The only opposition to our King are the universities, their philosophers and the lawyers, and nowhere more so than in Paris. To cut to the chase, Hugh,' the Frenchman's face was now pale, and sweat beaded his temples, 'I truly think we have all been brought here to be murdered, well away from our homes. We are an inconvenience, to be shed like the skin of some fruit, as well as a warning to others back in Paris.' Crotoy paused as a servant came up to serve them ale laced with nutmeg. 'No wonder Philip agreed for us to journey to England. Take poor Etienne; by the time his corpse is prepared, packed with spices and ointments, it will be too late for any physician to make a rigorous scrutiny of his body.'

'But the *Secretus Secretorum*?' Corbett asked. 'Doesn't your master want it translated, the cipher broken?'

Crotoy sipped from his ale. 'What are we really looking at, Hugh? True learning, or a farrago of nonsense, a fardel, a basket of stupidity fixed on our backs, a cunning device, a subtle ploy, arranged for very many different reasons? Oh,' he waved his hand, 'Philip likes his secrets, be they those of Friar Roger or the Templars. He knows about the black powder that can turn into fire. True, Friar Roger can describe wonderful things, but so can a child.'

Corbett grasped his tankard and sniffed at its warm tang, which brought back memories of a flower-filled garden with its heavy spices and fragrant aroma. If Philip was plotting mischief, he wondered – and that was more than a possibility – why was Edward of England involved? What was behind all this?

'Last night,' he said abruptly, 'after the banquet, Destaples and his comrades returned to their chambers. According to the evidence, Destaples changed for bed, drank his mint water and suffered a seizure. He did have a malady of the heart. What other explanation can there be?' He smiled at Crotoy. 'Your thoughts are too dark, Louis. If Destaples was suspicious he wouldn't let de Craon into his chamber, and he would rigorously check anything he was offered to eat or drink.' Corbett paused. 'I must ask you this, would Destaples let you into his chamber?'

'No.' The answer was emphatic. 'Oh Blessed Virgin guard us,' Crotoy breathed. 'We don't trust de Craon and we certainly don't like each other. According to the rest, none of us visited Destaples after he retired. I certainly didn't, whilst the other two were deep in their cups. I would take it as a certainty that Destaples would never have permitted de Craon to be alone with him, in France, never mind here. It was the same on board ship and our journey from Dover. You see, Hugh, for all we know, one of us, including myself, learned professors of the Sorbonne, could be in de Craon's pay.'

'Why are you telling me this?' Corbett asked.

'I was trained in logic, Hugh, to create a hypothesis based on evidence and develop that logically, but as the years have passed,' Crotoy rose to his feet, 'I'm aware of other feelings and thoughts.' He patted Corbett on the shoulder and leaned down. 'God forgive me, Hugh, but I think I have been brought here to die, and if that happens, whatever you think of me, I want justice. Oh, I'll be careful, but there again,' he laughed abruptly, 'so was Destaples.' Crotoy strode away.

Corbett finished his ale and thought of that locked chamber, of Destaples writhing on his bed. Surely Crotoy was wrong? Nobody had done any violence. If the dead Frenchman distrusted his own, he certainly wouldn't trust an English clerk. He placed his tankard on a nearby table and stared around the hall. Gazing up at the dais where they had feasted so well the night before, he tried to recall what he had seen and wondered if Louis Crotoy was right. As they all had eaten and drunk, had murder been planned?

When Corbett left the hall, the snow was falling so heavily the castle folk had retreated to the stables, outhouses or their own cottages built against the wall. He entered the Lantern Tower and quickly climbed the staircase. Destaples' chamber was now empty, except for a guardsman dozing on a stool just inside the doorway. Corbett told him not to mind as he quickly walked around the dead man's room. Destaples' robes still hung on a peg, but as he expected, the coffers and chests had been packed and removed, probably by de Craon, for safe keeping.

'I was here, you know.' The man-at-arms sitting on the stool, cradling his helmet, gestured at the bed, his dirty, podgy fingers jabbing the air.

'I beg your pardon?' Corbett answered.

'I was here when they broke down the door, that's why Sir Edmund left me here.'

'Did you see anything suspicious?' Corbett asked.

'Nothing but that old man sprawled on the bed.' The guard pointed at the small four-poster, its curtains tied tightly back.

'And was it like this?' Corbett asked.

'Sir Edmund was most careful. The body was twisted,' the man-at-arms said, 'as if the old man had tried to rise. The bed curtains were pulled back, there was a goblet on the table, and that small coffer, but nothing else.'

'And the door was certainly locked?' Corbett asked.

'Oh yes,' the man replied. 'Some of the castle folk,' he continued, 'whisper that this is a cursed place.'

Corbett threw the man a coin and, as he went back down the stairs, idly wondered if the guard had spoken the truth.

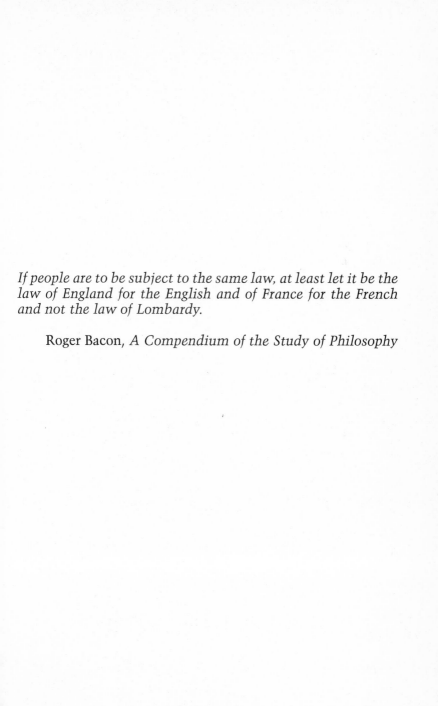

If people are to be subject to the same law, at least let it be the law of England for the English and of France for the French and not the law of Lombardy.

Roger Bacon, *A Compendium of the Study of Philosophy*

Chapter 6

'I do not believe such things are possible; they are fanciful notions. It is my belief Friar Roger was a great scholar with a lively imagination.'

Louis Crotoy sat back in his chair, pushing away the manuscripts in front of him as if they were soiled. Corbett, sitting at the end of the table, wondered whether his old friend had decided to confront the danger; by rejecting Friar Roger, he was implicitly demanding this meeting be brought to an end. De Craon, however, at the other end of the table, appeared unruffled. He had taken his cloak off and unlaced the quilted jerkin beneath.

'I agree.' Jean Vervins leaned forward, staring down at de Craon. 'In his *De Mirabile Potestate Artis et Naturae*, Concerning the Marvellous Power of Art and Nature,' Vervins translated the title as if the others had no knowledge of Latin, 'Friar Roger claims,' he picked up one of the manuscripts before him, 'there are marvels created solely by the agency of art or nature. In these there is no magic whatsoever. Why?' Vervins lifted his head and smiled thinly. 'Because, so Friar Roger claims, it has been proved that all magical power is inferior to that of art and nature.'

'What are you saying?' de Craon asked.

'Nothing, my Lord,' Vervins retorted. He blinked his tired eyes and scratched the tip of his sharp nose. 'But it follows logically that if marvels are the result of art and nature, then they can be seen by all and there is no secret knowledge.'

'And yet he contradicts that,' Crotoy put in. 'Friar Roger talks of, and I quote, "marvellous devices constructed in antiquity and in his time, and he has met people who are acquainted with them explicitly".'

'He says that,' Vervins' voice rose, 'in his work *De Arte*—'

'Except for the instrument of flying,' Corbett intervened.

'Ah,' Crotoy retorted, 'but he claims to have met someone who has thought it through. Here is Friar Roger claiming that he has actually spoken to someone who at least, in theory, has constructed a device which can fly.'

'He is referring,' Pierre Sanson spoke up, fat face all flushed, thin hair damp; he too had loosened his cloak, throwing it on the back of his chair, 'he is referring,' his squeaky voice caused laughter amongst the henchmen sitting near the hearth, 'to Peter Marincourt.'

'Ah yes,' Crotoy shook his head, 'this mysterious philosopher who was supposed to have taught Friar Roger in Paris. Look,' he leaned his elbows on the table, 'I concede that Friar Roger made incredible claims. Listen.' He picked up a manuscript. 'He actually writes, "It is feasible that great ships and sea-going vessels shall be constructed which could move under the guidance of one man, and go so much faster than a galley full of oarsmen", and again, "It is feasible that a cart could be made to move with incredible speed and such motion will not depend on man or any other creature." Later on,' Crotoy dropped the manuscript, 'he talks of a device which, if constructed, could take a man to the bottom of the sea, unscathed. Now,' the Frenchman warmed to his theme, 'what happens if I claimed to have built a set of wings to fly from the top of the keep of this castle? Is there anyone here who would like to try it?'

The question provoked a burst of laughter. Corbett, hiding the lower part of his face behind his hand, glanced at de Craon slouched in his chair, face all puckered up as if he was following every jot and syllable of this debate. He had concluded that, apart from the plump Pierre Sanson, the French scholars had very little respect for Friar Roger's claims and were deeply suspicious of the *Secretus Secretorum*. They had also quickly come to terms with the death of their comrade; there was little sign of mourning, except for Crotoy, who had asked Father

Andrew to celebrate a Requiem Mass later that day. De Craon had received Sir Edmund's promise that the body would be cleaned and gutted, packed with ointments and spices and sent by cart to Dover for the journey back to France. Once they had all gathered here, Crotoy had led the attack, fielding the hypothesis that if Bacon's claims in other manuscripts, which could be read, were ridiculous, why should they take notice of some secret manuscript indecipherable and totally resistant to translation? In other words, Corbett wryly reflected, the French scholars wanted to go home.

'But you have proof of this,' Bolingbroke broke in. 'When I was in . . .' he paused and stopped himself in time, 'in the Halls of Oxford, a lecturer had to prove his case either by logic or experiment.'

'Precisely!' Crotoy seized on Bolingbroke's words. 'In his work the *Opus Maius*, Friar Roger claims that if you cut a hazel twig in two and separate the pieces, the two isolated parts will try to approach one another; you will feel the effort both ends are making.' He leaned down and picked up a hazel twig, placed it on the table, took a knife, sliced it in two and held the pieces apart. Sir Edmund, seated in a high chair to Corbett's right, rose to his feet, watching intently.

'Do you see any movement?' Crotoy declared. The Constable came round the table. Crotoy thrust the twigs into his hands. 'Do you experience any sensation of these twigs, like lovers, yearning to meet?'

Sir Edmund held them for a while and shook his head.

'In other words,' Crotoy finished his declaration with the classic phrase of the schools, 'that which is to be proved has not been proved. Therefore the hypothesis on which it depends cannot be valid.'

'And yet,' Bolingbroke declared, 'in that same work you quoted, Friar Roger talks of 'certain igneous mixtures, saltpetre, charcoal and sulphur which, when wrapped in parchment and lit, creates great noise and flame'.

'But is that proof?' Vervins jibed. 'If you throw a slab of meat into a hungry kennel you will hear great noise.'

'Ah yes,' Bolingbroke retorted, 'but that is to be expected. What I am saying is that Friar Roger did prove that mixture would lead to that effect, as he does in Chapter Seven of the

Opus Maius, where he demonstrates how a rainbow can be measured.'

'What if,' de Craon's voice cut like a lash; the French envoy was clearly annoyed at the cynicism of his companions, 'what if the solution to all these riddles lies in the *Secretus Secretorum*? Perhaps,' he waved a hand, 'the answer to how a cart can move of its own accord, or the split ends of a hazel twig attempt to meet each other, might be resolved there? Doesn't Friar Roger claim,' de Craon closed his eyes to remember the words, ' "for the wise have always been divided from the multitude, and have hidden the secret truths of wisdom, not only from the vulgar, but even from common philosophers"?'

'Arrogance,' Crotoy jibed. 'If Jesus could reveal divine truths then why can't Friar Roger confess his secrets?'

'Ah no,' de Craon retorted. 'Didn't Jesus himself say that he spoke to the multitude in parables but bluntly and openly only to his own followers? Gentlemen, we are here not to debate Friar Roger's claims but to break and translate the cipher of his secret manuscript; that is what our royal masters have demanded.'

De Craon glared down at Corbett, willing his support, but before he could reply, the door was flung open and a messenger came in and whispered into Sir Edmund's ear. The Constable nodded but gestured at Corbett to continue. The Keeper of the Secret Seal opened the leather bag at his feet and drew out his copy of Friar Roger's *Secretus Secretorum*.

'Monsieur de Craon is correct,' he began. He patted the cover, noting with amusement how de Craon had produced his own copy of the same work. 'Everything depends on this manuscript.' He undid the clasp and turned the crackling parchment pages. 'At first sight it looks easy, a Latin manuscript, here and there strange symbols, but the words make little sense. If translated they are like the babblings of a child.'

'Which they are,' Crotoy intervened.

'We don't know that. Now, Friar Roger actually lists seven ways of writing a cipher. First, behind characters and symbols; we all know that method. Secondly, in parables, stories which are known only to the writer and his chosen reader. There are other more technical ways, such as,' Corbett ticked the next

three off on his fingers, 'the use of words where only conson-
ants are deployed; or different alphabets. Friar Roger studied
Hebrew and Greek as well as Latin, so he could have used any
of these, or a language not known to anybody. The sixth method
is the rejection of letters and the use of mathematical signs;
and finally, much more subtly, the writer creates his own
alphabet, his own language, consisting of different types of
symbols and marks which are known only to him and those to
whom he has revealed them. Now, as far as we know, the
Secretus Secretorum was written by Bacon and a copy made.
We are not too sure whether the English King owns the original
or his Grace the King of France, but we are assured – are we
not, Monsieur de Craon? – that these two manuscripts are
identical in every way.' De Craon nodded slowly. 'So I propose,'
Corbett continued, 'we compare the manuscripts one more
time. We can spend the rest of the day doing this. I recommend
therefore that Master Bolingbroke and Magister Sanson carry
this task through.'

'What if,' Ranulf, who'd sat fascinated by the argument,
tapped the table with his hand, 'what if a key does exist?'

'A great search has been made.' Pierre Sanson shook his
head. 'There is not even a hint or a whisper that such a
document exists. What we have to do here is understand the
Latin words used as well as the different symbols and characters which separate them.'

'As a gesture of goodwill,' de Craon pulled himself up in his
chair, 'and by royal command from my master, I can reveal
that Magister Thibault, before his unfortunate accident,' de
Craon glared at Bolingbroke, 'actually found a key, and was
hopeful that he could translate the entire manuscript!'

The French envoy revelled in the consternation his remark
caused. Corbett glared in disbelief. Ranulf leaned over to
whisper to him to keep calm.

'Monsieur, you jest?' Ranulf protested.

'Monsieur does not jest. If you turn to the last page of the
Secretus Secretorum,' de Craon waited until Corbett had done
so, 'in the second line there is an apparently meaningless phrase
"Dabo tibi portas multas", "I shall give you many doors".'

Corbett, staring intently at the last page of the manuscript,
studied the particular line as the Frenchman explained how, if

certain letters were removed and specified characters transposed, the words he had quoted emerged from the jumble on the page. Sir Hugh could clearly make out the word *dabo*.

'I'm afraid,' de Craon spoke again, 'that that was all Magister Thibault was able to decipher.'

The manuscripts were passed round, all animosity forgotten, as the various scholars studied the letters and began to argue amongst themselves. Corbett sat back, puzzled. He had had the opportunity to look at the French copy, and even a glance at the first page, the colour of the ink, the shape of the letters and symbols, the texture of the manuscript, proved the two manuscripts were a fair copy of each other. At the same time de Craon had been most helpful; indeed, his remarks had surprised not only Corbett but also his own colleagues. Why, Corbett wondered, were the French being so co-operative?

The discussion continued for at least an hour, parchment and quill being used; de Craon, like a schoolmaster, moved round the table, explaining what Magister Thibault had done, though expressing ignorance at how he had reached such a conclusion.

The castle bell chimed for the midday Angelis and they paused from their discussions while Corbett led them in the famous prayer, 'The Angel Lord declared unto Mary'. He noticed, with some amusement, that those clustered around the table fairly gabbled the words and returned immediately to the matter in hand.

Soon after, Sir Edmund announced that food would be served in the hall below, and Corbett brought the meeting to order. He and de Craon agreed that they would adjourn for the rest of the day whilst Bolingbroke and Sanson compared the manuscripts. Chattering volubly, de Craon led the rest of the group along the passageway into the hall. Corbett and Ranulf stayed to have a word with Sir Edmund. The Constable closed the door behind his guests and, plucking Corbett by the sleeve, took him over to the fireplace, gesturing at Ranulf to join them.

'The snow's ceased falling,' he murmured. 'A peddler has reached the castle; he came in from one of the coastal villages. He brought rumours of the Flemish pirates being seen much closer to the coast than normal.'

'In this weather?' Corbett exclaimed. 'The seas are swollen, there will be few vessels leaving port. So what are they waiting for?'

'What are they looking for, more like?' Ranulf retorted.

'I feel nervous,' the Constable confessed. 'This castle is well fortified and manned, but sooner or later you and the French envoys must leave. Think, Sir Hugh, of the disgrace if you or Monsieur de Craon, either on land or sea, were ambushed or captured by Flemish pirates. I would hear Edward's roars from Westminster here, whilst Philip of France's anger, well . . .' He shrugged.

'But there is no real danger, surely?' Corbett replied. 'The pirates are at sea; they are looking for plunder, a careless merchantman, or some unprotected village where they can slaughter fresh meat and retreat to their ships.'

'I know, I know.' The Constable shook his head. 'You are a clerk, Sir Hugh, skilled in the matters of the Chancery. I am a soldier. It is rare for pirates to come in so close at such a time, with the weather so bad. Yet they could use it to their own advantage. They could beach their ships, teeming with men, desperate veterans. If they made a landing, it might take days, or even weeks, for a message to get through the snow to London or one of the Cinque Ports. I thought I should tell you.' He gestured towards the door. 'Will you join us in the hall?'

Corbett didn't feel like eating; he made polite excuses and went out, slipping and slithering on the icy cobbles, to his own chamber in the Salt Tower. He waited before the fire until Ranulf and Chanson returned and, whilst the groom guarded the door, he tried to settle the chaos seething in his mind.

'I understand none of it, Ranulf.' The red-haired clerk sat at the small desk, and dipped his quill into the ink warmed by the fire. 'It's like being in the countryside when the mist comes down. Do we go forward or wait until it's cleared? Anyway, let's list the obstacles.'

Corbett walked up and down whilst Ranulf's pen scratched the parchment, writing in a cipher only he and Corbett understood.

Primo – Why is our King so interested in Friar Roger's secret manuscript? What has he discovered which so intrigues him yet he won't even tell me? He has gone through all of Friar Roger's writings and brought the Secretus Secretorum *from his Treasury of Books at Westminster. Is it because he has heard that Philip of France is equally interested, or is the opposite true? Is Philip simply, like I am, deeply curious at Edward's close interest in the writings of a long-dead Franciscan?*

Secundo – Is the Secretus Secretorum *a genuine manuscript? Does it contain a treasure house of secrets or is it mere babble? Is there a key to the cipher? A genuine key. Edward of England hasn't translated it, but has Philip of France? According to de Craon, and he showed some proof this morning, one of the lines can be translated. But is that a mere accident?*

Tertio – Why did the French agree so readily to Edward of England's request? Indeed, insist that such co-operation was in accordance with the Treaty of Paris? Why did they concede to come to England and ask that the meeting take place in a lonely castle near the coast?

'Because they knew,' Ranulf lifted his head, 'that Edward would agree to that. He does not like you in France. If Philip insists that the two courts co-operate, it's the least Edward can expect.'

'True, true,' Corbett murmured. He paused before the fire and stared at the faces cut into the wooden shelf. The sculptor had tried to imitate the faces of gargoyles seen in churches but in the end had satisfied himself with simple roundels, the eyes, nose and mouth cut roughly into them. Corbett continued his pacing.

Quarto – De Craon brings experts on Friar Roger's writings from the Sorbonne. These men are also experts on ciphers and secret letters. One of these has already died in unfortunate circumstances. My old friend Crotoy confesses that none of these periti, *or experts, are friends of the French*

King. They oppose his ideas of kingship. Crotoy is convinced that Destaples was murdered but there is not a shred of evidence to prove that. He is also of the mind that he himself, and the others, are marked down for death, that they have been brought to England to be killed, that they will all die in unfortunate incidents. Louis Crotoy believes such 'accidents' will be dismissed, and if there is any suspicion, it will be laid firmly at the door of the perfidious English.

Quinto – The business in Paris. Ufford and Bolingbroke maintain that one of the masters of the University, in return for gold, informed them where Magister Thibault's copy of the Secretus Secretorum was kept. Ufford and Bolingbroke stole this, but for some unknown reason, Magister Thibault and the young whore he was entertaining went down to the strongroom at the very moment of the robbery. From what I gather, Magister Thibault was reluctant to go down. According to the evidence, he was probably showing off to his lady friend. Yet why should a Paris courtesan be interested in an old manuscript? Was she told to take Magister Thibault down there at that time? If so, the person who betrayed Philip, this mysterious master of the University, also tried to betray Ufford and Bolingbroke. Indeed he nearly succeeded. Ufford was killed and Bolingbroke only escaped by mere chance and his own skill.

Corbett shook his head. 'I can make no sense of that.' He sipped at a beaker of wine.

Sexto – The deaths in this castle. I have sworn to find the killer. But why are hapless young maids being killed by a crossbow bolt? They are not ravished or robbed, their corpses are being found both within the castle and outside. The killings began after the Feast of St Matthew. First, a young woman disappears, but the rest have been found in or near the castle. Some attempt has been made to blame a coven of ragged outlaws. I don't believe that. First, why should they harm local girls – they would only stir up hatred in the local community against them. Secondly, that's why those

outlaws were waiting for us in the cemetery. They know
that a King's man has arrived in Corfe and they don't want
to be hanged for murders they haven't committed. I wonder
what they meant about the horror in the forest?

'We could ride in there.' Chanson, crouching by the door,
grinned eagerly at Ranulf. 'We could go deep into the forest and
follow the ancient trackways.'

'Why don't you go?' Ranulf snapped.

'Pax,' Corbett declared. 'Let's go back and see what we know.'
He seized a quill and a piece of parchment and drew a crude
map. 'This is Purbeck Island – there's sea to the east and to the
south. Corfe lies here, high on the downs which stretch down
to the sea. Further north, just as we enter the forest, is the
church of St Peter's and the Tavern in the Forest, with a small
village lying further to the east. Now, most of the victims have
been found in or near the castle, the only exception being poor
Rebecca, who was killed on a trackway outside the cemetery.
These young women had little in common except that they
lived in the castle and met every Saturday with Father Matthew
in the nave of his church. They were all killed by a crossbow
bolt loosed so close the quarrel was embedded deep in the
flesh. From the little I have learnt, the girl Alusia journeyed to
the cemetery to pay honour to a dead friend buried there, also
a victim of this malevolent killer. She went down on a cart
with Mistress Feyner, who takes laundry between the castle
and the Tavern in the Forest. Apparently Rebecca was supposed
to go with her but she didn't arrive in time.' Corbett went and
stood by Ranulf's shoulder. 'Tell me, Ranulf, why should
someone murder young women? If it's not to ravish them or
rob them?'

'Revenge, hatred?'

'Look, Chanson.' Corbett snapped his fingers. 'Go down to
the castle yard, bring up Alusia and Mistress Feyner. Tell them
the King's man wants a word with them.'

When Chanson had left, Corbett sat in the chair as Ranulf
read through what he had written. The clerk of the Chancery
of Green Wax was impatient. The day was almost halfway through and he had not yet seen the Lady Constance.
He'd received a small scroll last night tied with a purple

ribbon in which Lady Constance had assured him that if he wished to walk the castle gardens with her, his company would be most acceptable. Corbett watched his companion most closely and hid a smile. In any other instance he would have teased him, but Ranulf was so quiet, it was clear he was smitten.

'We will have to go to the woods, Ranulf. We need to meet that outlaw band and find out what they mean about the horror in the forest.'

Ranulf agreed. He stared across at the black wooden cross, the yellowing figure of Christ writhing there, and hid his fears. The King had often plucked him by the sleeve, taken him to one side and showed him what could be his; ambition burned fiercely within him. Sometimes he considered the Church as a path to advancement, but now he thought that the Lady Constance would be a good match, her father a friend of the King. He felt Corbett's hand on his shoulder.

'Be careful,' Corbett whispered. 'Remember, Ranulf, we are guests here.'

Before Ranulf could answer, there was a knock on the door and Chanson led in Mistress Feyner. 'I could not find Alusia,' the groom announced breathlessly. 'No one has seen her.'

'Probably gone off with that Martin,' Mistress Feyner sniffed, plumping herself down on a stool. 'Well, sir.' Mistress Feyner pulled off her woollen mittens. Corbett glanced at the chapped red hands. The cloak was patched and she pulled it closely around her whilst staring round the room. 'My husband made some of the furniture here; he was a carpenter. What do you wish? I'm a busy woman, and tongues will clack.'

'Let them clack.' Corbett smiled. 'Mistress, would you like some wine?'

Mistress Feyner's small black eyes creased into a smile. 'Why, sir, that would be most welcome; heated with an iron would be better.'

Corbett nodded at Chanson to do it. The groom took a pewter goblet, filled it with wine and, taking an ember from the fire, placed it in the cup before sprinkling in a little nutmeg and mace from the small spice box.

'You are chief laundrywoman of the castle?'

Mistress Feyner's black eyes were cold and watchful, one

thin hand combing her tangle of grey hair. She quickly grasped the pewter cup wrapped in a cloth, nursing it before taking a sip.

'You know what I am, sir. What do you want?'

'When did your daughter disappear?'

'Just after the Feast of the Exaltation of the True Cross. It was Harvest Sunday, that's right. Father Matthew had organized a special mass in which the Holy Rood would be taken in solemn procession around the cemetery. Phillipa was there.' The black eyes blinked. 'I thought she was with the other girls, but that afternoon she never came home. Sir Edmund was kind and organized a search, but nothing was found.'

'Do you think she has run away?'

'Run away, sir? Why should my daughter run away? She was the apple of my eye. A good girl, Sir Hugh, with fine skin and lovely eyes, gentle as a baby fawn she was. Father Matthew's best scholar, or that's how he used to tease her. She had many friends.'

Mistress Feyner held the goblet in one hand and tapped her chest with the other. 'I carried that girl for nine months. I would like to tell you, sir, that she ran away, that she is safe in some city or town, but a mother knows, sir, here, in the heart. Phillipa's gone.' Her voice broke. 'If only I could have her body back for burial, sir.'

'What do you suspect happened?'

'Killed, like the rest,' came the tired reply. 'The forest is full of swamps, marshes and morasses, but I would like her back, just to hold her one more time.'

Corbett opened his purse and drew out three silver coins. 'Here,' he urged, 'take them for yourself and for a Mass offering.'

Mistress Feyner nodded softly.

'Now, the morning Rebecca's corpse was found?'

Mistress Feyner lowered her head, a formidable woman, determined not to let this man see her cry.

'I apologize for my questions, Mistress,' Corbett pulled his chair a little closer, 'but the people of this castle want justice.'

'Alusia and Rebecca planned to visit Marion's grave. They wished to place greenery on it, they wanted a lift on the cart. Alusia arrived but Rebecca never did. I had to leave. I stopped outside the cemetery, on the trackway. Alusia climbed down, I continued. You see, sir, Master Reginald has a fierce temper and a sharp tongue. The linen from the tavern is brought to the castle to be washed and cleaned. Master Reginald pays well, he buys supplies from Sir Edmund and often sells goods to our Constable. There's a good understanding between Corfe and Master Reginald. However, when the taverner wants his clean washing, he wants it immediately.'

'Mistress?'

She looked at Ranulf. Corbett she liked, felt comfortable with, with his soft dark eyes and smiling mouth, a man who could speak in honeyed tones, but this one, with the hair the colour of the devil and eyes like the castle cat, she would have to be wary of. 'Yes, sir?'

'You went along the trackway that winds past the church. It was there that Rebecca's body was found. Did you see anything?'

'Well of course not, though her corpse may have been there. You must remember the snow was falling. I kept my eyes on the horse and the trackway ahead. Bitter cold it was. Alusia said the same, huddled in her cloak sitting beside me.'

'So,' Ranulf put his quill down, 'Rebecca might have gone to the cemetery beforehand and met her killer?'

'But why didn't she wait for me? What I think happened,' Mistress Feyner drank from the cup, 'is that she must have left the castle after me and met her death.' She glanced at Corbett. 'I can tell you no more, sir. People blame the outlaws, but I do not.' She drained her goblet and got to her feet. 'I thank you for the money.'

'Mistress Feyner?' She lifted the latch and turned round. 'If I put you on oath, if I formed a jury and asked you under the law to name a suspect . . .' The laundrywoman dropped the latch and came back.

'Why, sir, would you do that? If you did, you could not summons me; my daughter is one of the victims, I'm certain of that. But I shall tell you something, sir, and I think of it every time I visit that tavern. Mine host is a former soldier. Many of the girls have worked in his tap room, and Master Reginald, well, his hands and his lips are always hungry. My Phillipa served there as a slattern in the kitchen. She called him as lecherous and hot as a sparrow.'

'But he is not of the castle.'

'Oh yes he is, Sir Hugh. He often brings his cart here; his purse is always jingling and his eye always bright.'

'But none of the girls were ravished?'

Mistress Feyner returned to the door. 'Ask amongst the girls, Sir Hugh. Master Reginald, how can I put it, may be a cock in a small barnyard, but he's a gelded one.'

'You are repeating rumour,' Ranulf mused.

'No, sir, whoever you are.' Mistress Feyner grinned over her shoulder. 'Master Reginald has tried to finger my bodice and got nothing for his pains. He's tumbled others; the soil has been fresh but the plough has been weak. Master Reginald secretly knows that, for all his crowing, he's mocked by the very ones he pursues. You should go down to the tavern, Sir Hugh, and ask your questions. He does business with Horehound.'

'Horehound?'

'Oh, he and his coven take the name of herbs and plants, but they are not as fierce as they sound. Petty thieves and poachers,' she sighed, 'men and women trapped between the castle and the forest. So, if that's all?' and not waiting for an answer, she opened the door and left.

Corbett began to put on his riding boots.

'Oh no,' Ranulf groaned. 'Are we going hunting, Master?'

'Let's eat.' Corbett got to his feet, strapping on his war belt. 'We'll visit the tavern and taste Master Reginald's cooking, then we'll visit the church. I understand Father Matthew celebrates Mass late in the day.'

Ranulf and Chanson prepared hastily, and booted and spurred, they collected their horses from the stable. The snow had stopped falling but lay ankle deep. Corbett carefully led his horse across the slush-strewn cobbles, then mounted.

'Sir Hugh?' Corbett turned in the saddle. Bolingbroke hastened down the steps from the Hall of the Angels and, cloak flying, came running across. 'Do you wish me to accompany you?' The clerk pushed back his thinning hair and wiped the drops from his face. 'I'm wasting my time here. Sanson and I are comparing the manuscripts. They are the same, but as for their meaning . . .'

Corbett leaned down and patted Bolingbroke on the arm.

'No, no, stay here and watch what happens.'

They crossed the outer bailey, silent under its carpet of snow. Most of the garrison had now withdrawn indoors. They clattered across the drawbridge, the smells of the castle fading as they reached the trackway leading down to the fringe of trees. It was a bitterly cold landscape, the sky iron-grey and lowering, and beneath it only two colours, black and white. The trees and bushes, stripped of their leaves, made a sharp contrast to the silent whiteness around them. Corbett was glad of his heavy cloak and warm gauntlets. He guided his horse carefully along the trackway whilst above them two crows disturbed from their tree cawed noisily. He could tell from the track that few had left the castle. Here and there he could see the prints of birds and animals. A splash of blood and a few pathetic feathers showed where an animal had gorged on warm flesh in this icy wilderness.

Slumped in his saddle, Corbett reflected on the various problems facing him. He was so absorbed, he started with surprise as Ranulf called to him that they were approaching the Tavern in the Forest. They entered by the main gateway, an arrowshot from the trackway. The inn was a two-storey wooden-plaster building on a red stone base; it boasted a tiled roof and a small stack for the smoke to pour out. The yard was empty apart from two ostlers, one breaking the ice in the water trough whilst the other swept manure into a pile in the corner. The reek of horses mingled sharply with the sweetness from the nearby bakehouse and kitchen.

Corbett, throwing back his cloak, walked into the tap room. Ranulf followed, noticing the various doors and windows, just in case they had to leave more quickly than intended. It was a comfortable room with clean, whitewashed walls, and a black-beamed ceiling from which small sacks of vegetables and rolls of smoked meat hung to dry in the heat, well away from the rats and mice. A brazier stood in each corner, a large one in the centre. At the top of the communal table a fire glowed in the hearth built into the outside wall. At one end, near the kitchen, were a range of vats and barrels, and from the kitchen Corbett could hear the clatter of pans and pots, the shouts and cries of slatterns and servants. A few villagers were seated around the table; they looked up as Corbett entered and huddled closer to discuss the newcomers. In the far corner, grouped around a brazier, were five men, their dress almost hidden by cloaks and cowls. They too turned. Corbett glimpsed swarthy faces, black beards and moustaches.

The three newcomers took a table just near the door. One of the villagers turned and gave a chipped-toothed smile, lifting his hand, palm exposed, the customary greeting for peace. Corbett responded. A tap boy came running up with a tray of leather blackjacks full of ale, and without being asked, placed them on the table.

'Is Master Reginald here?' Corbett asked him.

'I'm here.'

The taverner emerged from the shadows around the barrels and vats where he had been working, a dark-haired, sour-faced man, small and thickset but quick and soft-footed. Unlike other taverners, there was none of the hand-wringing or wiping of the hands on the apron, the greasy smile or bowing of the head.

'You are strangers here? Why should strangers be travelling in such weather?' Master Reginald glimpsed Corbett's silver chain; now he did smile, the quickest of bows, and snapping his fingers, he called the tap boy back, gesturing at the blackjacks. 'Proper tankards,' he demanded, 'and the best ale from the barrel.'

He paused as an old woman, resting on a cane, staggered out of the kitchen and came to sit in a chair directly opposite him. She had a scrawny neck and the face of an angry chicken, hair piled high on her head. She beat her cane on the floor as she glared at the newcomers.

'My mother.' Master Reginald's smile was genuine. 'Sirs, would you like something to eat? I have a fine venison stew, the meat is fresh and cured, newly baked bread and a bowl of onions and leeks fried in butter?'

Corbett nodded. He took his horn spoon from his wallet and waited for the taverner to bring the food from the kitchen.

'You're the King's man, aren't you?' Corbett nodded and made the introductions, then pointed at the tankards. 'There should be four. I would like you to join us, sir.'

'I'm busy.'

Ranulf grasped his wrist. 'We are King's men,' he whispered hoarsely.

'I want some food,' the old woman shouted.

'Ask the cook,' Master Reginald shouted back. He tried to pull free from Ranulf's grasp.

'We are King's men,' Ranulf repeated, 'and carry his seals. We wish to buy you a tankard of ale and share local gossip.'

The taverner agreed reluctantly and sat like a prisoner at the bar. Corbett ate hungrily, while Master Reginald became more nervous and wary. When he had finished his meal, Corbett wiped his bowl with a dollop of bread, cleaned his spoon on a napkin and put it away.

'Do you know the outlaw Horehound?'

'I've never—'

'Yes you do.' Ranulf picked up his dagger, which he had used to share out the bread. 'You're a taverner, on the edge of a forest where outlaws lurk. They come to you for food and sustenance, they sell you fresh meat, they tell you who's on the road.'

'Tell the outlaw Horehound,' Corbett continued, 'that the King's man wants urgent words with him. It will be to his profit. You won't forget, will you? Secondly, these young women who have been killed. Some of them served in this tavern. Do you have a crossbow, Master Reginald?'

'Yes, I've got a crossbow, as have many of the villagers and castle folk. I also have a longbow, a quarterstaff, a sword and a dagger. I served in the Earl of Cornwall's retinue in Gascony. My mother owned this tavern, as her grandfather did before her.'

'And you have made it splendid with the plunder of war. Did you know any of those dead girls?'

'Of course I did.' The taverner kept his voice low. 'I often need help in the kitchens and tap room. In winter trade is poor, but once spring comes, the roads and trackways are busy with people coming into the castle.'

'Did you have a grudge against any of them?' Ranulf asked. 'Were they surly or impudent?'

'Some were, some weren't. Some had light fingers, others were prepared to sell themselves to customers. Some I liked, others I did not.'

'And you often go to the castle?'

Corbett was now closely watching the group in the corner.

'Well of course I do. I consider myself Sir Edmund's friend.'

'Who are those?' Corbett asked, nodding toward the group he had been watching.

'They are Castilians, trapped here by the snow. They are visiting the farmsteads and manors. They wish to buy up this year's crop of wool. Such visitors are quite common now, Sir Hugh.'

Corbett nodded; English wool was as precious as gold in foreign markets. Many cities and powerful groups of merchants sent their envoys to England to buy the wool direct.

'I go to the castle, and Mistress Feyner, the laundrywoman, comes here.' Master Reginald chattered on. 'Sir Hugh, I know which path you are leading me down, but I am innocent of any crime.' The taverner finished his tankard. 'I do not know why these young women were killed, but now, sir . . .' He scraped back the stool, got to his feet and walked away.

Corbett asked for the tally, and as he paid he studied the wool merchants, heads together, chattering in a tongue of which he caught a few words. He paid the boy and walked over to the foreigners. At his approach one of the Castilians turned, then rose to his feet, hand outstretched.

'Monsieur,' he spoke in accented Norman French, 'you have business with us?'

Corbett gripped the outstretched hand.

'No, sir, I am only curious.'

He glanced quickly at the man's companions; black-haired, moustached, swarthy-faced, about the same age, they could have been taken for brothers, although up close Corbett recognized the differences in both dress and manner. Two were apparently merchants, whilst the others, by their ink-stained fingers, were clerks or scribes. The table in front of them was littered with scraps of parchment and a small box of lambswool.

'You have been in England long?' Corbett asked.

'About six weeks.' The Castilian now spoke English, in a harsh, guttural way; lean-faced and weary-eyed, he glanced over Corbett's shoulder at Ranulf standing in the doorway. 'Sir, I understand you are a King's man?'

'In which you understand correctly, sir. I wonder if I can see your letters of commission?'

The smile faded from the Castilian's face.

'Sir, we are merchants. We have letters of protection.' He sighed at the way Corbett kept his hand outstretched, then talked quickly to his companions, one of whom handed over a large leather wallet. The Castilian introduced himself as Caratave; he undid the leather pouch and took out a sheaf of documents. Corbett scrutinized them. They were written in Latin and Norman French. The first was from the King of Castile asking that these merchants be given safe passage. The others were letters from the English Chancery. Corbett even recognized the clerk's hand on licences issued to enter Dover.

'I thank you, sir.' He handed the documents back. 'But now, if you are approached by the sheriff's men, you can say that Sir Hugh Corbett, Keeper of the Secret Seal, has confirmed your documents. May I buy you some wine?'

The offer was curtly refused. Corbett bowed and walked out into the stable yard.

'What do you make of that?' Ranulf whispered.

'Curiosity, Ranulf, curiosity, that's all.' Corbett gazed up at the sky and turned his face against the stinging cold wind. 'Here we are, Ranulf, in the King's own shire of Dorset, at Corfe Castle. Monsieur de Craon weaves his web and spouts his lies. Offshore Flemish pirates come close to land, and now we have Spanish merchants.' He shrugged. 'They seem legitimate enough.'

Chanson brought their horses from the stable and paid the grooms. Corbett grasped the reins and led his horse out on to the trackway. He had hardly mounted when it shied violently at the boy who burst out of the bushes on the side of the path, knocking the snow from his hair and ragged clothes. Corbett steadied his horse and quickly dismounted.

'You served us.' He recognized the boy from the tavern.

'Aye, Master, I did, and my ears are sharp.'

'Are they, boy?'

Corbett patted his horse's neck and, feeling beneath his robe, took out his money purse. The boy's eyes rounded.

'I'll make sure Horehound gets your message.' He deftly caught the coin Corbett threw.

'And the foreigners?' Corbett asked.

The boy, grasping the silver coin tightly, shook his head. 'They talk in their own tongue; sometimes it's difficult to understand. All they are interested in is wool and which farms are to be visited or which manor lord has the best flocks. They gave Master Reginald good silver for that information.'

'You didn't come for that, did you?' Ranulf drew his horse alongside Corbett's.

'No I didn't.' The boy licked his lips and looked furtively back towards the tavern. 'It's the young girls who were killed. I don't like Master Reginald, too free with his fists, and he is always trying to put his hand up some wench's skirt. They make fun of him, you know.'

'Who?' Corbett asked, leaning down again.

'The wenches. They composed a song about him. One night, just as autumn broke, they came down and sang it beneath his window, a truly rude song with lewd words. Master Reginald drove them off.'

The boy jumped with glee as Corbett spun him another coin. He caught this and, quick as a rabbit, disappeared back into the bushes. Corbett turned his horse and glanced at the gateway. He thought of Master Reginald with his cart going in and out of the castle, of that crossbow carefully stowed away.

'Some of the wenches,' Ranulf declared, reading Corbett's mind, 'might have been friendly with him; they would allow him to come close.'

'Aye, they would,' Corbett replied. 'I wonder if we have just supped with their assassin.'

They continued their journey down to the church, and by the time they had hobbled their horses just inside the lych gate, they could tell by the tolling of the bell that Father Matthew had already begun his Mass. Corbett walked into the church and paused in the porchway, sniffing the air. It was not the usual incense or wax, or even the mustiness of an ancient place, but an odour he couldn't recognize or, as yet, place. Ranulf was also intrigued, and pulled a face at Corbett's questioning look.

From the small sanctuary Father Matthew's powerful voice echoed.

'*Respice mei Domine, respice mei Domine.*' Look at me, Lord, look at me.

Corbett joined the small congregation of villagers, charcoal burners and woodmen who had drifted into the church for the

Mass arranged to suit their hours of labour. They worshipped God, ate and drank in the nearby tavern and worked until it was too dark to continue, a motley collection in their fustian jerkins, hose and shabby boots. The women wore high-necked gowns and dresses, dark greens or browns; they stamped their mud-encrusted boots against the sanctuary floor, pulling back hoods to reveal faces turned raw by the biting wind. They were friendly enough, peering shyly at these King's men, openly admiring the leather riding boots and Ranulf's quilted jerkin.

Father Matthew, however, standing at the altar in his purple and gold vestments, was intent on the Mass. Corbett listened carefully to the Latin and recognized that the priest had not only a good knowledge of the classics but a sure grasp of the Roman tongue. The Latin of many village priests was sometimes difficult to understand, but Father Matthew enunciated every syllable. Corbett watched with interest as he celebrated, turning to lift the Host, calling on the congregation to adore the Lamb of God.

Once Mass was finished, Corbett waited in the porch for the priest to join them.

'Well, well.' Father Matthew came striding down the nave, black robe fluttering. He clasped Corbett's hand. 'Sir Hugh, you wish to have words with me?'

'First, Father, the smell?'

'A little sulphur,' the priest replied. 'Sometimes I leave the door open; we've even had the occasional vixen nest her cubs in here. They always leave their offerings to the Lord!'

'Could we go to your house, Father?'

'I have to take the Viaticum to some of our sick,' the priest apologized. 'But one day soon, Sir Hugh . . .' His voice trailed off.

'Tell me, Father, do you have a crossbow?'

'Yes, I do,' the priest replied wearily. 'And a quiver of quarrels. I wondered when you would come and question me, Sir Hugh, yet I've told you all I can. As regards those young women, I school them here in the nave, I hear their confessions, and on Sundays and Holy Days I share the Eucharist with them.'

'They are not unruly or disobedient?' Corbett asked.

'Sir Hugh, if you wish to find out what they think of me, why don't you ask them? On the morning I found poor Rebecca, I was here in the church. I heard Alusia scream. It cut like a knife.' Father Matthew stared at this sharp-faced clerk and the other one standing deep in the shadows. 'I really must press on.' His words came out in a rush. 'Soon it will be the Feast of the Immaculate Conception and after that comes Christmas. I must start collecting wood for the crib, as St Dominic taught us.' He gestured towards the door. 'Sir Hugh, you are always welcome to return.'

'I think he wanted us to go.' Ranulf grinned as they unhobbled their horses.

'He did seem nervous,' Chanson intervened.

'Yes, yes, he did.'

Corbett gathered the reins in his hands and stared back at the church, an ancient building with crumbling steps, though the door was new and reinforced with iron studs.

'A strange one, Father Matthew,' he mused as he thrust his boot into the stirrup and swung himself up into the saddle. 'His Latin is perfect, yet he held the Host in a way he should not. After the consecration, Ranulf, the priest is to keep his thumb clasped against his forefinger; it's a petty part of the ritual.'

'Perhaps he was cold, as I was,' Ranulf snapped.

'And for a poor parish priest he seems to know a great deal about the Virgin Mary and the teaching that she was conceived without sin, and yet,' he urged his horse on, 'he doesn't seem to remember that it was St Francis, not St Dominic, who fashioned the first crib.'

The Secrets of Nature are not to be committed to the skins of sheep and goats.

Roger Bacon, *Opus Maius*

Chapter 7

Horehound sat on the edge of the snow-fringed marsh. He was freezing and famished. He wanted to sleep and dream about a charcoal fire above which venison steaks, basted with oils and herbs, slowly roasted. He shook himself from his reverie – he had seen men of the woods lose their wits; hadn't that happened to Fleawort three winters ago, when he had run himself to death chasing a stag no one else could see? The cold was intense. Horehound's belly had had nothing more than watery viper soup, and he realized how desperate the situation had become. Game was growing scarce, or was it simply that they were losing their skill? Foxglove had died chattering his sins whilst Horehound pretended to be a priest and mumbled words which sounded like Latin. One day he would ask a priest if Foxglove would have escaped the pains of Hell. Horehound stuck a finger in his mouth and rubbed his sore gum. The idea which had occurred to him in the warmth of Master Reginald's kitchen had grown like a seed in the ground. He'd crouched behind the tombstones and watched that King's man. The stranger was like Sir Edmund – a just, honest officer of the law.

'I'm sure it is here.' The outlaw known as Skullcap nudged his leader.

'I'm not getting too close,' Horehound snapped. 'If there is something here to show me, what is it?'

Skullcap edged forward, forcing aside the brambles and the thick hardy bushes. Horehound glanced quickly around. They were not far from the Tavern in the Forest, close to the trackway leading to the castle. He had to be careful. Sir Edmund's verderers were not unknown to go on patrol even in this weather.

'Come on,' he snarled.

Skullcap, eager to prove his case, was now crawling forward. He reached the snow-encrusted reeds and pulled these aside.

'There!' he exclaimed.

Horehound edged nearer and moaned quietly at the sight of the corpse bobbing in the shadows. Skullcap, stretching out his cudgel, forced the corpse to turn. Horehound glimpsed a mud-encrusted face with long hair; the dried blood ringing the mouth had mixed with the slime. He stepped back and stared around; whoever had killed that woman, and it must be a young woman, had brought her down here, murdered her and thrown her corpse into the marsh. He padded back, searching the ground for any sign, yet he could find no trace of a horse or a wheel in the frozen snow. Here and there a disturbance, but Horehound's own footprints, as well as those of Skullcap, would be difficult to distinguish from those of an assassin.

'What do you think?' Skullcap crawled close, crouching beside his companion, his thin spotty face flushed with excitement, eyes gleaming, the tip of his nose as red as a cinder glowing in a fire. On any other occasion Horehound would have made a joke of it and stretched out his fingers to what he always called this fiery ember. 'I saw it this morning, it wasn't there last night,' Skullcap hissed. 'Or I don't think it was.'

Horehound made his way back to the marsh to take a second look; this time he was bolder, allowing his boots to sink into the icy mud. He took his own cudgel and tipped the corpse. Yes, it was a woman, a young woman, probably from the castle. Her features were hard to distinguish, but he glimpsed the dried blood round that awful wound high in her chest. He retreated hastily, aware of the sombre silence. There was no birdsong, none of that flurrying in the thicket, the sounds of the forest which always reassured him. It seemed as if the winter snow had smothered all life. Horehound curbed his panic. He ran back, grasped Skullcap by the shoulder, and hastened with him into the trees.

'What shall we do?' Skullcap demanded. 'Now we have another horror. You know what they'll say.' Horehound tried not to flinch at his companion's sour breath. 'They'll say she was going for a walk down to the church or tavern and one of us killed her.'

Horehound didn't disagree. If this continued Sir Edmund would be forced to go hunting. He would summon up the levies and they'd enter the forest and see the horror hanging from that oak; it would only fan the fire of their anger. Horehound and the rest of his gang would be tracked by verderers and huntsmen; they would bring hunting dogs and not rest until they had cornered them in some glade. Justice would be quick. They would be either hanged there and then, or taken back to swing from the castle walls.

Horehound looked up through the bare black branches, the melting snow dripping down, splashing his face. A sudden sound made him start, and a rabbit sped from one bush to another, but Horehound was so frightened, so cowed, he couldn't even think about hunting fresh quarry.

'I wonder how long?' he muttered.

'And we are hungry,' Skullcap moaned. 'The meat we are eating is rotten. What can we do?'

Horehound crouched, assuming what he thought was his wise look. What *could* he do? Master Reginald's generosity had been stretched far enough. And Father Matthew? Horehound recalled that fire leaping up and shuddered. The villagers? He breathed in. They had little enough to share, and once they heard about that girl's corpse, every peasant's hand would be set against them. So who was responsible? How could a young woman's body, a crossbow bolt embedded in her chest, be floating in that marsh so near to the tavern? Was Master Reginald responsible? Had the wench gone down there? The taverner could be a brutal man, well known for his liking of the ladies. What about Father Matthew? Was the priest a warlock? Why should he be sprinkling powders on his own at the dead of night in his church?

'At least another quarter to spring,' Skullcap moaned. 'Milkwort wonders if any of us will be alive by Lady Day.'

Horehound sprang to his feet and hurried away. Skullcap, in surprise, followed him.

'What's the matter?'

But Horehound, shoulders hunched, ran on, deeper and deeper into the forest. Skullcap paused to catch his breath.

They weren't going back to the camp, but towards that glade ringed by ancient oaks, and with that horror hanging from one of the outstretched branches. Horehound was going to break his own rule, and Skullcap had no choice but to follow.

They reached the glade, but this time Horehound didn't stop. Ignoring Skullcap's cries, he raced across and halted directly beneath the corpse for the first time ever, staring up at that hideous face, made all the more gruesome by the passing of time and the pecking bites of birds and animals. The eyes had gone, leaving only black staring sockets, and the neck was all twisted, head to one side. Horehound wrinkled his nose at the smell of death. Although hideous in aspect, the corpse had now lost its horror. It was only the pathetic remains of a young woman, who had climbed up the oak, draped part of her long fustian skirt over the branch and fashioned a noose. Horehound could see how easy that would be; even the ancient ones could climb a tree like that. She must have moved along the sturdy branch, knotted one end around her throat and one end around the bough and simply let herself drop. Horehound walked around the corpse. Or *had* she killed herself? Had someone else brought her here and murdered her in this macabre way? He stared at the hands, the pared nails, then at the twisted cloth strong as rope. It would take some time before it rotted and allowed the body to fall.

Horehound drew his knife and scrambled up the trunk of the oak. Using the gnarled knots for steps, he edged along the branch and, positioning himself carefully, sawed through the cloth until it ripped and the corpse plunged to the forest floor. The sheer effort and tension had exhausted Horehound. He put the knife between his teeth and dropped lightly to the ground. Using the frozen, sodden leaf meal, the outlaw covered the corpse, trying not to look at that face, praying quietly to himself, begging Christ's good mother to help him.

'Who is it?' Skullcap drew closer.

'Just another girl. The flesh is beginning to decompose.' Horehound went to a nearby rivulet to wash his hands. 'There's nothing to be frightened of, not yet, not until they find her.'

Horehound picked up his cudgel, took one last look at that forlorn heap, and found the pathway which would lead him back to the hidden cave where the rest of his band sheltered.

He was almost there when he caught the first smell of wood smoke and the delicious tang of roasting meat. He stopped so abruptly Skullcap collided with him.

'Do you remember Fleawort?' he muttered. 'And the fantasies he saw? I can smell roasting meat.'

'So can I,' Skullcap retorted.

They ran through the tangled undergrowth, desperate to seek the source of the smell. Horehound couldn't believe his eyes when he reached the glade. The outlaws had left their cave and built up a great fire, and were roasting strips of meat and drinking greedily from the small cask being handed around. Horehound drew his dagger, then smiled as one figure emerged from the rest, pushing back a tattered cowl. It was Hemlock! Horehound hurried across to hug this comrade who had left shortly before the eve of All Souls, saying he would try his luck further to the east.

'What brought you back?' Horehound demanded.

Hemlock pushed aside his strange hair, thick and black with white streaks like the fur of a badger. He was a tall, sinewy man, the bottom half of his face hidden by a moustache and bushy beard. Horehound noticed the scar just under his comrade's left eye. The wound was still fresh.

'I have my own men now.' Hemlock jabbed a finger towards the fire. 'I brought two of them with me, just in case. They fetched the meat and the cask of ale.'

'Where from?' Horehound demanded.

'Ah!' Hemlock smiled and put a finger to his lips. 'I must tell you what I have seen and then you must see what I have witnessed.' He shook his head and laughed at Horehound's protest. 'Come,' Hemlock gestured, 'fill your belly, then I'll solve the riddle . . .'

Corbett sat on his bed, leaning back against the bolsters, body slightly crooked as he bent over to take full advantage of the candle glow from the nearby table. The fire had been built up, the braziers crackled. Corbett was pleased to be out of the freezing cold. At the foot of the bed, his back to the great chest, Chanson was busy repairing a strap, while across the chamber Ranulf was teaching Bolingbroke how to cheat at hazard, showing him how to switch good dice for cogged ones. Ranulf moved so quickly, so expertly that Bolingbroke protested, so Ranulf demonstrated the sleight of hand more slowly.

'You must be fast,' he warned. 'If you are caught, knives will be drawn.'

Bolingbroke took his own dice out and cast a few winning throws, causing loud laughter as Ranulf realized the other man was, perhaps, as adept at cheating as he.

Corbett went back to studying the King's own copy of Roger Bacon's *Opus Tertium*. He quietly mouthed the words the friar had used to describe his life of study: ' "During the last twenty years I have worked hard in the pursuit of wisdom. I abandoned the usual methods."' Corbett glanced up. The usual methods, he reflected, what were they? Disputation? Argument? The exchange of ideas with other scholars? 'I have spent more than twenty pounds,' Friar Roger had written, 'on secret books and various experiments, not to mention languages, instruments and mathematical tables.' Corbett pulled himself up, resting the heavy tome in his lap, keeping the place with his finger. What, he wondered, were these secret books? What experiments? Had Friar Roger really discovered or stumbled on secret knowledge? He opened the book and read again, following the words with his finger, translating the Latin as he read. He moved the manuscript to study more closely the phrase 'twenty pounds'. He noticed the manuscript was marked, the ink rather blotched, as if someone had tried to scratch the words out, blurring the letters.

Corbett, exasperated, closed the book and put it on the table beside him. For a while he watched the two gamblers, marvelling at Ranulf's persistence. He had learnt from Chanson how, as soon as they had returned to the castle, Ranulf had done some studying of his own, searching out the Lady Constance; they'd sat, heads together, in front of the great hearth in the Hall of Angels.

'They talked, Master. Oh, how they talked!' Chanson had reported. 'And the Lady Constance, she laughs a great deal.'

Ranulf looked across, caught Corbett's stare, smiled and raised a hand. You always make the ladies laugh, Corbett thought, that's one of your talents. Ranulf, sharp of wit and tart of tongue.

Bolingbroke had reported back how he and Chanson had

compared the two manuscripts, which were identical in every aspect.

'Like peas in the same pod,' he concluded, 'but as for understanding it, the French have retired to their own quarters to study the mystery.' Corbett too had decided to go once more through Friar Roger's writings to find a clue, some key to the mysteries.

Chanson scrambled to his feet, still clutching his stirrup leather.

'What hour is it?' Corbett asked.

The groom went into the far corner and took the hour candle from its lantern holder.

'Somewhere between six and seven in the evening. It's dark outside. Master, I am hungry.'

Corbett picked up the manuscript he had been reading.

'Say after me, Chanson, *Opus Tertium*.'

Chanson repeated the words.

'Now,' Corbett ordered, 'go and give my compliments to Monsieur Crotoy. Ask him may I borrow their copy of Friar Roger's work of the same name.'

'But you already have a copy,' Chanson protested, pointing to the calfskin-covered book. 'And it's cold out . . .'

'Do as you are told, groom of the stable,' Ranulf snapped, eager to retaliate for Chanson's teasing about the Lady Constance. 'Oh, never mind.' He pushed back the stool and put on his boots and cloak. 'I'll fetch it myself.'

'Ah, and that's the last we will see of you before midnight.' Chanson ducked as Ranulf went to cuff his ear.

Corbett swung off the bed. He followed Ranulf out on to the stairway, flinching at the blast of cold air.

'There's no hurry,' he whispered, 'but even if you do meet the Lady Constance, don't forget what I've asked.'

Ranulf grinned and, whistling under his breath, padded down the steps. Corbett returned to the chamber, washed his face and hands, and chattered to Bolingbroke for a while about the secret manuscript. A servant brought up some bread, cheese and a pot of slightly rancid butter. Corbett asked him of any new of the castle.

'Not very good,' the servant replied. 'The girl Alusia has not been found.' He went to the door and looked back, 'You seem to have missed the excitement, sir. You heard the clamour?'

'I did.' Bolingbroke cleared the table of dice. 'I heard shouting from below, though I didn't hear the tocsin ring.'

'Oh, it wasn't much.' The servant lifted the latch. 'One of the guards on the curtain wall saw a fire at the edge of the forest.'

'A fire?' Corbett asked. 'In the snow, in the depth of winter?'

'Sometimes it happens,' the servant replied. 'There are outlaws in the forest, travellers and tinkers, wanderers who do not like to come under the eyes of the Constable. They collect dry bracken and light a fire; sometimes it gets out of hand. Two winters ago they nearly burnt the death house at St Peter's, but now Father Matthew keeps them out of the cemetery at night – he's very strict about that. Anyway,' the servant opened the door, 'Sir Edmund sent a rider out; the fire was nothing.'

When he had left, Corbett shared out the food and drink.

'If Alusia is still missing,' Bolingbroke spoke up, 'it must be serious. No wench would go wandering in the darkness on a freezing winter night. Sir Edmund will have to wait until the morning before he can send out a search party.'

Corbett stared at Bolingbroke's long, rather lugubrious face and mop of sandy hair. The pouches under his eyes gave him a sleepy look, belied by the laughing mouth. A good swordsman, Corbett reflected, Bolingbroke had been Ufford's constant companion in the Halls of Oxford and entered the Secret Chancery as a clerk.

'I'm sorry,' Corbett apologized. 'I'm truly sorry, William.'

'What for?'

'Ufford, you must mourn him.'

'I've had Masses sung for him in the Chapels Royal at Westminster and Windsor.' Bolingbroke looked away, leaning against one hand on the mantle, staring down at the floor. 'Ten years in all.' His voice was muffled. 'I met Walter in a tavern near Carfax. Like Ranulf, he was cheating at dice. I had to rescue him.'

Chanson, mending the leather on the floor, stopped. He liked nothing better than to listen to the stories of the clerks. He always hoped Sir Hugh would send him to the school in the transept of the manor church at Leighton.

'Did he leave any family?' Corbett asked.

'A young woman in London. I gave her the news myself that Walter would not be coming home.'

Corbett sipped at his tankard. Sometimes he deeply regretted what he was doing. Both Ufford and Bolingbroke had come to his attention because of their skill, their knowledge of tongues, particularly Norman French and the patois of the countryside. They had both served in the King's wars in Scotland, and such a background made them ideal students for the Sorbonne.

'Do you resent de Craon being so close?'

'No,' Bolingbroke sighed. 'There are clerks in the Chancery offices whose fathers fought mine in Wales. It's like a game of hazard, Sir Hugh; if you lose, what's the point of cursing the victor? One day,' he lifted his own tankard in toast, 'I shall return to the table and pay Monsieur de Craon back in similar coin.'

'Tell me once more,' Corbett sat down on the great chest at the foot of the bed, 'how this magister at the Sorbonne provided the information.'

'I've told you, he left letters at our lodgings.'

'Did you trust this King of Keys?'

Bolingbroke pulled a face. 'He was a thief from the alleyway; despite his pompous title, he was a housebreaker. He would not have become involved if he hadn't been paid so well. In the end he died with Magister Thibault.'

'And both you and Ufford knew about the coffer in the strongroom?'

Bolingbroke nodded.

'And who hired the King of Keys?'

'Walter and I did that.'

'And the girl?' Corbett asked. 'The one with Magister Thibault?'

'I'm not too sure,' Bolingbroke scratched his neck, 'but if I had to hazard a guess, I would say our traitor hired her. We waited in the gallery upstairs until Thibault was, well . . .' he shrugged, 'otherwise engaged with her, then we went down. We must have been there an hour before the old fool appeared.' He chewed on some bread. 'We were trapped,' he declared slowly, 'and I still am.'

'What do you mean?'

'I often wondered why the trap wasn't sprung at Magister Thibault's home, but now Destaples has died, I realize we were meant to kill Thibault. The same is true of my escape.' He glanced sharply at Corbett. 'Don't you see, I was meant to escape, allowed to return to England with that manuscript. If I hadn't, there would have been no meeting at Corfe.' Bolingbroke snapped his fingers. 'That's it! As I approached the Madelene Quayside, I'm sure I was being followed. A beggar-man told me the Hounds of the King were in that quarter. After a while, all signs of any pursuit disappeared. I got safely out of Paris, on to the road north, but I was meant to. I was simply a piece on de Craon's chessboard,' he added bitterly. 'So God knows what that bastard is plotting. My only comfort is that we might do some good here. I mean,' Bolingbroke nodded towards the door, 'about these poor wenches.'

Corbett got up from the chest and walked around the side of the bed. 'And what do you think about these killings, William? What does logic tell you?'

'First,' the clerk replied, 'the victims trusted their killer, which is why he was allowed to approach so close. Secondly, therefore, it must be someone who lives in the castle or close by. Thirdly, the assassin must be someone skilled in the use of an arbalest and . . .' He paused.

'And what?' Chanson asked.

'Someone,' Bolingbroke pretended to glower at Chanson, 'who is not afraid. He is prepared to kill for no other reason than the killing itself. Have you seen a fox raid a hen run, Chanson? There may be sixty, and he will take only one, yet he will kill until no bird is left alive.'

'Which means,' Corbett concluded, 'the assassin is killing not for profit or sexual pleasure but out of sheer hatred or revenge.'

Corbett reflected on the number of men he had hanged for the assault and rape of women. They had all been different, criminals who had taken secret pleasure from their sin, but the killer at Corfe . . . ?

'Chanson?' He snapped his fingers. 'Of your kindness, go down into the castle yard. If you see Ranulf, remind him why I sent him, but search out a young red-haired woman called Marissa, and tell her that the King's man who asked about her cloak would like to meet her. Once you've done this, ask Marissa about a man-at-arms friendly with Alusia and any of the other girls who have been killed. Tell her she will be rewarded for her pains. If she names someone, bring that person to me. Oh, and you know where the laundrywomen have their vats?' Chanson nodded. 'Seek out Mistress Feyner, say I want fresh words with her.'

Chanson put on his boots and left. Corbett went and sat opposite Bolingbroke, who had picked up one of the manuscripts.

'What do you think, William? Are we chasing will-o-the-wisps here? The *Secretus Secretorum* – is it a puzzle which can be solved?'

'I went through the script with Sanson, Sir Hugh. It's written in Latin but I hardly recognized a word. Now, Magister Thibault,' Bolingbroke grew enthusiastic, 'what he did was very clever. He formed the hypothesis that if Friar Roger wrote a secret cipher, like all people who use such devices he would have become tired at the end and made a mistake. That phrase "I shall give you many doors" is a fine example of it. Now, as you know, Sir Hugh, once you have one line of a cipher, it becomes easy to tease out the rest. But this is where our problem begins; in this case it does not.'

Corbett closed his eyes and groaned. 'I advised the King of that,' he whispered. 'Friar Roger may talk about his marvels, and the *Secret of Secrets* may hold the truth, yet I've read the friar's works.' He opened his eyes. 'He truly was an arrogant man with a contempt for other scholars. What if he wrote that book in a cipher used once only and understood solely by himself? If that is the case, the key will never be found and the cipher will remain unbroken.'

Corbett opened the *Opus Tertium* he had been reading, but found he couldn't concentrate. He took the psalter Lady Maeve had given him and leafed through the pages. The illuminations always fascinated him; the use of colours and vivid schemes, Christ stretched like a piece of vellum on the Cross. He read the prayer on the adjoining page, and allowed his mind to drift. The Lady Maeve had given him the psalter on his birthday, the previous August. He glanced up. Bolingbroke was asleep in the chair. Corbett stretched out on the bed. He couldn't forget that girl's corpse, sprawled on the hand barrow, and the priest, Father Matthew, was a strange one. Why had he made those mistakes in church? Corbett's eyes opened wide with a sudden realisation. When he brought the corpse in, he thought, it was Father Andrew, the old priest, who insisted the last rites must be given.

He heard footsteps outside and rose as Chanson led the red-haired Marissa, followed by a young, pockfaced man-at-arms, into the room. Marissa looked freezing in her thin gown; the man was dressed in a sweat-stained leather jerkin over a linen shirt, padded hose and battered boots which looked a size too big for him. Chanson introduced the stranger.

'This is Martin.'

Corbett clasped the man's hand and ushered them both to stools in front of the fire. Marissa was friendly, happy at the chance to be warm. Martin, a local man from his accent, was quiet of eye and not overawed by Corbett. He asked bluntly why he had been summoned.

'I have been searching for Alusia,' he exclaimed, 'and I'm on sentry duty at dawn, the first watch of tomorrow.'

'I won't keep you long.'

Corbett served them steaming cups of posset wrapped in rags and sat between them. Bolingbroke had gone across to splash water on his face from the lavarium.

'Your name is Martin,' Corbett began, 'a friend of Alusia, the girl who is missing. Do you know where or why she may have fled?'

'Fled?' Martin's lip jutted out aggressively. 'Alusia has not fled. She was terrified at what she saw yesterday; she would not go out of the castle again until this killer is found and despatched to Hell.'

'So where is she?' Bolingbroke came over, wiping his face and hands.

'I don't know. She left her parents last night, sometime between Vespers and Compline, and never returned.'

'Were you to meet her last night?'

'No, I was not.'

Corbett studied the open, weatherbeaten face; he'd already glimpsed the leather wrist guard and the calluses on the man's fingers.

'You use a crossbow?'

'Yes, and I'm very skilled,' came the hot reply. 'I can hit my mark from ten yards, I do not need to get too close.'

'Peace, peace,' Corbett murmured. 'Did Alusia tell you anything about what happened yesterday?'

'No, I hardly saw her. She was resting, all disturbed. I did have a few words with her, nothing more.'

'And you knew the other girls, the ones who've been murdered?' Bolingbroke asked from his chair. The man-at-arms glanced sideways at Marissa, sitting beside Corbett as still as a statue.

'I knew some of them,' he mumbled.

'Especially Phillipa.' Marissa forgot her shyness and glared at the man-at-arms. 'You said Phillipa was sweet on you, or were you just boasting?'

'Just boasting,' Martin replied, flushed-faced. 'She was a strange one.'

'Phillipa?' Corbett asked. 'Mistress Feyner's daughter?' He looked over his shoulder. 'Chanson, where is Mistress Feyner?'

'She said she would come when she was ready,' Chanson replied.

'Oh, good.' Corbett turned back. Marissa was still shivering, and he put his cup down and went across to the cloaks hanging on a peg. He took one down and draped it over Marissa's shoulders.

'You're most kind.' She preened herself.

'It is yours,' Corbett replied. He took two coins from his purse and handed one to each of them. Martin accepted reluctantly. Marissa snatched hers, then drew the cloak close to her, treasuring the coin; she was flattered by the attention of this King's man who allowed her to sit so close to a fire and drink posset from a pewter goblet. Corbett, glancing down, saw a penny whistle lying on the floor, one Chanson used. He picked it up and absentmindedly put it in his wallet.

'You said Phillipa was a strange one?'

'Oh yes,' Marissa replied, 'full of herself. She claimed one of the outlaws, a mysterious man she called the Goliard, loved her, and said how they would meet under the forest greenery. She claimed he was a landless knight living in his own castle in the forest.' Marissa put a hand to her face and giggled. 'We said she was living in her dreams.'

'Were you close to her?'

'No. Some of the others may have been.'

'And when did she go missing?'

Marissa closed her eyes. 'On that Sunday when we gave thanks for the harvest. The weather was lovely. I remember seeing her in the cemetery after Mass, then she disappeared. We thought she had gone into the forest to meet her Goliard.'

'Did you take part in the search?' Corbett asked the man-at-arms.

'Yes, I did. From the forest down to the sea. We found nothing. And now, sir,' Martin scraped back the stool, 'I truly must go.'

'Before you do,' Corbett lifted a hand, 'did you have a trysting place?'

'A what?'

'A secret place,' Bolingbroke explained, 'where a man might meet the lady of his heart.'

'There's some ruins,' the man-at-arms replied, 'at the far wall beyond the keep. A passageway leading down to the dungeons and cellars; it was our place.' He ignored Marissa's giggle. 'I've been down there, it's deserted.'

He was about to leave when there was a knock at the door and Mistress Feyner came bustling in, the sleeves of her gown pulled back to her elbows, her hands and wrists red raw. She totally ignored Marissa and Martin and, without being asked, flounced down on a stool in front of the fire. When Bolingbroke served her some posset from a goblet kept in the inglenook, she snatched it from his hands.

'I can't be here long. Are you asking these two about my daughter?' She drank greedily from the cup. 'If you have questions about Phillipa then ask me.'

'She was last seen on the Sunday in the cemetery after Mass.'

'Yes, she was. She told me she was going to collect flowers.'

'Not to meet the man known as Goliard?'

Mistress Feyner threw a venomous glance at Marissa, and yet the way she moved her lips and blinked, Corbett could see she was on the verge of tears. She handed him her cup and got to her feet. 'Don't worry about Goliard,' she whispered. 'My poor Phillipa was lonely.'

'But she claimed to meet him.'

150

'Yes, yes, she did.' Mistress Feyner rubbed her hands down her gown. 'I can't tell you sir, I truly can't. My Phillipa has gone and so have the rest; now they are searching for poor Alusia.'

'This trysting place,' Corbett asked, 'the passageway leading down to the old dungeons?'

'That's a favourite place.' Mistress Feyner smiled. 'We searched it for Phillipa as we have for Alusia; there is nothing there. There's never anything there,' she added as an afterthought.

'I must visit it,' Corbett declared. 'Perhaps I will meet Ranulf! Mistress Feyner?' He took her hand in his, letting her grasp the concealed coin. 'I thank you for your pains.'

Once the three had left, Corbett put on his boots and took his heavy cloak from the peg, fastening the clasp under his chin.

'I wish to walk this castle; I want to see what's happening.' He nodded to Bolingbroke and Chanson, then paused. 'Chanson, for the love of God, go and find Ranulf. Tell him I want to speak to him before we meet the French, before we sup this evening.'

Corbett went down the freezing cold staircase and out into the bailey. Here and there sconce torches flickered bravely against the darkness. People ran across, moving hastily from one shelter to another, eager to escape from the chilling wind. Corbett pulled the hood over his head and walked around the keep. On one occasion he stopped, staring up at the masonry soaring into the skies, a forbidding, massive rectangle of stone. At various levels torches and candles glowed from the arrow slit windows. He walked along the side of the keep, passing through the small village where the castle folk lived in their wattle-and-daub cottages built against the walls and towers. A busy place, children still ran screaming about, dancing around the bonfires and makeshift braziers. The air was full of cooking aromas, the smell of tanned leather, the stench of horse manure and the sweet fragrance of hay from the barns. Now and again someone called out a greeting and Corbett lifted his hand in reply. He paused to talk to some of the men-at-arms and asked where the passageway was. They pointed deeper into the darkness.

Corbett was now on the other side of the keep. He climbed the brow of the hill which gave the keep its dominating aspect and walked through what must be the gardens of the castle, hidden under their cover of snow, down more steps, stumbling and slipping as he crossed what seemed to be a wasteland of snow and gorse only to realize it must be the castle warren. There were few buildings here: outhouses with empty windows and a few makeshift bothies. Nearby stood the engines of war, two catapults and a large mangonel. Above him on the parapet Corbett could see the sentries, only a few here, standing beneath torches lashed to poles. On the breeze he caught the faint strains of a song a soldier was singing to amuse himself. At last he reached the curtain wall and, going along the wasteland, found the crumbling passageway leading down to what must have been old cellars and dungeons carved out beneath the castle walls like a crypt in a church.

The steps were uneven, made more treacherous by the icy snow. Corbett held his breath as he went down, regretting that he had not brought a cresset torch. They were too steep. Corbett, cursing, clung to the wall and edged his way down. At the bottom the passageway ran on a little further. His hand felt the wall, and he sighed with relief as his fingers touched the thick tallow candle either left by the cellar man or, perhaps, brought by the lovers who met there. He took his own tinder from his pocket and, after a great deal of effort, lit the thick wick. Cupping the flame in his hand, he held the candle up. The walls of the narrow passageway stretched before him, shadows dancing in the candlelight, the beaten earth ending in a fall of masonry. Corbett walked forward, studying the ground carefully, but could find nothing. He returned to the steps and paused. The snow had turned into a muddy slush and he could tell that people had been here, probably looking for Alusia. He climbed the steps carefully. His search was futile, yet this was a lonely place. If a young woman had come here by herself and the killer had been waiting . . .

Corbett reached the top step and, cupping the candle, was about to walk through the ruined stone entrance when he missed his footing and slipped, just as the crossbow bolt smashed into the crumbling masonry above him.

From the flashing and fury of certain igneous substances, and the terror inspired by their noise, certain wonderful consequences follow.

Roger Bacon, *Opus Tertium*

Chapter 8

Ranulf of Newgate, Clerk of the Chancery of the Green Wax, was very pleased and self-satisfied. He had, by mere chance as he told himself, met the Lady Constance and her maid when he returned to the solar to find something he had lost. Of course he never mentioned that he had paid a groom a silver coin to keep him apprised of where the Lady Constance was. Now, with her maid perched strategically on a stool near the door, Ranulf was attempting to show Lady Constance the wonders of the miraculous coin trick so beloved of the cunning men at Smithfield Fair.

'Well, my Lady,' Ranulf placed the three pewter cups taken from the waiting table, 'which cup covers the coin?'

'That one.'

Ranulf's fingers brushed hers, heads drew together and he lifted the cup to show the coin had gone. Lady Constance's eyes danced with mischief as she swiftly tried to find the coin beneath the other two cups.

'You're a cheat!' she exclaimed.

Ranulf seized her wrist – he moved his chair so that the maid couldn't see.

'Sir,' Lady Constance's eyes widened, 'release me.'

'For a token,' Ranulf whispered, 'I'll release you for a while.'

'For words of love,' she whispered.

'*Vos, quarum est Gloria amor et lascivia atque delectatio Aprilis cum Maio.*'

'Which means?'

'If you were April's lady and I were Lord of May—' abruptly the tocsin sounded, the castle bell tolling like the crack of doom. Ranulf released her wrist, bit back his curse, and hastily remembered where he was and what he should be doing. Lady Constance jumped to her feet. At the door the maid was already standing, hands fluttering.

Corbett, his sweat-soaked body turning icy cold, also heard the tocsin as he crouched in the ruined doorway, staring out into the blackness. He wondered what it could mean. He could hear shouts; perhaps his assailant had retreated? Corbett moved, and hastily ducked as another crossbow quarrel hurtled into the stonework behind him. His anxiety deepened. That was the fourth time he'd moved, and the mysterious archer showed little intention of giving up. The sentries on the parapet walk were few and would not know of the deadly cat-and-mouse game being played out beneath them. Corbett had shouted, but his cry had not been heard and now the guards were leaving. He glimpsed one hurrying with a flickering torch to investigate the source of the alarm. They'd be totally unaware of the assassin below.

Corbett realized the murderous archer was watching the entrance to the dungeon. Any movement against the light-coloured stone, the slither of Corbett's foot on the gravel or the crackle of icy snow would alert him. Corbett was alone, unarmed, and he sensed that his attacker was drawing closer. The quarrels now smacked into the wall with greater force; he must be only a few yards away, probably crouched or kneeling down. Corbett shivered. The castle bell tolled again but then fell silent. His hand went to his belt but he wasn't even carrying a dagger. His fingers brushed the wallet and he recalled the penny whistle he had picked up. He took this out and, with all his breath, blew a long, piercing blast. He heard a sound in the darkness and began to shout the usual cry of a man being ambushed: *'Au secours! Au secours!'* He took a deep breath and blew on the penny whistle again. Corbett felt slightly ridiculous crouched here in the freezing darkness, his only weapon a child's toy. He shouted once more, heard scuffling sounds and blew a fresh blast on the penny whistle.

'Who's there?' Corbett relaxed as he recognized Bolingbroke's voice.

'William,' he shouted. 'I'm over here.' He edged out of the doorway. Bolingbroke stood a few paces away, sword drawn.

'What happened?' he exclaimed as Corbett came stumbling towards him.

'Nothing,' Corbett gasped, taking the sword out of Bolingbroke's hand. 'Did you see anybody?'

'I came out into the castle yard,' Bolingbroke explained. 'There's no real alarm. An accident, a small hay stall in the outer bailey near the walls caught alight. I looked around and couldn't see you. I walked past the keep and heard the blast of the whistle.' He laughed. 'Anyone lodging with Chanson recognizes that sound.'

'Did you see anyone, anyone at all?'

'Sir Hugh,' Bolingbroke caught him by the arm, 'people were running. I thought I glimpsed something, but—'

'I was attacked,' Corbett said. He suddenly felt weak, and dug the sword point into the ground, resting on the hilt. 'I went into the old dungeons. I was looking for the girl Alusia.' He described what had happened next.

Bolingbroke would have hastened off into the darkness for help but Corbett caught his arm.

'He's gone, William, there's nothing we can do. That's the last time I walk this castle unarmed. Where's Ranulf?' he snapped.

They walked back across the warren, past the keep. People thronged there, drifting back as the source of the alarm was known and the fire put out. Corbett glimpsed Ranulf standing on the steps leading from the Hall of Angels. He felt anger seethe within him and, striding across, brought the flat of the sword down on Ranulf's shoulder. His henchman turned, hand going to the dagger in his belt.

'Sir Hugh?' Corbett glimpsed Sir Edmund and his family in the doorway, watching him, and behind them de Craon's smirking face.

'I sent you on a task,' Corbett whispered, scraping the sword along Ranulf's shoulder, 'and while you were gone, I went looking for something and was attacked.'

'Sir Hugh, is there anything wrong?'

'No, Sir Edmund, I am just having words with a clerk who doesn't understand me.'

The hurt flared in Ranulf's eyes, and Corbett's anger ebbed. He turned, tossed the sword to Bolingbroke and grasped Ranulf by the arm. He could feel the muscles tense, a mixture of alarm and anger. Ranulf's fiery temper was difficult to control and Corbett did not wish to create a spectacle, or humiliate this man, his friend as well as his companion. In short, sharp sentences he told Ranulf exactly what had happened. The Clerk of the Green Wax heard him out, mouth and jaw tense, sharp eyes glittering.

'Where were you?' Corbett asked.

'I was talking to the Lady Constance.' Ranulf brought his hand down on Corbett's shoulder. 'Sir Hugh, don't blame me for your stupidity. How many times have I told you, the Lady Maeve begged, the King ordered? You are never to be alone in a place like this.' He pushed his face close to Corbett's. 'Don't worry, Master, there won't be a second time, and if there is, I'll take the bastard's head.'

Corbett drew a deep breath and stretched out his hand.

'I'm sorry, Ranulf; the truth is, I was frightened.'

Ranulf clasped his hand. 'You look as if you're freezing.'

They returned to Corbett's chamber. He was about to return the penny whistle to Chanson, then recalled how it had saved him. He crouched by the fire, drinking a posset, allowing the cold to seep away. A servant came to announce that dinner would be served in the Great Hall.

'Did you see Crotoy?' Corbett asked.

'No, I didn't.' Ranulf shook his head. 'In fact, when the tocsin sounded and everyone gathered in the yard, I looked for him, but he wasn't there.'

Corbett stretched a hand out to the fire and suppressed a shiver, like an icy blade pressed against his back.

'Where is he lodging?'

'He has his own chamber in the Jerusalem Tower,' Ranulf replied. 'The staircase up is blocked off; he's the only one who's lodged there.'

Corbett put on his war belt, got to his feet and took his cloak. 'Come with me,' he ordered his companions.

They went down into the bailey. Corbett wasn't aware of the

flurries of snow as he strode across to the Jerusalem Tower, a great drum-like fortification approached by a set of steep steps. He hurried up these and grasped the iron ring on the door to the tower but it held fast. He drew his dagger and beat vainly with the pommel.

'Chanson, go quickly, bring men-at-arms.'

Corbett walked down the steps and, looking round, glimpsed a window high in the wall, but there was no sign of light between the shutters. Covering himself with his cloak against the falling snow, he hastily pulled up his hood.

'There's something wrong?' asked Ranulf.

'Oh yes,' Corbett whispered. 'There is something dreadfully wrong.'

Sir Edmund came hurrying across. He had been changing for the evening meal and wrapped a cloak around him to protect him from the snow.

'Are you sure Monsieur Crotoy isn't elsewhere in the castle?' he asked.

'Sir Edmund, my apologies if I troubled you, but Louis is not a wanderer,' Corbett replied.

'Has he been seen?'

'What is the matter?' De Craon, followed by his cowled man-at-arms, came striding up.

'Louis Crotoy,' Corbett declared. 'Is he with you?'

'No, he isn't,' de Craon replied, wiping his face, 'and he should be. The rest are gathered in my chamber; I wished to have words with him. A servant came down and told me about this. I hastened across. Is there something wrong? Louis is a member of my retinue. Sanson claims he hasn't seen him since early afternoon.'

'Force the door,' Corbett urged.

At first there was confusion, but eventually Sir Edmund organized the men-at-arms to bring a battering ram, nothing more than a stout tree trunk with poles embedded along each side. Because of the steps, the men-at-arms found it difficult, and the pounding and crashing alerted the rest of the castle. The ward began to fill. The soldiers concentrated just beneath the iron ring, and at last the door broke free.

Corbett ensured he was the first through, almost pushing de Craon aside. The inside was cold and dark. Sir Edmund passed him a torch. Corbett held it before him and stifled a moan. Crotoy lay at the bottom of the inside steps leading up to the chamber, his head cracked, the dark pool of blood glistening in the light. Corbett glanced quickly to either side; there was no window. He took a step forward, shouting at Sir Edmund to keep the rest back. At first glance he knew his old friend was beyond any help: those staring eyes, the cold flesh, the blood like a stagnant pool. He moved the body tenderly; he could see no other wound or mark apart from the gruesome gash on the side of the head. He heard a jingle from the dead man's wallet, and opening it took out two keys, small and squat; he realized these must be to the door of the Jerusalem Tower as well as Crotoy's chamber. Meanwhile, the Constable's men had forced the curious down the steps, leaving only Corbett, Sir Edmund and de Craon standing in that draughty passageway. Corbett crouched down and glanced at the door that had been forced. The lock had been snapped, but he realized that when he inserted the key he could turn it easily. He took the key out, thrust it at Sir Edmund and hurried back down to Crotoy's corpse.

'Send a messenger for Father Andrew,' Corbett whispered to the constable.

Corbett plucked out the torch which he had placed in a sconce holder and, holding this out carefully, examined the steps leading up to Crotoy's chamber. They were steep and narrow, with sharp edges, and to the left of the chamber was a stairwell filled with fallen masonry. He looked back at the corpse. Crotoy had his cloak wrapped around his arm, its hem trailing down. Corbett sighed, went up the steps and using the second key opened the door. The chamber inside was cold and dark. Sir Edmund came up, and Corbett stepped gingerly into the room, allowing the Constable to light the candles and large lanternhorn which stood on the round walnut table in the centre. A neat, tidy room. Corbett felt a pang of sadness at the sweet smell of herbs.

'He always liked that,' he whispered.

'Liked what?' Sir Edmund asked.

'He loved the smell of herbs and spices.' Corbett went over and placed the torch in a holder on the wall. 'Very precise, was Louis. He loved the smell of spring and summer; his clothes, his chamber, his books, his manuscripts always had that faint smell of flowers and herbs.'

Corbett noticed the manuscripts piled high on the window, the candle pricket, the wax formed thick around the base, the clothes hanging from the peg. The curtains on the small poster bed were drawn and, on the far side, stood the lavarium, with napkins neatly folded next to a precious bar of sweet-smelling soap in a little copper dish.

Corbett heard voices from below. Father Andrew had arrived, busily intoning the prayers for the dead as he anointed the corpse. Ranulf came up the steps.

'What happened, do you think?' Sir Edmund sat down on the chair next to the bed. He glanced quickly at Corbett.

'Another accident?'

'That is for me to decide.' De Craon spoke up, standing in the shadows. 'I'm cut to the heart that my colleague is dead.'

'No, sir,' Corbett snapped. 'Louis may have been a member of your retinue but he was my friend and this castle is under the direct governance of the King of England. Sir Edmund,' Corbett called over his shoulder whilst holding de Craon's gaze, 'I would like to examine both the chamber and Monsieur Crotoy's corpse. Is his death an accident, misadventure, or is there some other cause?'

'I'll delay the meal,' Sir Edmund sighed. 'Monsieur de Craon, Sir Hugh is right. This is the King's castle, he has the right to act as coroner.'

'Then I will stay and help him.'

Corbett didn't object, and the Constable's men cleared the stairwell below, bringing back the broken door so as to block some of the cold night air. Corbett had every candle and torch lit and scrupulously began his search. He and Ranulf carefully examined the chamber, de Craon keeping close to the table, watching them sift through various manuscripts, loudly objecting when Ranulf picked up a piece of parchment to study it more closely. Yet they could find nothing significant. Crotoy's corpse, now laid out under a sheet at the foot of the steps, bore no mark other than the wound to the head, which was definitely the result of hitting the hard ground at the foot of the steps. Corbett fought back the memories of walking arm in arm with that clever scholar through Christchurch Meadows, or the orchards down by the Iffley Stream, or sitting in a tavern on the corner of Turl Street.

'Master,' Ranulf murmured, 'look at his boot.'

Corbett did so; the heel on the right boot was loose.

'He tripped,' Ranulf explained. 'The heel of the boot was loose, or his foot may have become caught in his cloak. He fell, bruising his head against the ground.'

'But would that kill him?' Corbett wondered. He returned to scrutinizing the corpse, and lifting it up by the shoulders noticed how the head hung slightly to one side.

'I've seen the same before,' Ranulf muttered, 'when a man has broken his neck.'

They stood aside as the castle leech arrived. He also inspected the wound to the head and, pulling up Crotoy's thick woollen cotehardie, pointed to the light bruising to the right of the dead man's chest and similar marks on his right arm and shoulder. He then examined the neck, moving the head slightly between his hands.

'An unfortunate accident,' he sighed, getting to his feet. He pointed to the door at the top of the steps. 'Monsieur Crotoy locked the door behind him, his cloak over his shoulder. He became confused, his boot may have slipped, his other foot caught in the cloak. Those steps are steep and sharp, and they bruised his body as he fell, but he died of a broken neck.'

Corbett glanced up. De Craon stood in the doorway above, staring impassively down at him.

'Sir Hugh.' Corbett looked over his shoulder. Bolingbroke was calling from outside. 'Sir Hugh, can I help?'

'Tell him to wait for me in my chamber,' Corbett whispered to Ranulf. He climbed the steps. The Frenchman didn't stand aside. 'Monsieur?'

'Yes, Sir Hugh?'

'Your colleague died of an unfortunate accident.'

'So it seems.' De Craon's eyes held Corbett's. 'I lay no blame on Sir Edmund or you. Crotoy should have been more careful, shouldn't he? I say the same to Vervins, who likes to stand on the parapet walk and stare out across your bleak countryside.' De Craon lifted a hand. 'What more can you do, Sir Hugh? Louis' death will be mourned by his daughter, his colleagues, and by my Grace, his master.' His eyebrows rose. 'Perhaps it was my mistake,' he continued silkily. 'Perhaps I shouldn't have chosen these old men and brought them to this cold castle. Well now, Sir Hugh, if you have finished, there are things I and my retainers must do.'

'Crotoy had a copy of Friar Roger's work, the *Opus Tertium*?'

'Yes, yes, he did.'

'I would like to see it.'

De Craon went back into the chamber and came back with a leather-bound book. He thrust this into Corbett's hand, 'Better still, borrow it for a while. You can return it tomorrow when we meet.'

Corbett thanked him and went carefully down the steps where Ranulf was waiting.

'Sir Hugh.' Corbett stopped and turned. De Craon was halfway down the steps. The English clerk did not like his look, the smirking eyes. 'Sir Hugh,' de Craon's words came like a hiss, 'don't grieve yourself. Accidents happen, we should all take great care.'

'Was it an accident?' Ranulf asked as soon as they were back in the chamber.

Corbett, slouched in a chair, kicked his boots off, vowing he must control his temper. He'd already had words with Ranulf; now he felt like grasping his sword, running back to the tower and confronting de Craon.

'Oh, he is a clever viper,' he snapped. He closed his eyes. 'A clever viper,' he repeated. 'Ranulf, bear with me. The steps to the old tower lead up to a heavy wooden door, which was locked. There's a small passageway beyond, no windows or gaps either side; the second set of steps are sharp-edged and steep. They lead up to Louis' chamber and another heavy oaken door. Louis had locked that just before he fell. To the left of that inner door there is a passageway, a small stairwell, now filled with fallen masonry, I must examine that again. Inside the chamber everything is in order. So,' he straightened up, 'according to all the evidence, Louis doused the candles, made sure everything was safe, picked up his keys and cloak, went out of his chamber, locked the door and fell to his death.'

'It must have been so,' Ranulf declared. 'I asked Sir Edmund, there's no other key to any door. Louis himself asked the same of the Constable and received assurances that that was the case.'

'Is that so?' Corbett murmured. 'Then it shows Louis was anxious, fearful.'

'What other explanation is there?' Bolingbroke picked up a stool and sat next to Corbett, spreading his hands to describe the passageway between the two doors. 'Louis must have been by himself. He had both keys in a pouch on his belt, Sir Hugh, it's a matter of logic; there's no other key to that chamber or to the outside door. He must have locked the door behind him, and was going down to open the other one when he slipped and fell, smashing his head and breaking his neck.'

'I would agree,' Ranulf added. 'Crotoy, by his own admission, was wary. He wouldn't allow anyone into his chamber unless he felt safe.'

Corbett remained silent. According to every item of evidence, Louis Crotoy had slipped, an unfortunate accident. Reason told him that, but his heart said different. He couldn't accept that those two French masters had come to Corfe and died by misadventure. Of course it looked suspicious, yet even if foul play was hinted at, it would surely be laid at the door of the perfidious English, rather than the wily schemes of the French court.

'We must eat,' Chanson grumbled. 'My belly thinks my throat is cut.'

'There speaks the last of the philosophers,' Bolingbroke mocked. 'We must go down.'

The evening meal, despite Sir Edmund's best efforts, was a sombre event. The castle kitchens served a banquet of Brie tart, fried artichokes, sorrel soup with figs and dates, followed by farmstead chickens stuffed with lentils, cherries and cheese, fried loach with almonds and a pear tart. The musicians in the gallery played sweet hymns and popular minstrel songs, the high table was covered with a white samite cloth and the trancher and knives were of silver, with precious goblets for wine. Sir Edmund's jester, a black-haired mannikin, could tumble, but the atmosphere remained dull. Corbett found it difficult even to look at de Craon. Ranulf sat embarrassed, this time rather wary of the Lady Constance, who gave up on her teasing and turned away to talk to Bolingbroke. Corbett, sitting on Sir Edmund's left, apologized to the Constable's wife for his apparent sullenness, claiming tiredness as well as a genuine sorrow for Crotoy's unfortunate death. Sir Edmund left him alone and Corbett, listening to the minstrel music, let his mind drift. One of the tunes he recognized.

'That's it!' he exclaimed.

'What is it, Sir Hugh?' the Constable asked.

'This outlaw band,' Corbett declared. 'Their members take the names of herbs and wildflowers, but young Phillipa, the first to disappear, said she had a lover amongst the group called Goliard. That's Provençal for a wandering minstrel, not the name of a herb or flower.'

He went back to his reflections, so immersed in his own thoughts he was almost unaware that the meal was ending and Father Andrew was making a hasty prayer of thanksgiving. Corbett excused himself and, followed by Ranulf and Chanson, made his way back to the Jerusalem Tower. The door still hung askew and the guard inside told him that both the corpse and the dead man's possessions had been moved.

'His body is in the church, sir. The other Frenchman, the one who looks like a fox, had everything packed away.'

Corbett stared at the ground still stained with Crotoy's blood, then climbed the steep steps. The upstairs door was open; he pushed this aside and glanced in, then turned to the ruined stairwell. The fallen masonry was as firm and strong as any wall, and nothing was left except a narrow shadow-filled alcove.

'Can I help you, Sir Hugh?'

De Craon stood in the doorway to the tower.

'No, no, de Craon, you can't help me.' Corbett went down the steps. 'Did you visit Crotoy today?'

'Yes, I did. I came by myself earlier. Louis was alive and well when I left him. Now, Sir Hugh, I must go up there myself.' He patted his stomach. 'I've drunk rather deeply yet I must make sure everything has been taken.' He brushed by Corbett and went up the steps.

'I want to pay my last respects to Louis,' Corbett declared, leaving the tower. He wished his companions goodnight and walked across the frozen castle yard. It had stopped snowing and, glancing up, he was pleased to see the clouds had broken and stars winked against the darkness. He spent some time in the narrow church, where three coffins now lay on trestles in front of the High Altar. He ignored the squeaking of mice, the cold which hung thick and heavy like a mist seeping through the very stones. He knelt, reciting the psalms of the dead, and started as he felt a brush on his shoulder. Father Andrew peered kindly down at him.

'I thought I would find you down here, Sir Hugh. I've seen Sir Edmund and the Frenchman. We've agreed the Requiem Mass will be sung tomorrow. Rebecca will be buried in the churchyard. The corpses of the two Frenchmen are to be taken to Dover, embalmed and put aboard a French cog. Both I and Master Simon, the castle leech,' he explained, 'have done our best. At Dover there are more skilled practitioners. Anyway, Sir Edmund has said there'll be no meeting tomorrow. The day will be given over to mourning.'

Corbett thanked him and left the church. He heard a sound deep in the shadows.

'I thought you'd gone to bed, Ranulf. I can smell the soap you've washed yourself with. The Lady Constance must be pleased!'

'I'll retire when you do.' Ranulf stepped into the pool of light thrown by the torches either side of the church door. 'I thought it best to make sure you were safe.'

'There'll be no meeting tomorrow,' Corbett declared, 'and I must attend the Requiem Mass.'

'I'm truly sorry, Master, about what happened earlier.' Ranulf swayed slightly on his feet. He had drunk deep-bowled goblets of wine too fast during the evening meal.

'Never mind.' Corbett slapped him on his shoulder. 'I've forgotten. Sleep well, Ranulf.'

Corbett returned to his own chamber. He knew Ranulf would follow him, at least to the entrance. He locked and bolted his door and made sure that the shutters were held firm against the window. Then he built up the fire and, taking his writing tray, sat for a while trying to make sense of the various problems which distracted him. He recalled the attack earlier in the evening, the crossbow bolts hurtling against the hard stone. How many people had seen him going there, how many people knew? But then he recalled striding across the castle yard. It would have been so easy for his attacker to see him,

seize an arbalest and follow him through the darkness. Was
that murderous bowman also responsible for the deaths of those
young maids, or was the attack planned and plotted by de
Craon? Was de Craon following orders, or was it simply that
the Frenchman's malice had got the better of him, unable to
resist an opportunity to strike at his sworn foe? And the
murders of these maids ... had he learnt anything new?
Nothing really, except the flirtation between the girls and that
young man-at-arms, but that could be found in villages and
castles up and down the kingdom. He wrote down the name
'Phillipa'. She was different, a lonely and intelligent girl who
spun fabulous tales about herself, about a landless knight, a
fictitious outlaw called Goliard.

Had she gone into the forest and died? Was her corpse
mouldering in some ditch, or had she run away? He recalled
Mistress Feyner's protestations. He rubbed his chin, wondering when the outlaw Horehound would meet him. Could
he know anything? He glanced across at the pile of Friar
Roger's books and manuscripts, including the one from
de Craon still lying on his bed. He placed the *Secretus
Secretorum* back in the Chancery chest and returned to reflect
on the deaths of those two Frenchmen, Destaples dying of a
seizure in a locked chamber, Crotoy found dead between two
locked doors, the keys to which he still had in his pouch.
Accident or murder? Corbett's eyes grew heavy. That would
have to wait ...

Ranulf of Newgate, Clerk of the Green Wax, was not as drunk
as he pretended to be, and although his companions protested,
he questioned both Chanson and Bolingbroke most closely
about what had happened during his flirtation with the Lady
Constance. Chanson, in particular, was only too ready to
chatter. Ranulf was clearly furious, especially with himself.

'I knew old Master Longface would go wandering off,' he
declared. 'I should have been there. Now tell me again, exactly,
what that red-haired wench said, and the man-at-arms and
Mistress Feyner.'

Chanson described in great detail Corbett's conversation
with all three; he also referred to Corbett's speculation
on Father Matthew, a matter Ranulf already knew about.

Bolingbroke filled in the gaps, and by the time he had finished his interrogation, Ranulf had decided upon his path.

'What we must do,' he declared to his sleepy-eyed companions, 'is meet with this outlaw Horehound. Something has happened in the forest which he knows about. I suspect we'll need his help over the murder of these maids.'

'Do you suspect the priest?' Bolingbroke asked.

'Possibly, or that taverner. What I can't understand is how the killer is able to place one corpse in a midden heap and another outside the castle, and a third on the trackway near the church.'

Ranulf kicked off his boots and, imitating Corbett, lay back against the bolsters. Chanson and Bolingbroke played a game of hazard, then retired. Ranulf sat listening to Chanson's snores as he turned over what he planned for the following day. Lady Constance, her sweet face, was a constant distraction. Ranulf tried to ignore it; he had failed Corbett and must make amends. Eventually he fell asleep.

He woke in the early hours. Quietly he washed and changed, laying out his war belt, ensuring the sword and dagger slipped in and out of their sheaths, and took an arbalest from the chest near Chanson's bed. Going down to the yard, he found the dirt and slush had been covered by a fresh layer of snow; only guards and cooks flitted like ghosts across to the bakehouses or kitchens. Men-at-arms were building bonfires, and few looked up as he crossed to the stable, shaking an ostler awake, urging him to prepare his horse.

'No feed,' he warned. 'I want it quiet. Check the hooves, make sure it is well shod.'

He returned to his chamber and roused Chanson, almost pulling the sleepy groom up out of the thick coverlet, tapping his face.

'Listen, Chanson, I'm leaving for the forest.'

'But, but . . .'

'Don't start stammering,' Ranulf warned. 'Tell Sir Hugh that I've gone to meet Horehound. I hope to be back shortly after noon.'

'But you're frightened of the forest.'

'Well it's time I cured that. Now, while I'm gone, you follow old Master Longface like his shadow.'

Ranulf collected his cloak and left. His horse was saddled and ready in the yard. He mounted and rode through the outer bailey and across the drawbridge. The snow on the trackway outside the castle was well over ankle deep, but although the morning was grey, Ranulf took comfort that the clouds had broken, and perhaps the worst was past. He glanced at the line of trees and quelled his own fear, letting his mind go back. He had seen or heard something yesterday, but he couldn't place it. He recalled the Frenchman's corpse lying at the foot of the steps, the blood seeping out like spilt wine from a cup, then thought of Corbett sheltering in that ruin while the cross-bowman took careful aim. He patted his horse's neck. 'Well, we will see who you are,' he whispered.

He entered the line of trees, allowing the horse to pick its way carefully along the snow-packed trackway. Occasionally he passed other lonely travellers. A chapman, his bundle piled high on his back, hood up, face visored, plodded his way towards the castle. He hardly lifted his head as he passed. Ranulf reached the church, which lay silent under its snow coverlet, the black crosses and headstones of the cemetery thrusting up, a sombre reminder of the shortness of life. He urged his horse on. He didn't want to tire it, but at the same time he wanted to be out of the forest before the day began to die or the snowfalls returned. He had a fear of getting lost.

When he reached the Tavern in the Forest he left his horse in the cobbled yard. The tap room was open and he was pleased to meet the boy Corbett had paid the previous day. He ushered Ranulf to sit in the inglenook. The fire had burnt down, and as the boy remarked, the tavern was as cold as the snow outside. He brought a pot of ale and some stale bread. Ranulf chewed on this, sipping on the ale to soften the bread in his mouth.

'Would you like to earn a piece of silver?' he whispered as the boy crouched like a dog in front of him.

The boy's eyes widened.

'Three pieces of silver.'

'Three pieces of silver!' The lad edged away. 'You're not one of those strange ones who thinks a boy's bottom is better than a girl's breasts?'

Ranulf laughed. 'No, I want you to come with me. I'll put

you on the saddle in front of me. I want you to lead me into the forest where I can meet Horehound.'

'I don't know him.'

'Oh yes you do,' Ranulf retorted. 'I know about outlaws. They always come to the nearest tavern to buy or sell, to collect information. I would wager a silver coin you've sat with Horehound out beneath the trees, haven't you, lad?'

'Meet him yourself.'

'Three pieces of silver,' Ranulf repeated. He put down the pot of ale and took out his purse.

'One now, one when I meet Horehound, and one when we return.'

The boy's eyes widened with amazement.

'Do you have parents?' Ranulf asked.

'Died five winters ago.' The boy's eyes never left the coins. 'Work here for Master Reginald I do.' He pointed to a table on the far side of the room 'Sleep under there at night and eat whatever scraps I am given.'

'Three silver coins,' Ranulf repeated again, 'and I'll find you a post in the castle. You don't have to come back here. How about that, lad, eh? Clerk of the kitchen, clean clothes.' He pointed to the leather cloths wrapped around the boy's feet. 'And a proper pair of boots.'

The boy jumped to his feet. In the twinkling of an eye he snatched the coin, scampered across the tap room and returned with a tattered cloak and a small pathetic bundle.

'Good.' Ranulf got to his feet.

'I've just got one more task. Master Reginald always tells me never to douse the fire in the morning,' and lifting his tattered tunic and pulling down his hose, the boy urinated into the fireplace, then, dancing like an imp from Hell, followed Ranulf out to his horse.

The Clerk of the Green Wax helped him into the saddle and swung up behind him. The boy stank, his hair was thick with grease, and beneath his cloak Ranulf could feel his thin body and bony arms. For a brief moment he went back years to when, garbed in rags, he had fought along the alleyways and runnels near Whitefriars. He was glad he had brought the boy; it dulled his fear of the forest, of becoming lost. The boy chattered like a squirrel, divulging all the secrets of the tavern, telling how Master Reginald was a bully but fawned on the foreigners who came and went as they wished and ate like lords. Ranulf listened intently. He did not want to prompt the boy, who, for a silver coin, would have told any lie about the taverner. So engrossed was he, it was a shock to realize how deep the forest had become. Only the occasional cawing of a rook or the rustling in the undergrowth betrayed any sign of life. On one occasion he thought he was lost, but the boy pointed their way through the trees and said they were safe. They reached a small crossroads where a forest trackway cut across their path. Here, the boy slipped down from the saddle, and stared owl-eyed up at Ranulf.

'You've got to stay there,' he warned. 'You mustn't move. I'll be back before you know it.'

Then he was gone, leaving the trackway, pushing through the undergrowth, disappearing into the darkness of the trees. Ranulf had no choice but to wait. He felt tempted to ride on. It wasn't the gloom, the snow or the greying sky above him, but that ominous silence, as if people were watching from the trees, waiting for him to make a mistake. His horse stamped and whinnied, and the sound echoed like the crack of a whip. Ranulf dismounted and hobbled his horse, which was restless at its master's unease. He stroked its neck, talking softly, reassuring it, trying to control the beating of his own heart. He thought of Lady Constance and wondered if she would give him a token, a light kiss perhaps, a brushing of the lips. His horse whinnied again and moved. Ranulf heard a click and turned slowly. Six men stood there, garbed in rags, tattered hoods pulled over their heads; three carried weapons, swords and axes, and the leader and the two standing either side of him brought their crossbows up, bolts in the grooves, the cords winched back.

'You have a fine horse. We could take that, the saddle and harness and sell them in the nearest town. Your weapons too. You also have silver coins.'

'Aye, you could do that,' Ranulf warned, 'and the King's men will see you hang. Are you Horehound? I'm Ranulf-atte-Newgate, Clerk of the Green Wax, a King's man. I have come to offer you a pardon.'

'I told you, I told you.' The tap boy appeared swift as a rabbit from behind a bush. 'I told you who he was.'

The crossbows were lowered, and the outlaw leader came forward, pushing back his cowl and the ragged cloth covering his mouth and nose. A dirty narrow face, the nose slightly twisted, a scar coursing down his left cheek. He had cropped grey hair, his moustache and beard were dirty and clogged with grease, his eyes were sharp and quick. Horehound stretched out his rag-covered hand. Ranulf grasped this and pulled the man closer, gripping him tightly.

'No, don't worry.' He saw the fear flare in the outlaw's eyes. 'I'm not here to trap you. The day you met us,' Ranulf half smiled, 'in the cemetery at St Peter's, you spoke of a "horror in the forest." What did you mean? You know something, don't you, about the maids who have been killed?'

'I know a lot of things.' The outlaw leader turned to the men on his right. 'Don't I, Hemlock? Isn't that right, Milkwort?' The two grunted in agreement. 'A full pardon,' he turned back to Ranulf, 'you promise that?'

'For every one of you,' Ranulf replied. 'Full pardon and amnesty, as well as silver to help you on your way.'

The outlaw fished beneath his rags and took off the crude-looking cross dangling round his neck; he thrust this into Ranulf's hand.

'That's been in holy water and blessed by a priest. Swear your oath and come!'

Ranulf never forgot the subsequent breathless wandering through that frozen forest. The outlaws left the boy with one of their gang to guard the horse, and in single file, Ranulf behind the leader, entered the trees; an ancient place, the outlaws confided, full of elves, sprites and demons. Ranulf hid his fear, for the forest was a truly terrifying place. The trees clustered in as if they wished to surround and trap him, icy branches stretched down to pluck at his hood or catch his cloak. Snow-covered briars and brambles tugged at his ankles. He could make no sense of where they were going; to all intents and purposes he was lost, yet Horehound trotted on like a lurcher dog, every so often stopping to warn Ranulf to follow him more closely as they avoided an icy morass or marsh. Occasionally an animal was startled or a bird burst out of the branches, making Ranulf's heart leap and the sweat start. They crossed a gloomy clearing where the sky was only slivers of light between the trees, then ducked back under the dark canopy, following paths as treacherous and dangerous as any alleyway in London. At last they stopped at the edge of a glade, and the outlaws fanned out behind Ranulf, reluctant to go any further.

'They be afeared,' Horehound taunted, 'but I'm not.' And off he went.

Suddenly, in a clearing, they came upon the 'horror in the woods'. Ranulf could tell that, despite the fresh fall of snow, someone had been here recently. Horehound pointed to the grisly find and, taking him back through the trees, brought him to the edge of the swamp and the second corpse. By the time they reached the morass, Ranulf's stomach was queasy at what he'd just seen: a girl, flesh decomposing, eyes hollowed, cheeks pinched. He agreed with Horehound, before they covered up the remains, that it was a young woman who'd been hanged from the oak branch above them. The second corpse was different. This time the outlaws helped scrape away the snow and ice and drag the body from the oozing mud. Ranulf used the snow and the edge of his own cloak to clean the face, trying to avoid those staring eyes. His hand moved across the corpse and brushed the quarrel embedded deep in her chest. Using his dagger, he cleared away the mud to reveal the purple wound, the feathered flight and the encrusted blood.

'Nothing to do with us,' Horehound announced. 'Neither of these deaths, that's what we tried to tell you in the cemetery. We will not be blamed and hanged for the murder of these poor wenches.'

'That's why I came,' Ranulf said. 'My master, Sir Hugh Corbett, wishes to have words with you.'

'I had heard that,' the outlaw leader replied. 'The taverner, Master Reginald, he told the boys to pass the message on, as if it was beneath him. I did not know what to believe. It may have been a trap but you've sworn your oath, haven't you?'

'I have.' Ranulf stared at the man squatting before him, the rest of his companions standing in a semi-circle around them. He glanced at the corpse sprawled in the snow, hair, flesh, clothing and blood-encrusted mud.

'The end of life.' Horehound followed his gaze. 'No better than a rabbit.'

Ranulf got to his feet, and in a loud voice repeated his oath. Then he told the outlaws to bring the corpses back to the castle; he would ride with them. Later they must bring the whole band. They would be given fresh clothing, hot food, money and a pardon written out by the King's own man and sealed in the Crown's name, so no one could lift a hand against them. Ranulf would have liked to examine the corpses more carefully, but he was aware of the passing of time, how cold and hungry he had become. He had done what he had come for and was determined to be free of this dreadful forest as quickly as possible.

When men and animals become angry they have a desire to do harm and possess a soul of malignity.

Roger Bacon, *Opus Maius*

Chapter 9

Corbett stared down at the two corpses. They had been stripped and washed, and Father Andrew had blessed both with incense and holy water, anointing the five senses with sacred oil. He had sighed, muttered prayers, then left the corpses to Simon the leech, who was now examining both carefully. Chanson and Bolingbroke had also withdrawn, driven out by the smell of decomposing flesh. Father Andrew had left the thurible open, and Corbett heaped incense on top of the glowing charcoal, welcoming the gusts of fragrance. Lady Constance, who proved not as squeamish as others, had also done her best, scattering rosewater and providing Corbett and Ranulf with pomanders saturated in perfume.

Ranulf's return with the corpses so soon after the funeral Mass for the other victims had created chaos and consternation which gave way to shock and grief. The remains were immediately recognized. Mistress Feyner had stared down at the sled and grieved, made all the more piteous by her soul-wrenching silence, her face contorted by the mute agony of loss. She opened her mouth to speak but could find no words, simply covering her eyes with her fingers whilst friends led her away. The parents of Alusia had sat for a while just staring down at the corpse until her mother began to scream, becoming so fretful Lady Constance and her maid, clasping her arms, took her into the Hall of Angels.

Corbett's anger at Ranulf's disappearance soon calmed when he realized what the man had done and the manner in which he had confronted his fears. Ranulf had ridden across the drawbridge like the figure of Death, hooves drumming on the wood. The garrison had already been alerted by sentries on the gatehouse who had reported a line of men emerging from the trees. Ranulf had tried to persuade Horehound and his gang to bring the corpses into the castle yard, but the outlaw chief had shaken his head.

'Only this far,' he declared. 'When the pardons are given, I shall come into the castle to receive the King's peace.' He and his companions had melted away.

Sir Edmund had sent out a cart to bring in the corpses, laying them out on a sled just within the gateway to the inner ward. De Craon and his retinue had excused themselves, whispering their condolences. The crowds around the sled had turned ugly, and Corbett had been reminded in no uncertain way of his vow to bring the killer to justice.

'Well, sir?' he asked now, breaking from his reverie.

'Well, sir,' the leech replied drily, 'both girls are dead. Phillipa, you can tell,' he pointed to the corpse, 'in life must have been comely and plump.'

The leech had covered her face with a coarse linen cloth. He had been pressing the girl's tummy and examining very carefully the purple weal around the throat before scrupulously inspecting the girl's hands. He got to his feet and covered his nose and mouth with a perfumed cloth, breathing in deeply.

'I have tended the dead on battlefields in Wales and Scotland; I've seen more corpses,' he blinked his watery eyes, 'than some people have seen summer days, but the horror never escapes you. Phillipa killed herself; she climbed that oak tree and used the fabric from her own gown. It's made of hempen, thick and coarse, strong as any rope. There is no other wound to the body, no blow, no bruise. Alive her flesh must have been as white as marble, and yet so soft and warm. A loving girl.' He edged up closer. 'I will not whisper this aloud,' he added. 'The girl should be given honourable burial. Father Matthew will see to that. She'll not be treated as a suicide, buried at the crossroads under a gibbet with a peg driven through her heart.'

'There's something else?'

'I am only a leech, Sir Hugh, I am not a physician.'

'Whatever you are, you are very astute.'

'Phillipa was expectant, possibly in the early stages. The lower part of her belly is swollen. I think her monthly courses must have stopped for at least two months; that's why she may have killed herself, steeped in shame, or what she thought was shame.'

'And Alusia?' Corbett glanced around the leech at the other corpse, the bloody quarrel lying beneath the sled.

'The same as the rest, but her killer must have been very close; it's a wonder the bolt didn't pierce her entire body. Yet what was she doing out in the forest, Sir Hugh? I've heard the whispers; Alusia was terrified of going there. Why should a young woman who knows about these deaths, who found one of the victims on a forest trackway, leave the safety of our castle?'

'Unless she was killed elsewhere?' Corbett mused. 'They say the marsh is near the Tavern in the Forest.'

Ranulf walked to the doorway and leaned against the lintel, sucking in the icy fresh air.

'Why should a girl kill herself,' he asked without turning, 'because she was expecting a baby? Phillipa's mother is most loving.' He gnawed on the knuckle of his hand. His journey into the forest hadn't frightened him, yet he'd felt a deep oppression as he brought these corpses in, as if the souls of the two girls were earth-bound, clustering by his side, begging ghostly for justice. He felt disgusted at what he'd seen. These were his people. He had grown up with girls like this in the fetid alleyways of London. They were full of life, eager for love, desperate to secure a grip on life, to marry well and settle down. Why should such a girl hang herself? To conceive a child was a natural thing and, whatever the Church said, blessed by God. He recalled what Chanson had told him about Corbett's interview with the man-at-arms and the red-haired Marissa; he imagined Phillipa that autumn Sunday morning walking into the forest to meet her Goliard.

'Sir Hugh, would you excuse me?'

Before Corbett could reply, Ranulf, taking his sword belt off the peg just inside the doorway, strode across the castle yard, strapping it about him. He approached the well where servants were filling buckets; he glimpsed the tap boy who had been brought from the tavern, crouched beside a fire, gnawing greedily on a piece of meat. He raised his hand. Ranulf replied, ignoring the dark looks of the servants.

'Marissa!' he shouted. 'Marissa, the King's man wishes words with you again.'

The red-haired girl stepped away from the group, fearful of this clerk with his sword belt clasped around his black leather jacket, those cat-like eyes studying her intently.

'Come here, girl.' Ranulf gripped her by the shoulder. 'I want to see you, and the man-at-arms known as Martin, in the council chamber on the bottom floor of the keep. You know where it is.' He took out his Ave beads from his wallet. 'I shall recite five of these; by the time I've finished you must be there.'

In fact Ranulf had reached only the fourth when Marissa and Martin, gasping for breath, hurried into that cold, murky chamber, the only light being the squat tallow candle in the centre of the table.

'Good, good.' Ranulf ushered them in, then kicked the door shut, pulling across the bolts. As he drew his sword and dagger, Martin's hand fell to the knife in his own belt. 'Please don't do that,' Ranulf asked. 'You're in no danger if you tell the truth. I want the truth.'

'About what?' Marissa stammered, stepping behind Martin for protection.

'Come here.' Ranulf beckoned to Martin. The man-at-arms edged forward and Ranulf grasped him by the shoulder and pushed him to the far end of the hall, then brought the flat of his sword down on the man's shoulder.

'I have done no wrong,' Martin declared.

'Except for Phillipa,' Ranulf replied. 'You are considered gallant with the ladies, aren't you, with your leather jacket and proper boots? You wear a sword belt and swagger like the rest of us. Phillipa lived in dreams, didn't she? You and she used to meet. Did you know she was pregnant? I am keeping my voice to a whisper so only you and I know what is being said here. Now, according to my law, there are two pleas, guilty or very guilty. Guilty is you and Phillipa lay together and she conceived. Very guilty is you and Phillipa lay together, she conceived but now you are going to lie.'

Martin gazed back, stricken-eyed.

'It's not a crime,' Ranulf whispered. 'I'm not saying she killed herself for that. I think I know why she killed herself. But are you the father of her child?'

Martin began to tremble and Ranulf moved the sword swiftly to the other shoulder, bringing it down with a slap.

'God have mercy on me,' the man-at-arms replied, 'but it must be me. She was a maid when I met her, her head full of dreams and fantasies. It was after Midsummer's Day; I followed her into the forest. I took some wine and bread, but after that . . .'

'Did you boast about it?' Ranulf asked.

'I dared not.' The man-at-arms glanced down the hall at Marissa, who sat on the edge of a bench. Ranulf followed his gaze.

'I was fearful,' the man-at-arms continued. 'Mistress Feyner has a fiery temper. I was supposed to be her Goliard. I did not know what to do, then Phillipa disappeared.'

'She wasn't liked by the other girls, was she?'

Martin shook his head. 'Phillipa was a dreamer,' he replied hoarsely. 'She had listened to tales about knights and squires; she even knew the tale of Arthur. She was clever with the horn book, she could count to one hundred and read the words of the missal. She was even learning some Latin and French.'

'And the other girls teased her?'

'They teased her,' Martin agreed. 'Harassed her like sparrows would an owl caught in the daylight.'

Ranulf resheathed his sword. 'And of course,' the clerk smiled thinly, 'once she had fled, they'd simply dismiss it, wouldn't they, as part of Phillipa's madcap dreaming?' Ranulf grasped the man-at-arms by the shoulder. 'One day in your sorry life, Martin, make a pilgrimage. Walk barefoot to some shrine, spend good silver for a Mass to be sung for the souls of that woman and her child who died before God's plan for them was complete.'

With a flick of his wrist, Ranulf dismissed them both and waited until they had left. He doused the candle and left the keep, striding across the ward to the death house. He was surprised to find Lady Constance and her maid waiting outside, deep in conversation with Corbett.

'My Lady has been making her confession.' Corbett smiled. 'She now realizes that on the night Monsieur Crotoy died, she distracted you.'

'My Lady is never a distraction,' Ranulf bowed, 'and the fault was entirely mine.' His heart leapt at Constance's beaming smile.

'I think we were talking about a token, weren't we?' she murmured.

Ranulf blushed.

'I felt guilty,' Lady Constance continued, 'then I recalled something. Early on the day he died, my maid and I visited Monsieur Crotoy. He seemed most friendly. I wanted to ask him about the fashions in Paris. We'd heard stories about new clothes and headdresses. Monsieur Crotoy was most helpful and charming. He took us up into his chamber, where we shared wine and a dish of marchpane. When we visited him, the outer door was locked.'

'I wondered about that,' Corbett said. 'How Louis could have heard anyone knocking on the door.'

'Oh, it's quite simple, Sir Hugh. The passageway between the doors creates an echo; you can hear any noise. I know. When I was young I used to hide there from my mother. Did you also notice, Sir Hugh, in the outer door there is a narrow grille, a small trapdoor. You pull back the flap and look through to see who is waiting. Now when Monsieur Crotoy let us in, I teased him about the doors being locked. He replied that if he had his way he would have bolts on the outside door as well. I asked him what he was fearful about, didn't I?' She turned to the maid, who agreed. 'Did he not trust my father? Or did he think all English men wore tails? Monsier Crotoy said something strange; he reassured me that he trusted my father completely, while he also talked warmly of his friendship with you, Sir Hugh. He added that, since the death of Monsieur Destaples, he feared his own kind rather than any other and had vowed he would let none of them into his chamber. He was quite insistent on that and repeated the remark at least twice. I felt sorry for him. When we left, he followed us down and locked the outside door behind us.' She shrugged. 'I thought you should know that.' She sketched a bow at Corbett, winked at Ranulf, tapped him gently on the shoulder and walked away. Corbett, frowning, watched her go.

'Now, isn't it strange, Ranulf – why should that viper de Craon claim he visited Louis? Louis was very careful! He wouldn't show de Craon the courtesies extended to Lady Constance. So why does that Frenchman lie? He claims to have visited Louis; I don't think he did.'

They returned to the death house, where the corpses lay covered in canvas sheets. Corbett crossed himself and was about to leave when he noticed the garments stripped from both young women lying in a heap on the floor. He went across and sifted through these. Phillipa's had grown threadbare, the colours running, due to the exposure in the forest; the only personal item found was a small set of Ave beads, eleven in all, which could be worn round the wrist. Alusia's were drenched in mud. Corbett put on his gauntlets and shook out each item, and exclaimed in surprise at what fell from the thick serge gown. He picked it up. It was a piece of wood, around which strips of wire had been wound to form a handle. He could slip three of his fingers into the gap. He stared curiously at it.

'Ranulf. What is this?'

'Where did it come from?' Ranulf asked.

'Alusia's gown is thick, it was caught in the thread.' Corbett pointed to the sharp end of the wire.

Ranulf took it out to the doorway, turning it over in his hands. 'It's a crude brush,' he declared, 'the type used to remove mud and dirt from linen. Once it has been weakened by the water you scrape it off. My mother had one. She carried it on a cord from her belt. Alusia must have been wearing it on the day she was killed.'

Corbett felt a tingle of excitement in his stomach. 'I wonder,' he whispered. 'Ranulf, go and ask someone where Alusia worked. Would she wash clothes?'

As Ranulf hurried off, Corbett went back into the death house and stood between the corpses; eyes closed, he prayed that what he had discovered would be of use.

'Sir Hugh!'

Corbett opened his eyes. Ranulf had returned.

'Alusia worked in the buttery. She never washed clothes.'

'Mistress Feyner,' Corbett whispered, 'she is the laundry-woman, Ranulf.' He crossed himself and led Ranulf out of the death house. 'Go and fetch her,' he declared. 'Bring her to my room but don't alarm her.'

Corbett was seated in the chair in front of the fire when

Ranulf ushered Mistress Feyner into the chamber. He rose to greet her, grasping those strong hands and guiding her to the high-backed chair opposite. Mistress Feyner had been crying until she was red-eyed, yet she was watchful, tense.

'Mistress Feyner, you are a widow. Your husband was a carpenter.'

'He was, and a very good one,' she declared.

'He was also a crossbowman,' Corbett continued, 'serving the King's armies.'

'What are you saying?'

'Do you still have his arbalest? His quiver of quarrels, perhaps two or three of those?'

Mistress Feyner remained silent. She glanced across at Ranulf.

'I don't want to talk while he is here.' She pointed at Ranulf. 'I don't like his eyes.'

Corbett glanced at Ranulf, pulled a face and indicated he should stand outside. Once he had gone, Corbett leaned closer.

'Mistress Feyner, Phillipa was your only daughter. A man can never understand a mother's love. You knew what was happening, didn't you? How your daughter was clever at the church school, quick with her numbers, able to read the words, but the other girls didn't like that, did they? Matters grew from bad to worse, especially when Phillipa began to talk about the mysterious Goliard, the landless knight who lived in the forest. In truth there was no Goliard. Phillipa was a dreamer, much taken with Martin, the man-at-arms. Mistress Feyner, did you know . . .' He paused, wondering whether to tell this mother what Ranulf had hurriedly informed him of while she had waited outside.

'What?' Mistress Feyner stretched a hand out to the fire but held Corbett's gaze. 'What are you going to say, King's man? That she flirted with Martin and made the others even more jealous. So what?'

'You know what I'm going to say,' Corbett replied. 'Those girls drove Phillipa out into the forest; their constant bullying, their cruel mockery forced your daughter away. They turned her wits. Only the good Lord truly knows what happened out there in the green darkness. Phillipa took her own life. You

sensed that, didn't you? You, the loving mother, knew she
would never return.'

The woman tried to reply, but her lower lip quivered. Despite
her roughened skin, her face had turned pale.

'Even when she had gone,' Corbett continued evenly, 'the
whispering didn't stop, the mockery. Did you hear the words
"good riddance" muttered? You were distraught, beside yourself
with grief. You hid it well as your sorrowing turned to anger.
You are a castle woman, Mistress Feyner, I suspect you have
been one all your life. Sometimes when the armies march, the
women go with them. Your husband must have instructed you
on the use of a crossbow; how to place the bolt in the groove
and wind back the winch, how to prime it well and have it
ready. Crossbows come in all sizes. I've seen one which can be
carried in one hand, but the bolts are always deadly. You are
strong after years of bending over the vats and scrubbing; you
have good muscular arms and wrists. An arbalest would be
easy for you to use, especially so close.'

The woman lifted her hand, but Corbett continued.

'You knew your daughter was dead, forced out by those other
wenches, cruelly treated and abused, so you waged war against
them. You reasoned,' he shifted in his chair, 'that something
must have happened to Phillipa. You would have liked her
body found, but you had no doubts about her fate and that the
people responsible had to be punished.'

'Are you sure, King's man?'

'Oh I'm certain. You had the motive and you had the means,
your husband's arbalest.'

'I am Mistress Feyner, not some soldier.'

'True,' Corbett agreed, 'you are Mistress Feyner the laundrywoman; who would suspect you? You moved amongst those
young women like a pike amongst carp, choosing your victim.
You could listen to all the chatter, who was going where, what
they had planned, where they would meet. You also have some
status in this castle. You could lure a wench here or there to
lonely spots, like midden heaps or outhouses.'

Mistress Feyner sat like a woman in a dead faint, head down,
hands resting in her lap.

'You have a covered cart inside the castle walls, full of dirty
washing or baskets of clean linen for Master Reginald. You can

move that cart around the castle on any pretext, such as collecting laundry or exercising the horses. Who gives Mistress Feyner a second glance? Who senses the murderous anger seething within you? Yes, Mistress Feyner?' She did not look up. 'I don't know how you lured the other victims, but as for Rebecca, well, you heard about her plans to visit her friend's grave in the cemetery of St Peter's in the Wood. You offered both Rebecca and Alusia a ride in the cart. On that particular morning, a cold December day, with the light hardly broken, Rebecca came first and you were waiting for her with the arbalest loaded. She hadn't even collected her cloak. She died in an instant, and you wrapped her corpse in a canvas cloth and lifted it easily into the cart where it would lie well hidden. I'm sure when we inspect the cart we will find traces of your murderous work. Alusia arrives, and of course Rebecca isn't there. You become impatient and leave. No one stops you, no one thinks that Mistress Feyner is an assassin, whilst your horses really pull a death cart. You reach St Peter's church, Alusia steps down and hurries off. You go to the tail of the cart, let down the flap, pull out the canvas-bound corpse, unroll it and leave it by the side of the trackway. Only for a few heartbeats are you vulnerable or exposed, then you are gone.'

'I could have been seen.' Mistress Feyner's voice was gratingly harsh.

'Seen? By whom? I've been along that trackway, it is too close for any of the outlaws to come. You can see back down the path and ahead, whilst the cemetery wall would hide you from Father Matthew locked away in his house behind the church. You have claimed one more victim but now you are wary. King's men have arrived in Corfe. I take a vow, at the time rashly, to hunt the killer down. You may have decided to pause for a while until I was gone, but Alusia was dangerous. She may have seen or heard something as she went into the cemetery. Perhaps she may have wondered why neither of you saw the corpse on your way down to the church. You knew she would never leave the castle. However, because of the chatter, you knew of her friendship with Martin. Alusia was nervous, stretched like a bowstring. Did you give her some false message from Martin to meet him here or there, some lonely spot? If things went wrong, you could always allege you made a mistake or were misled. On that night you were waiting for her, perhaps in the usual lovers' tryst, that ruined passageway leading down to the old dungeons. You killed Alusia, wrapped her body up and hid it. But you made one mistake.'

Corbett picked the wire brush from the sack beside him and held it under Mistress Feyner's nose.

'The dead don't just stand and watch, woman; they sometimes help. You made a mistake, one of your brushes was found on Alusia's corpse. Why should she have that? She never worked in the laundry room.'

Mistress Feyner lifted her head and smiled sweetly.

'Sir, how clever you are.' The smile faded. 'How clever you are,' she repeated. 'I really don't know what was wrong with my Phillipa. Sometimes I thought she was with child, but if she was,' the woman chatted on, 'she would have told me, wouldn't she? Sharp as a pin she was, King's man. Oh, she had her ways, her dreams and madcap tales. She listened too intently to Lady Constance's stories about mysterious knights, yet she was as bright as a button, my Phillipa, sharp as a dagger. Like her father she was, yes, he fought with a crossbow but he was also a skilled carpenter; he could carve out of wood and make such shapely things. Father Matthew complimented her. She understood a little Latin and French and he was teaching her to read from the lectern in church, and that was the problem. Those harridans were jealous of her! Harassed her, bullied her.

'On Harvest Sunday last, during Mass, I could see their spiteful glances, laughing behind their fingers. Phillipa, all pale, left the church, saying she felt sick. I never saw her again. Sir Edward was kind, a search was made, but I knew my Phillipa.' Mistress Feyner tapped her breast. 'Here, in the sanctuary of my heart, I knew something had happened. The weeks passed, Phillipa never returned, I accepted she was dead and grieved silently. I heard the tales, the gossip, about that skulker who calls himself a man-at-arms.' Mistress Feyner was looking at a point above Corbett's head, letting her heart gush out the hatred which curdled there. 'That horde of bitches never grieved, not a tear fell over Phillipa, no one ever comforted me, no one ever grieved. I knew they were guilty. I held them responsible.'

She glanced at Corbett and blinked.

'In the end it was so easy. My husband's arbalest was clean and oiled. I had three quivers of quarrels; I vowed to use them well. I began with those who gossiped and sneered the most; they came like flies to the honey pot. So stupid, so easily trapped. Rebecca, sidling up beside the cart when it was in the outhouse as I was loading Master Reginald's linen. All concerned she was about visiting her friend's grave. False tears in her eyes, stupid mouth pulled down in grief. Grief?' Mistress Feyner spat the word out, talking to Corbett as if he was a fellow conspirator. 'Grief? She had never once asked about Phillipa, my daughter who had no grave. I killed her so easily in that darkened place.' She paused, nodding to herself. 'You're right. The cart is high, it's so easy to hide a corpse.' She laughed sharply. 'She wanted to visit her friend; I thought, well, why not join her? As for Alusia,' she shrugged, 'she may have seen something so I pretended Martin wished to see her near the ruined doorway. It's a pity he didn't come. I judged him guilty as well.'

'You left her there?' Corbett asked.

'Oh yes. The next morning, before dawn, I decided to exercise the horses. No one gave me a second glance, why should they bother about me? They didn't even care to make a proper search for my daughter. It was a dark morning, the mist curling. I carted the corpse down to the marsh.' She sighed. 'I thought it would sink, but I don't really care. Phillipa has been found, she's back, and as for you, sir . . .'

Mistress Feyner got to her feet, stretching out her hands as if she expected them to be bound. Corbett, surprised, sat back in the chair and the laundrywoman moved as swiftly as a cat. She picked up the iron poker from the hearth, swinging it, aiming for Corbett's head. He threw himself forward, head down, and the iron bar whirled above him. He moved to grab Mistress Feyner but she had already dropped her weapon and was running for the door.

'Ranulf!'

Mistress Feyner swung the door open and Corbett followed in pursuit, only to realize Ranulf wasn't there, but at the foot of the steps. He came pounding up, alarmed by the noise and the crash of the door. Mistress Feyner turned right, fleeing further up the spiral staircase. Corbett and Ranulf followed.

The steps were steep, twisting sharply as they followed the line of the wall. Corbett felt a little dizzy whilst Mistress Feyner, light on her feet, raced ahead. On the storey above she stopped to send some wood, stacked in a window embrasure, rattling down, impeding Corbett's progress. He and Ranulf kicked the obstacle aside, and by the time they glimpsed her again she had reached the top, bursting through the door on the roof of the tower. She tried to bolt it from the outside, but in her haste was unable to draw across the rusting iron. Corbett paused, gasping for breath, his sweat-soaked hand slipping down the mildewed wall. The reek of this ancient place made him cough and splutter on the dust swirling through the air.

'I want her alive, Ranulf.' He put his hand on the latch. 'There is no place for her to flee. I want to know why she attacked me.'

They opened the door to be buffeted by the icy wind. Mistress Feyner had reached the battlements and stood with her back to one of the crenellated openings. She seemed all composed, a smile on her lips. Corbett edged gingerly across the hard-packed ice.

'Surrender!' he called out. 'Give yourself up to the King's justice.' He beckoned with his hand as he moved forward.

Mistress Feyner climbed up into the gap, holding the stone either side, bracing herself against the wind which sent her hair and gown billowing.

'Please,' Corbett begged, 'there will be mercy as well as justice.'

'What does it matter, King's man?' Mistress Feyner called back. 'What does anything really matter now?' And spreading her arms as if they were wings, she fell back.

Corbett and Ranulf, slipping on the ice, strode across. Steadying themselves against the battlements, they peered over. Mistress Feyner lay below, black and twisted against the snow. Already a dark puddle shrouded her head like some sombre nimbus. People were hurrying across, shouting at each other.

'God have mercy on her,' Corbett whispered. 'God give her peace.'

They went back down the steep stairwell. Corbett stopped to secure his chamber before continuing down into the yard. Sir Edmund and Bolingbroke were already waiting.

'I told them what had happened,' Ranulf whispered. 'Sir Edmund went looking for further proof.' Corbett stared down at the bundle at the Constable's feet: a dark-stained sheet, an arbalest polished and clean, next to it a leather pouch of crossbow bolts.

'We found them,' Sir Edmund declared. 'The crossbow was in a hole beneath her cottage floor. The cloth was folded neatly in the cart. So evil.' He turned and spat.

'No,' Corbett disagreed. 'A poor woman, driven witless by grief, revenge and hatred. Anyway,' he gazed up at the snow-laden sky, 'this bloody work is finished; we have other things to do.' He patted the Constable on the shoulder. 'Give her body an honourable burial. She sinned but truly believed she had been grievously sinned against.'

Already a crowd was beginning to gather, eager with questions; Sir Edmund waved them away whilst Corbett took his two companions up to his chamber. For a short while he sat hunched in front of the fire, warming himself, wondering if he could have done things differently. Mistress Feyner had killed, and killed again. The castle folk would have demanded justice and she would have received little mercy, being thrust in some dungeon then tried before the justices in eyre, before being dragged on a hurdle at a horse's tail to be hanged on some gibbet or, even worse, burnt alive outside the castle gate.

Ranulf brought Corbett some watered wine. He sipped it carefully, calming his mind.

'We will not meet de Craon today. So, let us draft the pardon letters for the outlaws.'

The two clerks muttered in protest, but when Chanson arrived they began the laborious process. Sheaths of vellum were smoothed with pumice stone. Corbett dictated the words, Ranulf and Bolingbroke writing them down before copying them into formal letters, dating them on the eve of St Nicholas, the thirty-first year in the reign of Edward the First after the Conquest. The hard red wax was melted, Bolingbroke carefully ladling it out on to the prepared parchments. Corbett opened the secret Chancery box and carefully made sure his own ciphers were there before taking out the precious seal and making the impressions. Certain places in the document were left blank to insert names of individuals, but they all read the same, 'that X be admitted, with full pardon and mercy, into the King's peace, and that this pardon was for divers crime, poaching, housebreaking, robbing the King's highway . . .'

'I must go,' Ranulf declared. 'I promised I would meet them, to assure Horehound and all his followers that all would be well. I also offered to bring supplies.'

When Ranulf had left, taking Chanson with him, Corbett replaced the secret Chancery box and, trying to forget that black figure, head soaked in blood, sprawled out in the snow, took out the *Secretus Secretorum* of Friar Roger and began leafing through the pages. He found it difficult to concentrate. Despite what justice would have been meted out to her he regretted Mistress Feyner's death; even more that he had failed to question her about the murderous assault on himself.

Corbett eventually composed himself and became engaged in a fierce debate with Bolingbroke over the value of the *Secretus Secretorum* and the cipher Friar Roger had used. The more he studied the strange Latin words, the more convinced he became that the Franciscan had invented a most cunning code. He and Bolingbroke tried every variation they knew, and Corbett had to check himself lest he inadvertently gave away his own ciphers used in the letters and memoranda issued to his agents across Europe. They tried position codes, code wheels and the most complex multiplication table codes, studying the vertical pattern with the letters forward or backward. Bolingbroke confessed to being almost certain that Friar Roger's cipher was based on one of these. Corbett, however, remained unconvinced and kept returning to the key Magister Thibault had found on the last page, *'Dabo tibi portas multas'* – 'I shall give you many doors'. He realized how the letters of this phrase were separated, transposed and confused by blocks of other letters which somehow gave the words a Latin ring, and isolated what he called these alien obstacles, but when he applied them to other lines and sections of the manuscript it failed to resolve the mystery. He and Bolingbroke must have argued for an age, and when Ranulf returned drenched in melting snow, Corbett welcomed the break.

'Yes, I met Horehound and his lieutenant Milkwort. They have agreed to come into the castle the day after tomorrow and accept the King's peace. Strange,' Ranulf sat on a stool to remove his boots, 'they were full of mumbles about the taverner Master Reginald, who drove them away, whilst Father Matthew was ill, claiming he was too weak to congratulate them on the good news. Sir Hugh?' He glanced across. Corbett had been half listening, staring intently at the copy of the *Opus Tertium* de Craon had lent him. He placed this on the bed and went to get his own copy, one finger on the text comparing the two pages.

'I've found it,' he whispered and glanced up. 'At least I know that!'

There are two methods of gaining knowledge: reasoning and experience.

Roger Bacon, Opus Maius

Chapter 10

Magister Jean Vervins wrapped his cloak about him and leaned against the parapet of Corfe Castle, oblivious to the bitter cold and the freezing wind tugging at his cowl. The walkway was slippery underfoot but Vervins wasn't frightened. In his youth he had served on a cog of war and had trod dangerous slippery decks which moved and twisted on heavy seas. He turned to his right; he was safe enough up here. Ten paces away a sentry crouched against the crenellated wall, warming his hands over the small brazier. He caught Vervins' gaze and lifted his hand; the Frenchman replied and turned to stare out across the mist-shrouded countryside. Vervins had climbed the steps leading up to the parapet walk resting on his cane, quite determined to escape the cloying atmosphere of Monsieur de Craon. He did not like the royal clerk; he resented his arrogance and above all was deeply opposed to this farrago of nonsense. He wanted to be back in Paris, to be closeted in his own warm chamber at the back of his spacious house on the Rue St-Sulpice. He wanted to return to his books and ledgers, to walk the narrow streets and meet his friends in the cookshops and taverns, or be back disputing terms of law in the cavernous schools of the Sorbonne.

Vervins had studied Friar Roger and dismissed the dead Franciscan as a dreamer and a boaster. He recalled Friar Roger's statement from the *Opus Minus*: 'there is no pestilence to equal the opinion of the vulgar. The vulgar are blind and wicked, they are the obstacle and enemy of all progress.' How could a follower of St Francis, a self proclaimed scholar, be so dismissive of others? Why all this secrecy? He recalled how Friar Roger had expressly said he had not seen a machine that could fly, yet added, 'but I know the wise man who has invented such a procedure'. How could he say that? What did it mean? Vervins leaned against the stonework, absentmindedly picking at the lichen and moss growing there. He liked nothing better than to visit the small squares of Paris where troops of travelling mummers and storytellers would set up their makeshift stages and recount legends and stories to astonish the crowd. Was that the case with Friar Roger? A man who hinted at wondrous things but never produced the truth? The English clerks were just as baffled as he over the cipher of the *Secretus Secretorum*. Was that just mummery cloaked in scholarship? Was there a cipher, or was it a cruel trick by Friar Roger? A way of taunting and teasing other scholars, cleverly hinting that this manuscript contained revelations which would explain the wonders described in his other writings?

Vervins stared along the parapet walk. He was tempted to take off the thick wool-lined gauntlets and warm his fingers over that fire, yet he desperately wanted to be alone. The *Secretus Secretorum* was one thing, but there were more pressing, dangerous problems; the deaths of his two colleagues had reduced him to a state of constant agitation. Of course, he had to accept the evidence of his own eyes. Destaples had died of a seizure, the door to his bedchamber locked and bolted, whilst Magister Crotoy had slipped down steep steps and broken his neck. How else could it be explained? There was no trickery there, surely? But why had they been brought here, plucked from their beloved studies, forced to endure a sickening sea voyage and the rigours of an English winter in a lonely castle?

Vervins returned to staring out at the countryside. The fields and hedges slept under their carpet of snow, and now and again the mist would shift to reveal the distant trees. From below he heard the sounds of the castle, and beyond the walls the distant cawing of ravens and rooks. He came up here to be alone; everywhere he turned there was smirking de Craon, or the French clerk's silent and grim-faced bodyguard Bogo de Baiocis.

'Are you well, sir?'

'I am well,' Vervins answered the guard, 'though freezing cold.'

He closed his eyes. Perhaps they would leave soon, and when they returned to Paris he would keep his silent vow. He would immerse himself in his studies and not be drawn, like the rest, into debates of political theory, or be party to veiled criticism of the power of the Crown, the real reason for his presence here. Vervins was certain that he and the others were being punished for what seemed to be disloyalty to the outrageous claims of Philip of France. They were being taught a cruel lesson to accept that axiom of Roman law, *voluntas principis habet vigorem legis* – 'the will of the prince is force of law'.

A particularly stiffening buffet made Vervins flinch. In Paris he loved to climb the towers of Notre Dame and stare out over the city; this was not the same. He walked carefully along the parapet ledge to the door of the tower.

'I'm sorry, sir,' the guard called out. 'It's locked, it always is.'

Vervins lifted the iron ring but it wouldn't turn. He sighed in exasperation and walked gingerly towards the guard, who rose from his crouched position to allow the Frenchman past to the approaches of the outside steps. Vervins was careful. He paused by the brazier and, taking off one gauntlet, spread his fingers over the spluttering coals. The guard, smiling at him, pulled the brazier closer to the wall to ensure the Frenchman had safe passage. As Vervins went to thank him he felt a sickening blow to the back of his head. He staggered, dropping the cane, and slipped over the edge, his body hurtling down to smash against the cobbles.

The sound of the tocsin alarmed Corbett and brought him and his two companions sprinting into the yard. A small crowd already ringed the fallen Frenchman, who lay sprawled, his head smashed like an egg against the sharp icy cobbles. Sir Edmund and his officers came hurrying up, followed by Father Andrew, his metal-tipped cane clattering against the ground. Soon after, Magister Sanson forced his way through, took one look at his comrade and immediately fell into a dead faint. De Craon arrived, shouting at Sir Edmund that Sanson should immediately be removed to the infirmary as he turned over the still, bruised corpse of Vervins.

Corbett did not interfere. A witness breathlessly informed him how he had seen the Frenchman on the parapet walk staring out over the countryside. He had begun to walk back to go down the outside stairs when he had apparently slipped and fallen. Simon the leech had the corpse placed on a makeshift stretcher and turned the dead man's head between his hands to the left and right, his fingers searching for cuts.

'The skull is fractured.' The leech looked up at Sir Edmund. 'It's like a piece of pottery, cracked and splintered. He must have hit the cobbles, and the force of the fall made him spin like a top. His head bounced like a ball hitting the ground.'

Corbett stared up at the parapet walk high above him. The brazier still glowed there. He recalled de Craon's remark about Vervins' liking to stand there. Had that most sinister of men already decided how another of his retinue should die?

'Where is the sentry, Sir Edmund?'

The Constable beckoned forward a thin, gap-toothed young man, all anxious-eyed and pale-faced, who kept wiping his sweaty hands on a stained jerkin. Corbett took him by the shoulder and led him away from the crowd whilst de Craon and Sir Edmund debated what should be done with the corpse.

'It wasn't my fault, sir.' The soldier broke free of Corbett's strong grip, staring fearfully at Bolingbroke and Ranulf, who had brought their war belts down and were strapping them on. 'I didn't push him, I was half asleep.' He gestured up to the soaring parapet. 'I'm on the dusk walk; I sit and warm my hands over the coals, out comes the Frenchman. I tell him to be careful. I couldn't understand much of his reply but he said he had served on cogs and would often climb the steps of No'dam.'

'Notre Dame,' Corbett corrected him.

'That's right, sir. He said he liked heights, wanted to see the countryside. I told him there wasn't much to see. I could tell he was talking to himself, he seemed worried.'

'And then what happened?'

'He went to the tower door at the end of the parapet walk.'

Corbett followed the man's direction. The tower, like a rounded drum, soared up from the bailey to dominate the curtain wall parapet, a fighting place with arrow slit windows.

He went round the back of the tower and into the narrow recess. He tried the door but it was locked. He came back to the sentry.

'Why is that door locked?'

'Ah!' The soldier half-smiled. 'The Constable is a strict man, he doesn't want people coming up distracting the guards.'

Corbett studied the tower. Built into the curtain wall of the castle, it jutted out slightly from the outside wall so that defenders could use it to assault the flanks of any enemy force trying to breach the wall with a battering ram. The door to the narrow entrance was on the far side of the tower, so anyone could enter unseen from the bailey.

'And the door at the top?' he asked.

'Also locked,' the guard conceded. 'Sir Edmund doesn't like us creeping in there and falling asleep.'

Corbett walked to and fro, staring up at the wall so dizzyingly high above him. The entrance to the tower was so well concealed it would have been easy for anyone to slip through. Yet that was locked, and according to the guard, so was the one at the top, whilst there had been no one on the parapet walk except Vervins and the sentry. Another unfortunate accident? Had the Frenchman slipped? Or had the dizzying height been too much for him? Corbett recognised why Sir Edmund had to be so strict. Doors to towers were often locked and sentries had to be kept in full view; many a castle had fallen because its guards had left their post.

'There's only one thing for it,' Corbett sighed.

'You are going up, sir? You should be careful! Even Sir Edmund only puts on sentry duty those who are used to such heights. I volunteer because it's better than digging latrine pits.'

'What precisely happened,' Ranulf asked, 'when Vervins fell?'

'I've told you and Sir Edmund,' the guard said. 'The Frenchman came up, he leaned against the wall, now and again he turned to greet me. He decided to go down. He tried the door to the tower but it was locked. He came towards me, very careful he was, carrying his cane. He took off his gauntlet to warm his fingers on the coals. I crouched against the wall to give him as much room as possible. I pulled the brazier away, he went to pass, he cried out, then slipped. I saw his body fall, it bounced on the cobbles, rolling, spinning like a top. I best go with you, Sir.'

Preceded by the guard, and ignoring Sir Edmund's shouts, Corbett and Ranulf gingerly climbed the steps, which were carefully sanded against the slippery ice. Corbett tried to remain calm and not look down, concentrating on the soldier in front. When they reached the top, the coals in the small brazier had turned a dusty grey, and the wind was strong and cutting. Corbett grasped the rope which ran the length of this outer wall. He edged along and turned, staring out over the battlements at the winter countryside. He understood why a man like Vervins would come here, away from the noise, smells and bustle of the castle; an opportunity to drink in the fresh air, and if the guard was right, Vervins was a man used to such heights. Edward, the King, was similar. On one occasion he had actually held a council meeting on the top of a tower, much to the horror of some of his advisers. Gripping the guide rope, Corbett carefully turned and stared down into the castle yard. A dizzyingly sickening drop which made his stomach clench in fear.

'Best not look down, sir,' the guard warned.

Corbett walked carefully along the parapet. From below it looked narrow, but it was in fact a broad thoroughfare, at least two yards wide. It stretched from the steps which bisected it to the tower at the far end and, more importantly, the door to the tower which Vervins had tried to open. Corbett gingerly walked towards this door. Of stout oak, it was strengthened with a thick tarry substance as protection against the weather, and reinforced with rusty iron studs. He grasped the cold ring; it held firm, so he walked back carefully. Ranulf had flattened himself against one of the crenellations. The guard squatted where Vervins had suffered his fatal fall.

'He was here, just where you are standing, sir, then he fell away.'

'And where were you?'

'As I am now, sir.'

Corbett crouched down and felt the parapet walk, sifting the grit and sand between his fingers. There was no ice here, no crack or crumbling which could explain Vervins' accident. He looked back towards the door. Something he'd glimpsed there intrigued him.

'So, Vervins . . .' Corbett quickly pulled up his cowl as a gust of freezing wind stung his face and made his eyes water. 'So, Vervins had his back to the tower, as did you. He was holding his cane?'

'Suddenly he gives a cry, sir, and falls to his death.'

Corbett returned to the tower, turning a deaf ear to Ranulf, who was already regretting following his master up to this soaring, freezing parapet wall. He examined the door. He'd noticed the spyhole just above eye level, a square of wood about a foot across on stiff leather hinges. He pushed at this but it held firm. He had seen the type before, a squint which could be opened from the inside so that the guard could see who demanded entrance, or who was walking along the parapet walk.

'It can only be opened from inside, sir. Two pegs keep it in place, rather stiff it is,' the guard called out.

Corbett thanked him and, followed by a grateful Ranulf, walked down the steps into the castle yard. Vervins' body had been removed. Sir Edmund, in his cloak, was in deep conversation with the leech.

'Another accident, Sir Hugh?' Corbett could tell from the Constable's eyes that something was wrong.

'You don't believe it was an accident, do you?' Corbett replied.

Sir Edmund shook his head, his lips twisted in a bitter grimace.

'I'd like to say, Sir Hugh,' he edged closer to Corbett, 'that an old man missed his footing, but de Craon tells me Vervins was used to such heights, in fact he revelled in them, while my soldiers tell me it was quite common for him to climb up on to the walls. He seemed to like it. You've been up there; the parapet walk is broad, firm and sanded.'

Corbett turned to the leech.

'Did you find any other wound?' he asked him.

'Nothing,' the man replied. 'His head is a maze of cracks, splinters, like a dropped pot.'

'But no arrow or dagger mark?'

'No,' the leech protested. 'Nothing like that! He could have been struck by a pole, the flat of a sword, or even a rock hurled by someone. Yet the guard reported nothing wrong. All I can say,' the leech concluded, 'is that the Frenchman's skull is a mass of bruises and cracks.'

'But all of them could have been the result of the fall, not the cause,' Corbett added.

'Exactly, sir. Now, I'm freezing and I have another corpse to strip.' The leech hurried off. Corbett pointed to the tower door.

'I have the keys,' the Constable declared. 'As the guard has probably told you, I keep both doors firmly locked. There's only one set.'

Sir Edmund called for a steward to bring the keys and a short while later the man came hurrying up, a large jangling ring in his hand. At Corbett's bidding he unlocked the tower door. Corbett, followed by Sir Edmund, Bolingbroke and Ranulf, stepped into the musty darkness. It seemed even colder inside than out. The Constable took a tinder from the ledge, lit a sconce torch and carefully led them up the steps, Corbett walking just behind him. In the poor light he could detect nothing amiss. One hand gripping the guide rope, they passed stairwells leading to deserted rooms and eventually reached the small passageway at the top, where they all stopped, gasping. Sir Edmund fitted the torch into one of the clasps on the wall, and the flame, catching the draughts, flared up, illuminating the door. Corbett noticed how this door was not only locked but kept secure by clasps at top and bottom. He stared down at the hard paved stone; again, there was nothing out of place. He could see the faint glimpse of light around the squint hole, and he released the pegs, caught hold of the leather strap and pulled down the squint to provide a clear view of the parapet walk.

'Sir Edmund, if you could?' Corbett gestured for the rest to stand back, whilst he adopted the stance of a man armed with a crossbow.

'What are you thinking, Sir Hugh?'

'I have no evidence,' Corbett gazed through the gap, 'but this squint folds away quietly. The hinges are leather, I loosened it with barely a sound. Is it possible that someone, armed with a crossbow and a blunted bolt, was watching Vervins from here? It would be easy to hit a man on the back of his head. Ranulf, wouldn't you agree?' He stepped aside as his henchman also pretended to be a crossbowman.

'An easy target.' Ranulf closed the squint then opened it again; the wood came away without a sound.

'It's possible,' Corbett declared, 'for the killer to have been here. Every so often he could open that slat and glimpse where Vervins was. Hiding behind this door, he would hear the Frenchman walking up and down.'

'But that's impossible!' the Constable protested. 'The door at the bottom is locked, there is only one key and my steward would never give it up, not even to you, Sir Hugh, without my permission.'

Corbett absentmindedly agreed. He thanked Sir Edmund and asked him to keep the bottom door open so that he could continue his investigation.

'Go down into the yard,' he told Bolingbroke. 'Search the cobbles, see if you can find anything suspicious.'

'But they are encrusted with mud,' Bolingbroke replied. 'Sir Hugh, it would be like looking for a needle in a haystack.'

'Look anyway, you may be fortunate.' Corbett returned to examine the squint, opening and shutting the wooden slat. He asked Ranulf to go down and order the guard to resume his watch on the parapet wall, and when he did so, Corbett began to play with the squint, opening and shutting it, shouting at the guard to tell him if he noticed anything amiss. After a while the soldier came to the door, pushing his face up against the gap.

'Sir Hugh,' he called out, 'I'm hardly aware of you being there. You could open and shut the squint and I would hardly notice. The door lies in a shadowy recess away from the light.'

Corbett thanked him, closed the slat and, crouching down, sat in the corner of the stairwell, blowing on his fingers. Ranulf, leaning against the wall, kicked the toe of his boot against the brickwork.

'Sir Hugh, you don't believe the assassin came up here?'

'I will tell you what I believe, Ranulf: we are lost in a forest where the mist hangs heavy and the trees cluster thick, and when they thin, it is only to expose some marsh or morass. I don't believe these deaths were accidental, I don't believe Destaples died of a seizure or Louis slipped on a sharp stairwell. Why should Monsieur Vervins, so used to heights, who came up on the parapet walk to relax and enjoy himself, a man who was very careful, why should such a man cry out and fall to his death? Very clever, mind you.' Corbett bit his lip in anger. 'Vervins' head has more bruises than he has hair and I am certain de Craon will assure Sir Edmund it wasn't his fault, that Vervins shouldn't have been up on the castle walls on an icy day.' He leaned across, plucking at Ranulf's cloak. 'Something is amiss, I don't know what. De Craon is secretly laughing at us.'

'If we tell him what we've found,' Ranulf declared, 'he will laugh even harder. One thing, Master, he cannot blame any of us for Vervins's death; we were with you in your chamber when he fell.'

'Aye,' Corbett retorted, 'but I wonder where Monsier de Craon and that silent retainer of his were?'

'They can't have been here.' Ranulf helped Corbett to his feet. 'The tower door was locked, you keep forgetting that.'

He and Corbett returned to the yard, where Bolingbroke was still sifting with his boot amongst the straw, dirt and ice. 'There's nothing here,' he grumbled, 'nothing at all.' He rubbed his hands together, blowing on his fingers.

'Sir Hugh, Sir Hugh!' The Constable came running across and handed Corbett a small scroll. 'Mother Feyner's corpse was stripped; we found this in the pocket of her gown.'

Corbett unrolled the parchment, a neatly cut rectangle, on it inscribed a few lines. The hand was clerkly, the words English: *And enough bread to fill the largest stomach, and damsons which a Pope could eat before singing his dawn Mass.*

'In God's name,' Corbett muttered, 'what on earth is this?' He handed it to Ranulf, who repeated the words loudly.

'It wasn't written by us, Sir Edmund,' Ranulf explained.

'I've shown it to de Craon, he claims to have no knowledge of it either. Apparently Mistress Feyner may have been taking it down to the Tavern in the Forest. It looks as if someone was trying to buy food from Master Reginald, but why so flowery?'

Corbett plucked the manuscript out of Ranulf's fingers and read it again. He felt a prickle of fear; he'd read enough ciphers to detect a secret message.

'We also found two freshly minted coins,' Sir Edmund replied. 'I can only deduce that Mistress Feyner was paid to take that parchment to Master Reginald, but the message is strange enough. I understand the reference to bread, but damsons in December?'

Corbett folded the parchment up and slipped it into his purse. 'And Vervins?' he asked.

Sir Edmund sighed in exasperation. 'The victim of an unfortunate fall. What more can be said?'

Corbett and the two clerks returned to his chamber. Chanson had built up the fire. For a while they discussed Vervins' death and the strange piece of parchment Sir Edmund had found. The day wore on. Corbett returned to his studies; at least he had solved one mystery and had shared it with his colleagues just before the tocsin sounded.

'Is that really why the King has sent us here?' Chanson had followed the proceedings carefully; he now sat opposite Corbett, who was comparing the two manuscripts on his lap.

'In the *Opus Tertium*,' Corbett explained, 'Friar Roger makes a very strange confession. Listen: "During the last twenty years I have worked hard in the pursuit of wisdom".' Corbett looked up. 'Then he goes on, "I have spent more than two thousand pounds on secret books and various experiments." Now this is what's written in the French copy of the *Opus Tertium*. However,' Corbett was aware how silent the chamber had fallen; Ranulf and Bolingbroke walked over, 'as I was about to explain fully, before Vervins' fall, in our noble King's version, Friar Roger claims it was only twenty pounds.' Ranulf whistled under his breath.

'Which is correct?' Bolingbroke asked

'The French version, it must be. Our King has tried to interfere with the manuscript. He's rubbed out two of the noughts.'

'Are you sure it's not French pounds?' Bolingbroke demanded. 'The *livre tournis* is only a quarter of the value of sterling.'

'No, no.' Corbett shook his head. 'Friar Roger was English, he's talking of two thousand pounds, a King's ransom. Let me give you an example, Ranulf. Remember when you became a Clerk of the Green Wax, you were instructed on the workings of the Exchequer. You do recall the assignment given to you?'

'Yes, yes,' Ranulf agreed. 'we were told to remember certain figures, it was a form of scrutiny.'

'In mine,' Corbett declared, 'many years ago, when I was

examined before the great Burnell, I was asked to memorize the income of the Crown at the beginning of our King's grandfather's reign. If I recall correctly, the entire Crown revenue in 1216 was about thirty thousand pounds; that's about the same time Friar Roger was growing up. Now we know that Friar Roger came from fairly poor people at Ilchester just across the Dorset border.' Corbett paused. 'Ilchester,' he muttered, 'it's only a day's journey from here. Isn't that strange? Yes, yes,' he continued talking to himself, staring at the dancing candle flame, 'very strange indeed, that the King should send us here, not far from where Friar Roger was born.'

'Sir Hugh?' Ranulf passed a hand in front of his master's face. 'Sir Hugh, what are you muttering about?'

'I'm not muttering, I'm just speculating why Edward the King is so keen on Friar Roger; why he wants the *Secretus Secretorum* translated. Here we have a Franciscan, vowed to poverty, declaring he has spent an amount equivalent to almost one fifteenth of the entire Crown revenue on the pursuit of knowledge. Friar Roger, of low to middling birth, a scholar and a Franciscan! Where did he get such money? How on earth could he spend two thousand pounds?'

'He's lying,' Bolingbroke declared. 'He must be.'

'Why should he lie?' Corbett asked. 'Shall I tell you something, William, I think Friar Roger made a mistake, he let something slip, and our King fastened on this. To disguise it, even from us, the King tried to change the text. He's the only person who's recently handled this manuscript,' Corbett added grimly. 'Look,' he picked up the manuscript, 'it's obvious, indeed quite clumsy. Edward has done his best to reduce that amount. I've read it a number of times. First I dismissed it as a mark on the page. It was only when I borrowed Crotoy's version that I realized what our wily royal master intends. Edward has spent treasure in his war against the Scots. He believes Friar Roger was an alchemist able to change base metal into gold. He also believes the *Secretus Secretorum* will demonstrate how he achieved this.'

'I don't believe this.' Bolingbroke sat down on the stool. 'I don't believe in alchemy and the philosopher's stone. And if our King does, why should he want to share such knowledge with the French?'

'Ah.' Corbett lifted his head and smiled. 'What you don't know, William, is that if the French are being cunning, so is our King. I am under strict instructions from Edward to compare notes with the French, to learn everything they know. I'm like a thresher in a barn. I have to separate the wheat from the chaff but make sure only the former is gathered by the King of England.' He laughed. 'I'm sure de Craon has received similar instruction.'

He tapped the bound manuscript. 'I will confront the King with what I know, I'll tell him not to be so suspicious. If he had told me this in the first place a great deal of hardship might have been avoided.'

'Can we translate the *Secretus*?' Ranulf asked

'Perhaps. We have discussed every single type of cipher, but there is one left, a secret language.' Corbett paused to collect his thoughts. 'Friar Roger wrote his *Secretus Secretorum* in Latin. He used that language as the basis to develop his own secret tongue, what clerks call "pig Latin" or "dog Latin". Let me explain. To all words beginning with a vowel, a e, i, o, u, you merely add the syllable "whey", so the word for is, *est*, becomes *estwhey*, the word for love, *amor*, becomes *amorwhey*. It is simple enough.' Corbett sat on the writing stool as the others gathered around. 'Any word which begins with a consonant,' he winked at Chanson, 'that is, a letter which is not a vowel, the first letter is moved to the end of the word and the syllable "ay" is added at the beginning. So, in Latin, the word for are, *sunt*, becomes *ayunts*. Now,' Corbett gestured, 'this is a very simple version; you can change the rules to suit yourself, but as long as you know what the secret word is, in this case "whey" or "ay", then any cipher becomes easy to translate.' He gestured at the *Secretus Secretorum*. 'Friar Roger based his secret language on that principle. If we could only find out what the key was, then the manuscript might give up its secrets and the King may have his treasure.' He threw his quill down. 'But it's easier said than done.'

Corbett went and lay on the bed while Ranulf and Bolingbroke began a heated discussion about what he had told them. He stretched out, half listening to Chanson, who, bored with the chatter of clerks, had returned to mending a bit which, he claimed, could be made more comfortable for the horse's mouth. Corbett stared up at the coloured tester above the bed. He didn't know whether to be angry or laugh at the King's considerable deceit, but that was Edward, suspicious and wary, a man who truly believed, though for different reasons than the Good Lord intended, that the right hand should not know what the left hand was doing.

Where had this all begun? Corbett reflected. Until late summer Edward had been engaged in trying to break the Treaty of Paris and escape the moral and legal obligation of marrying off the Prince of Wales to Philip's only daughter Isabella. The King had worried away at this as a mastiff would a piece of meat, giving Corbett no peace. The Keeper of the Secret Seal had, in the hot months of July and August, moved to the Tower as more and more reports flooded in from his spies in France, Gascony and Flanders. Edward had prayed, lighting great tapers in front of his favourite saints, that Corbett's spies would find some pretext for the English to repudiate the Treaty of Paris and all it entailed. Were Philip's troops massing on the Gascony border? Would Philip hand over the disputed castle of Mauleon? Would the French pay the dowry payments? Would the French insist that the Prince of Wales be sent to Paris for a betrothal ceremony? Were French ships beginning to gather in the Channel ports? Corbett had become exasperated with the King's constant demands for information. In the end, all he could prove was that Philip was as cunning and wily as Edward. In September there had been a respite. The King had travelled to the royal palace of Woodstock, just outside Oxford, and returned full of praise for the writings of Friar Roger Bacon. The libraries of the Halls of Oxford, Cambridge and elsewhere were ransacked as the King collected the dead Franciscan's books. He had become fascinated with the *Secretus Secretorum* and indulged in a royal rage when he learnt that the University of the Sorbonne in Paris owned a similar copy.

'Yes,' Corbett muttered, 'that's when the dance began.'

'Sir Hugh?'

'Nothing, Ranulf, I'm just talking to myself.' Corbett returned to his reflections. Edward had dispatched the most cloying letters to his 'sweet cousin' in Paris, asking if it would be possible for the French Crown to loan him their copy of the *Secretus Secretorum*. Philip, of course, had politely refused.

Nevertheless, the French King's curiosity had been piqued. Corbett didn't know whether Philip had been motivated by his arch-rival's interest or had been following a similar vein himself. Edward, of course, became deeply suspicious, and when his clerks, including Corbett, were unable to translate the cipher used in the *Secretus Secretorum*, the English King had given way to even darker suspicions. Was his copy of the book truly valid? Corbett had been given strict instructions to establish the truth.

He'd travelled to Paris himself to instruct Ufford and Bolingbroke. They had discovered how the French had already copied the *Secretus Secretorum*. Corbett had told them to ignore all other work but to steal or buy, by any means possible, the French version. Ufford and Bolingbroke had cast about, searching like good hunting dogs for a track to follow. They had been delighted when approached by someone in the University only too willing to sell them valuable information. They had been invited to Magister Thibault's revelry and everything should have gone according to plan. They had hired the Roi des Clefs, the King of Keys, and, for all Corbett knew, even the young courtesan who had kept Magister Thibault amused, but then something had gone wrong. Thibault had disturbed them and been killed whilst Ufford and Bolingbroke had to flee for their lives. Corbett recalled the gruesome details about the Roi des Clefs: how his hand had been so badly injured that Ufford had had no choice but to cut his throat. A grisly death, Corbett reflected, for a man who had boasted that no lock could withstand his secret keys and devices. Ufford, too, had been killed, Bolingbroke narrowly escaping with his life.

Officially, Edward of England had no knowledge of such dark deeds, so the cloying letters between him and 'his sweet cousin of France' had continued apace. Philip had been most amenable to sending a delegation to England, suggesting that, with the hardship of winter, the meeting should be in some secure place on the south coast, away from the hustle and bustle of London, but close enough to Dover. Edward had rubbed his hands in glee and immediately sent instruction that Sir Edmund prepare Corfe Castle. Now they were here. The French hoped they would learn from the English, whilst Edward prayed that, during these discussions, Corbett would stumble on the cipher which would translate the *Secretus Secretorum* and, perhaps, reveal the true reason for Friar Roger's wealth, not to mention other marvellous secrets. Ranulf had kept his own counsel but Bolingbroke had also advised both the King and Corbett that Philip had other designs. The French King was resented by many of the professors and scholars of the Sorbonne University, who were alarmed at the growing power of the French Crown and the outrageous theories of royal lawyers like Pierre Dubois. Bolingbroke had been proved right. Corbett had no proof, but he strongly believed that all three deaths which had occurred here were highly suspicious. Philip was not only getting rid of opponents but cruelly warning others at the University that they faced a similar fate. Like Pilate he could wash his hands, claim the deaths were accidental and, if suspicions were aroused, blame the insidious English.

What else was there? Corbett tried to ignore the bloody work of Mistress Feyner. He wondered what other news the outlaws had to tell him. He recalled Sir Edmund's worries about the fleet of Flemish pirates so active in the Narrow Seas. What was the loose thread here? Corbett recalled Destaples sprawled on his bed; poor Louis lying in a puddle of his own blood, neck all twisted; Vervins, dropping like a stone from the parapet wall. Were they all accidents? Corbett closed his eyes. He returned to the problem of the three deaths of intelligent, astute men who had no illusions about their royal master and took every precaution to keep themselves safe. They would keep well away from de Craon and yet, if it was murder, they had been killed by someone who could go through locked doors to commit such dreadful acts.

'Sir Hugh?' Corbett opened his eyes; the castle bell was tolling loudly. 'Sir Hugh, it is growing dark.' Ranulf leaned over him. 'We are going to the Hall of Angels.'

'To meet the Lady Constance?' Corbett teased.

Ranulf turned away. Corbett heard them leave, closing the door behind them. He got up, walked across to the table and sifted through the scraps of parchment Bolingbroke and Ranulf had used. They had, apparently, been searching for the ciphers Friar Roger had employed in constructing his pig or dog Latin. Corbett picked up the *Opus Tertium*, leafing through the pages, then turned to the front of the book where Crotoy had written

John, Chapter I, verse 6–7. He studied this curiously. What did Louis mean? Going across to his psalter, he leafed through its pages and found the first chapter of John's Gospel, 'In the beginning was the Word, the Word was with God and the Word was God.' He then followed the verses down to 6 and 7: 'A man came, sent by God, his name was John, he was not the Light but came as a witness to the light.'

Corbett closed the psalter and put it back on the table. Searching amongst the manuscripts, he found his copy of Friar Roger's *Opus Maius*. He had read this closely before leaving Westminster and the name John pricked a memory. He found the reference in Chapter Ten. Bacon had dedicated this *Opus Maius* to Pope Clement IV and sent it to the supreme Pontiff with a young man whom the friar had taught for the previous five or six years. Corbett now read this reference carefully. John was apparently no more than twenty years old at the time. Friar Roger described him as a brilliant pupil, an outstanding scholar, to whom he had entrusted secret knowledge. He had written, 'Any scholar might listen with profit to this boy. No one is so learned, in many ways this boy is indispensable.' And the even more startling claim, 'He excels even me, old man that I am.'

Corbett closed the book.

'Louis, Louis,' he whispered, 'what did you mean by this?'

He stood by the fire, watching the white ash break and crumble under the heat. Crotoy had been a master of logic; he had taught Corbett how there were often different paths to the same conclusion. Had Crotoy realized that the cipher couldn't be broken? But was there another way of resolving the mystery, of discovering who this scholar John was? Was he still alive, sheltering in England or France?

Corbett put on his boots and grabbed his cloak. He would join the rest in the Hall of Angels. As he doused the candles, he recalled that mysterious scrap of parchment found on Mistress Feyner. That was something he had forgotten, yet something he should probe. Why had she been carrying such a message? Who was it from? What did it mean? *And enough bread to fill the largest stomach, and damsons which a Pope could eat before singing his dawn mass.* What was the French for belly? *Ventre?* Corbett placed the grille in front of the fire. The message hadn't been written by him or any of his retinue. It was a mystery to Sir Edmund, so it must have been written by de Craon. What further mayhem was he plotting?

I have spent more than £2000 on secret books and various experiments and languages of instruments and mathematical tables.

Roger Bacon, *Opus Tertium*

Chapter 11

Horehound the outlaw was ready for the King's peace. He was cold, hungry and wished to be free of the malevolent force of the forest. He had lived too long among the trees to be worried about sprites and elves. Father Matthew had once talked of mysterious beings, the 'Lords of the Air'. Horehound truly believed in these beings he could not see but who crouched in the branches and stared maliciously down at him, who were responsible for the freezing darkness, the tripping undergrowth and the lack of any game to fill his belly and warm his blood. They hid behind that ominous wall of silence and peered out at him, rejoicing in his many hardships. Horehound was truly tired. He wanted to leave the cave and had convinced the rest of his coven to follow him. All were in agreement; even Hemlock had refused to go back and now hoped to be pardoned. Horehound had fixed the time with the red-haired King's man. Within two days he would be warming his toes in front of the castle fire.

Horehound had cleared the caves, dug up his few paltry coins, placed crude wooden crosses over his dead and pieces of evergreen on poor Foxglove's grave. He stood at the fire before the cave mouth and burnt their few pathetic belongings, items they would not need or could not take.

'We shall leave soon,' he called out over his shoulder. They planned to move to St Peter's, where they would wait for the red-haired one to bring more food and provender. Perhaps they could shelter in the cemetery, take sanctuary in God's Acre, perhaps even the church itself? Smoke from the fire billowed up as Horehound planned and plotted. He was still frightened of Father Matthew and his strange powders, but that was the priest's business.

'Do you think he'll help us?' Milkwort sidled up to Horehound.

'I hope so,' Horehound replied.

'He didn't last time.'

'That was because he was ill.'

'What happens if he is still ill?'

'Oh shut up!' Horehound snarled.

He'd plucked up courage to approach the priest but Father Matthew had just opened the casement window and shouted down that there was nothing he could do. Reginald the taverner was just as unwelcoming. He had met Horehound out near the yard gate and, red-faced, drove them away with curses. Horehound was now suspicious; he had listened very carefully to what Hemlock had told him about strangers in the forest. He sighed; but that was the forest, ever treacherous, ever dangerous.

'We'll go now. We must thank those who have helped us.'

They let the fire burn down and left the glade in single file, a dozen shrouded figures, men and women who had taken a vow to leave the forest for good. Horehound led the way through what he now called the Meadows of Hell, past strangely twisted trees with their branches stripped, all his secret signs and marks concealed by that freezing whiteness. Sometimes the trees give way to small clearings. Horehound reckoned he was on a line north of the church, castle and tavern, deep enough within the trees for safety yet not far from help. The outlaw trotted on, trying to ignore the cold seeping through his battered boots and the roughly hewn arbalest, slung across his back, knocking his shoulder. He clutched the knife in the rope around his waist, plodding carefully, wary of the silence. Here and there were the prints of some animals. Horehound hated the snow; in spring and summer you could always tell if someone had passed, but the snow kept falling, covering tracks and prints, making life even more difficult. An owl, deep in the trees, hooted mournfully. Horehound paused. Wasn't that an evil omen? True, the day was dying but it was not yet dark, so why should an owl be hunting?

They entered the glade where Waldus the charcoal burner's wattle and daub hut stood protected behind its weathered picket fence. Horehound paused. Usually the smell of wood smoke would be strong and there would be a glint of light between the shutters, but all lay silent, cold and black. Horehound climbed over the fence, treading carefully across the sparse vegetable patch. The door hung loose with no one inside. Horehound grew afraid; he wanted to be away from here. Waldus was gone. Horehound felt a shiver of unease. If the charcoal burner went into the forest, surely his flaxen-haired wife would stay?

They continued on past the charcoal burner's pit. On the edge of the glade something hung tangled from a bramble bush. Horehound picked this up. It was a rabbit skin, so fresh the blood was still glistening. It had been thrown there like a piece of rubbish. Now who would do that? Rabbits were scarce and precious enough. Who was skilled enough to trap this animal and throw away its skin? Horehound crouched down; he washed the skin in the snow, folded it neatly and put it in his bag. The rest watched carefully.

'Why throw away a good rabbit skin?' Hemlock asked. 'Even Sir Edmund would use it, and he is a travelled man. I was a soldier once in the castle.' Hemlock couldn't resist the opportunity to boast. 'Lady Catherine said that when she was in Paris, I don't know where that is, but it's a great city, even ladies' robes are fringed with rabbit fur.'

'Never mind that!' Ratsbayne, a small, furtive-faced man, thrust himself forward. 'I smell wood smoke.' Ratsbayne sniffed at the breeze with his pointed nose. 'Food!' he moaned in pleasure.

'It must be Waldus.' Horehound trusted Ratsbayne's acute sense of smell. They hurried along the narrow lane which snaked through the trees. Horehound glimpsed a glow of fire in the distance. Keeping to the line of trees, he approached the edge of the clearing and stared across the snow-covered glade. A fire crackled in the centre just where the ground rose before falling away the other side. He glimpsed the hunched figure of Waldus, but where was his woman, the flaxen-haired one? Why was he just sitting there? Milkwort pushed his way forward.

'I'm afeared,' he hissed. 'Ratsbayne believes we are being followed but he's always nervous. What's wrong with Waldus?'

Horehound strode across, kicking up flurries of snow. Waldus sat slumped, and when Horehound touched his shoulder he toppled on to his side, revealing dead eyes, gaping mouth and that awful cut to his throat from which the blood had slopped out to drench his legs and jerkin. Horehound looked down the rise. More blood stained the snow. He glimpsed some bracken tied up in a bundle. A hand was sticking out of it, and Horehound, terrified, recognized a wisp of flaxen hair. Gibbering with fear, he stared around, the dying light on the snow confusing him. The rest of the group hurried up. Horehound instinctively knew this was a mistake. A movement between the trees, the crackle of bracken, alerted the rest. Dark shapes were emerging. What new horror was this?

Horehound drew his knife, whilst trying to loop off his arbalest, but he was shaking, his fingers sweat soaked. All around the glade echoed those ominous sounds, harsh clicks and the twang of bows. Horehound was hit just above the chest; he dropped like a stone as the rest of his followers died around him.

Corbett felt disgruntled when he awoke. The fire had burnt down and Ranulf and Bolingbroke had not returned. He crossed to the lavarium and splashed water over his face, and for a while leaned against the mantle drying himself. He thought about Lady Maeve and his children; he wondered what they would be doing and quietly wished he was with them. Corbett recognized his own dark mood, so he opened the straps of his saddle bag, took out a small psalter of hymns and songs which he had copied down, and for a while stood in front of the fire singing softly the '*Felte viri*', a lament on the death of William the Conqueror, followed by three verses of '*Iam dulcis amica*'. He felt better afterwards but then recalled singing that second carol with Louis Crotoy in the porch of St Mary's church in Oxford. He thought of his old friend's cold, stiffening corpse, and this provoked him into action. He wanted to go back to the Jerusalem Tower; there was something about that death which puzzled him. He picked up his cloak, swung it about him and paused.

'Old friend,' he whispered, 'are you still teaching me?' That was it! He recalled Crotoy's corpse, the heavy cloak which may have made him trip. 'Nonsense!' he whispered at the candle flame. Louis was old and cold and the weather outside was freezing.

Corbett rubbed his hands together and absentmindedly put on his war belt. He recalled the times he had seen Louis around the castle, that heavy cloak around his shoulders; he wouldn't have carried it, he would have put it on! Why wait until you are in the freezing cold, especially if you are leaving a warm chamber?

Corbett blessed himself, whispering the *Requiem* for Louis' soul, and hurried down into the yard. He carefully crossed the cobbles, took a sconce torch from its holder, reached the Jerusalem Tower and climbed the steps into the cold ante-chamber. The door still hung open. Corbett went up carefully into the musty darkness. He found what he had expected: all of Louis' books and manuscripts had been cleared away, de Craon would have seen to that, but his old friend's personal possessions were piled neatly on the bed. Corbett sifted through these, picked up the dead man's boot and felt inside. He smiled as he gripped the loose heel and pulled it out. Taking it over to the far side of the chamber, where he'd placed the sconce torch in a bracket, he examined both heel and boot carefully. Hiding them beneath his cloak, he went back into the yard and stopped a servant.

'You have a shoemaker here, a cobbler?'

'Oh yes, sir, Master Luke, and a very good one too!' the man chatted back. 'Sir Edmund persuaded him to come from Dover—'

'Good,' Corbett interrupted. 'Then seek him out and tell him to come to my chamber in the Lantern Tower, I need his skill.' He thrust a coin into the man's hand.

A short while later, as he placed a log on the fire, there was a rap on the door. A thin, wiry man came in, almost hidden by the leather apron he wore, face all shaven, head as bald as a pigeon's egg.

'Ah! Master Luke.' Corbett wiped his hands on his jerkin and ushered the man to a stool. 'I want you to look at this.'

219

He handed him the boot and loose heel. The shoemaker asked for a candle to be brought across whilst he studied both of these, muttering under his breath, running his finger along the edge of the heel.

'Anything strange, Master Luke?'

'Oh yes, oh yes.' The man blinked, his eyes watering from the cold. 'Oh dear, yes! You see, sir, this is a good Spanish boot, genuine red leather, Cordova, with a fur lining within, work of a craftsman it is, though not English.'

'What's wrong?' Corbett asked, holding up a silver coin between his fingers.

'What's wrong? Why, sir,' the man laughed nervously, 'this heel is attached to the boot by a very powerful glue, as powerful as any stitching.'

'So it wouldn't work loose easily?'

'Oh no, sir, that's why I was examining the edge. You see, sir?' The shoesmith held up the heel, pointing to the rim. Corbett looked mystified, so Master Luke picked up the boot, returned the heel to its original position and thrust it in front of Corbett's eyes. 'Now can you see it?'

Corbett held the heel fast; now he could see that there was a small dent between heel and boot.

'It didn't break off,' he murmured. 'It was prised off, wasn't it? Someone thrust a dagger between heel and boot to force it loose.'

'Very good, sir. A foul trick. There's other signs, sir. You can see where the blade cut through the gum, and the outer edge of the heel is slightly hacked.'

Corbett examined this and could only agree. He gave Master Luke the coin and thanked him. Once the shoesmith had left, he sat and stared down at the boot.

'So what do we have here, eh, old friend?' Corbett talked as if Crotoy occupied the stool opposite. 'You didn't leave your chamber and trip. Someone broke your neck, threw your body down those steep steps, draped the cloak over your arm to make it look like you tripped and then loosened the heel on your boot. But how?' He closed his eyes, rocking backwards and forwards. Someone could have been with Louis in his chamber, but he was certain that, when the corpse was found, the key to the outer door was still in the dead man's wallet. How could that be?

Corbett rose, capped the candles, put the metal grille in front of the fire, locked his chamber and went back to the yard. He returned Crotoy's boots to the chamber in the tower and went across to the servants' quarters, where he asked to see Master Simon the leech. He found him in one of the stables, sitting on a stool cradling a blackjack of ale and deep in fierce argument with one of the stable boys over a sick horse. Corbett crouched beside him. The leech had apparently drunk deep and well; he gazed bleary-eyed at the Keeper of the King's Secret Seal.

'Another death?' he mumbled.

'No, an old death.' Corbett smiled. 'The Frenchman, Destaples?'

'What about him?'

'He had a weak heart.'

'That's true, no wonder he had a seizure.'

'Is it possible,' Corbett asked, 'to give such a man a potion, a herb, let's say at the ninth hour, the effect of which would only become apparent at the eleventh?'

The leech pulled a face. 'Of course it is. I can't tell you how, but mixed with wine, which already quickens the blood and excites the humours, such an effect is possible.'

'Thank you,' Corbett tapped the blackjack, 'and be careful what you drink!'

Next he went to the kitchens, where he begged the cooks for a bowl of hot broth, some fresh bread and a tankard of ale. He could hear the laughter and talk in the hall beyond but decided not to go there. His mind was all awhirl, images came and went; it was like leafing through a psalter where the small illuminated pictures catch your eye. He thought of Louis swinging his cloak about him, the French scholars' contempt for de Craon, Destaples eating so carefully at the banquet, Vervins falling like a stricken bird from the soaring walls of the castle.

Corbett returned to his own chamber, where he stripped, put on his nightshift and, for a while, knelt by his bed trying to clear his mind. Chanson came lumbering up, almost falling through the door.

'I've drunk far too much,' he confessed. Corbett stayed kneeling.

'Do you want to join me in prayer, Chanson?' Corbett asked.

'No, no, Ranulf is showing everyone how to cheat. I bring messages from the Frenchman; he says time is passing, tomorrow they wish to start early. He says he is ready to leave.'

'Oh, I'm sure he is.' Corbett crossed himself. 'Tell Monsieur de Craon I will meet him in the solar just after dawn. Oh, and tell Ranulf and William I want them clear-headed.'

The groom left and Corbett climbed into bed. For a while he lay humming in the darkness, the tune of the scholar song, *'Mache, bene, venies'*. He tried to recall all the words to soothe his mind, and slipped into sleep.

When he awoke, the fire had burnt down and the capped candle was gutted. Corbett was reluctant to leave the warmth but eventually braved the icy cold, wrapping a cloak around him and going down into the yard to beg for some hot water so he could shave and wash. A servant came up to build the fire and the brazier. Corbett dressed in the royal colours, blue, red and gold, carefully putting on the Chancery rings as he wondered what the day would bring. He was not surprised to find de Craon and Sanson waiting for him in the solar, fresh and alert, though Ranulf and Bolingbroke, who joined them later, looked rather haggard and heavy-eyed. They sat at a small side table eating bowls of hot oatmeal in which honey and nutmeg had been mixed.

De Craon was polite but distant. Now and again he would turn to whisper something to his sombre-faced man-at-arms. Corbett, however, watched Sanson. The French scholar appeared more relaxed, seemingly untroubled by the death of his comrades, and although they hid it well, Corbett could see that Sanson was de Craon's man, body and soul. I wonder, he thought, smiling across at Sanson, if you were the spy who gave that information to Ufford then lured him to his death. Well, we shall see, we shall see.

They gathered around the great polished walnut table. Corbett sent Ranulf back to retrieve certain manuscripts, whilst Bolingbroke laid out the writing trays with their ink horns, quills, pumice stones and small rolls of vellum.

'I think I may have a solution,' Corbett declared.

De Craon, on the other side of the table, raised his eyebrows in surprise, then turned to Sir Edmund, asking if the Catherine wheel of candles could be lowered to provide more light. Corbett described his theory of how Friar Roger must have used what he termed dog or pig Latin to hide his secrets, and when he had finished de Craon sat, fingers to his mouth, staring hard-eyed back.

'Well, Pierre.' He turned to Sanson. 'What would your reply to that be?'

'Sir Hugh is correct.' Sanson cleared his throat, his high-pitched voice cutting through the silence. 'I too,' he smiled smugly, his fat oily face creasing into a smile, 'reached a similar conclusion.'

He lifted his hands, snapped his fingers, and de Craon's man-at-arms brought across his copy of the *Secretus Secretorum* whilst Bolingbroke placed the English version in front of Corbett. At first the niceties were observed, but Corbett was soon drawn into fierce debate about which secret cipher Friar Roger might have used. He studied the manuscript and began to write down certain phrases which the Franciscan might have used to disguise his true meaning. Sanson countered with alternative explanations. Corbett deliberately increased the pace, scribbling down notes and passing them across the table, eagerly waiting for Sanson's reply. The hours passed. Outside the window day broke; the steward came in to say that the sky was clear, perhaps there would be no more snow, and did Sir Edmund's guests require some food? Both parties refused. Corbett kept concentrating on the French. He was not so much concerned about Friar Roger's cipher as Sanson's handwriting, and as the day wore on that became more hasty, but Corbett was sure he recognized the same hand as in those mysterious memoranda sent to Ufford, copies of which Bolingbroke had brought back to England. In the early afternoon Sanson declared he was exhausted, sitting back in his chair and throwing his hands up.

'There's nothing more we can do, there's nothing more we can do.'

'I'm sure there isn't,' Corbett agreed.

'Shall we eat, drink?' de Craon asked. 'Not to mention answer the calls of nature.'

His words created a ripple of laughter and he pushed back his chair. 'Sir Hugh, perhaps we can meet in two hours' time? Will you join us in the hall?'

'In a while, in a while,' Corbett replied. 'But, I too am exhausted. I must collect my thoughts.'

The solar emptied. Corbett remained seated, whilst Raunulf, who had seen the secret sign his master had given, returned as if looking for something.

'Not here,' Corbett whispered. 'Not here.' He led Ranulf out of the solar through the kitchens and into the castle yard, then up across the inner ward and on to the wasteland bordering the castle warren.

'Sir Hugh, what are you trying to do?'

'Forget Friar Roger, Ranulf, I now know why our King is interested. Friar Roger's cipher might take months, if not years, to break. We will make no sense of it. What I believe is that those three Frenchmen were murdered. No, no, listen. They were murdered and de Craon has come to Corfe Castle on some secret design of his own. Sanson is his creature. He simply sings the tune de Craon hums.'

Corbett clapped his hands against the cold.

'The mystery is beginning to unravel, Ranulf, but I'm not too sure which path to follow. I must keep things sub rosa. Whatever is decided,' he continued, ignoring Ranulf's look of puzzlement, 'these proceedings are coming to an end. We have made as much progress as we can and de Craon knows that.'

'I agree.' Ranulf gestured back at the hall. 'Last night de Craon was murmuring that time was passing. No wonder, if you're correct, Sir Hugh, that he brought those three men here to die; then his task is done.'

'Oh, there's more to come,' Corbett replied. 'Now, when are those outlaws to be admitted to the King's peace?'

'Tomorrow morning, but I did promise to take them supplies before this evening, a basket of bread and meat to be left at the church.'

'I'll go with you.' Corbett hitched his cloak about him. 'But for the rest, we'll eat, drink and sleep and see which way our French viper curls.'

They returned to the hall where Corbett, keeping his face impassive, chatted to de Craon and drew Sanson into discussion about the writings of Friar Roger. He was now certain that this French scholar was the one who had lured Ufford to his death, so he found it hard to talk, smile and practise the usual courtesies. Accordingly, he was highly relieved, when they reassembled in the solar, to hear de Craon's declaration that he did not wish to prolong the discussions any further.

'Sir Edmund,' de Craon pushed himself to his feet, 'we have trespassed on your kindness long enough. We have now reached certain conclusions regarding Friar Roger's writings. I agree with Sir Hugh,' he smiled blandly, 'that our Franciscan scholar invented a new language and only the good Lord knows how it can be translated. Nevertheless, this meeting at Corfe, despite the unfortunate deaths which have occurred, marks a new development in the ties binding our two kingdoms together. Scholars of both realms have met and exchanged knowledge – a matter most pleasing to our Holy Father the Pope. Perhaps these meetings will become more frequent and encompass a wider range of matters in the years to come,' De Craon was now beaming from ear to ear, as if announcing the most marvellous news, 'when the son of our sovereign lord will sit on the throne at Westminster and wear the Confessor's crown. However, I have an admission to make. A document was found on the person of that poor unfortunate woman who, I understand, took the lives of young maids in this castle. I now declare the document was written by me.' He raised his hand in a sign of peace. 'I wished her to buy supplies from the local tavern and paid her well to do so.'

'Why?' Sir Edmund broke in brusquely. 'Our castle is well stocked.'

'No, no, Sir Edmund, you have it wrong. Our meeting is drawing to an end, and although this is your castle, I insist that tomorrow night I be your host, that I buy the wines and food as a small thank you for your kindness and hospitality. However,' de Craon sighed, 'the best-laid plans of men can often go awry. Sir Edmund, I still insist that I host this banquet, that I pay your cooks and servants as well as for every delicacy served. You must,' he added silkily, 'accept the munificence of my master.'

Sir Edmund had no choice but to agree, even though he nudged Corbett under the table.

'If Sir Hugh is in agreement,' de Craon continued like a pompous priest from his pulpit, 'we will bring these discussions to an end. Tomorrow I must see to certain matters, the collection of our manuscripts and the packing of our valuable belongings. Our horses and harnesses must be prepared and, of course,' de Craon's face assumed a false mournful look, 'there is, Sir Edmund, the sad problem of conveyancing the corpses of my three dead comrades. Nevertheless, let us rejoice,' he continued, 'at our achievement. Finally,' he lifted a finger, 'Sir Edmund, I have stayed in your magnificent castle yet never once been beyond its walls. I would like to ride out with a suitable escort to visit this famous tavern so many of your servants talk about. I need to look at its wines, choose something special for tomorrow night.'

De Craon sat down, and Sir Edmund immediately rose to say what a great honour it had been to host this meeting, how he regretted the deaths of three of de Craon's retinue and that, of course, he would place his kitchens, his servants, cooks and store rooms at Monsieur de Craon's disposal. Corbett followed next, with what Ranulf later described to Chanson as a polite and pretty speech which echoed many of de Craon's sentiments. How pleased he'd been to renew his acquaintance with a French envoy and how he looked forward, with even greater pleasure, to future meetings. He did his best to keep the sarcasm out of his voice even though de Craon smirked throughout. At the end he added that he and his retinue would also be riding out on certain business and would de Craon accept his company and protection? The Frenchman quickly agreed.

A memorandum was drafted and transcribed by Bolingbroke in which de Craon, Sanson and Corbett briefly summarized their meeting regarding Friar Roger's writings and the conclusions they had reached. Corbett and de Craon signed the document, Sir Edmund acting as witness, before it was confirmed with the seals of both kingdoms. Bowing and shaking hands, offering assurances of eternal friendship, the French and English envoys separated. Once de Craon had left, Corbett slumped in his chair, resting his face in his hands.

'He is up to mischief,' Sir Edmund growled. 'You can tell that.'

'Up to?' Bolingbroke retorted. 'I think he has achieved what he came for. He has discovered what we know about Friar Roger's writings, which is the same as he now knows, that the *Secretus Secretorum* is written in a strange language, though

God knows whether that will ever be translated. More importantly,' Bolingbroke picked up his goblet and banged it on the table, 'three *magistri* from the University of Paris have suffered unfortunate accidents. Philip has rid himself of critics and sent a warning to the rest. Sir Hugh,' Bolingbroke got up from the chair, 'I'm not too sure whether I want to eat his food and drink his wine.'

'You will,' Corbett smiled back, 'simply because you have to.'

Bolingbroke sketched a sarcastic bow and walked out of the solar, leaving Corbett and Ranulf with Sir Edmund.

'So there is no mystery about that document found on Mistress Feyner?' Sir Edmund clicked his tongue. 'It was just the courteous Monsieur de Craon planning a surprise for us.'

'I still think he is planning a surprise.' Corbett got to his feet. 'I wish to God I knew what it was. Sir Edmund, we will get our horses prepared; we must take advantage of the daylight.'

A short while later, Corbett, feeling very self-conscious, led his own retinue and de Craon's across the drawbridge and out along the trackway leading down into the forest. The sun had grown stronger, the sky was a wispy white-blue, and although it was late afternoon, the countryside seemed bright under its canopy of white snow now melting and breaking up. De Craon chatted, saying he had studied Corfe and the surrounding countryside very closely before he had come to England, how it reminded him so much of Normandy, especially the fields, meadows and woods around Boulogne. Corbett half listened. Despite the break in the weather and the knowledge that his meeting with de Craon was drawing to an end, he felt a deep unease, a tension which stiffened the muscles of his back and thighs, like a jouster getting ready for the tourney, wondering what danger it might bring. He stopped at the edge of the forest, his gaze drawn by the blackened patch of burnt earth, the pile of charred branches and brushwood.

'That comes from the fire the other night,' Sir Edmund's steward, who was accompanying them, remarked. 'Travelling people. Often from the battlements you can see such fires glowing in the forest.'

As they entered the canopy of trees, de Craon continued his chattering, questioning the steward about hunting rights and the season for deer and did the forest hold wild boar? Corbett found the Frenchman's constant talking a source of deep irritation, and was only too pleased when de Craon reined in and summoned forward his man-at-arms.

'Go ahead of us,' he ordered. 'Sir Hugh, you talked of outlaws?'

'They are no danger,' Corbett reassured him.

'Never mind, never mind.' De Craon gestured. 'It's better to be safe than to be sorry. Follow the trackway,' he ordered his man-at-arms, 'but go no further than the tavern.'

The man answered reluctantly in French. De Craon's voice became sharp. The man-at-arms turned his horse, dug in his spurs and cantered deeper into the trees. 'As long as he keeps to the trackway,' de Craon muttered, 'he'll be safe.'

By the time they had reached the tavern in the forest, Bogo de Baiocis was standing in the yard shouting for the taverner and telling one of the stable boys to be careful with his horse. Sir Hugh and Ranulf stayed outside the gate with the rest while de Craon entered the tavern. A short while later he came out smiling to himself, his servant carrying two small tuns of wine.

'I paid him well.' De Craon gestured at Bogo de Baiocis to give one of the tuns to the steward. 'The best Bordeaux, imported four years ago; they say it's the finest those vineyards ever produced.'

For a while there was confusion as Bogo de Baiocis went back to the tavern to collect rope so that they could tie the tuns to the horns of their saddles. De Craon added that he had ordered certain items for the castle kitchens which Master Reginald would deliver personally to Corfe. Corbett declared that he and Ranulf were journeying on to the church and invited de Craon to accompany them, but the Frenchman politely refused.

'I passed the church as we entered Corfe,' he remarked, swinging himself up into the saddle. 'A lonely, gloomy place, Sir Hugh. You have business with the priest there?'

'More with certain outlaws,' Ranulf replied.

Corbett waited until de Craon and the rest were back on the trackway leading to Corfe.

'What's the matter, Sir Hugh?' Ranulf pushed his horse alongside.

'I wish I knew, Ranulf.' Corbett watched the group of horsemen disappear round the bend. 'I truly do.' He glanced up between the trees at the blue sky. 'The weather has improved, the sun is out; you remember the old saying, Ranulf: "Vipers and adders always come out to greet the sun"?'

He urged his horse on, Ranulf following slightly behind. The forest either side of them was noisy with the melting snow slipping off branches and the drip-drip of water. Here and there the trackway was slippery and Corbett had difficulty controlling his horse.

'Horehound and the rest,' Ranulf spoke up, 'will be nervous. I don't think they truly trust us.'

'In which case,' Corbett replied, 'let's tell them we are coming. Ranulf, you remember the words of the song *'Jove cum Mercurio'*? I'll sing the first verse to remind you of the words, then you can come in and repeat each line. If the outlaws hear us they will know that we mean peace.' And without waiting for a reply Corbett began the lusty student song, distracting Ranulf from his fears about the forest whilst assuring anyone in hiding that they came in peace.

As they reached the cemetery wall, following it round to the lych gate, Corbett's song died on his lips. The cemetery looked bleak in the sunlight, the crosses and headstones drenched in melted snow, and from the trees beyond came the cawing of rooks. No one was about. Corbett had expected the outlaws at least to build a fire, and even if they were hiding, to have left a scout or guard. They dismounted and hobbled their horses. Ranulf, uneasy, drew his dagger; Corbett followed suit. They walked round the church but could detect no sign of life. Both the main door and the Corpse Door were locked, and no glimmer of candlelight showed through the wooden shutters.

Corbett walked out of the cemetery along the path leading to the priest's house. He knocked at the door, but the sound rang hollow and the windows on both ground and upper floor were shuttered. He walked round the back, stopping at the water butt. He noticed how the ice had been broken, the water level much fallen. He caught the faint smell of food, of meat and bread and the tang of spices. The rear door was also locked. Corbett stepped back to look up and his foot caught a brass bowl, which clanged like a trumpet. Cursing, he picked it up, and was about to throw it further into the garden when he noticed how the inside was lined with black dust. He examined the bowl more carefully, weighing it in his hands. It was of good quality, heavy, not something a poor priest would likely throw away. He sniffed and caught the smell of saltpetre, the same odour he had detected in the church. He gently placed it down.

'Father Matthew!'

No answer. Corbett walked around the house again and knocked vigorously on the door.

'Father Matthew, I wish to have words.'

He heard a sound above him and looked up. The priest was visible through the top window shutters, his face pale and unshaven.

'Why, Sir Hugh. I'm sorry I can't come down. The sweating sickness, I believe. I've not been well.'

'Is there anything we can do?' Ranulf shouted back. 'Do you need anything, any food?'

The priest shook his head. 'I haven't eaten for days but I think I'm getting better.' He forced a smile. 'Perhaps I will make some gruel or oatmeal. Please give Sir Edmund my regards and tell the castle folk they must use the castle chapel. Father Andrew will look after them.'

'You know the outlaw Horehound?' Corbett shouted up.

'Yes, Sir Hugh, I do.'

'Have you seen him or any of his coven?'

The priest shook his head. 'I heard the rumours, Sir Hugh, about how they'd entered the King's peace, and I am pleased, but I have heard no sign of them.' The priest was now gabbling. 'Sir Hugh, it is cold. I will see you shortly.'

Father Matthew withdrew his head, closing the shutters behind him. Corbett walked back to the church steps and stood sheltering in the alcove, watching Ranulf go through the cemetery as if the outlaws were hiding there.

'What are you looking for?' he called.

'I thought they might have come and left, but there is no sign of them; no one has been here.' Ranulf walked back. 'Though,' he sighed, 'the snow is beginning to melt.'

Corbett stared across at the silent, forbidding priest's house.

'Why should a priest,' he asked, 'use a good bronze bowl to

mix saltpetre and other substances then throw it out into the garden? Why does he say he hasn't eaten when I can smell the odour of cooking?'

'He did say he was going to make some oatmeal or gruel.'

'True.' Corbett stamped his feet. The day was dying and they could not stay here much longer.

'Ranulf, something may have delayed Horehound. He knows where we are; let's return to the castle.'

They mounted their horses and rode back along the trackway. When they came to the tavern they saw the gates closed. Corbett glimpsed the light of lanterns and candles, and the faint, pleasing sound of a lute drifted out. They passed two chapmen, half bowed under the bundles piled up on their backs, eager to reach the castle before nightfall. They shouted a greeting; Corbett raised a hand in reply.

On their return to the castle, Corbett told Ranulf that he should begin preparations for leaving; he also asked his henchmen to bring some food and wine from the kitchens.

'You are not joining us in the Hall of Angels?' Ranulf asked.

'I'm tired of de Craon's smirking face. Anyway,' Corbett slapped Ranulf's shoulder with his gauntlets, 'I know you will be busy with the Lady Constance.'

Corbett went up to his chamber, where he checked the great chest at the end of the bed and carefully searched the room for any sign of an intruder, but could find none. He built up the fire, lit more of the capped candles and cleared the small writing desk. He took out of the Chancery box some ink, his writing tray and a smooth sheet of vellum. He intended to write letters to the King and Lady Maeve, but what could he say? He couldn't hide his growing anxiety as well as his anger at de Craon's smug arrogance, as if the Frenchman had told a very funny story of which Corbett couldn't see the point. He now accepted that de Craon had brought those three *magistri* from Paris to have them killed, but what further mischief was planned? He divided the piece of vellum into four, giving each column a heading, 'De Craon', 'The Deaths', 'The Castle', 'The Church in the Forest', then, using his own secret cipher, filled each of these categories with what he had seen and learnt, recording conversations, glimpses, who had been where when something had happened.

He thought of Father Matthew, his pale, unshaven face, that lonely house and deserted cemetery.

Ranulf came up with a tray of food. Corbett drank the wine too fast; he felt his face flush and his eyes grew heavy. He could understand the deaths, the murder of the three Frenchmen, but how, and who was responsible? He took a second sheet of vellum and, going back to the Chancery box, brought out all he had learnt about Ufford's stay in Paris. The hours passed and Ranulf returned to see that all was well. Corbett, immersed in his task, only mumbled a reply. He bolted the door once Ranulf had gone and lay down on the bed only intending to sleep for a short while, but he woke in the early hours, cold and tense, the fire gone down and many of the candles gutted. He pulled the cover over him and went back to sleep.

Corbett woke some time later and attended Father Andrew's dawn mass in the small castle chapel. The priest wore black and gold vestments whilst he offered the intercessory prayers for the dead. The day was proving to be a fine one. Outside the chapel both the inner and outer wards were bustling with people coming into the castle. Now the roads were clearing, a servant told him, more chapmen and travelling tinkers seemed to be on the move, all eager to take advantage of the break in the weather. Corbett went over to the kitchen to break his fast. The servants were busy preparing for de Craon's feast to be held that evening. He glimpsed the boy Ranulf had brought from the tavern, his hair and face all washed, an old jerkin about his bony shoulders. He even boasted a woollen pair of hose, and good stout boots on his feet. Corbett called him over. The boy, chewing on a piece of chicken, pushing the morsels into his mouth, came over wide-eyed.

'You don't want me to go back, do you?'

Corbett smiled, took a coin from his purse and gave it to the boy.

'What do they call you?'

'I think my name was Tom, but usually they call me Fetchit.'

'Very well, Tom Fetchit. Did you know Horehound the outlaw well?'

The boy's eyes slid away.

'Come on,' Corbett urged. 'There's no crime in speaking with men of the woods. Here, lad, you can have this coin too.

You know Horehound,' Corbett continued, 'was going to take the King's pardon? We were supposed to meet him yesterday. Ranulf, the red-haired one, took food down to him in the saddlebags.'

'And?' the boy asked as his curiosity quickened.

'Neither Horehound nor any of his coven appeared.'

The boy stopped his chewing.

'Are you surprised? Does that appear strange?'

The boy turned and dropped a piece of chicken on the floor; immediately a large mastiff snapped it up.

'That's not like Horehound, sir,' the boy replied. 'He would never refuse food; something must be wrong.'

Corbett gave the boy another coin and walked out across the yard. He heard the crack of a whip and turned as Master Reginald drove his cart into the inner ward, one of his ostlers sitting beside him. Corbett decided to return to his own chamber, to scrutinize everything he had written the night before. The others came up, Ranulf, Bolingbroke and Chanson, but they could see their master was distracted, and Ranulf was only too eager to return to the Hall of Angels and seek out the Lady Constance.

The day passed slowly for Corbett. Now and again he left to walk across to the Jerusalem Tower, and later in the afternoon he returned to that crumbling doorway and the dark, lonely passageway leading down into the old dungeons. This time he went armed, sword belt about him, accompanied by two of Sir Edmund's Welsh archers. He recalled the terrors of that night, of hiding in the freezing darkness as the assassin waited to take advantage.

He returned to the inner ward just as the coffins bearing the dead Frenchmen were blessed with incense by Father Andrew, before being loaded on to a cart to be taken on their long journey to Dover and across to France. Corbett couldn't tell which coffin was Crotoy's, but as he watched the cart leave, he crossed himself, quoted the psalm of the dead and quietly promised he would seek vengeance for his old friend's murder.

Ranulf was waiting for him on the steps to his chamber.

'Sir Hugh, you have been wandering this castle like a ghost. Sir Edmund is insistent that we show de Craon every courtesy.'

'Is he, now?'

Corbett took out the key and unlocked his chamber. Ranulf followed him inside. He helped Corbett shave, then laid out the red, blue and gold cotehardie, the white cambric shirt and the dark blue hose Corbett always wore on such formal occasions. Ranulf could see old Master Longface was distracted, even forgetting to put on his chain of office or take the Chancery rings from the small casket on the table. Even when they reached the Hall of Angels, Corbett remained silent and withdrawn, almost unaware of the lavish preparations Sir Edmund had made for the banquet: the fire roaring in the hearth, the dais covered in snow-white cloths glittering with silver and gold flagons, goblets, tranchers and knives. The air was rich with savoury smells from the nearby kitchens, soft music floated down from the minstrels' gallery and even the chill corners of the hall were warmed by fiery braziers.

Sir Edmund and his family were sumptuously dressed, Lady Constance looking truly beautiful in a gown of dark blue, a gold cord round her slim waist and an exquisite white veil covering her lustrous hair. Corbett greeted them distractedly, and, when de Craon invited them into the circle around the great fire, he just nodded and went and stood beside Father Andrew.

'I did what I could,' the old priest whispered. 'I know one of the Frenchmen was your friend, Sir Hugh, but in Dover their corpses will be embalmed again. I'm glad you were able to attend the Mass. I intend to say Mass again for them tomorrow, the Feast of St Damasus.'

'St Damasus?' Corbett queried.

'One of the early popes,' the priest replied. 'I think he was a martyr who died for the faith. Sir Hugh, what's the matter?'

'Damsons,' Corbett replied enigmatically. 'Damsons,' he whispered, 'which a Pope could eat before singing his dawn mass.'

Devices could be constructed to emit poisonous and infectious emanations wherever a man may wish.

Roger Bacon,
Concerning the Marvellous Power of Art and Nature

Chapter 12

Corbett tried to remain calm as he sat at the high table. He pretended to eat and drink but his mind was a blizzard of ideas, notions, excitement and fear. The anxiety which had gripped him crumbled in a release of emotion. At any other time he would have gone for a vigorous walk, saddled his horse for a ride, or even taken his song sheets out to chant some carol or psalm. The conversation at high table swirled round him like a breeze. What did it matter? It was all pretence. De Craon could sit there, stuffing his maw with the delicacies from the kitchen, preening himself and listening ever so graciously to Lady Catherine's chatter. You're an assassin, Corbett thought, steeped in wickedness. He almost exclaimed with relief when the banquet ended. Sir Edmund rose and volubly thanked de Craon, who gave some simpering reply. Corbett winked at Ranulf and pretended he was in his cups, lounging in his chair, legs sprawled as if half asleep. Once the rest were gone, however, he insisted that he, Ranulf and Sir Edmund meet in the Constable's private chambers. Corbett offered Lady Catherine his most profuse apologies.

'No, no,' she murmured, picking up a small bejewelled psalter from the table. 'I was watching you during the meal, Sir Hugh; there is something very wrong, isn't there?'

Ranulf, picking at a spot on his jerkin, looked up quickly. He had been so immersed in Lady Constance he had hardly given Sir Hugh a second glance, but now he could see the Keeper of the Secret Seal was not drunk or tired but tense with excitement.

'What is it?' the Constable asked, closing the door behind his wife.

'Sir Edmund, Corfe Castle is about to be attacked!'

'Nonsense,' the Constable scoffed. 'It would need a siege train, battering rams, scaling ladders—'

'I don't mean that way.' Corbett sat down on a quilted stool. 'It's to be taken by treachery.' He turned to Ranulf. 'For days we have talked about secret signs, ciphers and codes. Ranulf, remember the one I taught you? I told you to pick a coin from a pile on the table and concentrate hard. Which king was on the coin? I asked you to reflect carefully.'

'Ah, yes,' Ranulf smiled, 'and we astonished everyone because I always picked up a coin you could name.'

'What's the point of this?' Sir Edmund loosened the cords of his shirt. He had scoffed at Corbett's declaration but he knew this dark-faced clerk was both a soldier and a shrewd plotter.

'Sir Edmund, you remember that piece of parchment you found on Mistress Feyner about bread to fill the largest stomach, and damsons for a Pope to eat before his dawn Mass? De Craon has confessed that he wrote it. It's a secret cipher. When I taught Ranulf our trick I would use a certain word to denote a certain king. When I asked him to reflect, he would reply, "Yes, I've considered," or "Yes, I've reflected," or "Yes, I've remembered." Each word stood for a certain king. "Reflected" could be Henry, "remembered" could be Edward, "considered" could be Richard. It's a cheap fairground trick, but one which can be made more complicated. Now, de Craon knows that we are suspicious. We should never have found that message. At first he denied it until he realized that, by admitting to it, he can continue with his plot.'

'Which is?' Sir Edmund asked testily.

'To storm this castle by stealth. The message gives the time, the place and the method. Consider his message carefully. Bread to fill any belly; the word for belly in French is *ventre*; it can also mean, used loosely, the entrance to a castle. They aim to seize the gates.'

'When?' Ranulf asked.

'Ah, now we come to the damsons. De Craon is out of season; true, there may be some wizened plums, damsons preserved since autumn. However, he is not alluding to this. Damson means Damasus. He was one of the early popes. Tomorrow we celebrate his feast, and the reference to the dawn Mass names the time, before daybreak, when Father Andrew usually summons us to the first Mass of the day.'

Sir Edmund sat down in a chair and absentmindedly sipped from his goblet.

'But how?' Ranulf asked. 'Whom can de Craon use? Has he hired the outlaws?'

'I doubt it.'

'Suborned the garrison?'

'Impossible,' Sir Edmund declared.

'The Flemish pirates,' Corbett put in. 'Sir Edmund, we have good intelligence that Flemish pirates have been seen in the Narrow Seas, cruising close to our southern shore.'

'True, true, and they do land, though it's villages they sack.'

'This time it is different,' Corbett declared. 'They have the weather on their side. Corfe stands on the Island of Purbeck; to the south there is the sea, to the east the estuary. These Flemings are the most accomplished sailors; they have charts, maps and information they have collected. They can beach their ships in a lonely inlet or cove, assemble and move inland.'

'But they would be seen.'

'No, Sir Edmund, it's the dead of winter. When was the last time you left this castle? They would enter the forest, and God help anyone they met. I would wager a bag of gold that corpses now litter the woods: charcoal burners, chapmen, peddlers, tinkers.'

'The outlaws!' Ranulf exclaimed. 'Poorly armed, weak, they wouldn't stand a chance against such ferocious fighters.'

'It's possible,' Corbett conceded, 'which is why our outlaws did not meet us as agreed. God help the poor souls, they must be dead. In fact, Ranulf, we are most fortunate for I'm sure we almost met the Flemings ourselves.'

'Where?' Ranulf couldn't believe his ears. He often confessed to Chanson how old Master Longface could surprise him, but now he was truly astonished.

'We're talking about two to three hundred men,' Corbett

closed his eyes, 'and they have approached the castle as close as they can.' He opened his eyes again. 'I don't think Father Matthew is ill at all. On the day we visited him the church was locked and barred. If we had forced the doors we would have seen a sight which would have terrified us just before the air became thick with arrows.'

'You're saying they were there, in the house and church?'

'Yes, Ranulf, and even closer, perhaps in the tavern itself. They are going to use Master Reginald's cart, as they probably plotted to use Mistress Feyner's. When de Craon visited the tavern I'm sure he went to leave that same message which you, Sir Edmund, found on that woman's corpse.' Corbett shook his head. 'It could be done so easily, a piece of parchment dropped to the floor.'

'But the priest would have told us.' Ranulf spoke up. 'So would Master Reginald.'

'Both their lives are threatened,' Corbett explained. 'I'm sure that in the tavern, above stairs or in its cellars, lurk men with crossbows primed, or blades to the throats of Master Reginald's servants, and the same in the church. In fact, the priest did try to warn us. Do you remember, Ranulf, Father Matthew claimed he hadn't eaten, but we smelt the odour of cooking, and water had been drawn from the butt. Also there was that expensive brass bowl lying out in the garden. No poor priest would have thrown out something so costly.'

'What bowl?' Sir Edmund asked. 'What is this, Sir Hugh? How do you know de Craon is behind this? Why?'

'I don't know why, Sir Edmund, not yet, but the Flemings are mercenaries; they can be hired by the French King, or his brother, or a member of the royal council. Everything is done in secret. A sum of money is given to some banking house; more is promised when the deed is done. Do you remember that fire, Sir Edmund? Don't you think it was strange that your guards glimpsed a fire on the edge of the forest? And within a short while a similar fire started in the castle. De Craon was receiving and sending messages; like a chess game, all the pieces were moving into place.'

'I don't believe this,' Sir Edmund whispered, shaking his head. 'Sir Hugh, de Craon is an accredited envoy.'

'Precisely, Sir Edmund. He'll wash his hands of it, claim he knows nothing about it. If I'm wrong I will apologize to you and the King, but I would like the opportunity to apologize; I don't fancy having my throat slashed, or a crossbow bolt in my chest.'

Sir Edmund sat staring at the floor. 'If they wanted to kill you, Sir Hugh, why didn't they do it out in the forest, or in the tavern?'

'Oh, that would alert you. But what you say is significant, Sir Edmund. They must be looking for something else. I know you are Constable of the castle, but I am the Keeper of the—'

'And I have a wife and daughter,' Sir Edmund snapped. 'The solution is very simple, Sir Hugh, I'll double the guards. I'll secretly pass the word.'

'Don't let the French know the reason why.'

'Of course not. I'll order the outer drawbridge to be pulled up and the porticullis lowered.'

'The inner ward as well?' Ranulf asked.

'No, no. If something should happen,' Corbett explained, 'and the attackers get into the outer ward, the defenders must be given the chance to flee across the second drawbridge. If it was raised, by the time it's lowered again the attackers could follow the defenders deeper into the castle.' He got to his feet. 'Sir Edmund, I don't think I'll sleep tonight. Keep our preparations as secret as possible.'

'Why not send out horsemen?' Ranulf demanded, only to shrug as he realized the futility of his remark. 'Of course, in the dead of night, in the depth of winter . . .'

Sir Edmund reluctantly agreed to all of Corbett's requests. He had served with Corbett in Wales and along the Scottish march, and if Sir Hugh smelt danger, then danger there was.

Corbett and Ranulf returned to Corbett's chamber. The castle yards were now deserted; only the occasional servant hurried across, carrying a torch. The sky was cloud-free, the stars seemed like pricks of light. Corbett walked down to the entrance of the first ward. Officers of the garrison were already gathering around the main gateway, and even as he turned away, the rumble of chains echoed across. Corbett glimpsed some servants, the travelling tinkers and chapmen gathered around a fire. All seemed peaceful enough. As soon as he returned to his chamber he checked the great coffer and changed, putting on a stout leather jacket, testing his sword and dagger, drawing them in and out of their sheaths, whilst Ranulf took from their stores two crossbows and quivers of arrows.

'I had best tell the others,' Ranulf declared.

'No, no,' Corbett warned. 'Don't! I want you to stay with me. You can sleep on the bed if you want.' He pushed his chair in front of the fire and sat, recalling everything he had said to the Constable. He truly believed that the danger was real and insidious; all those little things he had glimpsed and heard in the castle, and beyond, now made sense. Yet he cursed his own tiredness, for there was something he had missed! He and de Craon had clashed swords for how long now? It must be years. And if de Craon was playing chess with other people's lives, he would have plotted secret moves and strategies to further his designs.

'*Causa disputandi*, for sake of argument,' Corbett whispered, 'let us presume that de Craon knows that I know what mischief he is planning. The Flemish pirates may be resolute fighters but they are not an army. They have no siege equipment.'

'They do have ladders.' Ranulf spoke up, sitting on the bed behind him.

Corbett smiled over his shoulder. 'Long enough to scale these walls, Ranulf?' He went back to his musings. 'The drawbridge is drawn up, the gates guarded. Oh God, I've forgotten something!'

For a while he dozed, starting awake at any noise, even the faint cries of the sentries. He placed another log on the fire and went across to check the hour candle. It had been lit at noon the previous day and the flame was already eating down to the fifteenth circle.

'If it comes,' Corbett glanced at Ranulf on the bed, fast asleep, 'if it comes, it will be soon.'

He returned to his chair, trying to recall what it was he had missed. He was falling asleep when he heard a sound outside, the slither of a foot. He sprang to his feet, drew his sword and tiptoed towards the door. He drew back the bolts, which had been recently greased, and turned the key in the lock, then lifted the latch, opened the door a crack and stared out. Nothing but shadows dancing on the wall. The cresset torch was leaping vigorously and he could feel the draught from the icy wind. He looked down at the floor; in the murky light he could see the imprint of footsteps. Someone had come up here. The door to the tower was unlocked. Someone had climbed those steps and tried his door.

Corbett, gripping his sword, went down the steps. As he rounded the corner to the bottom stairwell he heard the click of the latch as the outside door closed. Fear pricking the back of his neck, and fighting to calm his breath, he approached the door, lifted the latch and slipped through. The darkness was thinning; across the yard he could see the glow of a brazier, men lounging in the shadows wrapped in cloaks, fast asleep, nothing untoward or out of place. Corbett stepped back inside, drew across the bolt and returned to his own chamber. Ranulf was awake, already pulling his boots on.

'What is it? What's the matter?'

'Nothing, Ranulf, go back to sleep.'

'I've been dreaming about the Lady Constance. Sir Hugh, have you ever seen such a beautiful neck? I mean,' Ranulf added hastily, 'apart from the Lady Maeve's?'

'So you think Lady Maeve has a beautiful neck . . .'

'I mean I would love to buy the Lady Constance a necklace to hang round it, perhaps a silver cross or a costly stone?'

'Why not a silver heart?' Corbett replied. 'But you won't find anything like that in the castle. Perhaps when this danger has passed . . .'

'There's always the chapmen and tinkers,' Ranulf replied.

'Aye, there is.' Corbett's eyes grew heavy. He dozed for a while, thinking about the Lady Maeve and the silver collar he intended to buy for her as a New Year's gift. He had seen something in Cheapside he had liked. That was the best place to go. Travelling tinkers . . . Corbett opened his eyes, his stomach lurched. Going over to the hour candle, he noticed it was close to the sixteenth ring. He heard a sound from outside like the cry of a bird. He stared at Ranulf and realized what he had forgotten.

'Ranulf!' His henchman started awake. Corbett was already putting on his war belt, picking up the arbalest. 'Ranulf, do you have a horn, anything?'

'What is it? I have something somewhere.' Ranulf leapt off the bed. 'It's in my room. Sir Hugh, what is the matter?'

'Tinkers, travellers, chapmen. Ranulf, think! During the last few days a number of them have drifted into the castle.'

'Oh, St Michael and all his Angels,' Ranulf breathed, pulling on his boots and picking up his own weapons.

Corbett pushed him through the door and down the steps. The bolt to the outer door was stuck and he caught his hand pulling it back. Once in the yard, Ranulf would have run across to his own chamber, but Corbett pulled him back.

'It's too late for that. *Au secours!*' Corbett shouted, using the alarm signal for any military camp.

'*Au secours! Au secours!*' Ranulf echoed the shout. Slipping and slithering they raced across the yard.

Men-at-arms and archers, faces heavy with sleep, struggled awake and came out of the small cottages built against the walls of the inner bailey. They tried to challenge Corbett but the clerk was already racing across the cobbles, down to the second drawbridge. As he thundered across that into the first ward, he realized it was too late. The main portcullis was raised, the drawbridge was going down, and a group of armed men clustered in the murky light. One or two held torches, and there was the scrape of steel even as the piteous cry came from the gatehouse. Men-at-arms on the parapet walks above him were alarmed, roused by the clatter of chains and the crash of the drawbridge as it fell. The sentries were caught by surprise; they didn't know whether to face the danger in the yard below or the horsemen and carts which seemed to erupt from the darkness, thundering across the lower drawbridge. Corbett, Ranulf by his side, hurried across the cobbles.

The door to the Hall of Angels was open, a shaft of light in the darkness. Sir Edmund and his officers came hurrying down, half dressed in armour, swords drawn, helmets on their heads. Corbett glimpsed something moving out of the corner of his eye and turned, sword and dagger out. He recognized two of the chapmen he had glimpsed the other day. Now they carried no bundles; one held sword and dagger, the other, hurrying behind, was slipping a bolt into an arbalest. Corbett met the first in a clash of steel whilst Ranulf hurled himself at the bowman. A violent, vicious fight. Corbett was aware of a bearded face, glittering eyes, the foul smell of the man and the curses he muttered. He was a poor swordsman lunging with dagger; turning slightly sideways, he left his chest exposed and Corbett thrust in his sword even as Ranulf, clutching his opponent's crossbow, shoved it against his stomach whilst driving his dagger straight into his face. His assailant collapsed, blood gushing out. Ranulf danced behind him, clawing back his head so as to slit his throat.

Similar fights were already breaking out in the inner ward; individual duels, men rolling on the ground whilst the attackers surged through the main gate, massing in the bailey. A truly frightening force, they wore no armour but leather jerkins or long robes slit at each side. On their heads the pelts of foxes, badgers, wolves and bears. Well armed and organized, they were led by a line of crossbowmen, with fighters coming out from the flanks ready to take advantage. They had their backs to their gatehouse and were now advancing to the second drawbridge, whilst others were hastening up the steps to attack the guards and sentries on the parapet walks. As they edged forward Corbett realized that their main strength was on their right flank, and ignoring the whistles of the bolts and quarrels, he pointed towards the Hall of Angels.

'They intend to take it,' Sir Edmund, his face already cut, agreed.

'I'll defend that,' Ranulf whispered.

Sir Edmund was now bringing his own archers into play. A ragged line of arbalests, they did little good, being far too slow, but at least they halted the advance of the enemy. Behind this line, ignoring the hideous cries of the wounded, Sir Edmund and his officers tried to impose order. Ranulf, surrounded by a group of men-at-arms, was already protecting the steps to the Hall of Angels. Sir Edmund now drew back, sending forward more crossbowmen and, behind them, a line of men-at-arms with long oval shields and spears. At first Corbett, fighting for breath, body drenched in sweat, his ears dimmed by the raucous noise, thought Sir Edmund was acting foolishly, panic-stricken, unable to plan. However, line after line of Welsh longbowmen, marshalled by their officers, came slipping across the inner drawbridge and formed in kneeling lines with gaps between their ranks. The pirates, displaying their black and red banners and reinforced by fresh forces from outside, edged forward, ready to rush Sir Edmund's crossbowmen and the ranks of mailed men-at-arms. The outer bailey filled with these garishly garbed mercenaries. As in all battles Corbett could make no sense of it, only the sounds of shouting, men writhing on the ground, clutching at blood-gushing wounds, a body toppled from the parapet. He became aware of the enemy bowmen trying to shoot above their heads.

'Sir Hugh!' Both he and Sir Edmund were now protected by lines of men kneeling and standing before them, their shields out against the sickening thud of crossbow bolts. 'Sir Hugh!' Sir Edmund gasped. 'When I give the order you must run! You must not stop, and if you fall, God help you!'

A similar order was passed along the ranks. The enemy lines drew closer, their archers doing terrible damage. Sir Edmund gave the sign, a shrilling trumpet blast, and the castle defenders turned and fled, Corbett retreating with the rest. He passed men in leather jerkins, small and dark, hair tied back, straining on their great bows, quivers hanging from their sides, one arrow notched, another in their mouths. Two rows were kneeling, and in between them two further ranks were standing. The smell of sweat, leather, and that strange oil used to keep their yew bows supple was all around them. Corbett hastened through, wary lest he knock against one of these archers now bringing their bows down. The enemy, taken by surprise, stopped, baffled by these stationary ranks of men, the mass of barbed arrows, the long cords pulled back. A few moments of silence, then one of the enemy, face painted, head shrouded in a sealskin, leapt forward whirling an axe.

'Now!' Sir Edmund shouted.

'Loose!' a master bowman in the rear rank shouted. Corbett heard a sound something like the strings of a thousand harps being plucked, followed by a whirr as if some giant bird was fluttering its heavy wings. A black shower of shafts hung for a second against the lightening sky. The sight took Corbett back to a mist-shrouded valley in Wales and English men-at-arms in their red and gold livery falling like ripening corn under a deadly hail of barbed shafts. It was the same here. The first wave of attackers seemed to disappear, stagger back and fall; the rest, disconcerted, halted, presenting even easier targets for the second shower of arrows which fell thick and fast. The inner bailey became full of men staggering away clutching at arrows in the face, neck and chest; others lay still on the freezing ice. Corbett had witnessed the deadly effect of the massed ranks of longbowmen, yet he was still amazed at the speed and violence of such an assault.

The archers were now turning under the direction of their officers, moving into a horseshoe formation to sweep the entire bailey with their volleys. The speed of their arrows, their accuracy and the closeness of their foe wreaked a telling, devastating effect. The ground became carpeted with dead and dying. The attackers had no choice but to retreat. The Welsh archers advanced to shouts of 'Walk! Loose!' followed by that ominous thrumming. The pirates became disorganized. Some of their leaders were killed. Even as they retreated, the deadly hail continued. Panic set in, and the ranks broke and fled, desperate to reach the main gate. A few of the archers strung their bows and followed, a mistake as the enemy turned with sword and club. The archers were no match for these desperate men and their skill in hand-to-hand conflict. Sir Edmund summoned them back. Trumpets and hunting horns sounded through the air as the Constable called for the horses to be brought out and saddled for the chase.

Corbett stood back. He felt exhausted and wearied and had no desire to engage in the pursuit. The yard became full of horses milling about. Sir Edmund and his officers mounted, shouting at the men-at-arms to gather round them. The horn sounded again and Sir Edmund led the cavalcade across the outer bailey, archers running behind them. The rest of the castle folk now emerged from their hiding places armed with whatever weapon they could find. They moved amongst the dead, cutting the throats of the enemy, searching for loved ones. Lady Catherine and her daughter came out of the Hall of Angels, accompanied by Ranulf and a group of men-at-arms. Lady Catherine imposed order. The killing of the wounded stopped. Scullions and servants were ordered to light fires, boil water and bring sheets from the stores. Simon the leech was already busy, and behind him, Father Andrew, a stole round his neck, moved amongst the dead, now and again crouching to talk to a fallen man.

Corbett leaned against the wall struggling to control the nausea in his stomach. He tried to breathe in, clearing his throat, fearful lest he be sick. Ranulf and Bolingbroke hurried across. Both clerks had donned stiffened leather breastplates. Ranulf had his war belt slung over his shoulder and his sword and dagger were drenched in blood. Corbett turned away and retched. The dreadful silence which always followed a battle was shattered as the wounded cried in agony, or some woman finding her man began to wail. If Lady Catherine hadn't been present, accompanied by men-at-arms, a second massacre would have taken place. She insisted that the castle wounded be moved to the keep, the dead to the chapel, and those enemy prisoners able to walk quickly manacled and taken down to the castle dungeons. Corbett gestured with his hand for Bolingbroke to go and help her.

'Ranulf, I am finished here.'

With his henchmen helping him, Corbett returned to his chamber, trying not to look at the corpses sprawled in their dark puddles of blood. He reached the tower, opened the door and paused at the sound on the stairs above. Ranulf pushed him aside and went ahead; Corbett climbed the steps slowly. The door to his chamber hung open. He paused.

'I'm sure I locked it,' he whispered. 'I'm sure I did.'

He went inside the chamber. By the faint stains on the floor he could tell someone had been here; they had also removed a leather jerkin lying on the great chest. He crouched down and examined the locks.

'Where was de Craon during the attack?'

Ranulf resheathed his sword, wiping the sweat from his face.

'Hiding in the Hall of Angels, I believe.'

Corbett poured himself and Ranulf a goblet of wine. He drank greedily then lay on the bed. He felt as if he had hardly closed his eyes when he was shaken awake by Sir Edmund, his hair matted, face lined with sweat and dirt. The Constable looked furious.

'Sir Hugh, I need you now!'

Corbett struggled awake and sat on the edge of the bed. Sir Edmund unloosened his sword belt, slumped in a chair and rubbed his face with his hands.

'There were three hundred in all,' he began. 'We must have killed two thirds of them. We have forty prisoners.'

'What will you do with them?' Corbett asked.

'They're pirates,' the Constable replied. 'They carry no letters of patent, warrants or commissions. You know the law, Sir Hugh. Such men taken in arms are judged guilty and forfeit all right to life and limb.'

'You mean to try them?'

'Within the hour, Sir Hugh. You are a King's justice, I need your help. There's no other way. Ranulf here will act as your clerk, three justices under the law.'

'Wait, wait.' Corbett held his hands up. 'Have you questioned them? Why did they attack Corfe?'

'Their leaders have either fled or been killed,' the Constable replied. 'The captain of the fleet managed to escape. Those we've captured know nothing except that they were to attack the castle, ransack it, kill as many people as possible and withdraw to their ships beached along the estuary.'

Corbett accepted the goblet of wine Ranulf thrust into his hands.

'Sir Edmund, you seem to be in a temper. The attack was beaten off, you have achieved a great victory.'

'Have I? Have I?' The Constable took off a gauntlet and sucked at a cut on his wrist. 'I nearly lost my castle, my life, not to mention the lives of my wife and daughter. I risked your life, Sir Hugh. If you had been killed the King would have had my head. God knows what the Flemings would have done with the French envoys.'

'But they hired them,' Corbett mused.

'Did they?' Sir Edmund retorted. 'Monsieur de Craon sheltered in his chamber and came out all afluster.' The Constable forced a smile. 'He claims he is not safe here and wishes to leave for Dover. In fact he has ordered his retainers to pack and leave as swiftly as possible. He's demanding a heavy escort for the journey.'

'I'm sure he is,' Corbett remarked. 'I can just imagine your French guest throwing his hands in the air, eyes rolling, shouting that this place should be safer, that his person is sacred, and that he can't leave quick enough.'

Corbett toasted the Constable with his cup. 'Come, Sir Edmund, see the funny side. De Craon wishes to put as much distance between himself and Corfe as possible because he's failed, the attack was beaten off.'

'And yet, Sir Hugh,' the smile faded from Sir Edmund's face, 'we lost thirty-five men. I made a mistake. Apparently the pedlars and chapmen we admitted attacked the guard at the main gateway, cut their throats and lowered the drawbridge. I should have been more careful. The pirates were hiding in the dark; they brought in a cart, forced the gate, and the rest you know.'

'They were nearby all the time?' Corbett asked.

'Yes, yes. Now I'll come to the cruel part. The pirates landed in the estuary and moved inland. From what I gather, they swept into the forest, killing the charcoal burners and wood-men. They slaughtered and raped. Those who knew the paths were taken prisoner and forced to show them the way. They reached St Peter's in the Wood and used the church for shelter, as well as the priest's house. They threatened Father Matthew, telling him that unless he cooperated, pretended to be ill and drove away all visitors, they would cut his throat and burn their hostages alive. They then moved on to the Tavern in the Forest. Apparently those Castilian wool merchants were part of the plot; they were the ones who lit the fire. They forced the taverner to cooperate. They planned to use his cart and that of Mistress Feyner. They thought they would catch us unawares, seize the drawbridges and ransack the castle to their hearts' content.'

'That's why that bastard held his banquet,' Ranulf interrupted. 'He hoped we would all be fuddled with wine, deeply asleep. Sir Hugh, isn't there anything we can do?'

Corbett run a thumbnail around his lips. 'Continue, Sir Edmund.'

'They also cleared the forest.' The Constable joined his hands together. 'Poor Horehound and his coven were massacred. I sent riders into the trees. The pirates killed indiscriminately: Horehound and his group, foresters, charcoal burners. Good God, Sir Hugh, it'll be summer before we find all their corpses.'

'And Master Reginald?'

'They forced him to drive the cart this morning. He was killed just by the gateway, whether by design or accident I cannot say.'

'And Father Matthew?'

'Ah, we expected to find him dead. However, our priest has more nimble wits than they thought. He and the hostages managed to escape to the church and barred themselves in, just as the outlaws began to mass for their attack on the castle. Obviously the pirates hoped to deal with us first. The priest is shaken and nervous but he and the poor forest folk were found safe enough.'

'And the tavern?' Ranulf asked.

'Ransacked and looted. Most of the servants managed to escape into the forest.'

'And the Castilians?'

'From what one of the grooms said, one escaped, the rest were killed. They made a final stand just between the tavern and the church. I have brought the rebels' bodies back so that my people can see. They are laid out in a line, just within the inner bailey. I want everyone here to see that justice was done.'

'And the rest?' Ranulf asked.

'They will be hanging within the hour, but Ranulf is correct! Sir Hugh, what can we do about de Craon?'

Corbett rose, washed his face and hands and prepared himself carefully. 'Tell de Craon I wish to see him here.' He turned the high-backed chair to face the door. 'I want to see him here, by himself. You can be my witnesses.'

A short while later de Craon, booted and spurred, body shrouded in a thick woollen cloak, swaggered into the room. Bogo de Baiocis followed like a shadow.

'Sir Hugh, I'm glad to see you are safe.' De Craon looked around for a chair; Corbett didn't offer one. Ranulf lounged on a stool whilst Sir Edmund leaned against the wall, still picking at the cut on his wrist.

'Tell your servant to stand outside.'

'I beg your pardon?'

'Tell your servant to stand outside. This castle is the King of England's, I am his commissioner, I decide to whom I speak.'

Corbett rubbed his hands together. 'Now, he can leave of his own accord or I can have the tocsin sounded.'

De Craon lifted a gloved hand, waggling his fingers. Ranulf hastened to open the door and mockingly bowed as the henchman strode out, then slammed the door shut, drawing the bolts across. De Craon became alarmed.

'Sir Hugh, you seem in a temper. I truly object, as will my master, to the hideous attack launched on this castle,' de Craon gabbled. 'Perhaps, Sir Hugh, our two kings can meet and discuss the dangers posed by these marauders. At the same time I must remind you that I am an accredited envoy. I no longer feel safe here. I wish—'

'Oh shut up!' Corbett sipped from his wine cup. 'Monsieur de Craon, why don't you just keep quiet? Do you know, sir,' he continued, 'if I could prove who hired those pirates I would build a special scaffold outside the gate and watch him hang. However, I have no such proof.'

'Are you saying they were hired?' De Craon's eyes rounded in surprise. 'Sir Hugh, you have proof of this?'

'I said *if*,' Corbett retorted. 'The man who hired them is a murderer and assassin. He has the blood of innocent men and women on his hands. I call him a misbegotten knave, a cruel-hearted bastard who is not even worthy to wipe the arse of one of Sir Edmund's dogs.' Malevolence and anger began to seethe in the Frenchman's eyes. 'However, monsieur, you have made a very good point. Well, three, to be precise. First, we must gather as much information about this attack as possible, and you were witness to it. Secondly, you are an accredited envoy, and the King of England is personally responsible for your safety. Thirdly, there are still outstanding matters between us. So, to cut to the chase, I think it will be very unsafe, even with a heavy escort, to journey to Dover. These pirates may still be hiding along the roads.'

Corbett sipped from his cup, watching de Craon over its rim.

'Who knows, they may even launch another assault. Your person, Monsieur de Craon, is very special, I mean, very sacred to me. I must keep you close and safe.'

De Craon flushed as Ranulf sniggered.

'By the power given to me,' Corbett raised his left hand, 'I must insist that you be kept safe here at Corfe, given every comfort until we are assured that this danger is past.'

'And?' De Craon's voice was scarcely above a whisper.

'My sovereign lord the King,' Corbett continued, smiling with his eyes, 'will insist on reassuring you personally. He will want to know as much about this attack as possible.' He leaned forward. 'Within the week you will be escorted to London and given comfortable lodgings in the Tower. You can join the court's Christmas festivities.'

'I protest!' de Craon broke in. 'I must return to France.'

'Amaury, Amaury!' Corbett got to his feet, put his hand gently on the Frenchman's shoulder and squeezed tight with his fingers. 'We must make sure you are safe. We must show the Holy Father at Avignon the cordial relationship which exists between our two courts. Surely, Amaury, you are not going to refuse my royal master's invitation? I mean, he would take grave insult.'

Corbett's hand fell away. De Craon's face was a picture, a mass of controlled fury, white froth bubbling on the corner of his mouth. The Frenchman was breathing rapidly through his nose.

'You must be safe, Amaury, I would die a thousand deaths if anything happened to you.'

'I,' de Craon stepped back, 'I must think about your offer.' Ranulf was quietly laughing. This proved too much. At the door de Craon turned. 'One day, Corbett . . .'

'Aye, de Craon, one day, but for now, do make yourself available. Perhaps I may have other questions for you.'

De Craon drew back the bolts and disappeared through the doorway. Ranulf, laughing loudly, kicked the door shut.

'Can you do that?'

Sir Edmund came away from the wall, eyes watchful.

'I don't want him to leave,' Corbett declared, 'and I want to keep him in England as long as possible. He'll enjoy the Tower. He shouts he is an envoy; then he should at least present his letters to our lord. Perhaps the snow will return and, with a little luck, King Philip will have to do without his Keeper of Secrets until the spring.'

'You will accuse him of the murders?' Ranulf asked.

'He is a murderer,' Corbett replied. 'A malevolent black spider who spins his webs in dark corners. He hired those pirates. He tried to fill our bellies with food and wine and I think I know why. Sir Edmund, whatever happens, keep the drawbridge raised. Apart from myself, nobody must leave this castle. Now I believe we have other business to do.' Corbett roused himself, blew out the candles and strapped on his war belt. 'Ranulf, fetch Bolingbroke. Sir Edmund, where will the court be held?'

'In the council chamber in the keep.'

'Tell Bolingbroke to meet us there,' Corbett ordered. 'He is skilled in languages. Let these miscreants know why they are going to die.'

Any educated person may listen with profit to this boy, John. No one is so learned that this boy may be dispensable to him in so many ways.

Roger Bacon, *Opus Maius*

Chapter 13

The corpses, all bloodied, were stretched out on the cobbles, row after row like slabs of bloody meat on a flesher's stall. Corbett followed Sir Edmund as the Constable inspected each corpse on what was proving to be a dark, freezing morning, the sky threatening more snow. The pirates, even in death, still looked sinister and ferocious. Corbett had heard of their exploits in the Narrow Seas. The Flemish fleet comprised all the scum, cutthroats and murderers from the ports of Flanders, Hainault, France, even from Genoa, Venice and further east. They were dressed in a motley collection of gaudy robes and filched armour, hair grown long, faces almost hidden by thick moustaches and beards; here and there lay the occasional youthful, clean-shaven one. Their corpses were already plundered of jewellery; this lay piled high on a table brought out from the tower, and Sir Edmund's scribes were busy making a tally. The air reeked of blood and iron, and the sight of such corpses had tempered the rage and resentment of the castle folk.

'At least one hundred,' Ranulf whispered. Death had been inflicted in a variety of ways. Many still carried the feathered, barbed shafts of the longbowmen; others had hideous wounds to their head, face or chest; a few had been speared in the back; one had lost his head and this had been placed as a macabre joke under his arm.

'Did they have horses?' Corbett asked.

'No,' Sir Edmund replied. 'Only some sorry mounts they managed to steal from a farmstead.'

Once he had finished his inspection, the Constable climbed a barrel and gave a pithy address extolling the castle folk for their bravery, gesturing at the prisoners now bound and gathered in a huddle, promising that the King's justice would be done publicly and swiftly.

Once Sir Edmund had climbed down, he, Corbett and Ranulf, with Bolingbroke acting as interpreter, crossed to the council chamber in the keep. This had been transformed, lit by a myriad of candles and warmed by the many capped braziers lined up against the walls and placed in every corner. The great table had been turned round to face the door. Sir Edmund sat in the middle chair, beneath the crucifix, Corbett on his right, Ranulf to his left, with a worried-looking Bolingbroke at one end of the table and a castle scribe at the other. In front of Sir Edmund lay a sword, a small crucifix, and a copy of the chapel breviary. Corbett took out his own commission and unrolled it, using four weights to hold down the corners. At the bottom of the document were his seal and those of the King and Chancellor.

The prisoners were brought in, and pushed and shoved to stand in front of this crudely devised King's Bench. Sir Edmund declared that they were pirates, invaders, with no rights and subject to martial law. As he spoke Bolingbroke quickly translated. Sir Edmund then listed the charges against them.

'That they maliciously and feloniously invaded the noble King's Realm of England, causing devastation by fire and sword, pillaging and killing the King's good loyal subjects contrary to all usage and law...' Every so often he would pause for Bolingbroke to translate. At the end he asked if they wished to say anything in their defence.

'*Merde!*' a coarse voice shouted.

Sir Edmund asked again if any of them could claim innocence of the charges levelled against them. One of the pirates in the front hawked and spat. Corbett's unease at such swift justice receded as he studied these invaders. They looked what they were, violent, murderous marauders who had no fear of God or man and would have shown little compassion to any of their victims. He thought of the lonely charcoal burners, poor Horehound and his coven, corpses stiffening under the snow. Staring at these scarred, cruel faces he wondered what other cruelties they were guilty of. He tugged at Sir Edmund's sleeve and whispered quickly in his ear. Sir Edmund nodded in agreement.

'Is there anyone here,' he declared, 'who can claim innocence of any of the charges? I've asked before and I'm asking again, for the final time.'

He was answered with a tirade of abuse in at least half a dozen languages. Despite their shackles the pirates were still dangerous. Corbett noticed how they were shuffling towards the table in front of them, so much so that Sir Edmund's officers had to form a cordon between them, shields up, swords drawn.

'Listen!' Sir Edmund shouted. 'I am empowered to offer free pardon and amnesty to anyone who can lay evidence on who hired you and why you came here.' A deadly silence greeted his words. One of the pirates shuffled forward, almost pushing aside the guard.

'We don't know who hired us,' he replied in guttural English. 'Only our Admiral could tell you that, and he is frying in Hell or raping one of your women. You mean to kill us, why not get on with it?'

'In which case . . .' Sir Edmund stood and, one hand holding the hilt of his sword, the other his crucifix, intoned the death sentence: 'That they are all found guilty of the terrible accusations levelled against them, being the perpetrators of divers hideous crimes . . . and by the power given to me of high and low justice, as Constable of this royal castle, I condemn you to be hanged, sentence to be carried out immediately.'

His words did not need to be translated and were greeted with a roar of abuse. The pirates surged forward, only to be beaten back by Sir Edmund's guards. They were thrust out into the inner bailey and divided into batches of six. Corbett left the hall as the first prisoners were hustled up the steps to the parapet walk. The nooses had already been prepared, the other end tied round the castle's crenellations. Father Andrew stood at the foot of the steps, quietly reciting prayers; many of the pirates cursed him as they passed. Once they had reached the parapet walk the noose was put round their necks and they were kicked unceremoniously over the edge. The castle folk had already left, standing in the frozen fields outside to watch one figure after another be thrown over the castle walls to dance and jerk at the end of a rope.

'I've seen enough,' Corbett whispered. 'Sir Edmund, I ask you again to make sure no one leaves this castle.'

'Where are you going?' the Constable asked.

Corbett smiled. 'I need to talk to a priest.'

Corbett was relieved to put the castle behind him. The execution party was now moving round the walls, and as he looked back he could see those small black figures, some still, others kicking in their death throes. He turned away and whispered a prayer, patting his horse's neck, then pulled up the edge of his cloak to cover his nose and mouth, turning his head slightly as the bitter breeze stung his face. He held the reins slack, allowing his mount to pick its own way along the frozen track. Behind him, huddled on his mount, sat Ranulf, deeply silent. Corbett knew the reason. Many years ago he had rescued Ranulf from a hanging, and the sight of such executions always provoked bitter memories.

The snow had turned to ice, and on either side of the track Corbett saw signs of the recent attack, wet patches of blood, a shattered club, a buckle or button. He paused as Ranulf pushed his mount towards a thick clump of gorse where the corpse of another pirate lay, sprawled crookedly in death, one hand turned as if trying to pluck the yard-long shaft embedded deeply in his back. They entered the line of trees; here again were more scenes of the bloody pursuit: a corpse half hidden by the snow overlooked by Sir Edmund's men, and more and more of those dark bloody patches.

When they reached the tavern, its cobbled yard was deserted. Corbett dismounted, told Ranulf to wait and walked into the tap room. He was met by the chief ostler, who informed him that Sir Edmund had given the tavern to his care for the time being. 'We are still looking for those who fled.' His sad eyes held Corbett's. 'Young boys and maids out in the freezing forest. We've been out there and seen some terrible sights. Corpses, throats slit from ear to ear, tinkers and travellers, God's poor men, only looking for a warm fire.'

'The Castilians?' Corbett asked.

'Sir, we thought they were what they claimed to be. They would leave now and again; I always thought they were going to the castle. Then the others came, silently, just before dark, terrible men, Sir. They kept careful watch on the road. Some of the maids were cruelly abused.'

'Well they are either dead,' Corbett replied, 'or about to meet their final judgement.' He told the ostler to keep careful watch lest pirates who had survived the fight were hiding out amongst the trees.

'Is it going to end like that?' Ranulf asked as Corbett remounted. 'Bodies dangling from the wall? Who, Sir Hugh, will answer for the hideous murders in the castle? Your good friend Louis—'

Corbett held up a hand. 'I'm tired, Ranulf, of secret books and hidden ciphers, de Craon's treachery and his lust for my blood. There's still work to do.' He smiled. 'We have a priest to see. Always remember, the mills of God's justice may grind infinitely slowly, but they do grind infinitely small.'

The trackway outside the church and the churchyard itself bore witness to the recent conflict. Some of the crosses and headstones had been overturned whilst a pile of bloody rags lay heaped against the cemetery wall. Father Matthew was standing on the church steps, busy sprinkling water in all directions.

'I'm hallowing this place,' he explained, as Corbett and Ranulf dismounted. 'Well,' he held up the holy water stoup and the small asperges rod, 'it's the least I can do.' He sprinkled a little water in Corbett's direction. 'Sir Edmund told me about Mistress Feyner. You did well, clerk; another devil in our midst, though.' Father Matthew sighed. 'God rest the poor women.'

Corbett stared at this kindly priest with his heavy peasant face, now unshaven, eyes red-rimmed, and realized how shrewd a man he was; just a glance, a movement of the lips proved the old proverb that still waters run very, very deep. Corbett rested one foot on the bottom step of the church.

'I came to thank you, Father.' He laughed abruptly. 'And to congratulate you on your return to good health. When I came here last you were warning us, weren't you? You could smell the odour of cooking and so could I. And what poor priest would throw a beautiful bronze bowl out amongst the rubbish near the rear door?'

'I hoped you would see that.' Father Matthew kept his head down. 'God have mercy on me, Sir Hugh, I had no choice. They were in every chamber in the house and they held the hostages in the church; they were as fearsome as Hell. I thought I would never meet devils incarnate! Hell must have been empty, for all its demons came to Corfe.'

'You escaped?'

'A long story.' Father Matthew smiled. Corbett noticed how clean and even his teeth were, whilst the ragged black mittens on his hands couldn't hide the elegance of his long fingers. 'The pirates were leaving, eager for more mischief. I simply escaped into the church and barred the Corpse Door. Thanks be to God, if I hadn't I'm sure they would have slit my throat and those of the other people they brought in.'

'Where have they gone?' Ranulf asked.

'Oh, back to their homes. I gave them what I could.' Father Matthew made to turn away.

'John?'

Father Matthew whirled round, and if he hadn't been holding the water stoup so carefully he would have dropped it. He gaped towards Corbett.

'I, I don't . . .'

'You're not a priest,' Corbett replied quietly. 'You are a scholar pretending to be a priest. Your real name is John. Many years ago, in a different world, you were the disciple, the close friend, the personal messenger of the Franciscan brother Roger Bacon, scholar of Oxford and Paris.'

'I, I don't know.' Father Matthew had turned so pale Corbett strode up the steps and grasped him by the arm.

'I think you had best come into the church where you have hidden for so long.'

The priest didn't resist as Corbett led him into the dark, smelly nave which still bore signs of occupation by the pirates. Stools and benches were overturned; near the baptismal font was a pile of horse manure. The floor was stained and two shattered pots lay directly beneath the oriel window, catching the poor light pouring through.

Ranulf pulled back his cowl and absentmindedly blessed himself. Corbett's declaration had taken him by surprise. He found it difficult to accept that a great scholar of Oxford should be hiding in such a shabby church. Yes, old Master Longface had his own ways; if the King wouldn't let his right hand know what his left was doing, Corbett was even worse. The priest was deeply shocked, trembling so much Ranulf had to prise the water stoup from his grip and urge him to sit on the small high-backed chair just under the window. Corbett sat on the stool opposite.

'Would you like some wine, Father? I will call you Father, though you are not a priest. Oh, you tried to be, but you hold the Host the wrong way. Now and again you forget your duties, such as neglecting to administer the last rites to that poor maid found on the trackway outside.'

'I don't know what you are talking about.'

'Yes you do,' Corbett continued evenly. 'We could go across to that house, and sooner or later I will find a hidden compartment. I wonder what it will contain? An astrolabe, a calculus, a compass, maps of the heavens, charts of the seas, perhaps one or two books, and a jug of that fiery powder which the King uses to loose his bombards and hurl bricks at castle walls?' He paused. 'Why should a poor parish priest have such an expensive bronze bowl and use it so much it is caked with black powder? But there again, you know all there is to know, don't you, about Friar Roger's *ignis mirabilis*? You've read the formula, you know how to mix it.' Corbett smiled. 'You've committed no crime, Father Matthew, except one, I suppose. You will produce letters from some bishop which will declare you are a priest, yet I'm a royal clerk and even the best forgeries can be detected. I mean, it wouldn't be hard for you, would it, to buy the finest vellum, a quill, a lump of wax, and forge your own seal? How many people can read such a document? And who really cares? After all,' he waved around, 'St Peter's in the Wood, outside Corfe Castle, is not the richest benefice in God's kingdom. What are its tithes and annual revenues, Father, a mere pittance?'

'They'll burn me!' Father Matthew lifted his head. 'You know that, Sir Hugh. They'll ransack my house, take away the gold and silver I have hidden. They'll burn my books like they did Friar Roger's. For what? Because I'm a scholar? Because I want to probe the mysteries? What harm have I done anyone? True,' he nodded, ignoring the tears spilling down his cheek, 'I have no power to change the bread and wine into the body and blood of Christ. I have no authority to loose people from their sins, but if there is a God, He must be compassionate. He will understand.'

Corbett listened as this former scholar made his confession. How he had been born not far from Ilchester, orphaned young, and had travelled to Oxford, where Friar Roger had received him kindly. He explained how the friar had given him an education second to none, in the Quadrivium and Trivium, in mathematics, logic, astronomy and Scripture, as well as a variety of different tongues.

'He was my Socrates.' Father Matthew smiled. 'And I sat at his feet and drank in his wisdom. But,' he sighed, 'Friar Roger clashed with his own order in the person of the Father-General, the great scholar Bonaventure. He lost the protection of the papacy and spent years in prison. After his release, he travelled back to Oxford a broken man. When he died, the good brothers nailed his manuscripts to the wall to rot.' He shrugged. 'Or so rumour had it; by then I had fled. Friar Roger told me to hide, to keep well away from both his order and the Halls of Learning. I travelled back to Ilchester but no one recognized or knew me. I heard that this parish had no priest.' He forced a smile. 'Well, you know the rest. You're right, Sir Hugh, no one cared. The Bishop's clerk was so ignorant he couldn't even translate the Latin on the letter I had forged. But what could I do? I wanted to continue my studies.' His voice faltered.

'The secrets?' Corbett asked.

'Ah, I thought you would ask about that. I heard about the meeting at Corfe. I wondered if I should flee, but that would have provoked suspicion. Who would care about an ignorant parish priest?'

'Would the King know?' Corbett asked. 'Is that why he chose Corfe?'

'Possibly,' Father Matthew conceded. 'Perhaps he thought such a meeting might provoke the interest of Friar Roger's hidden disciples. The truth is, Sir Hugh, there's only one, and you are looking at him. When I met you,' he sighed, 'I did wonder. You are sharp of eye, keen of wit.' He paused. 'I don't want my house ransacked, I don't want my books burnt, I don't want to be dragged before some archdeacon's court or local justice. Sir Hugh, I have done no harm, I have done no ill.'

'I'm not going to pass sentence, Father Matthew, but I asked you a question. The secrets?'

'If I told you, you wouldn't believe me. You'd say I was lying. Friar Roger's secrets are described in his manuscripts. He talked of things, Sir Hugh, of men he had met in France, of mysterious documents, of marvellous machines beyond our comprehension.'

'The *Secretus Secretorum*?'

'Ah, that.' Father Matthew closed his eyes and breathed in. 'Friar Roger was very careful,' he began. 'Many people regarded him as a magician.'

'Was that true?'

The priest opened his eyes. 'Yes and no, Sir Hugh. Friar Roger was a member of a secret circle of scholars. In his letter *On the Marvellous Power of Art and Nature* he attacks magic as trickery.'

'So what was he frightened of?'

'That things which could be regarded as magic are really the creation of the human mind, of a newly found wisdom. Friar Roger often talked about the great scholar Peter de Marincourt, with whom he worked in Paris. Peter taught him great secrets, for example, how a glass could be built so that the most distant objects appear near at hand, and vice versa. Sir Hugh, how can you explain such a thing to an ignorant bishop or inquisitor? Friar Roger became frightened. He was also deeply resentful at the way he was imprisoned and silenced, so he wrote the *Secretus Secretorum*, his handbook of secrets. It's a mixture of the sources of his knowledge and future predictions, as well as how certain experiments can be conducted. He wrote it in a secret cipher, and before you ask, Sir Hugh, there is no translation. On his deathbed Friar Roger whispered to me that the key to that book was his own mind and that when he died that key would disappear. Now, Sir Hugh, you may drag me to London, have me tortured, threatened, I would say no different. The *Secretus Secretorum*,' Father Matthew raised his voice so it echoed round that sombre church, 'is Friar Roger's treasury of secrets. It is also his revenge on those who rejected him. He could have said so much but no one wants to die screaming, lashed to a pole with the flames roaring around you.'

Corbett moved on his stool. He had interrogated many men, some consummate liars, and on such occasions he rejected logic and reason and trusted his own feelings. He instinctively felt that Father Matthew was telling the truth.

'So that book will never be translated?'

'Never!' Father Matthew agreed. 'And the more it is copied, the more it is added to so the more difficult it will become.'

'And Friar Roger's wealth?' Ranulf asked. 'He talked about spending two thousand pounds. Did he discover the Philosopher's Stone? Unravel the secrets of alchemy?'

Father Matthew threw his head back and laughed.

'He had hidden wealth,' he replied, and sat chuckling to himself.

'Hidden wealth?' Ranulf insisted.

The priest gestured with his hand. 'Go back to Corfe Castle, Red-hair, and gaze upon its battlements. Men lived on that spot before the Romans ever came. It's been a royal residence, a place of power. Tell me, what do people do in times of danger? How do they protect their wealth?'

'They bury it.'

'That's one thing Friar Roger learnt from Peter de Marincourt. How to find hidden wealth. Speak to the country people, Sir Hugh, men of Dorset and Somerset. They will tell you how, with a mere stick, they can divine underground streams or wells. According to Friar Roger, Peter de Marincourt discovered a way of finding hidden treasure. Don't doubt me, Sir Hugh; even without such knowledge, tell me, how often is treasure trove found in London, gold, coins, silver from some forgotten age? That was the source of Friar Roger's wealth. He wasn't greedy for money; he just saw it as a means to an end.'

'Do you know that method?' Ranulf asked.

Father Matthew shook his head.

'I suspect it is one of the secrets he locked away in the *Secretus Secretorum*, which,' he spread his hands, 'to me, like you, is an impenetrable wall.'

'Yet you were Friar Roger's favourite pupil; he described you as a great scholar.'

'He also loved me dearly as a brother. He said the time was not ripe for such knowledge, that if he revealed his most secret thoughts it would only place me in deadly danger.' Father

Matthew slumped in the chair, weaving his fingers together. 'What more can I say?'

Corbett stared up at that sombre nave. A slight mist had crawled under the door and through the gaps in the shutters, so it looked like a hall of ghosts. The altar at the far end was bare and gaunt, dominated by a stark crucifix.

'Are you happy here?' he asked.

'Yes, Sir Hugh, I am. I come from these parts. I think I do something useful. I truly care for these people.' He pursed his lips. 'I have a little wealth hidden away, I have my books. It is an ideal place for a scholar to remain hidden and pursue his studies.'

'I shall tell you what I will do.' Corbett got up, scraping back his stool. 'In the spring I shall invite you to London and present you to the Bishop of London; he is a friend of mine, he will be only too happy to ordain you a priest and issue letters from his chancery. As for your friendship with Friar Roger,' Corbett rehung his cloak about him, 'why not leave that as one secret hidden amongst so many?'

'I have your word?' Father Matthew asked, the relief apparent in his face.

'You have my word, Father.'

'Then I shall tell you something.' The priest pushed himself up. 'You've a kind heart, clerk, and a good voice. When I was in the castle I became agitated. I met someone who, I thought, might recognize me.'

'One of the Frenchmen? De Craon?'

'No, the one who struts like a cheerful sparrow. Monsieur Pierre Sanson. But, *Deo Gratias*, it has been many years since he last spoke to me. About twelve years ago,' the priest continued, 'Pierre Sanson was part of a French delegation which came to Oxford. They stayed at the King's palace at Woodstock. You may recall the occasion? The marriage of the King's daughter Margaret to the Duke of Brabant? Naturally, scholars visit each other. Sanson claimed he was deeply interested in Friar Roger's work and came to ask him about his secrets. My master was old and frail. He never was sweet-tempered,' he added quickly, 'and gave Sanson short shrift. When the Frenchman asked him about his secrets, Friar Roger replied that he would conceal them in a document and make copies of it, and if the world could unearth these secrets then it was welcome to them.' Father Matthew blessed himself quickly. 'What I am saying, Sir Hugh, is that from the very start the French knew the *Secretus Secretorum* could never be deciphered.'

Corbett extended his hand and the priest grasped it warmly. 'I'll see you in the spring, Father. I'll send an escort to accompany you.'

Corbett and Ranulf made their farewells and returned quickly to Corfe. They tried not to look at the row of corpses clustered together like flies hanging from the battlements but thundered across the drawbridge and up into the inner bailey, where Sir Edmund's retainers were still busy removing all sign of the recent conflict. Corbett was lost in his thoughts, ruthlessly determined on his course of action. When Sir Edmund came to greet them, Corbett enquired about de Craon, only to find that the Frenchman was sulking in his chamber. He took the Constable out of earshot, even from Ranulf, and whispered urgently to him. Sir Edmund made to object, but Corbett insisted and the Constable agreed. Ranulf was keen to seek out the Lady Constance, but his plea died on his lips at Corbett's dark look.

'Ranulf, I need you.' He gave that lopsided smile. 'The mills of God are beginning to turn.'

They went up to the chamber, Corbett preparing the room, dragging chairs and stools in front of the fire which Chanson was building up. The groom had slept through most of the battle; consequently he had to suffer Ranulf's constant teasing and was only too pleased to escape to the kitchens to bring back ale, bread and cheese and strips of smoked ham. Bolingbroke joined them and Corbett ushered him to one of the stools in front of the fire.

'I would have gone with you, Sir Hugh.' Bolingbroke sat down and picked up the small platter on which Chanson had served the food. 'This is like the castle of the damned; virtually the entire curtain wall is festooned with hanged men.' He bit on a piece of cheese.

'We shall be gone soon.' Corbett sat in the chair and wetted his lips with ale. 'And what will you do then, William?'

'Oh, I shall journey back to London. I may ask for some

leave from the business of the Chancery. You will find me another post, Sir Hugh?'

'I shall find you nothing!' Corbett replied. Bolingbroke dropped the cheese he held.

'Sir Hugh?'

'Do you pray for his soul, William? Your good friend and companion? Your brother-in-arms Walter Ufford?'

Ranulf stiffened; even Chanson, sitting almost in the inglenook, forgot his food.

'You're a traitor, William,' Corbett continued, 'and I shall show you how. Two things in particular. First, let's go back to Magister Thibault's house in Paris. You remember it well: the Roi des Clefs who could open any door, chest or coffer?'

'Sir Hugh, I do not know what you are talking about.'

'Of course you do, you were there. The King of Keys was wounded, his hand and wrist spiked by a caltrop, pumping out blood, screaming until Ufford had to cut his throat. Do you remember what the King of Keys carried? A pouch of strange instruments, master keys, cunning devices to turn a lock or force a clasp. What happened to these?'

Bolingbroke's face grew pale, his chest rising and falling rapidly, the panic obvious in his eyes.

'They were left there.' He made to rise. Ranulf, sitting beside him, put a hand on his shoulder and forced him to sit back down.

'You took them,' Corbett continued. 'You picked them up. Who would notice? The King of Keys was dead, Ufford all a-panic. You used those keys on two occasions, the first when you murdered Crotoy and the second when you murdered Vervins.'

'I was with you when Vervins died.'

'Of course you were,' Corbett agreed. 'But you had given the keys to de Craon so that he or his henchman could creep up those tower steps. As the Gospel of St John says, "In the beginning was the Word",' Corbett sipped at his ale, ' "and the Word was with God". That is where all this began, Bolingbroke, with the pursuit of knowledge, used by de Craon and his sinister master to trap our King. Philip of France crows like a cock; he has Edward of England trapped by the Treaty of Paris, the Prince of Wales is to marry Philip's only daughter Isabella.

But there is a fly in the ointment: me and my spies in France and elsewhere. Philip would like to sweep the board. He knows about Friar Roger's secret writings but he also knows that those writings can never be deciphered, whatever Magister Thibault claimed. Philip of France studies Edward of England most carefully, as he has for the last twenty years. The English Exchequer is bankrupt, Edward has wars in Scotland and he must defend the Duchy of Gascony. Earlier this year, our fat little Sanson inveigled Edward into studying Friar Roger's manuscripts, a secret letter addressed only to our King. Perhaps it wasn't Sanson but Philip himself whetting his appetite. Anyway, Edward loves a mystery, particularly when he learns that Philip of France is also studying those same manuscripts. Edward's rivalry with Philip is legendary.'

'I know nothing of this,' Bolingbroke bleated.

'Don't you, William? I think you may have helped Sanson. Who knows? Perhaps you sent messages yourself through Ufford. Ah well, Edward of England prides himself on being a scholar. He reads Friar Roger's work and stumbles on, or is allowed to stumble on, a great secret: Friar Roger's bold assertion that he had spent over two thousand pounds, a veritable fortune, on his studies. Our King wonders, where and how could a poor friar, of common stock, draw on such wealth? He must have some great secret. And so the hunt begins.'

Corbett sipped from his ale, and before Bolingbroke could stop him, leaned across and plucked the dagger from its sheath on the clerk's belt.

'Oh, by the way, William,' he patted Bolingbroke gently on the arm, 'the Constable's men are now going through your possessions. They are looking for the King of Keys' tools; I'm sure they'll find them. So,' Corbett cleared his throat, 'let us go back to our own King, the prince to whom we both swore fealty. He tries to hide Friar Roger's reference to the treasure spent in the pursuit of knowledge. The King is also worried about his copy of the *Secretus Secretorum* being accurate. Perhaps Monsieur Sanson helped in this? Anyway, Edward of England wants to steal the French copy, so he instructs me to contact our clerks in Paris to move Heaven and Earth to obtain it. Of course, what we don't know is that Walter Ufford has been baited, teased into a trap, and this is where you come in,

William. You are a scholar at the Sorbonne, you have already been under suspicion as a spy, a clerk of the Secret Chancery in England. De Craon or Sanson approached you. Did they threaten you with the horrors of Montfaucon, or offer you gold and silver, a sinecure in France?'

Bolingbroke stared impassively back.

'Well, you know the story better than I do,' Corbett continued. 'So, we come to the night of Magister Thibault's revelry. You were invited to all that mummery. Magister Thibault is distracted by a nubile courtesan called Lucienne. Did you hire her? Was it de Craon? Or was it both? Anyway, she is under strict instructions to flatter the old fool, to persuade him to take her down to his treasure house to see the precious manuscript he is working on for the King of France.'

'But that's impossible,' Bolingbroke stammered. 'Magister Thibault came down by accident. He didn't know when we would be there.'

'That's a lie!' Corbett snapped. 'I suggest that when you went down to that cellar you passed Monsieur Sanson and gave him a sign. He would then hasten up the stairs to make sure Lucienne kept her part of the bargain. I agree, it would take some time to rouse that old goat from his bed, but Magister Thibault stumbled down into that cellar. As soon as he opened the door he was a dead man. Ufford cuts his throat and that of Lucienne. Walter was always a ruthless man. A short while later the King of Keys is wounded and later killed; you secretly seize his keys. Eventually you and Walter make your escape, two successful spies who have achieved the task assigned to them.'

'Why didn't they arrest us there and then?' Bolingbroke interrupted.

'That's not such a good question,' Corbett retorted. 'They needed you, William, they wanted you to escape.' He paused, rubbing his hands together. 'You and Walter did what any spies would do; you separated, though not before you made sure that you escaped with the *Secretus Secretorum*.'

'The dice!' Ranulf spoke up. 'You have cogged dice – that's the way I'd decide anything. You're as sharp as I am, Bolingbroke, you'd make sure you won.'

'Yet that was only the beginning of the mischief,' Corbett continued. 'De Craon constructed a plot of many layers. The first was to remove certain opponents from the University of Paris, scholars opposed to the outrageous claims of his royal master; that's the one thing Thibault, Destaples, Crotoy and Vervins had in common. Sanson was also one of these but, unbeknown to his colleagues, he was de Craon's man, body and soul. Philip of France later proposes this meeting. He wants a castle on the south coast, somewhere lonely for the next part of his plot. Edward of England rises to the bait and chooses Corfe, an indomitable fortress, not very far from where Friar Roger was born. Perhaps the meeting would arouse local interest and curiosity, particularly that of any disciples of Friar Roger hiding in the area. However, that part of Edward's stratagem,' Corbett winked quickly at Ranulf, 'failed to come to fruition. Have you communicated with de Craon,' he asked sharply, 'since the attack by the Flemish pirates?'

'I don't know what—'

'I wonder if he will betray you. If I offer him secret, safe and immediate passage back to France, he might sacrifice you. Why, William,' Corbett leaned over, touching the clerk's face, 'you are beginning to sweat. Are you hot?'

'Sir Hugh, you accuse me of treason and murder!'

'Yes, yes, I do. Your hands are stained with the blood of an old friend. Oh, you acted the part so well, William. You even declared that de Craon might be bringing those scholars to England to have them murdered. You spoke the truth yet at the same time posed as a perceptive, loyal clerk of the English Crown who had doubts about de Craon from the very beginning. Yes, yes,' Corbett blinked, 'you knew the truth because you were party to those murders.'

'I was asleep when Destaples died.'

'Of course you were. You had already murdered him. The French *magistri* were no fools. Destaples was more suspicious of de Craon than anyone else. Why should he distrust an English clerk? You sat opposite him at the banquet on the night they arrived. You had been told he had a weak heart, and with the cups being filled and platters being brought it would have been so easy for you to pour a powder into his wine cup. What was it, William? Foxglove, to quicken the heart? Destaples could have died at table or returning to his chamber. Who could have been blamed? He was not a strong man, he had just completed a most vexatious journey, and he suffered a seizure.'

'Ranulf,' Bolingbroke turned beseechingly, 'we have shared the same chamber . . .'

'We also shared the same friend,' came the reply. 'The same master, the same oath.'

'Louis Crotoy was next.' Corbett patted Bolingbroke on the arm, making him turn back. 'Louis was much more careful and prudent, but of course he never realized that de Craon had a spy in my retinue. Like Destaples, he would be wary of de Craon but not one of my clerks. Late that afternoon, the day he died, Louis heard a knock on the outside door. He came down, opened the squint hole and glimpsed William Bolingbroke, trusted colleague of his friend Sir Hugh Corbett.' Corbett kept his voice even. 'The rest was so simple. You were invited in. You're a strong man, William, Louis was fairly frail; you broke his neck and threw his corpse down the steps. You then loosened the heel of a good boot – I can prove it was cut – and rearranged his cloak, creating the illusion that Louis had tripped and fallen. To all intents and purposes an accidental death, an impression heightened when you placed both keys in his wallet. You locked the outside door using one of the devices you had taken from Le Roi des Clefs.' Corbett paused as if listening to the sounds of the castle. 'You made a number of mistakes, William. Most importantly, just after Louis was killed, you raised the possibility of it not being murder by pointing out how both keys had been found in his wallet.'

'Someone told me.'

'Was it de Craon? You weren't present when the corpse was found. I kept that information strictly to myself. Then it was Vervins' turn. What are you going to say, William? That you were here with me and Ranulf when he fell to his death? Well of course you were! But Vervins liked that parapet walk. It had become something of a routine. What happened was that, using one of the instruments from the Roi des Clefs, Bogo de Baiocis, de Craon's henchman, was given a free hand. The door into the side of the tower is hidden from public view. It would be easy for Bogo to slip through and up the steps with an arbalest and blunted bolt. He opened the small slat in the locked door leading on to the parapet; this provided an excellent view. The arbalest was well oiled, the bolt placed in the groove, the catches released. Vervins stumbles and falls to his death. The assassin slips down the steps out of the tower, quickly locking the door behind him. Nobody would dream of looking for a blunted bolt, and any bruise on Vervins would be considered as a result of the fall.'

'You asked him to search for it,' Ranulf declared.

'Oh yes, I did. If he'd found it he wouldn't hand it over. You're responsible for a number of murders, William. Magister Thibault; your good friend Ufford, a colleague of mine, a trusted English clerk. You have the blood of those three Frenchmen on your hands, in particular that of my good friend Louis Crotoy. Finally,' Corbett moved quickly and slapped Bolingbroke across the face, 'you tried to murder me! At first I thought it was the killer of those young women, but when I trapped Mistress Feyner I realized that though she could loose a crossbow bolt up close, she could not fire through the darkness with such accuracy and speed. On the night I was attacked only three people knew where I was going: me, Chanson and you. No, don't,' Bolingbroke had opened his mouth to protest, 'don't lie, William, don't say that I must have been followed. Mistress Feyner would never have done that. De Craon?' Corbett shook his head. 'That's not the Frenchman's style; he wouldn't want to be caught attacking the King's clerk on English soil.'

'But why?' Chanson, standing behind Corbett, listened to these accusations against a clerk he had grown to like, even admire.

'Why, Chanson? Well, now we come to the real business in hand. It wasn't the writings of Friar Roger Bacon but something much more serious. The *Secretus Secretorum* was written in a cipher. De Craon knew that our King's appetite had been whetted. This meeting was proposed,' Corbett waved his hand, 'to make it more palatable to our King, whilst the French insisted it should be in some castle along the southern coast, well away from any town or city. Corfe may be impregnable but there's not a castle built which can't be taken by stealth and treachery. The Flemish pirate fleet was hired, paid good gold and silver as well as offered the prospect of wholesale plundering. They appeared in the Narrow Seas and ravaged the coastline further to the west. De Craon also sent agents into

England: those Castilians pretending to be wool merchants. They took up residence in the Tavern in the Forest; others took the role of pedlars, tinkers and chapmen. I'm not too sure if they were taken directly to England or landed by the pirates; they could even have been Flemings themselves. Philip and de Craon are very cunning. It's wintertime, the roads are deserted, Corfe is surrounded by forest, and so the game begins. De Craon acts all innocent, but that fire at the edge of the forest, on the night I was attacked, was a signal that all was ready. The accidental fire which later occurred in the castle was de Craon's reply that the assault was to continue as planned. De Craon, of course, sent a message to his agents at the tavern giving them the time and place. He also arranged that banquet the night before, hoping the Corfe garrison would be caught unawares.'

'If you hadn't trapped Mistress Feyner?' Ranulf asked.

'Yes,' Corbett agreed. 'For all her evil, some good did come out of it.'

'But why?' Chanson repeated.

'Oh, a number of reasons. First, I'm sure de Craon and his party would have escaped unscathed, but me? The Keeper of the Secret Seal, de Craon's mortal enemy? The nemesis of his master? I would be killed along with Ranulf-atte-Newgate, principal clerk of the Green Wax, and Chanson, Clerk of the Stables; perhaps Sir Edmund and his family would have been taken for ransom.' Corbett snapped his fingers. 'Yes, that's it, the same fate would befall de Craon, though he would be tended to gently enough and later released under some fictitious arrangement.'

Ranulf watched Bolingbroke carefully. He had attended the King's Bench in Westminster and seen men sentenced before the justices in eyre or the justices of oyer and terminer. Condemned men always acted as if they were drunk, unable to accept what was happening. The same was true of Bolingbroke. He hadn't even touched his face where Corbett had smacked him, but sat, half turned in his chair, lips slightly parted, only the occasional blink or twitch of a muscle showing he was awake and listening.

'It wasn't just murder, was it?' Corbett continued. 'But also my destruction and that of Ranulf. On the morning of the attack I locked my chamber. You opened it. You hoped that the pirates would storm the Salt Tower, force that great coffer behind me—'

There was a knock on the door. 'Come in.'

Sir Edmund stepped through the door. Chanson, who had gone to answer, was handed a small leather sack.

'I found it, Sir Hugh, not in his chamber but in a crevice further up the steps. Keys, instruments you would use to pick a lock.' Sir Edmund's face was wary. 'Sir Hugh, what is going on here? I've tried one of the devices myself, it can turn a lock as quickly as any key.'

'If you could wait outside, Sir Edmund? I do apologize, I will tell you in due course.' The Constable made to refuse. 'Please, Sir Edmund.' The Constable sighed, shrugged and went out, slamming the door behind him.

'The attackers were after the Chancery box, weren't they?' Ranulf asked.

'Yes, they were. Can you imagine, Ranulf, what a great prize that would have been? The death of the Keeper of the Secret Seal whilst his ciphers, the ones we use to communicate with our spies abroad, the different codes, the variety of symbols, the tables and the keys, all falling into de Craon's hands. What a great achievement! The secret doings of the English Chancery would be ruined for months, even years. De Craon would be given access to every agent and spy from Marseilles to beyond the Rhine. He knew that I would bring them with me, not to a meeting in France but to a place in England. Of course, Bolingbroke would confirm this, especially as I was attending a meeting about secret ciphers and codes. They may have picked something up from my dialogue with Sanson, but that would be nothing to compare to the looting of this chamber and the removal of our own secret books and manuscripts. Philip would truly become the master. Edward of England, already bound by the Treaty of Paris, would have all his secrets laid bare. Philip and de Craon would act the innocent, publicly bewailing what had happened but privately rejoicing at their great triumph. It was never,' Corbett concluded, 'a matter of Friar Roger, just a continuation of the old game of who wields power in Europe. But why you, William?'

Bolingbroke's lips moved.

'Do you want to deny it?' Corbett asked. 'I can go and see de Craon, tell him what I know. I will wager that he will act the Judas and betray you for less than thirty pieces. Or I can have you bound and sent under guard to Westminster. You can stand trial before King's Bench; the charges will be high treason and homicide. The evidence against you is pressing, William. You will be lodged in the Tower and dragged from there on a hurdle to Smithfield, where they will hang you. Just before you choke to death they will cut you down for the disembowelling. Once you are dead your head will be severed, your body quartered and placed on spikes along London Bridge.'

'Gold.' Bolingbroke's hand went to the weal on his face. He coughed, clearing his throat. 'Gold and silver.' He stretched out his fingers to the fire. 'Last summer, just after the Feast of the Baptist, Sanson asked to meet me in his chambers. De Craon was there. They said they had evidence that I was a spy. They could arrest me and hang me at Montfaucon. They promised me life, wealth and honour in France. I was tired, Sir Hugh, tired of the rotten food, of the rat-infested garrets, of acting the poor scholar. It was so simple, so easily done. I was trapped.' He blinked away the tears. 'In the twinkling of an eye.' He talked as if speaking to himself. 'And once trapped? Well, it was like when I was a child running down a hill; once you begin your descent you can't stop. I thought, what did it really matter, serve this king or serve that king?'

'Would you point the finger at de Craon?' Corbett asked.

Bolingbroke snorted with laughter.

'What proof do I have? You can't play that game, Sir Hugh. You would have to confess that Ufford was a spy and de Craon would simply listen and laugh. The only proof you have is the evidence you laid against me. Not enough to hang him.' He shrugged. 'But certainly enough to hang me. I do not want to take that journey to Smithfield.'

'Do you confess?' Ranulf asked.

'In this chamber I confess. In your presence I admit to the truth. I have innocent blood on my hands, and of all the deaths it's Walter's I feel most bitter about. De Craon promised he would be taken prisoner, perhaps exchanged for one in England.' He pushed back his chair. 'But what's the use? You have the power of a justice, Sir Hugh.' Bolingbroke pleaded with his eyes. 'A swift death, a chance to be shriven by Father Andrew? Let it finish here.'

Corbett gestured at Ranulf. 'Take him outside, inform Sir Edmund of what we have learnt, let Bolingbroke admit his guilt. He is to be taken under guard to the chapel. Father Andrew can hear his confession, and whilst he whispers the absolution ask Sir Edmund to have the executioner prepared. Make it swift, a log and an axe. William, I do not wish to see you again.'

Ranulf seized Bolingbroke by his arm and pulled him to his feet. The clerk was unresisting; he even loosened his own belt, throwing it to the floor. He then took off his Chancery ring and let it fall at Corbett's feet. Chanson made to accompany Ranulf but Corbett pulled him back.

'No, no,' he whispered when they had left. 'You stand by the door, Chanson.'

Corbett took out his Ave beads and began to thread them through his fingers. He tried to concentrate on the words but let his mind drift, willing the time to pass as swiftly as possible. He heard shouts and cries from outside, the sound of running feet and the bell of the castle chapel tolling long and mournful.

'Chanson.' Corbett called the groom over. 'Go and tell Monsieur de Craon,' he spoke over his shoulder, 'that William Bolingbroke, Clerk of the Secret Chancery, has been executed for treason and murder. Tell him that one day our noble King will explain to the Holy Father in great detail what happened here. Oh, and Chanson, do tell de Craon that it is not the end of the matter; for me it's just another beginning.'

Author's Note

This novel reflects very important strands of English history at the beginning of the fourteenth century. The peace treaty of 1303 was forced on Edward I, and he spent the last four years of his life desperately trying to escape it. His son, the future Edward II, continued this policy but then had to succumb to French wishes. In January 1308 Edward II married Princess Isabella at Notre Dame de Boulogne. The marriage did not bring the lasting peace Philip had hoped for. Some eighteen years later Isabella led a civil war against her husband and deposed him. More importantly, Philip IV never dreamt of the nightmare possibility that his three sons would die without a male heir and so expose the throne of France to the claims of Isabella's son, Edward III. The consequent Hundred Years War plunged France and England into a savage, prolonged conflict which cost both countries dear in men and resources.

The outlaws described in this novel are an accurate reflection of those poor men and women who had to flee the King's peace and live out their lives deep in the forests of England. They were not Robin Hood and his Merry Men but desperate individuals living on the fringes of society with everyone's hand turned against them. The staple weapons of these outlaws were the crossbow and the dagger. The longbow had yet to make its impact on the battlefields of Europe. Edward I had learnt the terrifying possibilities of this powerful weapon during his Welsh wars. The use of the longbow as described in this novel was as important an innovation in military technology at that time as the submarine, tank or aeroplane was in ours.

The writings of Roger Bacon are also faithfully described in this novel. The quotations are from his Latin works. He did acquire the secret knowledge from the mysterious Marincourt. No one has ever explained Bacon's wealth or discovered the fate of his favourite disciple, 'John'. The *Book of Secrets* could well be the Voynich manuscript, discovered by the American Wilfrid Voynich in an Italian villa near Frascati in 1912. This manuscript comprised over two hundred semi-illustrated pages with an almost incomprehensible script. William Newbold, a professor at the University of Pennsylvania, declared that this was the secret manuscript of Roger Bacon. Since then controversy has raged over this find, which no one has successfully deciphered. Some claim it is Bacon's, containing his prophecies and discoveries; others stoutly maintain that it is the work of John Dee, the Elizabethan occultist and astrologer, a contemporary of Elizabeth I. What cannot be denied, however, is that Bacon had an enquiring mind and did imagine inventions such as the aeroplane and the submarine which are, of course, a part of our reality.